Checklist for the End of the World

J.R. Rickwood

DEDICATION

For all the Programmers who fixed the Y2K bug. After writing this book I finally understand how it feels to spend a year of your life working on something that most people will never see or even know existed.

RESOURCES

Special Thanks
Dan Atkins - Sonix Software
Beverly Rickwood
Cait Gabe-Jones

Websites
theprepared.com
oswreview.com
mashable.com
tunecaster.com
inthe90s.com
wordstream.com
www.inc.com - Geoffrey James - The day the world
didn't end
google.com - various
wikipedia.com - various
takemeback.to - various
ukchristmastv.weekly.com - various
cosmopolitan.com - various
halifaxcourier.co.uk - various

Media
Headlong: Surviving Y2K - Dan Taberski
1999 Queen's end of year speech

ACKNOWLEDGMENTS

Since I can remember I have been enamored with the thought of writing a novel. I can honestly say it has been an incredible journey, one of the most rewarding things I have ever done and it was something that I could not have done alone.

First of all, a big thank you to Cat, without your encouragement and support this would not have happened. You have truly been with me the whole of this journey and I am eternally grateful. Thank you to my Dad for proofreading and my Mum for giving me the push back to writing and editing the first version.

The technical aspects of Y2K were definitely a challenge to understand and get my head around (again!) so a massive thank you to Dan Atkins of Sonix Software for allowing me to rack his brains and then of course explaining everything to me in layman's terms.

Thank you to Cait Gabe-Jones my copy editor and finally to everyone who was part of this journey whether they knew it or not: Lily Hayden, Rob Hughes, Blue, Mike Price, Writers Menorca and the good people of Halifax, West Yorkshire.

1

The rain is pissing down, and I'm already regretting leaving my umbrella at the office - navigating the sea of faceless pedestrians, some aimless, but all moving in differing directions. It makes me feel like I am in a never-ending game of Space Invaders, and is one of the reasons I have always kept my head down as I walk home through Halifax town centre. Combined with this never-ending rain I couldn't shove my chin further into my coat if I tried.

Not long now, just a couple more streets and I can get out of these sodden clothes, put my feet up and have a glass of warming whisky, preferably with a nice soothing cigarette to ease away the stress of the day... fuck...where are my keys? I fumble around and can't feel them in any pocket, think of the lock on the door of my office or the little post box thing where we pick up our mail, and then it hits me. I must have left them on the counter in the paper shop when I was picking up the whisky and cigarettes that I am now desperately craving.

I perform a quick U-turn to the chagrin of some twat on a mobile phone behind me and head back to the paper shop where I stocked up on my evening supplies earlier, having to dig through my pockets for loose change after being told my credit card wasn't working. The girl in the Backstreet Boys t-shirt behind the counter said it wasn't her fault and muttered something about Y2K before staring at me blankly whilst I awkwardly pulled loose change from every available pocket: the beggar on the pavement outside not understanding the irony of his request for "any spare change" as I left.

I'm going against the traffic of pedestrians now, heading back towards the centre whilst everyone else is fleeing to get the fuck out of town. My shoes have stopped squelching now, given up and accepted the fact that along with my coat, hat and gloves they are going to get soaked through.

I slip off a glove that I strategically place under my arm and slide a cigarette out of the damp packet, patting myself down again, this time in search of my lighter which thankfully is still in working order. As I light my first Lambert and Butler of the day, the harsh smoky nicotine hit, soothing me slightly as I start to contemplate my credit card not working. It's not maxed it out, I pay it on time (in full) and it's a fairly newish card, so yeah... must be the machine. Perhaps I should just ditch the thing for good anyway, as I can afford stuff now and don't need to live paycheck to paycheck. I could even knock a chunk off my overdraft whilst I'm at it, actually make use of whatever I've got from the inheritance instead of leaving it sit in an envelope in my sideboard.

Debbie mentions the envelope pretty much every day. It's hard to know if she is curious or just after a weekend in Meadowhall shopping. Guessing she would probably be home now. She usually gets in just after me but with this detour I'm pretty sure she will be sat on the sofa with a glass of wine thinking of what kind of shit to throw at me when I get back. The inheritance was still a sensitive subject but then again so was the house, and so was me not wanting to have a baby in March so that we could enter a radio contest to have the first "Millennium Baby" in our county. Debs had a Tamagotchi for a few months a couple of years back and she couldn't even look after that.

I'd probably better pick up some wine for Debs whilst I'm at the paper shop again. She never buys it herself as it's apparently seeing me have a drink that makes her want some. Pretty sure she will have made short work of a glass by the time I get in though...ah crap...I have no cash and my credit card doesn't work. I'll pop back out later if I have to. All I want right now is to get home and out of these sodden clothes, preferably in that order.

Turning the final corner and nearly kneeing a toddler in the face at the same time, I step over the worldly possessions of the beggar on the floor outside the paper shop.

I scan the back of the counter for my keys. As I become first in the queue and approach the counter the girl in the Backstreet Boys t-shirt has already clocked me.

"You left your keys," she states.

I nod sheepishly in agreement. She doesn't say anything so we both stand in the emptiness of nothing but an awkward silence.

"Can I have them back?" I ask, breaking the enforced silence.

"The keys?" she replies.

"Well, yeah." I confirm, slightly confused as to what else she might have meant.

She sighs "I've put them in lost property. It's where we put stuff that's lost."

Another awkward silence...

"Can you get them for me?" I ask.

"No." she says flatly, "We lost them."

I chuckle. "You lost them?"

"Well, you lost them first. We found them and then we misplaced them. You remembered where they were so, hopefully, we will too tomorrow."

I stare in amazement at the girl, wondering if she was being serious or just in serious need of some help. "So, you have lost my keys?"

Quick as a flash she replies, "Like I said - misplaced them, and you lost them first."

I take a moment to let my brain process what is happening and offer a solution to the girl.

"How about I leave you my number and you give me a call when you find them again?"

The girl thinks this over before countering with "What? Like a date?"

I step back a little. "Err, no not specifically a date. Just, when you find the keys call me and I can come and collect them."

She seems signed up to the plan as she pulls out a pen and paper from under the counter and thrusts them towards me. "Give us your number then." I jot down my recently acquired new phone number and pass the sheet back. "Is that a mobile?" she asks.

"Erm, yeah it is." I reply.

Her eyes flash as she asks, "What you got?"

"Nokia 3210." I reply as she nods in admiration.

"Can I have a go on Snake?" she asks.

"What now?" I reply, "I'm in a bit of a rush."

The nod turns into a slight frown "Can't call mobiles from the shop phone. Costs a fortune. I'll text you." she offers.

"Thanks." I nod and turn to leave.

"But when you pick them up, I'm having a go on Snake." she smiles.

I keep walking and give a thumbs up. With my back turned I can't see if this is greeted with a smile or a sneer but at this point, I'm past caring. I step out into the rain and over the beggar's front room again, light a cigarette and pull my hood back over my hat.

2

As I turn onto the bottom of my street off King Cross Road, now completely soaked by the rain, I instinctively start patting myself down for my keys which I have now been separated from for the time being. I hope Debbie is home. I sent her a text to let her know I wouldn't be able to get in the house, so hopefully she's rushed back.

I think I can see a light on, but it could easily be any one of the many lights on the street. Debbie usually sits in the back room next to the kitchen so it would be unusual for the front dining room light to be on anyway. The street is unusually quiet. Must be the weather. The usual band of knobheads who hang around under the canopy of the old Grocers have stayed inside tonight... pussies. In fact, none of the usuals are out tonight: that feral kid who always wears an old grey Man United shirt with 'Cantona' on the back, the old fella who sits on his windowsill with a can of John Smiths, even Pat who I have only ever seen sat in a deckchair has abandoned her post to a warmer, dryer life inside.

I notice that the dining room light is on as I get to the front door. I ring the bell and knock three times shouting at the same time

"Debs it's me. I lost my keys."

I see movement in the front room, two shadows, one Debs and one mystery shadow. Have I forgotten something? Is someone over tonight? I can hear Debs and the mystery body moving around the front room now. The front light is off now and its eerily silent.

"Debs it's me. Don't worry it's not the Jehovahs." I shout again as the hallway light goes off and I can almost feel someone on the other side of the door looking through the peep hole.

"Debs is that you? It's me. Open the fucking door it's chucking it down out here."

Nothing…

"I've lost my keys Deb."

Nothing still. The presence I felt behind the door has gone now just the drips of rain water going down my collar. I reach into my pocket and pull out my mobile. Just as I start to punch in the numbers for the landline my phone beeps. It's a message from Clive, Debbie's dad.

DEBBIE DONT WANT U IN HOUSE

Well that was short and fucking sweet. To say I'm slightly confused is an understatement. I'm stood in the rain outside my own home being told via text message that I can't come in.

"Debs answer the door." I blurt out as I knock again and ring the bell, I can't see any lights on now and theorize they must be huddled in the dark in the kitchen right at the back by the garden. Probably with a glass of wine, looking at each other with unwarranted concern on their faces.

"Deb's its fucking freezing out here. Let me come in. What's going on?" I shout.

Still nothing. No response, no noise or movement just the sound of my phone receiving another message.

GO AWAY DEBBIE HAD ENOUGH

Her father always had a way with words. I am tempted to text back "fuck off" but that would probably exacerbate the situation.

I push open the letterbox.

"Debbie... this is mental. It's my house! I'm soaking wet and need to come in." I shout and suddenly hear a wail from the direction of the kitchen.

U MADE DEBBIE CRY

Another message from Clive, who has surprised me with his ability to text, albeit in caps. I probably have been drawn a poor hand with him as my go between.

GO

Either Clive is losing interest, or he is being as firm as a man hiding in the dark in his son-in-law's kitchen can be.

I open the letter box again and shout "Can I at least get some stuff?" as I admit defeat.

NO

Quick as a flash reply from Clive, he is getting good at this texting lark now.

"For fuck sake!" I shout to nobody in particular as I pound the door one final time. My pulse is racing, my chest is tightening, and my heart is pounding.

Suddenly I have gone from cold to boiling hot and feel like the layers of clothing I am wearing are constricting and tightening around my body whilst sweat now drips and blends with the rain. I am breathing rapidly, and my head is pounding as I reach into my pocket for my beeping phone.

IF YOU BOUGHT WINE FOR DEBBIE LEAVE IT ON THE STEP

3

I'm sat like a knobhead under the canopy of the old Grocers literally feet away from my own house. After Clive's final text I wandered around aimlessly for a while, I was pissed off and angry but mainly I didn't know where I was going to go. So, I find myself back here staring at my mobile hoping for a text message from Debs to say I can go in my house.

I have smoked half of my twenty pack of Lambert and Butler now so better slow down a bit otherwise I will have run out by the morning. I'd massively cut back on my smoking and I wasn't smoking during the day anymore, but I can't promise that for tomorrow.

My clothes feel like they have moulded themselves to my body now, and I can feel the wrinkles in the soles of my feet that have developed from my sodden footwear. She could have at least let me grab some fucking clothes and explained to me why I am suddenly being exiled. I'm fantasizing about just kicking the door down and running in now. What would I grab?

A warm jumper, my leather jacket, the green cargo pants and my waterproof boots. Gloves and hat on the radiator whilst I change. Grab some fresh work clothes, my bank book from the sideboard. Punch Clive in the face... I keep making mental checklists in my head of what I would have grabbed, and it all seems so necessary at this moment when I'm sat on the floor piss wet through in the cold with nowhere to go. If only that beggar could see me now.

I can't sit here all night. I need to think about work in the morning too but right now I need to get somewhere warm, dry and preferably with a bar.

Money is a problem... If my credit card isn't working. I literally spent my last available money on a bottle of whisky and some cigarettes, and unfortunately, I'd probably make the same decision again if I had known then where I would be sat at ten o clock at night. I should have just asked Debbie for my bank book. She wouldn't have deprived me of that. But saying that, she did deprive me of clothes so I guess anything is possible. There won't be a bank open till tomorrow morning anyway so I guess I will just have to be skint until then.

I'm still staring at my mobile, hoping that a text from Debbie or even Clive, comes through and I can waltz through the door into an apology, a nice warm shower and some dinner. Shit... what am I going to eat tonight?

Reality is starting to kick in and I need to get away from this idea of getting a message to come back. Even if I did, all likelihood is that Debbie would want to talk about it for hours which means more time sat feeling like shit in damp clothes.

I start to scroll through my address book on my

Nokia. It's a fairly small list of work colleagues, old uni friends, Debs and a few of her family. None of my own seeing as its only me left but I can be happy in the knowledge that I can soon add the girl in the Backstreet Boys t-shirt from the paper shop.

I need to go somewhere. I can't stay outside the Grocers all night and if Debbie were to see me on her way to work it would hardly do me any favours. I press down to go through my contacts. I discount Deb's family, especially Clive, work colleagues, the one2one top up line and the local taxi firm. My two options are Dave or Eddy, probably my only two friends in the world.

4

"Dave you are a twat." I press the red button to end the call and light up another cigarette, throwing my hood back over my hat and grabbing my bag as I move out of the cover of the old Grocers and back into the pouring rain.

I'm going to take a chance on the local pub. I'd not really been a 'local' since me and Debbie moved to the area but I felt sufficiently confident that I could get a drink or two by the log fire they had and figure out my next move before they closed in just under an hour.

Growing up, I had been a 'local' at two different pubs in the village of Haworth where I lived with my grandparents. These pubs were both very different, each having their own brand of pub 'etiquette'. The one I'm heading to now I have no idea what to expect as the only times I had been in there were with Debbie and her family for Sunday lunch and to watch some of the games from France '98 last summer.

Some pubs you could ask for a 'cheeker inner'

which was someone outside to slip you a couple of quid for your first drink to get you inside where you could subsequently sneak into a round. Other pubs it was fine to work up a tab and pay when you were flush again. If Dave hadn't been a twat I'd more than likely be over at his place now listening to his kids scream and figuring out my next move, not still pissing about in the pouring rain trying to figure out how I was going to get a free drink in a pub I'd hardly ever been in.

I stub out half of my cigarette and count the remaining ones in the pack; 6, probably enough for tonight but I'd need to get into my house somehow before work in the morning, except right now it's not my house its Debbie's, with her dad guarding the door like an overweight bulldog with a moustache and who's probably making his way through my drinks cabinet right now.

I can see the pub sign now, "Do un", formerly "The Dog & Gun", however now half illuminated as some of the bulbs have blown. I remember laughing with Debbie as it looked like it was telling us to "Do one" when we first saw the sign.

I look through the window. It's still open and still quite busy from the look of it, the 'cheeker inner' is off the table for tonight as nobody is outside thanks to this weather so I'm going the second route and asking for a tab. Once I've settled down in there, I'll give Eddy a call and see if he can help me out. I hate asking Eddy for stuff but I'm getting desperate and Dave is a twat.

The door to the pub is heavy and reveals a cloud of cigarette and cigar smoke to the street outside as I pull it open. I spot a coat rack tucked away with a few coats and a couple of umbrellas in its stand. I'll be better off putting my coat by the fire if I can,

14

somewhere I can keep an eye on it.

There's about twenty people in here and eighteen of them seem to be stood at or near the bar, I squeeze in and nod at a large ruddy faced man of around seventy adorned in gold chains, cigarette in hand and halfway through a pint of cider. Nobody seems to be talking except for a skinny man in an oversized coat in the corner who is shouting at a picture on the wall. What it's done to him I will never know but he looks outraged.

I walk across to the bar and a burly man in a polo neck with a lion tattoo on his forearm shifts his mass from leaning on the bar to face me. He is smoking a super king cigarette and doesn't look very interested in me

"Can I start a tab please mate?" I ask the burly man as I remove my wet hat. I'm greeted again by silence. Perhaps he is the father of the girl in the Backstreet Boys t-shirt and it's a family thing.

"I'd like to start a tab please". Still nothing. I take my credit card out of my wallet and place it on the bar between a packet of pork scratchings and a full ashtray. "I'll stick my card behind the bar. Just don't have any cash on me at the moment mate."

The burly man picks up my card puts on his glasses that are hanging around his neck and reads my name out loud. "Mr. Rain O'Riordan" as the band of locals burst into laughter

"Yes, that's me" I reply.

"Well Rain, could you kindly fuck off please?"

5

I press the bell on Eddy's front door and shake off the water from the umbrella I liberated from the Dog and Gun. I figured if they were keeping my card, I'd at least have an umbrella off them and whoever's parka coat was there too. I'd found a rolled-up tenner and a betting slip in the pocket along with a pack of Superking Blue cigarettes.

The outside of the house towers over me. Three storeys and an attic conversion with God knows how many rooms, the majority of which are either empty or with the furniture that came with the house. I stare up and have to take a step back to see the building.

"Ray what are you doing here man?" Eddy has his head stuck out of an attic window and from what I can make out looks happy to see me at least.

"I need some help Eddy" I shout back.

"I'll be down now mate, come in the door is open" he shouts to me.

I pull the handle and step inside wiping my

shoes on what I thought was a mat but as the lights go on, I see it is Eddy's mail. I take in the view in front of me and can't help but envy Eddy a little bit.

The stairs are in front of me. Behind them is the half open-plan kitchen, to my left a massive room that looks nearly empty and to my right his games room. He lives exactly how he wants and doesn't let anyone, or anything, shape who he is. From the 'Street Fighter' arcade machine I can see in his kitchen to the empty pizza boxes stacked against his TV unit in the games room, it was definitely all Eddy's design and how he wanted it.

"What's happened man?" Eddy asks as he descends the stairs in his dressing gown and Jurassic Park slippers.

"Can I stay here tonight mate?" I ask reluctantly, not because I don't want to stay, it's just since Eddy came into some money, he's had a lot of 'hangers on' taking advantage of him.

"Course you can mate, pick a room its yours. Do you want a beer?"

I give Eddy a hug.

"That would be great mate, I've brought something." I reach into my work bag and pull out the unopened bottle of whisky. "Was looking forward to having this when I finally got out of the fucking rain".

6

I savour my last bite of the pizza that Eddy has ordered in and wash it down with a swig of the cold lager we are drinking. I hadn't expected to be eating a double pepperoni with olives and anchovies with Eddy at gone midnight when I woke up this morning, but at least it was a good end to one day and a good start to another.

"What's the plan with Debbie?" Eddy asks halfway through grabbing a potato wedge.

"I don't know mate; I've heard nothing from her still and I'm not texting via Clive forever."

"Who's Clive?" Eddy asked.

"He's her dad, and current gatekeeper of what used to be my house. The one who complained about the food all through the wedding."

Eddy grabs the pizza box and chucks it on top of the rest of the stack by the TV unit.   "Why don't you just go in tomorrow when she's at work and get all your stuff, lock up and just come back here mate."

"I don't have any keys mate. I lost them, someone found them and then they lost them."

Eddy frowns processing it all.

I take a swig of my beer "And to top it off my credit card doesn't work and is currently in the custody of the friendly bloke who runs the Dog & Gun."

"What about your normal card? For your bank account?" he asks.

"It's being posted to the house that I currently can't get into." I take my last swig of beer.

"Fresh one mate?" Eddy nods at my empty bottle.

I shake my head "Work tomorrow, can't be fragile" declining Eddy's offer of another.

"You used to be indestructible at uni." Eddy laughs heading towards the fridge.

"None left, I'll go grab another box from the cellar" he says through a mouthful of pizza.

"Cellar? how big is your house mate?" I laugh.

It's dangerous leaving me on my own with a drink. I just seem to ruminate about past glories or failures, like those Uni days when I would have stayed up all night drinking with Eddy, laughing so hard that our stomachs hurt the next day and with no hangover whatsoever. Now I will be lucky if I manage it past 9a.m. without a pounding headache, dry mouth and acid reflux that could burn a hole through a steel door.

Eddy and Dave had been like brothers to me at Uni. Having a beer and sharing a pizza with Eddy envelops me in a comforting nostalgia. Although we had been selected wholly at random to be housed in a dorm together, I felt like I'd known both him and Dave for years when we first met and, until I got kicked out, we were inseparable.

I was only two terms or six months, off finishing my course when I got kicked out. I was feeling depressed after the death of my grandmother and lashed out at some knobheads in the student's union after a few too many drinks. I'd been drinking heavily to calm myself down, ease my worry, fear, non-stop sweating and pins and needles, I'd get points where I couldn't breath and I never knew why.

Eddy left Uni with me because he didn't really have anything else to do. He was on his second attempt of the first year of a Computing course but decided to leave in protest when I left. He wrote a letter to the Chancellor and everything and tipped over a load of shelves in the Library.

Eddy and I moved out of the dorm we shared with Dave and got a flat together in Huddersfield near the Uni we had both just left, I found a job with Calderdale Council that I have never left and Eddy continued messing about with computers with both of us living quite happily until Debbie came along. Eddy kept the flat for a few months after I moved out but then got this place off Skircoat Moor Road, near me and near Halifax town centre and seems as happy as he has ever been.

The high ceilings in this place have huge light fittings that hang over you like a hovering seagull just readying itself to swoop down and steal a chip from your tray. Eddy seems to have settled here and has definitely left his stamp on the place, having minimal furniture and multiple piles of 'stuff' hanging around every room like bits of old computer and games he has picked up from various places.

I go past this place sometimes, usually on the

way to Debbie's parents place. I never pop in, not even for a quick chat and a beer. I always argued with myself that I have somewhere more important to be. It's a shame because I like spending time with Eddy and it pains me that Debbie looks down on him because he just does what he feels like all the time including buying this house and smoking a lot of weed.

"I was just thinking," Eddy says re-appearing from the cellar, "the best room is one floor up, has a proper bed laid out and everything. Think it was the master bedroom on the house plans."

"Thanks mate" I smile "I promise I'll get stuff sorted mate. I just don't know what the stuff is right now."

Eddy shrugs his shoulders and lights up a joint. "Stay here as long as you need mate. There is loads of room and, whatever you need, just let me know. Eat what you want, drink what you want and smoke what you want."

I give Eddy a knowing nod and pick up my bag to head up and find a place to kip. "I appreciate it Eddy I really do, but I'll be getting my shit together tomorrow and hopefully sort all this out."

Eddy looks at me with a grin "Am I going to wake up and find one of your famous lists pinned to the fridge again?"

I head towards the stairs "It's better than one of Dave's post it notes telling you to stop cleaning your bong in the sink."

Eddie laughs. "Dave's a twat" he chuckles. "One request if you're staying here though; let's have a whisky before you hit the hay."

7

It feels like a bomb is going off in my head. I turn over on the bed and realise my mobile is ringing. I glance over at the screen and I am greeted with the name 'Clive'. Fuck that! I throw the pillow back over my head and try to blur out the custom ringtone Debbie's sister had made for me on my new Nokia.

I'm thirsty now. I'd had the best part of a case of lager with Eddy and a couple of whiskies before and after that. I am now remembering why I don't drink much mid-week. The fucking phone is still going, and I can just imagine Clive sat there with his cup of tea with seventeen sugars, dialing my phone over and over again.

I sit up and a rush of blood to the head starts the pounding headache I can expect to have all day. The acid hasn't started yet but give it a few hours and I'll be drinking Gaviscon from the bottle. The phone has stopped ringing now and I can hear Eddy shouting from wherever he decided to sleep.

"What the fuck is that noise?" he wails.

"Eddy it's just my mobile phone" I grab a cigarette from my pack.

"I know it's a phone, but what's that ringtone? Its shit."

I nod, because it is shit. "Debbie's sister made it" I shout back.

Eddy emerges from the hallway wrapped in a duvet. "What's wrong with Grande Valse? People don't need to go pissing about making new ones. What's it supposed to be anyway?"

I light my cigarette and try and remember. "I think it's supposed to be Livin' La Vida Loca."

Eddy goes to grab a cigarette from my empty pack. "Fuck La Vida Loca, especially at this time in the morning. Next time just let her play snake instead".

As Eddy walks back towards his room my phone beeps with a text message, another stormer from Clive.

WHERE R U?

I'm still refusing to communicate via this chosen mediator so I chuck my phone in my work bag and root around for any painkillers that might have dropped to the bottom. Glancing at the time on my watch, I reckon I have around half an hour before I need to leave, probably just enough time for the pain killers to take effect - if I can find them.

I seem to have quite a random assortment of generic crap that I have picked up along the way in my work bag along with some essentials; my work ID and folio with recent meeting notes, and other ridiculously mundane jottings. I pick out a pack of gum, my old Walkman containing a tape of Nevermind by Nirvana and a half-drunk bottle of Lucozade. I decide it would be both safe and worthwhile to down the Lucozade and examine the betting slip I found in the parka.

RIVALDO – BALLON D'OR – TO WIN, BECKHAM – 2, SHEVCHENKO -3

Looks like the burly man from the Dog and Gun was planning on having a punt on the winner of the Footballer of the year. I'm assuming that I nicked his coat, mainly to make me feel better about it but it's a 2XL and he was definitely smoking Superkings - they are a half an inch or so bigger than normal cigarettes. Regardless, I'm hanging on to it all for now seeing as he has my credit card.

Looking up at me from the bottom of the bag next to a little blue Argos pen is a half-crushed pack of Ibuprofen. I grab my now empty bottle of Lucozade and navigate the bits of computer and various items of laundry Eddy has strewn around his landing to make it to the bathroom at the end of the landing.

I run the tap as cold as I can make it and fill up my Lucozade bottle, downing the first top up and half of the next. I use the rest to swill out my mouth after squeezing a dollop of some of Eddy's toothpaste into my mouth and rubbing it on my teeth with my index finger. Living like a king. I fill my bottle back up and quickly head back to the room, throwing on my now warm clothes from the radiator and sweeping my worldly possessions into my bag.

I make a valiant attempt at making the bed, mainly draping the duvet approximately where it should be and separating the two pillows back into one on each side. It's quite refreshing to not have to fight with an army of decorative pillows or have my bed-making skills examined and graded by a towel clad Debbie for once. As I turn to leave, I hear another beep from my phone, hoping it's the Backstreet Boys T-Shirt girl from last night. My hopes are dashed when I see it's another blinder from Clive.

WE NEED 2 TALK

Fuck him. I navigate Eddy's massive staircase and spot him cracking open a beer in the kitchen. He must have had a few before I got here last night and is hoping the 'hair of the dog' will help him. This technique was always a favorite of Eddy's along with the 'wake and bake' and the 'pill and chill'. Basically, any excuse not to accept the fact that the fun was over, and a new day had begun.

I throw on the stolen Parka I'm holding and make a beeline for the kitchen where I am hoping Eddy has coffee for me.

"Morning mate," I direct at Eddy who nods and raises his beer.

"You off to work mate?" Eddy asks between a sip and a cough. "What is it that you do again?"

"Planning and Environments Admin Supervisor for the Council and yeah, I'm off now. Going to try and call past the house first, and then the paper shop and then I have a meeting about about Y2K compliance," I tell Eddy as I start looking through the cupboards for some coffee.

"Why is your phone going off all the time?" Eddy moans.

"It's fucking Clive!" I groan, "he's texting me all the time."

"Perhaps he's heard you're single" Eddy jokes,

taking another sip of his beer. "Coffee is in the top left one next to the cat food, there's a in the sink," he directs.

"Fuck it. I'd better head off anyway mate. I'll grab one at work. I'll nick a ciggy though if that's ok?"

Eddy points to the same cupboard as the coffee. "I got some 'baccy in there, help yourself. Do you need a lend of any cash today Ray?"

This was the thing I was trying to avoid. "No mate, I found a tenner in my bag and hopefully I'll get my stuff from the house now anyway." I head for the door hoping to cut the conversation there.

"Ray, just borrow some cash, give it back whenever." Eddy throws one last bone my wayl I just need to dodge it now. I'm not going to be taking money from him like every other fucker does.

"Seriously mate I'm fine. I'll probably be back later seeing as Debbie will only speak to me via a negotiator."

Eddy shrugs his shoulders and nods. "Anytime, just come straight in. I'll either be high playing computer games or high making them. Who knows?" he cracks a smile as my phone buzzes again. It's not anyone I actually want texting me but once again Clive.

DNT IGNORE ME

I'm starting to wish I'd never bought Clive a fucking phone for his birthday.

8

I close the gate on Eddy's place and start to roll a cigarette for the walk back to my house. I'd better give Debbie a call before showing up. Hopefully she will be at the house and can let me in to get some stuff at least. Change of shirt for work would be nice and some proper shoes in case it rains tonight. Most importantly though my bank book and possibly my phone charger as its not been charged for a few days now.

I light the cigarette and pull my mobile out of the parka pocket. I'll call Debbie and let her know what I'm doing. That way she can get the stuff ready if she wants. I dial the number and hope she can hear the phone wherever she is. It's ringing at least but she usually makes it to the phone by the fourth ring and I'm on five now... still ringing... three beeps over and over now... she's pulled the line out. Shit! Perhaps this is her way of showing me I need to go via her chosen mediator in Clive. I'm slowly running out of options now and might have to talk to him. I stare at my phone and like magic it beeps and shows me I have a new text from Clive.

DON'T CALL ANYMORE

Well I guess Clive is still in my house, probably making his way through the biscuit tin right now and my coffee I reckon. It will be pointless going to the house now, especially after this charade. Debbie is making her point, writing it in blood and then stapling it to my forehead. If I turned up now she would scream at me, tell me that I was making a 'scene' whilst in the process of making a scene herself. It would be more productive to turn up with my cock hanging out singing God Save the Queen.

I take a right towards the paper shop instead of onwards home and re-light my now extinguished roll-up, my phone beeps again.

LEAVE HER B KNOBHEAD

Well that's a charming one from Clive. He was upset I was ignoring him an hour ago and suddenly I am a 'knobhead' for calling.

I take a nice deep drag on my cigarette and reach for the Walkman in my bag which should pass the time in between Clive's texts. Did he mean 'leave her be' as in forever leave her or just temporary? See there isn't much to digest with Clive's texts as it seems he feels if he goes over the characters into a second text message the world is going to end. Funny thing is he hasn't even paid for the messages; I have as he's had the same top up credit on the thing since I got it for his birthday. He bought me a Twix for mine.

Getting closer to the centre of town, the hustle and bustle of the morning commute to work starts to become more apparent. Kids in swarms making their way to school and gangs of old ladies waiting for shops to open, but inevitably getting in the way of the stampede of unsatisfied and monotonous office workers like me.

When I first started this job I needed it; I wanted to do well and I had pride in being one of the smart ones walking through town in a suit, sometimes with a nice woolen overcoat and smart scarf. I'd made it. When I thought I would never 'fit in' and be 'normal' I had made it; my mother had had a lot to do with that.

The graph of highs and lows in my life would have three highs and the rest a constant line of less than adequate. Meeting Debbie, getting my first and only job and buying my first house, my three highs: one gone now, one I don't care about much anymore and one I currently have held in the safe hands of Clive.

I step over the beggar in front of the paper shop and tiptoe around all of his worldly possessions. Perhaps I should sit down and join him, compare our treasures as I think he would be winning right now.

Same fucking queue as yesterday, the British really do love a queue. One lady has a newspaper this time and a six pack of 'Special Brew' so she is either anticipating something terrible in the news or this is a normal day for her. Either way she's getting hammered and seems comfortable with that choice. The bald fella in the Leeds United coat in front of me is bobbing his head to the radio in the background; 'Smooth' by Santana, whilst tapping his fingers on the box of condoms in his hand, not so smooth.

The noticeboard by the counter has some interesting adverts: "Psychic Sue" a local medium, spaces on the over 70's bowls team, a Land Rover for sale and a missing tortoise. I grab my 'borrowed' tenner and root around for any loose change that might be in this 'borrowed' parka. I feel a couple of five pences and a penny or so but nothing significant so it will have to be just the cigarettes today, meaning I will have spent all the money I have access to on my vices.

As I get to the front of the queue a middle-aged lady in an apron half smiles at me as I wonder if she'd been baking or perhaps wandered into the wrong shop for work. She has no reason to be wearing an apron.

"Ten pence copy of The Sun?" she asks almost as if programmed to do so.

I scan the front page of The Sun and the other papers laid out on the counter. They are pretty much all reporting the same thing just from different viewpoints. I usually get my news from Gordon and his viewpoint almost daily at the office, so I'll wait for my briefing. I'm sure Gordon will come and find me when he is bored, and I am at my busiest.

"Do you want t'paper or not?" apron lady interjects my thoughts.

"No, I'm alright ta."

"Oh, have you come to ask about the Land Rover then?" she asks.

I shake my head, "No. I'll have 20 Lambert and Butler please and I lost my keys here yesterday. Have they shown up yet?"

Apron lady fetches my cigarettes and ponders my second request, "What sort of keys?" she asks taking a sip of her tea.

"Well, the normal kind really, on a keyring,

opens stuff," I offer for some clarification.

Apron lady takes another sip of her tea and a lightbulb goes off "Oh yes; we found some keys. Well R'Kelly did but misplaced them. Hopefully they will turn up." Lightbulb goes off and she's back to the tea.

"R Kelly? The singer?" I ask with some hesitation.

"Who?" Apron Lady replies.

"You said R Kelly found some keys? R Kelly, the famous singer, I believe I can fly? You're saying he came in here and found my keys and then lost them?"

"Misplaced them I said. Anyway, you sound barmy lad. R'Kelly don't even like singing, she'll not even join in a Karaoke at social club. And flying? you been on that wacky baccy love?"

Time for my lightbulb to charge up. "I get it now; Kelly is the girl who works here. She found and then lost my keys, not the famous singer from the movie Space Jam."

Apron lady slams her tea down "Yes, of course she is! And she misplaced them, they are not lost."

I nod and give apron lady a smile as she stares directly back at me, probably wondering what flavour 'Space Jam' is. "Well your Kelly has my number. Can you make sure she calls me if she finds them today?" I ask.

"R'Kelly has your number? Do you know her then?" Apron lady seems to be joining the dots but in the wrong order.

"We met yesterday. I only know her from working here."

Apron lady seems surprised. "Well she only works here! Don't work anywhere else R'Kelly."

"Okay, cheers," I say, stamping a full stop on the conversation.

31

"Why did she have your keys? Are you two dating or something?"

I shake my head almost too quickly. "No. How much are the cigarettes please?"   "Three fifty-two," apron lady replies as I hand over my rolled-up tenner "I'll tell R'Kelly you were asking after her" apron lady informs me with a cheeky grin.

"Alright, thanks" I tell her. "Oh, and the keys too. Call me if you find the keys", I add watching Apron Lady smile and give a sort or wink. Either that or she has something in her eye.

As I leave the shop, I take the wrap off the cigarette packet and pat the top of box into my palm a few times to 'pack' the cigarettes for a tighter smoke. As I draw one out, I go to step over the beggar and decide to offer him a smoke.

"Fancy one mate?" I offer him a smoke.

"Ta," he says as he smiles and takes one. He must be in his forties; short and skinny with small beady eyes but a massive smile, full set of teeth and a big mop of black hair.

I light his cigarette and then mine and take a look at his front room laid out over a blanket on the floor; a Styrofoam cup, sleeping bag, half eaten pack of digestives, a newspaper, one of the new 'Metro' ones they started giving out on buses and trains this year and a dog lead.

"Where's the dog?" I ask.

"Gone for a walk" he replies taking a drag of the cigarette "about six months ago."

I nod as if it was a normal thing and move on to the coffee cup. "Do you want a coffee?" I motion to the empty cup.

"Nah, I had one earlier, I'll be right for the day now" he replies with a smile, taking another drag on the cigarette. "Thanks for the fag. What's your name mate?"

"Ray mate, and you?"

"Michael," he replies reaching his grubby hand out. I shake it as he takes my hand in a vice like grip smiling the whole time.

"Strong handshake Michael," I compliment.

"Get used to it in my trade," Michael replies offering me a digestive biscuit to which I shake my head.

"Been a carpenter for twenty years. Had me own business and everything until I lost it," his smile fading slightly as he taps his head. "But they can't take this," and then back to full smile as his reveals a tool box hidden under his sleeping bag "Or this! The bastards," he laughs.

"Aye, have a good one mate," I give Michael a nod and step over his front room.

"Catch you later," I say as he nods back still enjoying his cigarette.

9

I flash my ID badge at the tiny receptionist Angela who is lost in a sea of Christmas decorations and head towards the lift area.

"Nice Parka Ray," she calls after me.

"Thanks," I shout back pressing the button to go up.

"Where's it from?" she shouts around the corner.

"The pub," I reply back imagining Angela's confused face and smiling a little. Usually it is a bright face, full of joy and hope and general loveliness which is a pleasure to see first thing on a dull miserable morning, so I feel guilty and I need to clarify for her sanity.

"I borrowed it from someone at the pub Ange," I tell her.

"Ah okay, it's nice" she shouts.

It's nice to have her there right at the front and most importantly happy. When Geri left the Spice girls last year, she was inconsolable and walking past her every day was becoming a challenge. Thank God that's over.

I press the lift for the sixth floor, looking in the mirror and adjusting my haggard appearance as best as I can. I'll just shut myself off this morning until the meeting with the Y2K compliance supplier. Nothing I'd like better than to chuck myself into a meeting room and lock the door but at least it's Annabel that's hosting the meeting with me and not Gordon.

I stop messing about with my hair as the lift stops at the first floor and a man I have worked with for at least three years enters the lift. I don't know his name. I probably never will, but we both exchange a courteous smile, as you do, and both know that there will be no conversation for our trip to the sixth floor. It's the unwritten rule of the lift.

After about twenty seconds of silence the lift stops on the fifth floor as another colleague gets in the lift. I share a disgusted glance with the first passenger at the cheek of this lazy bastard for taking the lift one flight of stairs. I stare at the back of passenger two's head. He must feel ashamed as he's avoiding eye contact by facing the front. Didn't even give the traditional courteous smile to me or passenger one.

As we reach the sixth floor and the awkward self-imposed silences end, we scatter our own ways never to speak of the journey again. I open the door off the hallway to my department and as usual Gordon is stood centre stage in the middle of the office with a cup of coffee talking about something that he has seen or heard and most definitely has nothing to do with anything or anyone at work.

"Morning," I offer the crowd as I head directly to my desk tossing my bag in the corner and searching for my mug to go and get a brew.

"You're in later than usual. You missed the tea round." Tina turns in her seat like a Bond villain.

"No worries, I'll go make one." I grab my mug and head past Gordon's one man show again to the corner of the office with the kettle.

"Bit later today? Assume you are owed some time?" My fellow 'supervisor' Tim shouts at me just loud enough that people can hear.

"Didn't realize it was non-uniform day," I jab back at Tim who is dressed in double denim with a tight white vest and now shooting me a frown under his gel spiked fringe.

"I have an appointment, none of your business really," he spits back.

I nod and give him a smile, "Trying out for East 17 again? Still no excuse for the double denim." He processes it but can't think of a comeback, so goes back to flirting with the new office temp. "Make sure you show her your new tattoo Tim," I shout as I spoon in a heap of somebody else's coffee.

'BE CONSIDERATE - Refill kettle after use'

That's a new one. I notice the pink post-it note stuck above the kettle that I will inevitably not refill.

I take my phone out of my pocket whilst the kettle boils. Three messages: Clive, Clive and Dave. I select Dave's first and it's a typical Dave text, mainly apologizing for last night…. his kids were asleep blah blah blah. Clive is back on form though.

WHERE IS THE TOASTER?

WHERE IS THE BREAD?

I'll keep him guessing for a bit longer. He can search high and low around the house. He may find the toaster, but he will never find my bread because there isn't any. If Debbie doesn't eat something it doesn't make it past the front door.

Kettle seems to be taking ages to boil, so I turn my back on it and examine the pantomime that's unfolding in front of me. Gordon has one foot on a desk now and is still probably only a third of the way through whatever story he is telling. He's lit a cigarette now so is in for the long run. I spot the meeting rooms at the other end of the floor are empty so I could just go hide for a bit? Better not, Tina would find me anyway. In a way she's always somewhere, as her passive aggressive post it notes are dotted on every communal object around the office, including the one she's recently put above the sink.

'Please wash up after yourself, I am NOT a maid'

I admire her handiwork as I turn back to the now boiled kettle and add water to my mug, blowing on the top a bit before taking the first sip. Definitely feel a bit better now. I look back over at the show and can see Tina has taken offence to something Gordon has said, and she is red in the face and pointing her finger at him. Gordon is still going which seems to be making her even angrier. What's funny is everyone else is just sat at their desks just getting on with stuff not even paying much attention to the Gordon show featuring Tina.

I will have been with the council for six years next week. Lots of different faces, but Gordon and Tina remained the same. I am 99% sure that Gordon is wearing the same shirt and tie as he was the first time I walked through the door as a University drop out full of hope on a new adventure in the wonderful world of administration for the council. "Once you have been here as long as me, you'll enjoy coming to work," Gordon had bestowed upon me that first day. "Make sure you don't move anything around" Tina had added. They then both had a huge argument and Tina went home for the afternoon 'sick'.

Nothing changes much. Not Gordon. He is in his element now, surrounded by oblivious colleagues and Christmas decorations, his portly frame bulging out of 1993's Christmas shirt, his face ruddy and sweat dripping off his moustache as he laughs at his own jokes which are mostly taken from whatever television programme he has seen the night before.

I went to see a film earlier in the year with Debbie, 'American Pie'. It was about half way through the film that I realized I knew exactly what was going to happen as Gordon had acted it all out to me, even the sex scenes, most of which Tim had stood sentient, hand on hips with a sly smile, occasional winking and saying ridiculous shit like " like it when they do that."

I make my way over to the sofa area where I spot Annabel sat. She is smartly dressed today in a white blouse and pencil skirt with her chestnut brown hair pulled back behind her ears and falling to the nape of her neck. Her huge brown eyes are looking over the notes we put together last week and the red lipstick she has on is being left behind on the pen she is chewing. I think I am going to enjoy my coffee sat in comfort and, most importantly, without the theatrics of Gordon, daily update from Tina and as far away from Tim as possible.

In the nearly six years since I started here, I hadn't really got to know anyone, well by choice anyway. Gordon had always forced everyone to socialize in the local pub which was really an excuse for him to get pissed and talk to you. Tina was always talking to the back of my head when she was bored and I was busy working on something so I knew a lot about her. And Tim I just blanked out. Annabel however, was around my age, slightly younger, had also been to and left University albeit voluntarily in her case and was incredible at ignoring Tim and avoiding Gordon and Tina.

"Any news on the computer geeks?" Annabel asks as I sit down.

On closer inspection she looks a bit like Mia Wallace today, Uma Thurman's character in Pulp Fiction, but it's probably me that needs the adrenaline shot to the heart.   "Due any minute now" I reply back taking a sip of coffee.

"Have you got a hangover?" she asks looking at me with a wry smile.

"Yeah I have actually" I say sheepishly.

"Fucking hell Ray" she playfully slaps my wrist "we have to explain all this to the boss on Monday morning. Don't expect me to remember all this shite."

I shake my head and manage to hold back some rising stomach acid "Don't worry, I'm fine."

"Shit. Late night was it? What did you get up to?" she asks.

"No not nice really. Debbie kicked me out the house and I was walking around for ages, so I went to a mate's house and we got drunk."

"Sounds fun," Annabel says as she offers me a cigarette.

"Thanks, and yeah wasn't that bad actually in the end. I just wish I could have changed my shirt. I'm starting to feel a bit like Gordon wearing the same shirt two days in a row." I take the cigarette and light it up.

"Don't worry Ray, I'm sure the computer geeks aren't going to be bothered about your two-day old shirt. Pretty sure they just want to sell us some stuff" Annabel says, inspecting my shirt for any marks. "It's a nice shirt actually, suits you, even though I'd always recommend double denim."

I laugh and take a long drag of my cigarette. "Thanks. What are we being sold again?"

Annabel thinks for a second, "It's new software for Y2K compliance purposes. Apparently, the council have been all over putting it in but it's down to each office what level and contract and so on."

"Sounds fun," I say, forcing a smile before finishing off my coffee.

"I'll go grab my stuff. Let's get this over with and then pop out for something to eat."

Annabel smiles, "Sounds good to me."

I stand up and head back to my desk sneaking behind Tina and quickly grabbing my folio, just narrowly avoiding a conversation with a rabid Tina as she turns in her chair a second too late. I can see Annabel back on the sofa laughing as I dodge a now thrusting Gordon and nearly knock over an inflatable Santa as I head towards the door.

10

As he takes a sip of well-deserved water, both of our eyes are fixed on the geek in the suit pointing at the slides flickering on the wall of the meeting room with his pointy stick. He is definitely not so much a geek in appearance, being an extremely well dressed, tall, slightly muscular man with an impeccable haircut. I can see Annabel next to me out of the corner of my eye and she seems as interested, yet confused, as I am.

As the man finishes, Annabel glances towards me and mouths "What the fuck?"

The man puts down his glass and focuses his gaze back on the two of us. "I don't expect you both to understand fully what I am saying to you, but I want you to take the key messages from this presentation."

He moves closer to us.

"There are only a few opportunities left to ensure that all the computers and software you run, the ones that are pivotal to the council, will be safe and secure."

He points his pointy stick thing at Annabel. "How many computers do you think there are?"

Annabel shrugs her shoulders.

The salesman continues. "There are over fifty major computer programming languages. Fifty. It's a huge amount, and what's scary is that in addition to the major languages, there are the minor ones! How many of those are there?"

Both of us remain still and silent.

"Over fifteen hundred minor programming languages exist in the world, which means there are multiple languages in all the computers in your office. Who knows which ones have been used and if they will be safe?"

I see Annabel put her hand up like a schoolgirl. "What do you mean safe?" It's a good question.

The man seems eager to answer. "We have known about the issue for a long time. Back in 1996 people first began discovering problems with the programmes that started with us saving precious space."

He points to my Casio wristwatch. "Back when computer programmes were first being put on microchips, your watch there would probably be the size of the door to this room. When programmers inputted the date, they did it with two digits to represent the year, to save time and to save memory."

"99 instead of 1999?" I chip in.

He slaps his thigh. "Exactly! So, all these different computer programming languages, most of them use two digits for the year, so when next year rolls around its going to tick from 99 over to 00."

Annabel smiles. "So we are going to have to manually edit a load of dates?"

He shakes his head and sips his water. "No. Think of all the computers and microchips in the world and then think of manually updating them. For some, yeah, it won't matter, and you can always know a 00 means 2000, but for some they are going to think its 1900 and that's going to confuse the hell out of them! These ones are just going to stop."

When I first started working here, we didn't have computers so maybe that's not a terribly bad thing. "So, we don't have computers for a while until they are fixed?" I ask the man.

"You don't have computers at all." He says, staring me dead in the eye. "It's a problem. It's a problem we have caused by not planning ahead and here we are in 1999 and we still haven't completely solved the problem and we are staring down the barrel of a gun because it's going to happen soon! Russia isn't doing anything. Don't be like Russia."

He paces around and opens his briefcase that is full of shiny CD cases. "Now I can't solve this for you but all I can offer is software that will protect your computers, your systems and your place of work. I also offer my expert advice to not ignore this threat."

I could see Annabel was a bit worried. I suddenly have a flashback to the card not working in the shop and my debit card having to be re-issued due to 'Y2K', or how it had been sensationalized in the media as 'The Millennium Bug'. Perhaps there is an issue here, and because the majority of us are technological cavemen when it comes to computers, we have been turning a blind eye.

The salesman interrupts my thoughts. "If we don't do something now there are consequences, bigger consequences than your email not working or

43

not being able to print. Hospitals could lose power as the grid goes down; oil pipelines could stop pumping and leave us with no fuel. Cash machines stop paying out money, all your savings are gone in a flash. Land deeds, records, insurances all wiped in a blink of an eye! Trains stop running, traffic lights stop working and planes fall from the sky, all because these little chips think its 1900 rather than 2000. They don't know what's happened. They fail, they stop, and they shut down."

My hangover was really kicking in now. I didn't expect to be dealing with this first thing this morning. I hold back the acid now forming in my stomach.

Annabel raises her hand again. "How do we know this could happen? Why isn't anything else being done? I mean, there isn't much we can do about planes is there?"

She's asking good questions. That's why I asked her to come with me as I knew I wouldn't have a fucking clue.

"All the major corporations and nations across the world are preparing for this bug." the man says as he reaches into his briefcase and pulls out a magazine. "This is TIME Magazine, January 18th, 1999 with the headline 'The End of the World'. They know about this. Microsoft released advice a few months ago recommending wholesale replacement of corporate PCs. The UK government are spending billions in preparation for this. In fact, we have an estimate that two to five percent of the microchips in the world are going to fail and we better make damn sure that they fail in your Casio watch rather than our necessary computer systems or we are all fucked."

I think he got the sale from Annabel on the word 'fucked'. I, however, couldn't stop thinking of how

I'd been screwed over by the credit card machine yesterday and how different my evening could have been. It had already started in my eyes and I had little hesitation when I shook the man's hand. "Just install what you need to and bill us," I tell him before walking out.

11

Gordon is waddling back from the bar with a pint in each hand and a packet of pork scratching clenched between his teeth, squeezing past me and Annabel to wedge himself at the head of our table with a couple of other loud men from some department downstairs.

We are sat by the slightly cold window and from my seat I can actually see Tina sat in the office, still at her desk making a point that she was working when we had all skived off. It was pointless as there wasn't anyone around to give a flying fuck. She has been looking over once in a while with a sad, lonesome face like a lost puppy. She was invited but always likes to pretend she's busy and important, despite spending two hours today arguing with Gordon about whose idea it was to use post- it notes on the holiday calendar.

Gordon had raised the idea of a lunchtime drink at The White Horse pub just as me and Annabel had got back from the software presentation, so at least he had waited until half ten in the morning. Despite Tina's peacocking, there wasn't anyone around this close to Christmas that actually cared if we were working or not.

My manager, Heather, or 'The Boss' as she is known, lives in Manchester and has only been to our office a handful of times. I sent her an email telling her me and Annabel had agreed to the 'Y2K' software updates and they would bill the council directly. I'd told her how helpful Annabel was, wished her a good weekend, asked about her kids and said I was looking forward to seeing her next week. Her one word reply of 'OK' made Clive seem like a wordsmith. She's probably waiting until Monday to kick off about anything.

Even Tim had come along, oddly suggesting we take the afternoon to 'chill', and had rolled his sleeves on his denim jacket as high as he could get them to reveal his barbed wire band tattoo on his right arm. His new one was right at the top of his arm so me and Annabel had a pool going on when his denim jacket would finally come off.

"That guy was a bit intense, wasn't he?" Annabel says, taking a sip of her glass of coke.

"Yeah, he was. I guess I hadn't thought much into all this Y2K stuff until this morning." I pause to light a cigarette, "I don't have my own computer, just the one at work so I haven't paid it that much attention honestly."

"Same here" Annabel replies.

"Load of wank if you ask me." Tim shouts, taking a swig from his bottle of lager. "If it was a big deal, I'd be running the updates or someone senior would, no offence."

Annabel flashes a fake smile. "Thanks Tim. Nobody asked you but next time we will make sure we send you in to meet with them."

Tim takes a swig of his lager and from under his immovable gelled hair, casts another frown our way before moving his attention back to the office temp.

I turn back to Annabel, "I never realised it was such a massive..."

"Sorry to interrupt," Gordon interrupts, and he wasn't sorry, "but I think it's scary how we are so influenced by technology nowadays. I've never been one for computers, but they are a waste of space and money in my opinion. What's wrong with a good old pencil and a bit of paper?" Gordon smiles triumphantly to his audience and takes a gulp of his pint of 'Landlord' bitter.

"Love having your little pencil in your hand don't you Gordon! Ready to jab it at that Tina," one of the loud men from another department growls.

"You use a pen anyway Gordon, not a pencil." Annabel jokes.

Gordon goes into full theatrics mode. "Back in my day, we had pencil and paper and nobody died, nobody wanted for anything, and we all did well for ourselves. They replaced Mary from accounts with a computer. Some bloody spreadsheet replaced her."

I interject, "Mary from accounts was shit at maths. She kept messing up the forecasts. That's why she was let go.

Annabel giggles and Gordon's face goes red. "Well I can't be replaced by a computer. No computer can do what I do!"

I nod and smile at Gordon. "That's because nobody has a clue what you do Gordon." Gordon shakes his head and stands up, "I'm going for a piss".

"I think it's coming off," Annabel whispers. I glance over at Tim who is now almost pressed against the new office temp. He's sat really awkwardly as he's trying to flex his left bicep.

"You said after two beers," I say to Annabel as she scrunches up her nose.

"What is he doing with his arm?" She asks and lets out a chuckle.

"I think he's clenching his biceps," I reply.

Tim does the universal sign language for drink and clenches again as he listens to whatever the poor girl has chosen as her drink. He puffs his chest out and starts making his way through the crowd to the bar, barging past a fragile looking old man and shooting back a wink to the temp.

"New bet!" I bang the table. "I bet he doesn't get a fucking round in."

Annabel shakes her head, "I'm not taking that bet."

"What's your bet on the whole Y2K thing then?" I ask her.

"I don't know. I mean it's scary that all the things the guy said this morning could happen if nothing is done, but the government and businesses are doing stuff. People like us are actually required to do something, so in a way it's comforting that everyone is trying to stop whatever could happen. Just scary that all it takes is for someone to not do it and things could come crashing down."

I nod back at Annabel in agreement, "Yeah, that's the scary part. I mean if we had said no to that guy this morning then potentially some records get lost; names, addresses, money paid, money owed but we would still have Gordon ready with his pencil and paper. If a hospital, power plant, prison or bank doesn't do anything then what could happen there? How effective would Gordon and his pencil be?"

Annabel nods, "True, but I am deeply offended by the imagery of Gordon standing there, pencil in hand. It sounds crude!" She sticks her fingers in her mouth, "and can we agree that it's a pen! Gordon uses a pen! That will remove the possibility of that image ever invading my brain again."

She has a point as I now have that image in my head. "OK, pen! And, as scary as that image is, imagine this image: waking up on New Year's Day with nothing working, no cash machines, no TV, no phones, no anything."

"That's worst-case scenario though" Annabel says.

"It is, but little things are starting right now" I add.

"Shots for the lady." Tim announces in some weird accent as he reappears with a tray, placing two shots each in front of himself and the poor temp. "Aftershock and Apple Sourz, top shelf price for a top shelf girl," he announces to the group with that stupid smug grin of his, not quite realizing what he had implied.

"Gordon gets his magazine from the top-shelf, don't you Gordon?" another loud man growls.

"Do you want another shot m'lady?" Tim flirts with the temp.

"No, I'm fine thanks," the temp replies.

"Is that your FINAL answer?" Tim laughs.

Annabel turns to me and groans, "Remember that phase when he kept saying 'Shagadelic'?"

"Yeah, I am undecided if the end of the world due to a computer glitch is worse or better than that," I joke as Tim slides off his denim jacket to reveal his white vest and newest tattoo right at the top of his upper arm.

"Or that," Annabel adds to the equation.

"Yeah that's pretty bad too," I agree as we are all finally witness to Tim's latest piece of artwork which is some sort of tribal sun design.

"New tattoo?" Annabel shouts across to Tim.

"Oh this?" Tim points at the mess with a nice bit of faux surprise. "Took three hours, cost two hundred quid."

"Is that supposed to be the sun?" Gordon asks.

"It's tribal," Tim grins smugly.

"What part of Halifax still has tribes?" Annabel laughs.

Tim does a fake laugh and focuses his attention on the temp again. I reach into the coat of my stolen parka to see if I have enough cash left to get a round in for me and Annabel at least. I feel a few coins, but it doesn't feel at all promising.

"Ray, I'll get these," Annabel offers like the angel she is.

"I'm just having a feel around in my pocket, probably got enough on me," I say back, hoping secretly that she can see that I probably need all the cash I have.

"Save what you have until you get your cards back or go to the bank or steal another coat, whatever works for you." She smiles and reaches into her bag for her purse.

"Y2K is screwing me over already," I tell her.

Annabel screws up her face. "Err, how so?"

"Well, the bank re-issued my Debit Card a few weeks ago because of some issue with the date, said it was something to do with the Y2K glitch," I tell her.

"How? It's only the 16th!" Annabel asks.

"Something to do with the expiry date. Probably that numbering error the guy was talking about."

"Well at least they are identifying problems" she offers.

"How many are there though? You know my credit card was declined last night and the girl in the shop was saying something about the card machine and Y2K."

Annabel just stares at me. I've probably just sounded like I should be wearing a tin foil hat in a bunker somewhere. "I'm not paranoid, it just seems that too much can go wrong from something so small. Imagine if the computers in the hospitals fail, or the airports. It's going to be messed up everywhere." Yes, that made me sound completely sane.

"I get what you're saying Ray, but why wouldn't they be doing the same thing we have done today and get it sorted before the new year? And it seems like most places are doing that aren't they?"

The salesman and his pitch are still ringing in my ears. "That's the problem though Annabel, Russia aren't doing a thing are they? Yeltsin is too busy getting pissed up and trying to conduct the Berlin Orchestra."

Annabel laughs and takes a cigarette from my pack. "Look, we have done our bit now, there isn't anything else we can do is there? Shouldn't you be focusing on getting back into your house and talking to Debbie?"

I suddenly remember that I hadn't checked my phone since before the meeting, I'd been more concerned with the Y2K bombshell that was just dropped on us and getting to the pub for my own hair of the dog.

"Where are you going tonight Ray? You can't be

in those clothes all weekend!" Annabel asks.

"I don't know really. I'll probably go back to my mate's and try and call Debbie again." I rumble around in my work bag for my mobile.

"You can always kip at mine if you want," Annabel offers, "Just probably wouldn't be the best thing if Debbie finds out."

I grab my phone out of my bag. "Cheers Annabel, means a lot, but I'll be fine at my mate's place." I look down at the phone. 2 messages from Clive.

"You should really try and talk things over with her Ray. I mean, what is it that made her kick you out?"

I shake my head and tell her the truth. "I honestly have no idea." I look back down at my phone and open the first message.

DNT COME BACK AFTER WRK

Well that rules out that option I think, Annabel has a worried look on her face and I can't tell if it's still the Y2K problem or genuine concern for me.

She grabs my hand and sighs. "Maybe a couple of days apart will help out? Let her clear her head and think things over before making any decisions, especially if one of you does something you regret."

I nod at her and focus back on my phone to click on the second message from Clive.

DEBBIE SAYS ITS OVER

"I think it's too late for that" I say to Annabel sliding my phone into my pocket. "I'll take a lift to my mate's if it's on your way home though?"

CHECKLIST FOR THE END OF THE WORLD

12

I pour myself a glass of the whisky I'd bought from the shop around 24 hours previously. I hadn't heard a thing from Debbie, Clive or the girl with the Backstreet Boys t-shirt. Guess I should be calling her 'Kelly' now I know her name.

Annabel had dropped me off outside Eddy's, and I was still kicking myself for breaking one of my own core beliefs of never mixing work and personal life by letting her know what was happening between me and Debbie. Well, more of what was happening to me as I had no idea what was going on with Debbie. We hadn't spoken for over twenty-four hours now.

Eddy is sat in a beanbag chair in his front room playing 'Ready 2 Rumble' on his new SEGA Dreamcast. It looks pretty cool to be honest, and a huge difference from the SEGA Mega Drive that we had in our Uni Dorm room. Just thinking about the hours we invested in Street Fighter 2 and Streets of Rage, it's no surprise neither of us ended up with a degree.

It's the weekend tomorrow, a week until Christmas Day, and whilst I would usually be putting up the last of the decorations and undertaking some last-minute Christmas shopping, I need to focus on getting some semblance of normality back into my life right now.

I have a pen and paper in front of me (Gordon would be pleased) and I'm trying to figure out what I need to get a sense of normality back. I write checklists a lot. I get it from my grandmother as she would always have a list for everything that required a bit of thought. She said she started making them during the war and just carried on as she liked to make sure things were done and done properly; unlike my late mother who lived her life off the bag of a fag packet.

It's getting harder to remember my mother's face. Since she died it has slowly faded every day. It's been over two years now and the after effects have never really gone away. My drinking became heavy again to mask the pain and I withdrew more into myself than I had when my grandparents died, one in 1991 and the other shortly afterwards in 1992. It was more the unanswered questions of why that threw me into a dark depression.

The only thing I have left of hers is whatever is in that envelope in my sideboard. The will was all done and dusted and distributed out by some trust and whatever is left is in the envelope. I think it's the only thing she has ever given to me since she left and, although I'm pretty sure I know what it is, part of me doesn't want to accept that part of her life, the part that was chosen over me.

She left me to go live on a commune in 1977; I was five. I'd written a similar list to the one I'm writing now; albeit in crayon and less detailed but the purpose was the same; to make sure I got everything I needed before starting off somewhere new.

I'd left our small, rented room and walked down the street to my grandparents' house. The look on their faces when I just turned up was one I'll never forget. So much concern and worry but so much love too. They had adopted my mother back in Ireland at a similar age so why not do it all over again, I guess.

My grandmother saw the checklist I was clutching in my hand and made sure I had everything on it whilst we unpacked my rucksack of possessions into their attic room. It was from this point in my life that I found the need to compartmentalize anything and everything to make it easier for me to understand, and that's why I made lists.

I wrote a checklist when I left for University, a list when I got kicked out, a list when I bought the house and two when both my grandparents died. Each time everything turned out all right.

I start with a heading to give myself some perspective on what I am trying to attain. 'Things I need' - no, too generic. I scribble it out. 'Getting back on track', sounds like I was somehow on track which I don't think I was. I cross that one off. 'Checklist for...' I can't think of what I am preparing for, a new life? A different life? Life without Debbie?

Eddy interrupts my train of thought. "I'm making a sandwich, do you want one?" he asks as he saunters over to his fridge to hunt for some ingredients.

"Yeah go on then," I reply, still nursing the whisky in my one hand and pen in the other.

"Writing your checklist?" Eddy asks whilst pulling out some packets from the fridge.

"Yeah, just stuck on the title," I reply.

"That's a good start," Eddy mocks as he knocks the fridge closed with his elbow. He dumps his chosen ingredients down on the kitchen island in front of me. "All this okay?" he points to the mound.

"Yeah, whatever," I dismiss. "Problem with the list is I need to know the end goal before I write it mate, otherwise it's just a list of shit with no goal at the end. The title, the purpose is the main thing."

"Just put on there: Credit Card, Debit Card, Clothes, Money, Phone Charger and new Girlfriend" he shouts over from inside his cupboard.

I roll my eyes. "That doesn't cover much Eddy, I mean I can't live in your spare room forever."

Eddy looks back over, "Why not? I mean I have more room here than I need and you need somewhere to stay, just move in with me. Easy!" he smiles.

I appreciate the offer but I can't keep sponging off Eddy like so many others had done. "Thanks Eddy but I need to sort something out for myself. I'll happily stay here with you till I do though if that's cool?"

Eddy looks a little disheartened, "Yeah, whatever you want mate, it's cool with me."

I look back at my blank piece of paper covered in scribbles and decided a fresh piece of paper will help me. I screw up the sheet and toss it at Eddy.

"I'm trying to make you a sandwich you twat." he moans and continues with his masterpiece whilst I am staring blankly at mine.

I start to think about the previous lists I had made and which bits I could steal or modify for my current situation. The one from when my mum left was my first and probably my most successful, but I doubt that I will be needing my Teddy Bear, Star Wars figures and Stretch Armstrong this time, although they were essential back then. Perhaps that's the key though: what is essential to me right now? What do I want from life? A few days ago, I would have answered Debbie and my house but I seem to have survived without those four walls and Debbie's lukewarm embrace, so what is it I actually want and what do I actually need?

It's two weeks until the new year so that seems a good starting point for me, gives me a fortnight to prepare and start fresh. 'Checklist for the New Millennium,' I write down. It looks hopeful and optimistic, so what sits under it? What is it I actually want and need?

I remember that during my first bout of depression the counsellor showed me a triangle with every basic need at the bottom and then some more on top. I wish I had paid attention and could remember it. That could be a good starting point and be useful right now. I look over at Eddy who by now is drizzling olive oil with his arm above his head. He had been infatuated by the new 'Naked' TV chef Jamie Oliver and had suddenly started using his kitchen and had bought a Vespa moped.

"Eddy you know anything about a triangle with basic human needs?" I shout across to him.

Eddy who has now started juggling some tomatoes seems perplexed. "No idea mate, look it up."

"I can hardly look up triangles in an encyclopedia mate. It's not going to help is it?" I reply, wondering if Eddy has an encyclopedia.

"Ask Jeeves mate," Eddy tells me.

"Who the fuck is Jeeves?" I reply as Eddy sits down the tomatoes and grabs a knife.

"He's the online butler mate. It's pretty cool.

Just ask him a question and he will find the answer for you."

"You ask a question, any question, and he will answer it?"

Eddy nods "Yeah, pretty simple programming. It's a search engine. Basically, just uses the words you input to run some algorithms and bring up what you need. Wish I had thought of it."

Eddy already had enough money rolling in from the 'dot com boom', I doubt an online butler or search function could be worth that much.

"Which computer has Jeeves on it mate?" I ask as I raise from my stool.

Eddy laughs.

"What?" I ask.

"Use the one next door, just make sure the modem is plugged in and..." Eddy pauses as he sees my bewildered face, "I'll load it up for you. Give me a sec."

Eddy abandons the sandwich station and grabs a cigarette as he drags me to the computer with Ask Jeeves on it.

"That's the modem there." Eddy points at the wall, "This cable connects to the PC and you click on the picture of the computer with the phone next to it to get onto the internet."

I nod, pretending to understand everything as the computer makes a weird squeaky noise a bit like the fax machine in the office.

"Click on Internet Explorer and in the bar at the top type 'AskJeeves.com' and he will pop up."

I sit back and smile as the face of a butler slowly appears on the screen. "Can I get this programme at work?" I ask.

Eddy laughs again. "It's a website so any

computer attached to the internet will be able to access it. Just use Internet Explorer and type in Askjeeves.com."

"Cool, I get it," I say, still not quite understanding how this will all work.

"Use this PC whenever you want though mate. It's a good one, Windows 98 and 128MB of RAM so quite quick really."

"I don't know what any of that is, but I don't think I'll need to use the internet much, just want to ask this Jeeves about the triangle."

Eddy laughs. "It's full of porn you know."

My mouth must have dropped, "What is? The Internet?"

"Yeah! It's like 90% pornography, 5% Chat rooms and 5% other!" he chuckles.

No wonder Tim took his laptop home from work every day.

Eddy points to the screen. "Jeeves has loaded up now, ask him what you want mate."

I replace Eddy in the swivel chair in front of his desk and start to type my question for Jeeves.

13

"Maslow's Hierarchy of Needs," I announce to Eddy as I re-enter the kitchen. Eddy is finishing off his sandwich and points to mine on the counter.

"Sandwich, that's probably a need," he says through a mouth full of food.

I sit down and pull the sandwich towards me, lifting the top slice up to see what Eddy had constructed for us.

"Honey roast ham, Emmental cheese, pickles, tomato and English mustard" Eddy informs me on his way to the dishwasher.

"Nice one, cheers," I reply, grasping both sides of the thick wedge with my hands.

"Maslow, that's the triangle then is it?" Eddy asks.

"Yeah, it's all your basic needs at the bottom, then your psychological needs through to self-actualization," I reply before stuffing the sandwich into my mouth for a bite.

"What's self-actualization?" Eddy asks.

I take a pause from my sandwich. "Well, from what I could gather from Jeeves, it's about reaching your full potential."

"Not sure I understand," Eddy frowns.

I grab my pen and pad with my one free hand (the other clinging to my sandwich) I draw out a rough triangle and divide it into five sections.

"On the bottom of the triangle are the basic needs, so first the physiological needs like water, food, shelter, heat. Then. in the next section safety and security."

"Right" Eddy nods.

"Then the next two layers are psychological, so you start with belongingness and love and then esteem. Then, right at the top of the triangle, self-actualisation."

"How does it work then?" Eddy scratches his chin.

"Well Maslow put it together to show how human's motivations generally work, so for the motivation to happen at the next stage the previous stage needs to be fully satisfied."

"I'm still lost" Eddy sighs.

"So, basically, you need to complete each level to move onto the next. The goal is to get to the top which is self-actualisation."

"Reaching your full potential."

"That's right," I tell Eddy before stuffing the last bite into my mouth.

"You could have just printed that out," Eddy points at my sketch.

"Didn't know you had one," I laugh.

"Yeah, it's got everything hooked up and installed on it. Everything you need mate; Tomb Raider,

Championship Manager, MSN Messenger whatever you want."

I put my sandwich down on the pad and head back to the PC to print off the page on Maslow's Hierarchy of needs.

"Have you got that software CD that prevents the Y2K bug?" I ask Eddy as I search for the print button.

"Software CD?" Eddy shouts back from the kitchen.

"Yeah for the millennium bug thing," I yell. "How do I print by the way?"

Eddy walks into the front room and finds the print button for me. "Should print now. What do you mean about software for the Millennium Bug?"

"You know, the date thing where it's two digits instead of four and if it's not compliant the chips will shut down, you must know about it you work with computers!"

Eddy chuckles and puts his hand on my shoulder tapping me patronizingly. "Well, firstly, it's not a bug it was designed that way to save space and secondly, I don't know what software you are talking about."

I grab the sheet of paper from the printer tray. "I thought you worked with this stuff?"

"I do," Eddy says, "but I actually go in and fix the problem for major companies and I have never used a CD. "

"Isn't everyone using them?" I ask.

"No, and not everyone is fixing the programming errors either," Eddy says. "High risk industries are the priority and they have been fixed for months."

"Well if everyone did their bit we wouldn't have

to worry, would we? I mean if were not fixing everything and countries like Russia aren't doing anything at all what's the point in anyone being prepared?"

Eddy laughs. "Don't chuck me and Russia into the same sentence. It's hardly the same is it mate!" He points to the PC. "That PC there controls that printer and nothing else. If some run programme fails or breaks who cares? I'll buy a new one."

"That's if there is anywhere left to buy a new one," I scoff.

Eddie sighs "Ray, nothing is going to happen. Or at least, nothing major."

"The guy selling the software at work said 3-5% of computer chips or something like that would fail."

Eddy shrugs "Look Ray, I have friends in the industry who say it's happening, and friends who say it won't. There's a guy online who has a website dedicated to busting it as a myth. On the news it's the same: one day it's essential, next it's a massive waste of money. For me, all I can do is make sure I'm using four digits when entering a year when I programme from now on."

"It just feels like we should be doing more than we are," I argue.

Eddy lights a cigarette. "The media are blowing it way out of proportion. They didn't even bat an eyelid about September. We use 9999 in programming to specify an unknown date, so everyone was worried about the date actually being 9/9/99. SEGA even released the Dreamcast on 9/9/99 as a massive 'fuck you'."

I shake my head. "But what if it's not hype? Nuclear missiles in Russia are programmed to go off if they even think they are under attack, which they will if millions of chips start to fail. What about the chips in banks' computers? All our records just wiped; everyone starts with zero." I join Eddy by lighting a cigarette as he looks at me with some concern.

"Mate your hangover is terrible today. Triangles, self-actualization, Y2K. You need a proper smoke."

I raise my eyebrows "I'm alright thanks Eddy."

He shrugs. "Suit yourself. I'm going to roll one up and play some WCW/NWO Revenge on the N64."

I grab my printout and head back to the kitchen.

"Oh, and it's the pay per view on Sunday so I'm having some people over to watch the wrestling, so try and finish your triangle by then," Eddy shouts at me from his beanbag chair.

I rest my cigarette in the ashtray on the table and place the printout of 'Maslow's Hierarchy of needs' next to my pen and paper. Eddy's solution to everything was to have a drink or roll up a joint. He had been on his Dreamcast or Nintendo 64 for most of the day and apart from making me a sandwich hadn't done anything else. I couldn't do that. If I had a problem, I needed to solve it and await the problems that always arose from whatever I had decided was the solution. Eddy was happy enough in his beanbag chair when he probably could have earnt a couple of thousand pounds today working on one of his contracts for web design, programming or fixing the Y2K problem. Sometimes I wonder if he knows how lucky he is to be part of the 'dot com boom', as the media call it.

I look at printout in front of me: 'Physiological Needs' makes sense; food, water, warmth and rest. These were part of the basic needs and I'd pretty much taken them all for granted until last night when I had been deprived of them all albeit not for too long.

'Security and Safety' is next. It is categorised as a basic need too, but also falls into the psychological section. All part of the progression through the pyramid, I guess. You need to feel safe and secure.

'Belongingness and Love' has intimate relationships and friends listen underneath it. I look for sex in there but apparently, he classed it as a 'physiological' need to much controversy. I guess it fits in all the sections depending on the individual. Teenage me would chuck it in as a basic need.

'Esteem', both higher and lower versions covering prestige and accomplishment. Not sure about this. I'll have to come back to these in more detail. Probably best to work on the basics first.

And, again, sitting as a goal at the top of the pyramid is the big blue triangle of 'Self Actualization', reaching one's full potential, something that I can't help but think I have always had a problem achieving.

My phone suddenly beeps so I reach inside my pocket and pull it out. It's an unknown number.

Found ur keys c u soon Kelly xx

14

"Where were they?" I ask Kelly, no Backstreet Boys t-shirt today.

"Fell into the cola bottles," Kelly says as she points at the jar of sweets behind the counter. One of many in a row of future tooth decay.

"Thanks," I say as I turn to leave.

"Is there any reward?" Kelly asks.

"Err, I don't really have any money to be honest," I offer as Kelly processes this.

"Fancy taking me out then?" she suggests.

My mouth drops open slightly, "Um, yeah?" I manage to get out.

Kelly smiles, "Cool, where shall we go?"

I struggle to come up with either an excuse or an answer, so I just say what's on my mind, "I'm busy this weekend but I'll text you."

Kelly flicks her hair "Well, it's up to you."

"I will," I tell her "I promise."

Kelly leans over the counter slightly "Where

shall we go?"

"I don't know, I'll think of something."

"My mum really likes you by the way, said you were very polite."

I don't know whether to be relived or worried. "Great, like I said, I'll text you yeah?" I offer as I inch towards the door.

"Cool, see you then," she shouts as I push the door to escape.

I see Michael outside reading his newspaper and give him a nod. He smiles back and goes back to whatever story he is currently engrossed in. My eyes focus on the headline under his gloved fingers: 'Y2K Bug Minister – Funding Cut'. Something I'll have to 'Ask Jeeves' about later.

At least now I have my keys, I can get into my house and get some stuff I need, and I don't have to go through Clive or face the wrath of Debbie. It's a Friday night so Debbie is most likely still out with her work colleagues having a drink. Clive has hopefully eaten or drank anything of value and gone, so fingers crossed I should be able to get in and out without anyone knowing I have been there.

I'm planning it out in my head like precise military operation: phone charger from lounge, bank book, passport and documents from my sideboard, clothes and underwear from my side of the wardrobe. Chuck it all in the big 'France 98" duffel bag I got free from the petrol station. Toiletries from the bathroom, photo album from the spare room and out of the house. I reckon I can do it in five minutes or less which should be ample time. Debbie hasn't been home before ten on a Friday for months now. I just hope that she has stuck with her routine and I can get in and out without any confrontation.

I can see the 'Do un' pub sign in the distance, probably halfway between the shop and my house now. I could go in and get my credit card on the way back. I wouldn't have to come back here for a while then, or unless I wanted to which currently I don't. I can see the burly landlord through the window, his bald head shimmering under the backlights of the bar and his big, tattooed arm pulling at the Black Sheep Bitter pump. He could probably throw a mean punch, but it would probably kill him as he looks severely out of shape. Too many pints a day I reckon.

The rain has held off tonight which is good. Debbie would notice muddy footprints in the house, and I don't have time to be without my shoes whilst I'm inside. I want to be as quick as possible. The last thing I need is to be caught halfway through by Debbie. Not that she would say anything anyway. She would just cry and shout and make a scene. Clive would be round like a flash and I wouldn't achieve anything. The time for talking has been and gone. She has said it is over; well Clive has, and she has made no attempt to speak to me or even let me know what I have done that warrants being banished from my own home.

The kid in the old grey Man United shirt with 'Cantona' on the back boots a ball in my direction which I expertly dodge and shout:

"Cantona retired two years ago. Your haircut is out of date too." I chuckle at the 'curtains' flopping around his face. The bunch of knobheads who hang out by the old grocers are back and manage a snigger as I walk past. I can't see the old fella with the can of John Smiths, or Pat as her deckchair is empty.

The front room light is definitely off. I can't see

any light from the house at all, but I'll need to get up to the doorstep before I am sure. I step over a recently laid dog turd on the pavement and past the final house before ours on the terraced street. I quietly open the gate and tip toe up to the front door where all I can hear is the sound of distant cars, the kid shouting 'CANTONA!' and someone in the vicinity singing along to 'Livin' la Vida Loca'.

I walk up the short path to the front door and look at my watch. It's ten to ten and time to get in and out as fast as I can. I gently kneel down so I am at the same height as the letter box, I raise it slightly and peek through.

I feel a wave of relief as I see no movement at all. I reach in my pocket for my keys and slowly inch them into the lock and turn, hearing the click as I rise to become eye level with the house number on the door.

I gently push the door open and slither into almost pitch black, being careful not to leave any footprints on the mail that has landed on the mat. I slowly close the door and in the glare of the streetlight spot a letter addressed to me on the mat I have just stepped over. I pick it up and it feels like it contains a card. Bonus! I shove it in my pocket and head to the lounge feeling my way towards the wall by the stairs and grabbing my phone charger from the drawer in the huge dresser there along with a couple of my cassettes from next to the music station that sits on its main shelf.

I haven't turned on a light yet, so It feels slightly like I am robbing a house. This being my own house and the fact I had a key slightly dampens the buzz, but I'm still feeling a slight adrenaline rush.

I head upstairs and to the bedroom where I feel

on top of the wardrobe and grab the unopened plastic bag containing the 'France 98' duffel bag, quickly opening the plastic covering and shoving it into the main section followed by some socks, boxers, jeans, chinos, popper pants, t-shirts, jumpers, hoodies, work shirts, scarf, pair of gloves and a couple of hats; at least that's what I think I have grabbed in the dim light from the street.

I empty my pockets of the phone charger, letter and cassettes into one of the side pockets and throw in the parka I am wearing. take my favorite leather jacket from its hanger in the wardrobe and slide it on.

Onto the bathroom next. I flick the switch for the light in my shaving mirror to fish out a travel toiletries bag from the below the sink cupboard. I manage to grab it throwing in a toothbrush, deodorant, aftershave, shaving cream, razor and a couple of washcloths from the airing cupboard. I shove the toiletries into the main compartment of my duffel bag along with a towel from the airing cupboard, turn off the mirror light and head back to the landing.

Next, the sideboard; I open the central drawer and take out my bank book, passport and big folder full of all my important documents placing them at the top of my duffel bag. I rearrange what's left in there to try and cover my tracks and spot the envelope containing my inheritance from my mother's will. Weird; it seems to have been opened.

I put the duffel bag down and pick the thick green envelope up. Sure enough, the top has been sliced open with a letter opener. Whatever was inside is still there I think, but it's definitely been opened.

Of all the things I'd have expected from Debbie this was not one of them. She knew I didn't want to open it. I wasn't ready. But her curiosity, or Clive's, must have got the better of them. I decide to take it with me. It's open now so I guess that choice has been made for me. I rip off some of the front of the envelope and look for a pen in the 'pen drawer' but as per usual there is everything but a fucking pen in there I reach into my bag and sure enough I find the little blue Argos pen.

I needed to get some things, sorry but I had nothing. I'm staying at Eddy's, we can talk when you want.

I start to write 'love you' but I can't bring myself to do it. I don't know why but I think I'm more angry now than upset, so I just leave the note on her pillow as it is. Hopefully the note will let her know I can't just be erased from her memory like my mother tried to do to me, and also it leaves a little hint that I know she's opened something I didn't want to be opened.

I head back downstairs and towards the kitchen, switching on the hob light above the stove near the drawer I am after. I can see Clive has made his way through all the beers I had in the fridge and there are two empty bottles of wine too. Debbie must have had a secret stash; I'd imagine she will be having a bit of the 'hair of the dog' herself as well today.

I pull out the corner drawer where we store all the loose odds and ends that have no real place anywhere. I find my 'Swiss Army' knife that my Grandad got me for my tenth birthday and his old tobacco tin which I hope still contains something I stashed in it earlier in the year. I pry open the top and sure enough inside is a roll of ten-pound notes from my bonus at work and, more interestingly, a selection of old coins and little plastic pockets with rare stamps in them from my grandmother's collection. She told me the coins and stamps were worth a few quid.

I palm off one of the tenners and shove the knife in my pocket along with the tin and turn off the hob light. My watch is showing 21:57 now. I'd better get out before Debbie and/or Clive gets back. I make sure everything is how I found it so they don't actually think they were burgled and walk slowly towards the front door, feeling the blood rush to my head as I realize I have everything and just need to get out now.

I reach the front door and look through the peep hole. I can't see anyone in the front. It's now or never. I open up the door quietly, using the handle as a crutch as I step over the mail onto the front step, and closing it as quietly as I can, ensuring I hear the click of the lock. I almost don't want to turn around but I do and thankfully nobody is there, apart from the kid with the curtains in the 'Cantona' shirt.

15

I pull open the heavy door to the 'Do un" Pub and once again I'm greeted by a waft of smoke and the gaze of around a dozen 'locals' who are propping up the bar. The ruddy faced old man adorned in gold is here; so is the skinny fella in the oversized coat, shouting at the same picture. I spot the scene of my theft last night and I'm suddenly glad I made the choice to swap the parka for my leather jacket.

"Oh look, it's Rain man! After a tab again are we?" the burly landlord greets me to a chorus of chuckles from his band of merry locals.

"No." I walk up to the bar. "Could I have my card that you took last night please?" I reason it would be better to get to the point.

The landlord laughs "What card is that then?"

I can see he is either a massive twat or extremely bored and wants to get into a pissing contest in front of his mates. "Don't remember any card from last night."

I breathe out deeply and shake my head.

"Perhaps you left it in a gay bar in town?" he quips, and his audience burst into a chorus of chuckles and coughs.

I can feel the adrenaline building up inside me. I want to say something, but I can't get any words out at the moment. I just want to get my card and get out of this shithole.

"Shall I call your mummy and daddy? Let them know you've wandered off again,"   he laughs as the band of locals resume their cackling as if on timer.

"What is it you get out of this?" I ask.

The landlord just laughs and looks around at his audience of clowns.

"No seriously, what do you get out of this?" I say sternly.

"You what? Shut up!" he dismisses.

"Do you really have the time for all this? Is your life that dull you have to rope me into your shit?" I ask him.

"Shut up you dickhead," he tuts.

"You the big hard man, are you? Making funnies to impress your mates? Acting all hard like it's some sort of badge of honour that you're a violent prick?"

"Watch yourself," he warns.

"The big hard man... does it make you feel important? Better about yourself? What is it that makes you such a cunt?" I don't fancy my chances against this burly oaf, but pleasantries got me a stolen card and a 'fuck off' last night so I'm employing different tactics.

The burly landlord smiles, presses a button on his till and takes out my credit card, he stares at me whilst placing it on the bar. "Go on then Lad, take it, I dare you".

I step forward and reach out to grab the card as his shovel hand grabs my wrist and squeezes and twist it with a vice like grip.

"Take the card then!" he shouts in my ear squeezing harder as I wince. "Go on, grab your fucking card!" The locals are laughing now. He is pushing my left wrist down into my forearm and pain is searing through each of my fingers. I can see tears of laughter forming in the eyes of the gold clad ruddy faced man who is banging his fist on the bar in laughter.

"For fucks sake let go!" I shout at him, but all I can see is his few teeth in a sadistic grin as he squeezes tighter and I hear a pop in my left wrist as tears form in my eyes.

"I told you not to mess we me lad!" he shouts in my ear as I spot something hanging on the wall next to the bar. "I'm gonna break your fucking ar..." He is silenced as I grab a cricket bat hanging on the wall and connect it with the side of his head. His eyes roll back and his huge frame crashes back into the wall of spirits and liquors behind him.

Ruddy face man is staring at me now, his mouth wide open as I look over the bar at this beached whale dazed and confused on the sticky floor of the bar.

Ruddy face man rises slightly out of his stool "Is he dead?"

"Nay, he's just had the senses knocked out of him," advises another local who must be a doctor. At least I haven't killed him.

I drop the bat and pick up my card from the bar, blood now appearing near one of his eyes and my left wrist still throbbing and searing with pain.

"All I wanted was my card," I direct at the locals as they all nod along encouraging me, probably fearful they will be next up to bat.

I walk round behind the bar and look at the landlord still half laid on the floor, covered in various liquids and the blood dripping from a gash on the left side of his bald head. I grab a whisky glass and push the optic of the one remaining bottle behind the bar; Jameson's. I down a quick double before walking back around to where I had been assaulted. I shove the card in my pocket, pick up my duffel bag and throw it over my shoulder. I kick the bat to the other end of the pub and head out the door.

16

I'm sat in Eddy's kitchen again. I have a bag of frozen peas on my left wrist and a glass of whisky in my right hand. I'd almost sprinted back after my confrontation at the pub. I hadn't been in a fight since the one that got me kicked out of Uni. The adrenaline was wearing off now and my wrist was starting to hurt. I had tried to get on with something but failed as I'm just staring at the table in front of me, switching between the green envelope from my mother's will, the start of my checklist and the diagram of 'Maslow's Hierarchy'.

My wrist has started to swell quite badly. I don't want to go to A&E. I hate waiting and the people I'd be waiting with are horrendous, but also, if anyone from the pub has called the police, they will be looking out for someone of my description checking in there. He knows my full name for fucks sake and there are precisely zero other people I have met with my first name.

I don't think my wrist is broken but might be

dislocated or sprained. When I got back, I asked Jeeves 'What is a broken wrist like?' and the fact I can still move my wrist seems to be a plus. The pop I heard when the burly landlord was squeezing it back isn't good but at least I didn't hear a crack.

Eddy was in bed when I got back here. He had left the N64 running Super Smash Brothers so was probably hoping I'd be back for a game with him before he passed out. I can see around twenty empty bottles of 'Stella' around his beanbag chair. He's had those today. I am starting to wonder if he's drinking too much as he has polished off a case since I arrived yesterday.

My own drinking, of course, is purely medicinal. I reassure myself of that as I gulp down the whisky. It's easing the pain in my wrist so it must be good for me. It's in lieu of hospital treatment. I have swallowed a couple of Ibuprofen too so I should be fine in a few hours, especially with the bag of peas bringing the swelling down.

I'd not had any messages since Kelly's earlier about my keys. I'd plugged my phone in for charging next to the PC whilst I was asking Jeeves about my wrist; might be worth checking it in a bit just in case Debbie or Clive have figured out what I have done, or the police came knocking there after my run in with the Landlord at the 'Do un'.

Jeeves had also told me about the headline I saw today: the government have announced a permanent cut of funding for all work on programming issues for the Y2K 'bug'. The 'Millennium Bug' minister, Margaret Beckett, had fought it but it's being cut with current spending hitting over a hundred million and nearly fifteen billion spend privately; the decision being made to follow Italy and Russia's lead of doing pretty much fuck all and calls from some to invest the money elsewhere such as in England's bid for the 2006 World Cup and a new Wembley Stadium. We were officially now doing nothing more.

'Checklist for the New Millennium' stares back at me. It's gone midnight now and I'd come no closer this evening to sorting out what I need to do over the next fortnight. All I have achieved is robbing my own house and knocking someone out with a cricket bat to retrieve my own credit card.

The thoughts of the salesman this morning and my disagreement with Eddy over Y2K are dancing around my mind. Perhaps that's what it will come to in a few weeks anyway, knocking people out with cricket bats just to get back what is yours. Everything I had gone to great lengths to get tonight was originally mine in the first place - the keys, the credit cards, the debit card, the stuff from my own house.

It makes me angry because it is my house, not Debbie's at all. She hadn't paid a penny towards it but was happy to claim it as her own now. Technically it was half hers when we got married but I'd spent my money from the sale of my grandparents' house to buy it. Five years ago, I'd agreed to buy a small cottage in the countryside near Haworth off one of my late grandparents' friends. Debbie had sulked for months until I agreed to buy the one in town, said we would be 'outcasts' if we moved so far from the town centre.

I don't want to go back there. It was never me. It was a life I had designed for me and no wonder I wasn't happy in it. I want to make my roots somewhere new and watch them grow. I'd been uprooted so many times as a child. I'd settled at my grandparents but nowhere else really, and even then I never knew if my mother would turn up and try to take me to her commune or - my biggest fear - a stranger turning up and announcing they were my father.

I'd gone to see The Matrix with Debbie a few months back and suddenly parts of it are starting to make sense. Right now I could easily take the 'blue pill' and ignore everything that is happening around me, the things I have seen and learnt in the past few days, and wake up happily in bed next to Debbie for the rest of my life; whether that be two weeks or much longer. Or, I could take the 'red pill', and carry on with what I am doing, learning more, potentially growing more and coming out of it alive. I roll the pen between the fingers on my good hand and decide that I am taking the red pill. I scratch out part of my title to my checklist and re-write with my new chosen words. I sit back and admire "Checklist for the New Millennium End of the World".

I sip my whisky and look at the envelope containing my mother's first, last and only gift to me. I pull it towards me with my good hand and examine it. Just full of papers, nothing else really. I push the bag of peas off my injured wrist and grip lightly with it at the bottom left corner as I pull out what's in the envelope, unfolding the bits of paper and spreading them out across the table in front of me. What she has left me is exactly what I thought it would be. I'd been told and heard second hand but never seen the details myself.

Maybe I am ready now, ready to face the past and also ready to move on.

17

The wind is howling and pounding at my body and exposed face. Perfect for the nearby wind turbines but relentless in its assault on me.

I look out across the moors ahead of me and amongst the purple sea of heather sticks out a patch of green and some buildings - the commune. A two-floor farmhouse with a stone-walled barn to the side of the farmhouse and some smaller outbuilding in front of it. We have come as far as the metal gate and there is still the large front field between us and the farmhouse's front door.

This was where my mother had gone to go live when she abandoned me in 1977. High in the moors that separate Hebden Bridge from the small village of Oxenhope; close enough to Hebden Bridge for all their needs but far enough away to live how they wanted.

All I can remember was her saying goodbye and leaving in a battered old camper van full of smiling people. That's when I made my checklist to emigrate to my grandparents' house down the road.

My mother visited once after that, on my 6th Birthday, after which I never spoke to her again. I remember her telling me that no matter what happens I was never to live with my father. I'd never even met the guy, so he obviously wasn't too bothered about me.

The breakdown I had after she died crippled me. I had so many unanswered questions and I was now completely alone. Debbie was there for me, but all of my family were gone. The breakdown (and depression) was one of the reasons I never opened the envelope; I knew it would bring me here. She was the last here before she died. I just wasn't ready to come here.

"It's bloody freezing up here," Annabel says, shielding her face from the wind. She wasn't wrong. It was colder than in the town centre and I was grateful I'd worn the stolen parka.

"Sorry, I do appreciate the lift though", I reply, trying to figure out how to open the gate.

"No worries, I didn't have any plans today anyway" she says, locking her Renault Espace.

I pull the lever back and push the gate open. "I would invite you in for a cuppa but…"

"Don't worry, I brought my own," she smiles showing me the Thermos flask in her bag. At least someone came prepared.

Walking across the field towards the front door of the farmhouse I can see where the crops and vegetable patches used to be. There are still some planters in place made out of railway sleepers and some definite animal pens in front of the barn. I make out what looks like a water well to the side of the main building and some abandoned chicken coops, sheltered by an awning off the side of the barn, that need a bit of renovation.

From what I heard about this place from my grandparents it was completely self-sufficient and the only reason they went into Hebden Bridge was to have a few drinks, some work and to sell their crop of weed. My grandfather had told me that my mother had worked in the Trades Club in town and did so right up into the 90's apparently.

"So, all this is yours?" Annabel asks.

"Yeah, I guess so," I reply, noticing that she almost seems to be enjoying this.

Annabel nods "And it was your mother's and she left it to you?"

"That's what I understand, yeah. She was the last one here and it was all hers before she died. I think I need to file a few things or send some things off, but its mine, everything within the drystone walls according to the plans".

I wasn't quite sure what I needed to do 'legally' to be completely sure everything was mine, but seeing as I was now preparing for what I believed to possibly be the end of the world in a fortnights time it wasn't high on my new agenda. I'd give Dave a call. Being a solicitor, he should know.

"How did your mum end up here then?" Annabel asks whilst kicking a dandelion.

"It was a commune. From what I know people either died or moved away or gave up and it ended up dwindling down to just being my mother here by herself, and by default it hers." Saying it out loud made it sound a bit like the book 'Battle Royale' I had read a few weeks ago.

"Sounds like Battle Royale," Annabel said almost as if reading my mind.

"You can read minds," I chuckle back.

I didn't imagine my first trip back to the commune being like this. As a kid I'd always imagined riding in on my bike and saving my mother and whisking her away to safety, which blended into my teenage years where I'd imagine riding in on my motorbike, calling her a piece of shit and a terrible mother before whisking some young hippy girl away who hopefully had some weed on her.

As an adult I didn't even think about coming here. I was too scared of what I would find. What did it look like? What did my mother look like? Sound like? Would my father be here? Would my mother tell me about why she abandoned me? All questions I was too afraid to get the answer to but I was just fearful as she had chosen them over me. And then I became so obsessed with it all after she died.

This wasn't how I had imagined it either. How I was feeling or what I can see. There isn't any life here at all. I'm trying to visualize this place twenty years ago with a congregation of people all working the land, playing guitars and singing Bob Dylan songs, some twat in the corner with a Harmonica ruining it for everyone else. I just can't quite see it.

On approaching the farmhouse, it looks even smaller now than when I first caught a glimpse coming up to the main gate. A front door in the middle with two windows either side of it and two on the upstairs. Probably only two rooms on either floor. The outbuilding isn't that big either, but the barn is a decent size, around twice the size of the house.

"How do we get in?" Annabel asks as I start to realize I hadn't thought of how I'd get into the place.

"I haven't got the set of keys yet," I tell her.

"Story of your life Ray," she jokes as she peeks around the side of the house.

"If there's another door I don't have a key for that either," I shout after her.

"Ray, there's a ladder here, we can try the windows."

"No, it's all right. I'll come back when I've got the keys," I quickly shoot her down.

"You gonna knock me out with a cricket bat as well then?" already mocking the story I had told her from last night.

Annabel circles the house, checking the ground floor windows with no luck before grabbing the ladder. "Come on Ray, hold the ladder, I'll go up."

"My wrist is still a bit fucked," I argue.

"Just hold the damn ladder Ray" she snaps as I nod my head in forced agreement.

I wince as I help her position the ladder. It's damp and extremely rusty but looks like it might hold Annabel's weight. It would be pushing it if I tried, especially with my messed up left wrist.

"No, let's try that window," Annabel directs whilst pointing at a window that looks like it could be slightly ajar. I shift the ladder into place with my good hand as she readies herself for the climb.

"Are you going to be able to catch me if I fall?" she asks with one step on the first rung.

"Try and fall towards my right side," I advise, half-joking and half completely serious.

Annabel shoots up the ladder at a great pace, probably afraid each rung would crumble with the slightest weight. She reaches the summit, pulls at the bottom of the old window frame and it pulls out squeaking on its hinges.

"I'm going in," Annabel shouts down and I steady the ladder with all my body weight to ensure she has a decent platform.

As her feet disappear into the depths of the building, I wonder what to do next. Should I go up as well? Is she going to come back down? What if she can't get back out? What if she falls? Then I hear a loud creak and look back around the corner.

"Door's open!" Annabel smiles at me, "Bring my bag so we can have a cuppa will you Ray?"

18

Entering the farmhouse, I am immediately overwhelmed by the smell of stale smoke, partially from cigarettes but mainly from the massive fire that takes up the majority of the left-hand side of the building, Within the set-back alcove is not only a huge section with a fireplace, but also a pretty nice-looking old range cooker and separate area for hanging clothes and what looks like meats for smoking.

Neatly stacked in the left-hand corner is some firewood and a basket half full of kindling. There is a large bulky wooden table in the centre of the room where I put Annabel's bag just next to an old newspaper. Eight matching wooden chairs surround the big hunk of wood, four on each side still pushed into place. Underneath is a large rug that covers the whole length and width of the table.

The back wall and the front wall have been plastered over and some pictures hang on them. I can't make out what they all are, but one is definitely the outbuilding in front of the barn. The two remaining walls are exposed stone, one containing the huge alcove with the fireplace and the other containing both a door leading to a second room on one side, and a set of stairs on the other.

I walk across the flagstone flooring to the second room where Annabel has positioned herself in one of the pretty awesome wingback leather chairs.

"Think these are Chesterfields," she comments as I run my hand over the smooth leather.

"Yeah, pretty nice," I add sitting down on the matching three seat sofa.

My eyes start to take in the rest of the room. The sofa I am sat on backs onto the main dividing old stone wall. Annabel's wingback chair is in the back right hand corner of the room. Opposite my sofa is a smaller fireplace than in the kitchen. The other wingback armchair is between the fire and the front window with its net curtains just about hiding the outside.

"No telly," Annabel states.

"No power," I add pointing to the empty oil lamps hanging on the walls.

"What's the upstairs like?" I ask Annabel.

"Go have a look for yourself," she says standing up, "I'll pour us a tea".

She follows me back into the kitchen as I point to her bag on the table. I look at the staircase. The stone has been covered with a thin carpet all up its tight and winding path. I look for a bannister but there isn't anything to hold on to; probably not the best to navigate after a few drinks.

I emerge into a large dark room with shiny oak wooden floorboards. There are four beds, almost military style cots, against the left side of the wall, all of them unmade with bare mattresses, apart from one, which I guess was my mother's, still covered with a duvet and two pillows at the head.

There is a book next to it and a dusty glass. Maybe the last remnants of her presence here, or even possibly on earth. On the right side of the wall are some bookcases, a dresser and a wardrobe, all in a dark thick set wood that has been roughly, yet beautifully, made. The bookcase is dotted with some dusty old books; 'Moby Dick', 'Wuthering Heights' along with a few handwritten journals and wooden carvings.

The dresser has a funky tie dye sort of cloth draped over the top of it on which sit a mirror, hairbrush, small bowl and what looks to be an old shaving set. I open the drawers one by one. All empty apart from a small tobacco tin in the back-left hand corner of the smallest drawer.

I feel the soft, thick wood on the wardrobe and enjoy its beauty and the craftsmanship of whatever carpenter build all of these. Perhaps my father did? Whoever did them didn't make a bed, but at least they did something. I open the wardrobe and suddenly feel like I am being sucked back into a dream. I'm looking at one sole dress hanging in there; the one my mother was wearing the day she left.

I quickly close the wardrobe doors. I can't process all of that right now. I can see her all over this room. I can feel her presence and it's making me feel extremely agitated. I need to go back downstairs.

"Cool isn't it?" I hear Annabel shout from the kitchen.

"Yeah, the wood here is amazing," I shout back down as I steady myself for the trip down the staircase, navigating the small carpeted steps until I see Annabel sat at the large kitchen table with a steaming cup of tea.

"Would have made you one but there's only one cup," she grins.

"No worries, we'll just have to share then," I joke taking a seat opposite her.

"When's the housewarming party then?" Annabel asks taking a sip of her tea.

"New Year's Eve," I reply gesturing for a sip of her brew. "Well, I want to be all sorted by then, but if you're planning on sending me a Christmas Card you can send it here." I take a sip of the hot tea and pass the plastic thermos mug back to her.

"You've got a fair bit to sort out before then Ray, I mean; where is the toilet?"

I nod, she has a point. "I'll go have a look at the barn and the other outbuilding. I'm guessing the toilet is in one of those."

19

The barn doors aren't locked from the outside, so I am able to lift the heavy metal bolt out and pull one of the hefty wooden doors open with my good hand which is a relief. It reminds me of the expression 'shutting the stable door after the horse has bolted' as they clearly didn't bother locking away whatever is in here.

The flooring is a mixture of old hay and dried mud. Looking up at the roof it looks in pretty good condition, considering its abandonment. Someone had obviously cared for it meticulously in the past.

The barn has separate sections on the left for what I can only assume to be different animals once upon a time, and a mezzanine floor above them that contains a load of hay and a small seating area. To the right of me I can see tyre tracks, probably from whatever vehicle they drove, and larger tracks from whatever they used to work the land - both long gone.

Right at the back of the barn I spot a large, corrugated iron structure housing some cobweb covered firewood, a few buckets and an axe. Nothing else to see in here really.

"Bit of a disappointment," Annabel sighs.

"What were you hoping for?" I chuckle.

"Dunno, a toilet maybe?" she laughs.

We walk back towards the front of the barn, carefully pulling the door to a close and re-applying the heavy metal bolt. The wind is now howling and battering our faces as we walk to the other building which is about thirty feet away from the front of the farmhouse. This time we don't have the same luck as the door is firmly locked and there are no windows for Annabel to squeeze through. I give the door a push, but it stays firmly in place.

"No getting in here without the key," I tell Annabel who is hugging herself as the cold wind batters our bodies.

"Aren't you going to kick it in like in the movies?" Annabel asks.

"Err, no," I reply.

"Shall we go back inside?" Annabel suggests as I give the door one last push and twist of the handle.

"Yeah, probably best," I concur, as we both turn into the direction of the wind and start to fight our way back to the farmhouse.

"Whatever is in there is locked down tighter than anything else here," Annabel says. "Must be where they keep the booze," I chuckle as the wind freezes my face.

I make it through the front door of the farmhouse and walk over to the remnants of the last fire and toss some of the kindling into the pit. I roll up a bit of newspaper and set it alight with my zippo lighter, positioning the flaming ball in the centre of the kindling, placing some more on top and letting the flame take.

"Check you out Ray Mears!" Annabel comments.

I have no idea who that is but smile back to her and play it cool. "It's just a fire. Learnt all this in Scouts." She giggles as I turn back to the fire and pop a couple of smallish logs on the now burning pile of kindling. I take the opportunity to warm my hands as a nice orangey glow fills the dark fireplace.

I walk towards the framed pictures hanging on the back wall, looking for the one I spotted earlier. I need to know what's in that outbuilding. I see a photograph of a group of people by a vegetable patch, next a drawing of the moors, then another photo of a couple of bearded fellas working on the construction of the wind turbines, and one of loads of people in front of the farmhouse and its outbuildings. I spot my mother wearing the dress from upstairs; smiling and sat next to a lady with a guitar. I can see now what I was trying to visualize earlier when I arrived here. There are patches of vegetables being tended by men and women, a lady with a bucket is using the well, a Volkswagen Camper Van is sticking out of the recently renovated barn and there is a stack of the military style cot beds between the farmhouse and the outbuilding. Ten of them. That's odd as there are four upstairs, perhaps the others ended up in the barn?

The outbuilding in the picture is freshly built here. I can see two men with beer bottles in their hands just in front of the open door doing a 'cheers' and something in the doorway - a head?

"Annabel have a look at this" I shout over.

Annabel gets up from her seat and joins me. I point to the outbuilding on the photograph. "Does that look like a face to you?"

Annabel squints "Yeah, definitely a head. Perhaps someone is lying down?"

I take a closer look and the face is in profile facing the left, not the camera. "Well they would have to be pretty short. There is about two feet of space and then nothing but brick in front of them."

Annabel looks at me and scrunches her eyebrows "So... They are in some sort of hole?"

I nod back at her "Looks like it."

Annabel takes her seat back at the table and tops up her tea, her eyebrows still scrunched and now chewing slightly at her bottom lip. "Perhaps they were digging the hole for the toilet?" She theorizes, eyebrows now raised.

"You are obsessed with where the toilet is," I joke. "Could be though I guess," I add half-heartedly as I stare at the picture. How did they lose six cot beds?

"There are ten of those military style cot beds on this picture, there are four beds upstairs and clearly more than four people on the picture, so where are the other six?"

"Maybe they broke?" Annabel suggests.

"The ones upstairs are military cot beds, they last forever," I argue.

"I don't know Ray!" she shrugs her shoulders. "I'm not Doc Brown. I don't have a time-machine."

"Why would they lock the front door, and the outbuilding but not the barn or the windows? They must have locked it because it was important. The cars, the vans and the animals were gone from the barn so why shut the door after the horse has bolted? Well, they didn't, so there must be something in that outbuilding for whoever it was, probably my mother, to lock it."

"Your mother?" Annabel sighs. "I'm lost Ray, what does the outbuilding have to do with your mother?"

"Somebody locked it. They locked the house and the outbuilding but not the barn. There is something in there they didn't want people to find and the last person here was my mother."

The connection clicks in my head and I dash up the staircase.

"Ray! Why are you going upstairs?" Annabel shouts as I make it to the top of the staircase and onto the creaky solid wood floor. I go straight for the dresser drawer and the tobacco tin right at the back. I hope that my mother learnt the same thing as I did from my grandad, which was hiding important stuff in tobacco tins at the back of drawers. I prise open the top and look in at the contents. Sure enough, there they are on top of some bits of paper - a set of keys tied together with a worn piece of string.

20

"I don't get it Ray. How did you know there would be something upstairs? Are those keys?" Annabel asks as I dash out the front door towards the outbuilding.

"I saw it earlier," I shout back. "It reminded me of where I stash stuff in my house."

Annabel catches up with me looking flustered, "Just slow down and explain what's going on!"

"My Grandad gave me a tobacco tin when I was about seven or eight and he told me to keep my treasures in it away from prying eyes. He must have done the same to my mother. I saw an old tin in one of the drawers upstairs and it had these keys in it."

Annabel sighs. "Fair enough, open it then!"

There is one key that is bigger than the other and it definitely won't fit this lock, so I go with the smaller key that slots in; turns and clicks like a charm. I pull the door open towards me and can see that there is a load of hay and tools on top of where the man's head was in the picture.

"No toilet then," Annabel sighs.

"No, not much of anything really," I say unable to hide my disappointment

"Move some of the tools and hay. Perhaps there's one of those holes you have to squat over," she directs.

"You are obsessed!" I kid, "Why are you so desperate to find a toilet?"

"Why do you think Ray?" she asks, giving me a knowing look.

I use my good hand to move the tools out of the outbuilding and use the rake that is there to push the hay back as far as I can. Underneath I have revealed what looks like an old 'For Sale" sign that was probably acquired by someone in the last few years as its in pretty good condition. I shift that to the back, and I can see a few wooden boards now. The same wood that is in the bedroom at the farmhouse.

"What the fuck were they hiding?" Annabel gasps.

I pull each board up in sequence and move them outside, revealing a large circular hatch where all the crap was piled up. It's a faded red colour, made of some sort of metal and probably around fifty inches in diameter.

"What is it?" Annabel asks leaning in to take a closer look.

"I don't know. I'll need to open it and have a look," I tell her.

"Are you sure about this?" she asks.

"Might as well," I grin. I can't see a handle, so I grab the flat shovel that I had just moved and decide to prise it up. I get a slight surge of pain in my left wrist and wince. Annabel pushes down on the shovel to help as the hatch rises slowly.

"Hold this," I tell Annabel as I give her control of the shovel. I grab the edges of the hatch with my hands and lift it up so its ninety degrees, and then let it fall back on itself down onto the hay with a crash, a cloud of dust forming and getting in my eyes. I wipe the dust away and see a hole beneath where the hatch was.

"What the fuck?" Annabel's jaw is on the floor.

A ladder straddles the side of the hole and seemingly heads down to whatever is at the bottom.

"I'm going to have a look," I tell her.

"You didn't want to go in through the window earlier, now suddenly you want to go down there!" Annabel laughs, "I don't know Ray, who knows what's down there?"

"I'll go down. You go back in the farmhouse and keep an eye on the fire."

"Okay, but shout when you're down the bottom and I'll come check on you in a bit."

I salute her, "Yes captain."

"Just go," she sighs.

I kneel down in front of the hatch, turn and slowly make my way down the rungs. I count forty-five before my feet hit the hard floor at the bottom. Looking upwards it looks around twenty to thirty feet to the surface, so a fair way down.

"I'm at the bottom!" I shout back up to Annabel. It's pitch black down here but it doesn't feel like I imagined it would. There is a little smell of damp and its extremely dark, but the walls feel warm.

I am not going to get very far without a light. I pat myself down and locate my cigarette lighter. It's a Zippo so fortunately will hold a flame quite well. I spark it up and suddenly I can see a door in front of me. It's metal and the same red colour as the hatch. I push the handle and it opens, creaking a little and revealing a small room, almost like a porch. There are a couple of small stools on the floor, some boots still covered with mud and another metal door, this one silver.

I walk to the back of this porch area and again push against the large vertical handle on the door. It doesn't move. I grab the larger key from my pocket and turn it in the lock. I hear the click and push the handle again and it creaks open.

I am immediately hit with the smell of stale cigarette smoke. My lighter has only illuminated the first ten or so feet, but I can already see that the floor below me is now carpeted to the right and there is a light switch on the wall with a cable running all the way back through to the porch area. I step into the room towards the switch on the wall and with one flick suddenly the whole expanse in front of me is revealed as it is filled with light.

21

The sturdy old wooden table in the farmhouse kitchen has been toppled on its side with the large dusty rug flung over the top of it.

"What the fuck is down there? "Annabel asks whilst staring down the steep stone staircase. She still looks shocked, though not as shocked as when I started knocking on the hatch hidden underneath rug and table.

"Well the missing six cot beds are there," I chuckle.

"Why does your new house have some kind of sex dungeon Ray?" Annabel playfully groans.

"There is one staircase here, and a ladder in the outbuilding. I'm guessing it was the basement and they expanded it outwards and converted it into their hidden weed growing emporium." I reply.

"How do you know it was for growing weed and not sacrificing kids or something?" Annabel asks, probably still trying to decide if she's going to venture down for a guided tour.

"I'm guessing it's weed due to the left-over planters, the lighting system they have rigged over the planters, the insulation on the walls, the ventilation shafts and that they have gone to great lengths to hide whatever they were doing."

Annabel still isn't convinced about setting foot in my mystery dungeon.

"And I happen to know, as the discarded son of one of the former occupants of said dungeon, that the commune here was well known for selling weed and not well known for sacrificing children or goats or anything like that. I didn't see anything remotely sacrificial; I promise Annabel!"

"But where did all the animals go Ray?" She replies with a grin.

I laugh and motion down to the staircase, "Go have a look. I'll come with you, so you don't trip over the sex swing."

Annabel steadily starts down the dusty stone stairs keeping a hand on the opening hatch when she is almost fully submerged by the floor. I start to follow her as my nose tickles with the dust that has been agitated after who knows how many years undisturbed.

As we get to the foot of the stairs the light has illuminated all but the darkest corner of the basement. The stone stairs come out in the middle of a wall, looking out at a far wall and two slightly narrower walls either side that make up the room, one wall containing the door I first came through. I look over at Annabel and her mouth is half hanging open, either in intrigue or disappointment.

"It's massive!" Annabel declares, as she walks towards an old tea chest that had been turned upside down for use as a table. "You could actually live down here. It's like Mr. Bean's bedsit but massive!" Annabel's eyes are surveying the huge room, "It's very seventies," she adds walking towards the bottom left of the room and what looks like the 'lounge' section.

"What makes you say that?" I joke.

"Orange shag-pile rug, half the walls being wood paneled, the G-Plan furniture and that 'Isle of White Festival 1970' poster sort of gave me an inclination. It does smell a bit funky down here though."

"I think most of that is the toilet," I say, pointing at the far corner by the door I first came in through.

"I'm just glad you finally found me a toilet" she laughs.

"It's going to take more than a bottle of bleach to sort that bad boy out, I reckon. They flushed half the stash before shutting this place down."

"So, I can't even use it?" Annabel groans.

"You can try but I'm not sure you'll want to."

"I'll go behind the barn," Annabel frowns.

I point towards the 'growing' section of the basement to the left of the lounge. "That's what I think they were hiding down here; from the look of it probably around fifty weed plants if you count five to a planter, with an irrigation and lighting rig set up. Probably the most technologically progressive thing in the whole place."

"Gordon would love it down here, no technology and plenty of shag pile to make never-ending sexual innuendos," Annabel replies.

"He's not exactly on my list of potential bunker buddies," I tell Annabel, wondering why I am suddenly referring to the basement as a bunker.

"Oh yeah, do I make this VIP list then?" Annabel asks with a slight smile.

"Well, I haven't really put much thought into it," I say honestly, "and it's a basement I shouldn't have called it a bunker."

"It looks like a bunker to me," Annabel says.

"It does have a very bunker-like feel, I grant you that, but in all reality, it is definitely more of a basement," I re-affirm.

"You're right. I'm only messing and it's definitely a basement. A nice normal farmhouse basement with a kitchen, lounge, toilet, bedroom and dedicated Cannabis hydroponics area."

22

"Who's next please?" The barman shouts across a sea of raised hands in front of the bar of 'The William IV', each clasping five pound notes in an eager attempt to get the attention of the lone barman. It's not a bad pub, but the rest of the staff seem to have forgotten they are working in a pub. There are probably ten or fifteen of us wanting to get served but room for about five of us at the bar, as the 'locals' are refusing to give up their posts on a busy Saturday night. I try and make eye contact with the lone remaining barman but he has already given the nod to a tall girl in a boob tube who seems to have appeared from nowhere - a bit like boob tubes before the Spice Girls.

"Can I have a packet of nuts?" I hear Eddy shout from the corner table we managed to steal to by slightly rearranging the furniture around an old man who had fallen asleep with his pint in hand.

"Yeah no probs," I shout back "If I ever get served that is."

The tall girl in the boob tube has just given her money to the barman so I am trying to make eye contact again, but I don't think my eyes are what he is looking for. I gaze towards the sour faced barmaid perched on the far end of the bar who is having a cigarette and reading 'Take a Break', trying to use some Jedi mind trick to urge her back to work whilst some twat behind me is pushing at my back and all I can hear apart from the noise of the crowd is the 'local' sat sentient in front of me, tapping a pound coin on the bar.

"Same again Albert?" The barman asks the local who gives a halfhearted nod and pushes his pound coin slightly further towards the barman.

"That's all you have to do is it?' I ask the local, 'tap your fucking pound coin, and you get your drink?"

The local pulls back his pound coin from the bar and shoves it into his grubby cardigan pocket while his pint of Bitter is placed on the beermat in front of him. "Stick it on me tab," he tells the barman who nods and manages to completely miss my gaze again. As I am looking for his gaze, I meet that of the local in front of me who is looking me dead in the eyes like a fucking owl. "Better keep me coin otherwise I'll have nowt t'tap next time you're at the bar, you sad bastard," he laughs and gulps down a mouthful of Bitter.

"Ray, get two packs of nuts," Eddy shouts over.

"Yeah no probs Eddy," I reply, noticing the barmaid un-perch, adjust her tits and stub out her fag.

"Oh, and a Bounty if they have one," Eddy adds as the barmaid lights up a fresh Superking cigarette and re-perches.

"A fucking Bounty?" I shout back. "Who orders a Bounty in a pub? Or anywhere to be honest?"

Eddy shrugs and goes back to chatting with Annabel, a position I would most definitely trade with him right now especially as I'm now queuing up to ask for a fucking Bounty.

"Who's next?" the barman asks as if anyone has any fucking idea.

"Let the soft lad get a Bounty for his boyfriend," chips in a second chubbier local to a sputtering of laughter and then coughs from the 'locals' blatant homophobia (and misguided at that). But fuck them. At least I have the gaze of the barman.

"We don't do Bountys mate" the Barman shoots back to me, half turned in motion towards the next victim of his charm.

"Can I get some drinks then please mate?" I fire back, stopping the barman in completing his turn away.

"They don't do Ribena 'ere, soft lad," interjects the chubby local to another round of chuckles and coughs.

"They don't do pies either so you can fuck off." The chubby local looks like a bulldog chewing on a wasp as his chin disappears further into where his neck once was. Before he can fire back his latest homophobic masterpiece, I turn my attention back to the barman "Six pints of lager please."

"What took you so long?" Annabel asks with a grin.

"They need some sort of ticket process like the butcher's or something," I sigh as I carefully place the tray of six pints down on the old wooden table.

"Wrist feeling better?" Annabel asks.

"Yeah it's much better thanks, glad I didn't go to the hospital now."

"Why have you got six pints?" Eddy asks.

"There is no way I am going back to that bar," I tell

him.

"I can only have one. I'm driving" Annabel says.

"Don't worry, I'll have one of yours," I tell her before taking a long gulp of the frothing pint.

"This is the strangest Bacardi and Coke I have ever seen" Annabel quips, wiping the froth off the glass with a beer mat.

"What about the nuts and the Bounty?" Eddy chips in.

I take the nuts from the pocket of my stolen parka and chuck them across to Eddy.

"Nuts but no Bounty," I tell him taking a gulp of my pint.

"Do they do any food here?" Eddy asks whilst shoveling some nuts into his mouth.

"I don't know mate. It hardly seemed the right time to be asking for a menu. We're lucky to have some drinks," I shoot back, focusing my attention back on my pint.

"I'm proper starving" Eddy moans with a mouthful of nuts, mid chew.

"Maybe you shouldn't have had a massive joint before walking down here to meet us?" I tell Eddy.

"I had to try it out before the party tomorrow night, and I'm glad I did because I am going to need a lot more food than I've bought," Eddy says, still shoveling nuts into his mouth.

"I'll go ask at the bar," Annabel says and pushes her heavy wooden chair back along the stone floor. "Where's the toilet? Down some stairs in a creepy bunker?" she adds flashing a smile at me.

"Very funny. They are at the back of the bar, turn left, behind the sex swings," I joke back and polish off my first pint.

"I don't think I want to know what you two did today," Eddy says, pouring the final bits of nut dust into his mouth.

"You do know they are going to give you a massively bad dry mouth," I tell him.

"Yeah but I have two pints to keep the cotton mouth at bay so I'm fine. Don't worry, I weighed all this up Ray," Eddy says breaking open the second pack." So what was your mum's place like then?"

"Sort of what I expected until we found an underground bunker and weed hydroponics set up. Your standard kind of commune farm I guess."

"I could help set you up growing something down there if you want," Eddy offers with a glint in his eye.

"Maybe something edible if you're offering," I say to Eddy.

"Not my thing mate, but I can pretty much grow anything though. My grandmother showed me her greenhouse a lot when I was growing up. That's how I managed to get those weed plants so massive when we had that Uni flat. Why would you grow them inside though if you have a farm? I must advise you though, it would be far more beneficial to everyone involved if we grew something smokable."

"I have been thinking a lot about this Y2K thing and I think if I am going to start over, why not just prepare for if I really need to start over?"

"Well you do have a bunker now apparently," Eddy chuckles.

"It's a basement. And just finding this farmhouse, along with all this crap happening with Debbie, seems too much of a coincidence to ignore. Especially with the Y2K problem looming around the corner."

"I don't see it myself, Ray, but if that's what you

110

want to do then whatever. Thinking about it, I would probably hide myself away in a bunker to get away from Clive anyway. Has he been messaging you again today?"

"Nothing today," I reply taking a swig of my second pint.

"Perhaps he's found your stash of porn then," Eddy laughs and shoves some more peanuts in his mouth.

"No food, but there is a chippy down the road and you can bring it in here," Annabel tells us as she sits back in her seat.

"I'm all right now," Eddy says tipping the last of his nuts down his throat, "Getting thirsty now though."

"Toilets smelt nearly as bad as yours Ray," Annabel jokes taking a sip of her recently acquired Bacardi and Coke.

"How were you served so fast?" I ask.

"Just made eye contact with the Barman. You should try it sometime," Annabel says with a smile.

"Ray has been telling me about his Y2K bunker," Eddy announces.

"Oh yeah, have you made it onto his VIP list?" Annabel asks Eddy with a grin.

"Didn't realize there was a list," Eddy says looking at me.

"There isn't a list, well not a person list, just a list of things I need to do."

"Ah, one of your checklists," Eddy says with a nod.

"Yes," I reply, "a checklist".

"Checklist for filling up a creepy bunker after your wife has kicked you out?" Annabel jibes causing Eddy to spit some of his pint.

I shake my head and wonder if what I am going to announce solidifies my descent into the matrix:

"Checklist for the end of the world."

"Fucking hell, that's a bit morbid," Annabel says with a frown.

"If the computers fuck up it will be," I say back.

"They won't fuck up," Eddy adds.

"But if they DO fuck up then I'll be prepared and if they don't fuck up, I'll still have everything I need to start a new life up at the farm."

Annabel takes out a cigarette and offers one to me and Eddy. "So, you're seriously going forward with all this?" she asks.

"Yes," I reply, taking a cigarette from her pack, "right now what have I got to lose?"

"Shouldn't you wait for all the legal stuff to be sorted with the farmhouse? I mean I'm not an expert in that sort of thing but is it worth the risk now?" Annabel says taking a long drag on her cigarette.

"I spoke to Dave and…"

"Dave's a twat though," Eddy interrupts.

"Yes, but a clever twat who knows this stuff. He said my mother transferred all the titles to me somehow so it's mine to do with as I please unless I get a challenge from someone during probate. But they are all dead or long gone now. You saw the place Annabel; nobody has been there in years."

"Yeah, I have seen it and honestly, even if it is all yours, it's in a bit of a mess Ray. Hardly ready to move into and that's a lot of work to take on at this time of year."

"Well I literally have nothing else to do and it won't take that long. The structure of the place is fine, it's all decoration and actually filling it with supplies." I take a long drag of my cigarette, "plus, if I use the pareto principle then 20% of the work gets me 80% prepared which is good enough for me, and enough to keep me alive."

"You're right, this is morbid," Eddy interjects.

"If it's what you want Ray, then go for it" Annabel says. "Just make sure it's what you really want."

"It is, and right now all I want is somewhere I can call my own, where nobody can lock me out or take anything away from me and fuck around with me or disappear into the distance leaving me with fuck all" I stub my cigarette into the half full ashtray in front of me.

"Well I'm really regretting having that joint now," Eddy almost whispers as Annabel looks at me with some concern and confusion.

"If it helps, I can give you a lift up to the farmhouse with some stuff tomorrow evening before my parents visit," Annabel offers.

"No!" Eddy interjects "PPV party tomorrow. You can't bail out on me now. It's Starrcade and the biggest wrestling show of the year so I am putting my foot down on this one."

"Okay" Annabel sighs. "Watch the wrestling show with your friend and we can move all your toys and games up next week after work."

"He's only got two bags," Eddy buts in. "Probably easy enough to get the bus."

"Thanks Annabel," I smile at her. "I'll start getting some stuff together and tick a few things off my list." I pick up a beer mat and fling it at Eddy's head, "By the way dickhead, this place is up on the moors. You can't get a bus there. You can't get anything up there. It's just nothing for miles."

Eddy lobs the beer mat back at me and smiles, "Neighbours will probably wish I'd held the party there then."

113

"Just don't get too drunk. We need to present the Y2K software updates to the boss on Monday and I am not carrying you through this one," Annabel says with a stern look. "I'm being serious now Ray. You seem to be the expert in this Y2K stuff anyway so if you're going to stock a fucking bunker and order all this expensive shit for the office you could at least explain to her highness why it's necessary," she tosses a beer mat in my direction.

"Oi! Stop tossing t'beer mats!" The barmaid had put down her 'Take A Break' and was scowling at us from the side of the bar with yet another cigarette dangling from the corner of her heavily made up mouth. "Behave or fuck off," she adds as a fitting full stop.

Annabel cups her hand and starts to whisper to me, "I don't see a cricket bat anywhere, but I reckon you could take her anyway!"

23

I'm weighing up whether or not it's worthwhile finishing off my checklist or sticking some wax in my hair for the party. I am currently not party ready by any means, in boxers and a vest, half laid on Eddy's spare bed with my list in one hand and my little blue Argos pen in the other.

I'd chilled out with Eddy for most of the day playing Goldeneye on the N64 and then watching Twin Town. We had both seen it so many times now that we could quote the whole film. It was part of a growing wave of culture out of Wales that had been nicknamed Cool Cymru.

My phone has been beeping for the last few minutes. I should have been downstairs an hour or so ago, so it's probably Eddy. I came up here to freshen up a bit after helping set up the projector and the ring downstairs, but time is ticking, and I need to get some plans down before it's too late. I saw the guys arrive with the ring and then the DJ with his decks, but he has been set up a while now as I can hear the music downstairs now. Must have been turned up as more people started arriving and I can hear Foo Fighters clearly now after muffled Blink 182, The Offspring and even some Slipknot, along with a lot of banging around - that will be the wrestlers I'm guessing and probably my cue to stop hiding upstairs.

I have gone high level with my list. I don't have a lot of time or cash to be going into specifics, but I am making sure it fits the triangle, or the 'Hierarchy of Needs', its proper name.

I lean across the bed and grab my pack of cigarettes, lighting one with a deep drag and looking for the empty beer bottle that is my current ashtray. Probably something I will need to cut down on, the cigarettes, and the alcohol too. I chuck the packet back to the other side of the bed and reach down for my beeping phone. It's a message from Clive, Well, five messages from Clive.

I KNOW U WERE HERE

I KNOW U WERE THERE

Good to see Clive is texting me again. Looks like he has figured out I went into the house, even if he doesn't quite know how to communicate that. Wonder what gave it away. The whole point of leaving a note was to highlight the fact I had fucking been there.

THE HOUSE Y DID U BREAK IN?

WOT DID U TAKE?

*U CNT GO BREAKING IN 2 THE HOUSE AND THEIVING
STUFF*

He doesn't seem to have the strongest grasp of the
law, accusing me of breaking into my own house and
stealing something that may or may not be mine, as he
isn't sure what the item actually was. I am pretty
confident it won't stand up in court.

*WAS IT U OR DID U BRING A MATE 2 AS THEY R IN
TROUBLE NOW*

WAS IT THE MONEY IN THE LOFT?

WAS IT FOOD FROM THE KITCHEN?

DID UR MATE TAKE ANYTHING FRM THE BEDROOM?

It's getting harder to concentrate on adding to my
checklist with the ever-growing noise downstairs from
Eddy's party and the constant beeping and vibration
from my Nokia as Clive is now playing a never-ending
game of "Cluedo" with me, trying to find out what I
took from my own house and if I had any accomplices.

*I WILL FIND OUT WOT U TOOK N REPORT YOU 2
POLICE*

He's back with a bang. Debs has probably told him I
came and took some stuff and he's now gone all Poirot
trying to solve the perceived crime. I can't be bothered
with Clive now. I'm shutting that part of my life down.

Deb's has said it; it's over. I flick on silent and toss my phone to the end of the bed and chuck the generous whisky that I had poured myself an hour ago down my throat. Standing up and stretching as I take another long drag of my cigarette, I hear the door creak.

"Not the bathroom then?" A tallish girl with jet-black hair and a lip ring steps into the room, glancing around the mess.

"Nope," I reply, pointing further down the hall.

"What you got going on in here?" she replies, flicking a blonde streak from her fringe out of her face and back into her jet-black hair, looking around at my mess and edging further into the room.

"Nothing, just getting changed, bathroom is down there."

"Are you going to the party then?" She eyes me up and down. "Do you even like wrestling?"

"Yeah, I'm going. I used to watch wrestling but haven't watched it much since Owen Hart died, he was my favourite."

"His brother, Bret, is headlining tonight," she tells me. "He's my idol. They got trained in their father's dungeon, the Hart's did. Proper hard, all of them."

"Yeah, best there is, best there was, best there ever will be."

"Can I have a drag?" she asks as she takes the cigarette from my. She looks at me as I stand just in my boxers and probably with a confused look on my face. "Not bad," she says, "walked into shittier rooms than this. What's that triangle for?" she points at the printout on my bed.

"Maslow's Hierarchy of Needs," I reply.

"Never fucking heard of it," she says.

I reach down to my bag for the bottle of whisky to break the silence. "Do you want a drink?" I ask her.

"Don't drink mate, don't smoke really either but just fancied some of yours. Is that Nevermind on tape?" she asks, pointing at my open Walkman. "Can I borrow it?"

"Yeah, sure, if you want," I tell her taking the cassette out of the Walkman and handing it to her.

"Cheers," she says, taking the tape and sliding it into the pocket of her tight denim shorts. She's got black tights on her long legs under the shorts and a pair of knee length laced up boots with spikes on the toecap.

"Just in case," she says, noticing me staring at the boots. "Are you living with Eddy then?" she asks, flicking the cigarette end out of the window.

"No. Well, yeah, but only for a few more days." I reply.

"Think a few people will be here for a few days," she says. "Last party for Wrestlemania went on for nearly a week. Police tried to shut everything down. We scared them off and the fuckers came back, slashed the projector screen and smashed the speakers to make us leave."

"Bloody hell," I gasp.

"I'd get your homework done now on that triangle, if I was you, or just sack it off and enjoy yourself," she says, as she starts to look through my pile of clothes on the floor.

I grab my cigarettes from the bed and light one up, "What are you looking for?"

"Something to wear," she says.

"For me to wear?" I ask.

"No. For me." She sighs and keeps rummaging.

"What's your name?" I ask her.

"Bea," she replies.

119

"Cool. Well Bea, I'm Ray and I'm going to get changed now."

"Fine," Bea replies, now weighing up two t-shirts from the pile.

I shrug and grab my jeans from the floor, pulling them on. "Can you throw me some socks please?" I ask Bea.

"Jeans before socks? You're weird," she tells me before taking off her t-shirt to reveal a purple bra and sliding on my old red and black flannel shirt.

"Looks good on you," I tell Bea.

"Aw thanks. Hey! Perhaps we can be friends?" she says sarcastically taking the cigarette from my mouth and throwing a t-shirt at me. "Get changed, you're missing the party."

24

"How fucking awesome is that!" Eddy beams to me pointing at the full-size wrestling ring set up in his back garden next to the covered-up swimming pool.

"You know what, I might even buy one to have out there permanently. It looks amazing," he says, grinning like a kid at Christmas.

"Fair play mate, it's a pretty awesome set up," I tell him. "You going to have a go later?"

"Yeah definitely! Big Nick is going to teach me how to do a moonsault!"

"Isn't that flipping backwards over your own head? Might want to start with a headlock or something," I say.

"Maybe you start with that. I'm going big or going home. Here, have some confidence." Eddy tosses me a cold bottle of Stella from one of the many ice buckets laying around. "Heard you already met Bea. What do you reckon?"

"Yeah, she walked in on me just as I was about to get

changed. Nice girl. Smokes a lot for a non-smoker," I crack open the cold beer. "How do you know her?"

"Met her at the wrestling show. She was in a ladder match with Big Nick's girlfriend."

"She's a wrestler?" I ask Eddy with some surprise.

"Yeah, she's been doing it for a few years now. She's really good. She might even get in the ring later!" Eddy motions to Bea who is stood in front of the new massive projector screen set up in the lounge. "She's a huge Bret Hart fan. He's in the main event tonight so she'll be around till the end."

"I might not be," I tell Eddy. "I have the boss visiting tomorrow so need to be on form otherwise Annabel will kill me. I'll get my shirt back off Bea at some point and head up at a decent time."

Eddy laughs, "Don't piss off Bea or she will actually kill you."

I laugh and nod back "Okay Eddy."

"I'm serious Ray, don't mess with her," Eddy says, scaring me slightly as I wonder how I will ever get my shirt back. Probably not worth the hassle. I'll buy a new one.

"Do you want a drag on this Eddy?" a tall well-built man with a Limp Bizkit t-shirt and backwards cap interrupts.

"Yeah pass it here Buttercup," Eddy says, taking the cone shaped spliff and taking a long drag.

"Good isn't it?" Buttercup asks as Eddy takes another drag.

"I'm not getting anything mate," a confused Eddy replies, shaking his head before taking another drag. "You have rolled this like a carrot Buttercup. I'm not getting anything."

"It's very subtle," Buttercup adds.

"Nothing, sorry. Here Ray, you try," Eddy says, offering the huge carrot shaped spliff in my direction, "Try it, see if you get anything."

"No, I'm okay thanks," I say before Eddy hands the huge carrot spliff back to Buttercup.

"Where did you get this stuff from?" Eddy asks.

"Tesco," Buttercup replies. "Oregano and nutmeg, heard its really good."

"Who did you hear that from? Delia Smith?" Eddy laughs back.

"Well, I like it," Buttercup snaps.

"Let me get you something proper mate," Eddy says, wrapping his arm around Buttercup's massive shoulders and leading him away.

I spot Bea who has moved to the kitchen. Leaning against the Street Fighter arcade machine I flash a smile. She fires one back in return so I make my way over to where she is standing by the projector "I hear you're a wrestler?"

"I hear you're getting divorced," she shoots back.

"Err, not sure yet but seems that way," I reply, not quite sure how I should be handling this.

"Did you chuck her, or did she chuck you?" Bea asks.

"It's complicated," I stutter out in reply.

"It always is though," Bea says. "If it wasn't complicated then there wouldn't be any arguments would there? Can't imagine just one person was in the wrong. It's not black and white, good versus fucking evil. You are human beings, so likelihood is you both fucked it up."

I take a sip of my beer, not quite sure how to respond, so I just sort of bite my lip.

"Oh, and a bit of advice," Bea continues "don't go smiling across a room like a fucking rapist before speaking to people, its creepy as hell."

"Okay," I nod "Thanks for the advice."

"It's fine," she says. "It's starting soon so I'll see you in a bit."

As Bea walks off, I do a double take in my head as to how the conversation just went and my internal review deems it a disaster, probably couldn't have ended any worse. I check the level of beer in my bottle and decide I need a new one, especially if I'm going to be drowning my sorrows now.

The music from the DJ is just about drowning out the thuds coming from the wrestling ring in the garden. The guy Eddy referred to earlier as 'Big Nick' is currently holding a smaller lad above his head ready to 'powerbomb' him down onto the mat. I can only see a Nick's face from my vantage point by the big kitchen window, but I'd imagine the fella on his shoulders Is shitting himself.

Buttercup sidles up next to me. "I used to do that," he says staring at the ring.

"Wrestle?" I ask.

"Aye, way back in my younger days."

"It looks painful," I tell him as Big Nick slams the lad onto the mat with a thud.

"It takes a toll on your body, that's for sure mate," he sighs "every night over and over, taking some nasty bumps."

"Were you any good?" I ask him.

"Oh aye," he says nodding, "had the belt, went undefeated for about two years give or take."

"Was that at the same place as these guys put on

shows?" I ask him.

"No, never made it there, long retired."

I grab another beer from the Ice bucket and hand one to Buttercup. "Did you wrestle anyone here?"

"Nah, mainly family," he says taking the cold beer from me.

"Family?"

He nods "Yeah, mainly me sister," he says taking a sip.

"Right," I say.

"Mainly in the bath when we were younger. She never beat me once in all that time," he tells me eyes fixated on Big Nick body slamming the poor volunteer.

"Alright mate," I say to Buttercup as he keeps a fixed glaze on the match in progress outside as I begin edging away slowly towards the lounge.

"Are you watching this fucking show with me or what?" Bea grabs my arm from nowhere. "It's about to start. I grabbed us some good seats near the back on the two-seater sofa." She pulls my arm and moves me towards the lounge.

"I didn't think you were... I thought that...." I struggle to find some words to explain to Bea my confusion at her actions so settle on "Okay."

I sit down on Eddy's two-seater on the 'back row' of the re-arranged seating area. There is a three-seater and a single lay-z-boy recliner to the left and another three-seater to the right of us with plenty of cushions and bean bags in front providing ample room for the twenty odd people here at the party.

Bea takes the seat next to me and immediately turns, placing her legs over my lap. And here I was thinking I'd messed something up with her. Perhaps she does like me, or she doesn't, or she's just impossible to read.

25

I don't know what the time is but it's late, or early, depends how you want to look at it. The PPV just finished and some sort of screwed up ending to the Bret Hart vs Goldberg match has resulted in people here lobbing their drinks at Eddy's new projector screen.

"Hey! Chill out! That's a brand-new screen!" I can just about hear myself saying over the noise of the party, to whom I don't really know. There are around four or five really drunk guys near the front of the lounge who are starting to take the piss a little bit, getting aggressive and overly dick-ish, and this is after they have all let their aggression out on each other in the wrestling ring Eddy had set up outside.

"Hey!" Buttercup shouts and gets to his feet. "Stop it!" A can brushes past Buttercup's ear and lands on the projector screen. "Hang on a second now," he shouts as the rabble calms down a bit. "Has anyone seen a blue clipper lighter? I think I've dropped it somewhere," he asks, as the volleys continue again.

"What's the issue?" I ask Bea who is half asleep now with her head on my lap.

"Shitty finish to the match," She says with a yawn.

"Eddy has disappeared somewhere. Should I calm these fellas down?" I ask her.

Bea swings off the seat and stretches. "Leave it to me," she says and steps over the piles of empty drinks, food packets and bodies sat and asleep on the floor. "You four," she points "get the fuck out now, and you!" she points at the loudest one, "clean this mess up."

The singled out drunken lad seems to find this all a bit amusing and starts to chuckle. Bea sighs and strikes him with the loudest backhand I have ever heard in my life.

"I won't ask again," she smiles and starts to hopscotch her way back over to the sofa. The group of lads make their way to the door as the designated cleaner starts to pick up the mess laying around Eddy's new screen. Bea has made it back to the sofa and is pulling on my arm. "I'm tired," she moans.

"Do you want me to call you a taxi? I don't know if they will be running at this time on a Sunday to be honest," I say.

"I'll just take your bed," she says yanking at my arm. "You can sleep next to me or on the floor or wherever, just don't wake me up."

"Yeah sure," I say, not quite sure what I am agreeing to at this point. I push myself up out of the sofa and check my pockets for my cigarettes. My mouth is really dry, so I better down a pint or two of water before bed if I'm going to avoid a hangover in the few hours when I wake up. "I'm going to get a pint of water; do you want one?" I ask Bea.

"I'll see you up there," Bea says before leaning over and giving me a kiss on my cheek. She vaults over the sofa and walks towards the stairs before turning around, "just don't wake me up if you come in and I'm sleeping, unless it's important."

I take Bea's message to heart and understand none of the consequences really as I head towards the kitchen where Eddy is half passed out but still attempting to share a bong with Big Nick on the kitchen table. "Do you want any water mate?" I ask Eddy, pouring myself a glass from the cold tap to ease my already pounding head.

"No mate, the bong has plenty," Eddy replies.

"Not for the bong, for you," I tell him taking a big gulp of the cool water.

"I don't understand what you're saying," he manages to mumble before taking the bong from Big Nick and reaching for the lighter. "I can't grip" he mumbles as Big Nick tries to work the lighter for him.

I down the rest of my glass and top it up again "Sure you don't want a drink mate?"

"Just a Stella please," Eddy mumbles. "I wish I had opposable thumbs," he whines as he tries to pick up the lighter.

"Night Eddy," I tell him and leave him to his struggle.

26

I push open the heavy door to the office and immediately regret my decision as the wails of Angela the receptionist feel like daggers piercing my sensitive skull. I raise my head ever so slightly to check what the situation is without drawing attention to myself, and am relieved to see that someone is already trying to comfort her, and she is not being stabbed by someone who had lost the plot and snapped. Tina came to mind.

"Morning," I mutter as I move past the scene unfolding in the reception area. A lady I had never met before is almost cradling Angela, whilst another stands behind her, arms folded, shaking her head and shouting something I can't quite hear over Angela's screams.

I press the lift button and pray that it comes quickly this morning. I'm an hour late and I really don't want to get involved in whatever is happening down here. Whatever it is may be causing me irreversible damage as my head feels that way right now.

The lift arrives just in time as I hear Angela

shouting my name from down the hallway. I hop inside as quick as possible and press for floor six, immediately switching to the close doors button. Just as the doors start to shut a hand appears stopping them - Sadsack.

Sadsack gives me a look of surprise and disgust, a bit like he had just found a turd in the lift. He shuffles in with a sad looking machine coffee in his limp hand and presses the button for the first floor, all the time his face the picture of agony.

I contemplate the life of Sadsack. Why is he so sad? Does he just need a nice coffee for once? Why can't he use stairs? As he gets out of the lift on the first floor, I wonder what does he do here? Does it make him sad? Does the six seconds we spent together in the lift make him sadder? I'll ask him one day but today my hangover is stopping any sort of social interaction.

I'm not that late. It's an hour, not anything too massive and it's not like I do it often. Hopefully, being a Monday, nobody has noticed yet and I can slip quietly behind my desk blaming traffic or a damsel in distress. Yes, good plan, I was helping somebody. If anyone asks, I was helping somebody.

I push the door of the office and to my surprise nobody is there. Very odd. I can see Gordon's briefcase, Tina's handbag and Tim's stupid denim jacket but there is nobody here. I chuck my bag behind my desk and head over to the break area, flicking on the kettle and taking a scoop of someone's coffee into someone else's mug. Pretty sure I bought the sugar though.

I look around and I can see the blinds closed in the meeting room at the bottom of the office. Perhaps Gordon has died? Or Tina has organized another team meeting about the stationery cupboard, or perhaps the cleaners just didn't open them back up? I chuck the now boiled water into my coffee and fumble around for my phone. Surely if something was going on Annabel would have at least messaged me? If it's nothing, then she wouldn't have bothered. I pull my phone out of my parka pocket. Fuck. Six missed calls, all from Annabel.

It's clear now. The hangover had clouded my vision, my phone has been on silent since last night. I can see people in the meeting room. I can bloody hear it! I grab my coffee and head down the office, taking off my parka as I march and trying not to spill the hot coffee all over my creased shirt. I chuck the parka onto someone's desk and push at the meeting room door.

"Afternoon," Tim chuckles with a smug grin. He's stood up with one leg on a chair like he's trying to project his cock into the room.

"Ray, nice of you to join us," a familiar voice from the corner greets me. I get a cold shiver from the top of my head, down my arms and to my stomach as I see the tall lady with the high bun and shoulder padded trouser suit and realize my boss is here early. She's never here early, always late morning as she travels from Manchester.

"Are you taking a seat or just going to stand in the doorway?" she asks me, pursing her red lips as I nod and make my way over to a chair.

"Miss your bus, did you? Oh no, you walk in usually." Tim stirs the pot as I take a seat next to Gordon who notices I have his mug with a frown.

"As I was saying, it's not a decision that was taken lightly but none the less it is one that is necessary to modernize and streamline the workplace." The boss takes a sip of her coffee and continues, "You probably have a lot of questions about what comes next and what to expect but please rest assured that Ray and Tim will be able to answer those questions for you." I jolt up in my seat, me? I don't have a fucking clue what's going on.

"Oh Ray! when did you know about this?" a near tearful Tina wails.

"Come on now, this has been on the cards for some time," Tim butts in, "besides, it's necessary to cut out the dead wood once in a while to keep the house strong."

"I say if it isn't broken don't fix it!" Gordon bellows.

"Ray, Tim can you two please say something please?" the boss directs as I sit in silence wondering what I can say when I have no idea what has been announced.

"You want me to say something?" I gasp.

Tim stands up and moves in front of me with his backside nearly in my face. "As a supervisor I will be conducting a full, fair, independent and objective review of all personnel and processes within all areas."

"Can you move out of my face please Tim?" I plea.

Tim moves back to his cock projection pose. "This isn't personal, but please be aware that I know some of you personally so will already have a good idea about who you are, which should quicken things up a bit."

"You can't sack us before Christmas!" Gordon barks.

"You are not being sacked. There is a restructure. If your role isn't in the new structure then it will be redundant and it's effective as of the first of January, so well after Christmas," the boss replies.

27

The room is nearly empty now, just me, Tim and the boss. Annabel was the first to leave, followed by the other ten or so people in the office. Gordon and Tina were the last, fighting their corner for nearly two hours and both leaving with severely bloodied noses and bruised egos.

"What the fuck was that Ray?" The boss shouts at me.

"What the fuck was that exactly!" I say back. "I didn't have a clue any of that was going on!"

"That's dodging responsibility a bit mate isn't it?" Tim chuckles.

"What do you mean? I have no responsibility here!" I nervously laugh.

"That's very concerning as a supervisor," Tim snorts.

"What's concerning is your constant bullshit mate," I fire at Tim.

"I briefed you last Friday mate, it's okay we have all forgotten things after a few pints," Tim pats me on the shoulder.

"You did not" I snap.

"I did before you left to go over to the pub," Tim fires back. "I tried to have a chat with you over there as well about the finer points, but you'd had a few."

"Are you serious?" I spit back at him.

"Look, it's done now. Don't worry about it mate. Everyone has had a few too many before." He pats me again as I bite my tongue and restrain the urge to knock him out.

"Leave it now Ray," the boss instructs coldly "As Tim said, it's done, the announcement has been made and it's all about next steps now."

"Exactly, next steps," Tim says like a parrot.

"I want both of you to submit your proposals for the restructure to me by Thursday via email and I'll sign off on the one that best fits the new vision on the Friday morning okay?"

We both nod.

The boss gathers up her papers and shoves them into her bag, grabbing her long dark trench coat off the coat stand. "I'll let the lucky one of you two break the news to the rest of the staff whenever you can on Friday. So 'Merry Christmas' and I'll see one of you next year."

28

It's quieter in the pub than the office. The lack of noise and the pint in my hand are both helping with my hangover. Walking back down the office I felt like a condemned man passing each of his victims' families. Gordon and Tina looked so disgusted I actually wondered if I'd not shit myself too. There wasn't anyone remotely interested in me being in the office, so I decided that the only thing to do was to come over here for lunchtime hours at The White Horse.

Tim had printed out the briefing and put it on my desk this morning. This had worked out perfectly for him and he had played it like a professional - a professional dickhead. The brief was short and sweet, but knowing the content on Friday would have at least given me time to understand what was going on rather than being dropped in it on the spot.

"What the fuck was all that about?" I look up and see Annabel stood in front of my table with an umbrella in one hand and her bag in the other. "Are you able to explain any of that? It's a pretty fucked up way to start the last week of work before Christmas," she says putting her bag and umbrella down.

"Take a seat," I say "Do you want a drink?"

"No Ray, I don't. Not everyone drinks during the day you know," she says taking off her coat and sitting down.

"I didn't know any of that was coming, I swear," I plead.

"I know that," she says. "I spent most of Saturday with you and you didn't mention anything. You're not that much of an arsehole, but Tim is so what is going on?"

I take a sip of my pint. "They are restructuring the department, and everyone will need to re-apply for their jobs."

"That's the part I know," Annabel says.

"They want me and Tim as supervisors to put forward a proposal each for how the re-structure would look. They called Tim on Friday and asked him to give me the brief, but he didn't of course."

"Surely the boss could see it was clear that he didn't?"

"He had planted some seeds with her Friday, even pushed for us to take the afternoon off after Gordon suggested it. He was setting it up to look like I'd been on the piss all weekend and forgotten."

"And you being on the piss all weekend didn't help" Annabel says sternly.

"No, I guess not."

"But why you? No offence but why is it you and Tim making these proposals?"

"I thought the same but a couple of months back the Boss mentioned a possible Manager role and I threw my hat in the ring. So, apparently, did Tim."

"And he's played you like a flute already?" Annabel sighs.

I take a sip of my pint. "He definitely did."

Annabel takes out her pack of cigarettes and offers me one. "So, what do you have to do for this proposal?"

"Reduce staff numbers and modernize the processes. In essence we are replacing some people with computers." I light the cigarette and take a deep drag. "Angela on reception is gone. She will be replaced by the new internal email and diary system. We are cutting at least two people in our area and moving most of our work onto an internal records system. So, computers for everyone all the time."

"That's why they want all this Y2K stuff then" Annabel suggests.

"Seems so. Still think it's all going to screw up myself, but if the computers make it through then we are going to be tied to them for everything we do."

"That's if we have jobs to go back to" Annabel sighs. "I think I might get a drink actually." Annabel grabs her purse from her bag. "Same again?" she asks.

"Yeah why not," I tell her as she forces a smile and turns towards the bar. I hadn't really thought about how this will affect her. She obviously wants and needs her job and what has happened is probably making her feel terrible but she has come and seen to me to make sure I am okay, make sure I am alright and I haven't even given her or Tina or Gordon a second thought so far. Tina was obviously outwardly devastated and visibly upset by the news and Gordon was outraged and also slighted at the suggestion that he could be redundant in his job, something that he took a lot of pride in.

"What do you think Tim will propose?" Annabel asks

placing our drinks down on the old copper table.

"I have no idea, but he obviously wants this Manager role so I'm guessing he will do exactly what he said in the meeting and get rid of what he sees as deadwood." I gulp down the last of my pint and move on to the fresh one in front of me. "Thing is, with everything going on in my life currently, including the fact I believe the world will most probably end in eleven days, I really couldn't care less about being the Manager right now." I take a long drag at the end of my cigarette and stub it out in the large ceramic ashtray. "It's him fucking me over that has annoyed me. The consequence of that is everyone at work thinking I am a dickhead and what I should really be concerned about is that people might lose our jobs. You might lose your job, but I'm sorry Annabel, I honestly haven't even thought about that."

Annabel stubs out her cigarette and puts her head in her hands, rubbing her temples and then moving her chestnut hair behind her ears to recompose herself. "Look, I know you give a fuck," she says sternly. "Gordon and Tina are upset. Tina was supposed to be finalizing the Christmas Party today with everyone, but she's been crying in the toilet since you left. Gordon is re-enacting the whole meeting over and over to the canteen staff and you are becoming a bigger knobhead on each successive performance. Tim is walking around smug as fuck telling everyone how he saw it coming and he's even put on a tie."

"Great, can't wait to get back," I chuckle.

"It's shit news, but you have had shittier news this week. I get it Ray. I haven't had shittier news for quite a while so I am quite upset about it and the fact I need to spend the next few days not knowing if I will have a job next year," Annabel says lighting another cigarette.

I smile at Annabel. "Let's just hope for the end of the world and then none of this will matter anyway."

"I might just join you in that bunker of yours Ray."

29

At least the rain is holding off as I push forward through the icy gale that's blowing in my face and trying to force me back to the office. Whoever invented Yorkshire was obsessed with hills and shit weather. Fortunately, Eddy's place is closer to work than my own house, well Debbie's house now, so at least I have a shorter walk home than usual. Every cloud.

Wonder what state Eddy's place will be in now. There were a few people still awake when I dragged myself out this morning, but more were still sleeping, such as Bea who I left in my bed. I reach for my cigarettes as I feel a pang of guilt thinking about me and Bea sharing a bed together. I thumb one out the packet and stop in my tracks to light it with the zippo flame that's dancing around in the wind. The guilt starts to ease with the nicotine and the realization that my marriage is effectively over and, in all reality, why shouldn't I be sharing a bed with another woman as a single man?

What about Bea though? She pecked me on the cheek and at one point during the night I think she cuddled me, but that doesn't really clarify anything. She spent most of the evening verbally kicking me in the balls so am I reading too much into her sleeping fully clothed in my bed? I have no idea. She doesn't have my number so I can't expect a text or call soon; that's if she wants to call me at all.

I think I need to get away from Eddy's as soon as possible. He is still living like we did back in uni and it's going to be nearly impossible to get anything prepped with all the weed and alcohol around all the time. Time is running out and I really need to get into the farmhouse as soon as I can.

My head is spinning now: Debbie, work, Bea, Eddy, the farmhouse everything suddenly at the forefront of my mind spinning around in a constant merry go round of plans and ruminations. I take a long drag on my cigarette. I can feel my palms and forehead starting to sweat and my chest is getting tighter. I pick up the pace walking as I just want to be somewhere quiet and isolated.

I'm breathing heavier and I can feel a tingling down my arms to my fingertips and I struggle to grip my cigarette. I toss it to the floor and just keep walking as fast as I can with my head down, hoping nobody notices me. I stop dead in my tracks and my body feels like jelly, my legs are filled with pins and needles and I feel acid rising up my throat. I try to reach for another cigarette, deciding I shouldn't have tossed the last one, but I can't get my hands in my pocket as they are shaking uncontrollably now. I need to sit down. There is a wall in front of a house just across the road, but it seems so far.

I push myself into the road and walk as fast as I can, gasping for air as I make it to the wall, not realizing I had been holding my breath. I stick my head into my hands and screw up my eyes to get complete darkness.

My eyes are still closed. I can hear the hum of cars in the distance, getting closer and louder and then passing as the noise disappears again. The wind is cooling my face a little bit, but the sweat is still there as I wipe my palm across my forehead, breathing deeply and less frantic as I do so.

I should really go back to the doctor but I just can't face it; the whole process of getting an appointment, waiting in a room with people who are coughing and sneezing all over you and it was horrendous last time. When this happened after my mum died, the pills they gave me made it worse, then better, and then worse when they ran out, so I just stopped them. This I can handle, being in bed for a fortnight I can't. Especially right now.

The pins and needles have subsided now, and I have enough of my balance back to force myself to stand. I exhale deeply and open my eyes. There is a young boy on a bike opposite me who is looking at me with curious eyes. He's probably about nine or ten, has all of the fun parts of life ahead of him - and moments like this where he will be no use to anyone in the world and completely lost in himself. He probably thinks I'm some sort of mad man.I step forward, leaving him behind me and take out a cigarette, light it up and inhale the thick smoke.

"Smoking is bad for you," I hear the boy say behind me.

"It is. Don't smoke or you'll end up like me," I reply, hearing the boy speed off on his bike to tell his friends about the weird man.

I start walking and grab my phone out my pocket. Three missed calls from Clive. I can't deal with him now. I need to sort my head out and start marking progress with my list too.

30

"Ooh look 'ere, it's Casanova," Apron Lady announces as I enter the paper shop. "What have you come to lose this time, ey?" She winks, not so subtly, at me.

"Alright," I nod back at her.

"Hey Fred, he's after our lass he is," Apron Lady informs the hunched man at the counter who turns to grin at me. Fred flashes a smile that resembles a coconut shell with a number of teeth knocked out and only a select few remaining.

"You filthy bastard!" Half-dead Fred grins.

"If you're after R'Kelly then you're in luck, she's about to come relieve me for half hour."

"Bet that's what he's come for too," Half dead Fred cackles.

"Shut up you!" Apron Lady swipes Fred with her sausage fingers.

"Just after some essentials," I shout back, turning to browse the selection in the one open fronted fridge.

"Nice to see some old-fashioned courting," Apron Lady shouts over to me.

"Pardon?" I reply.

"You know, courting. Pretending to lose your keys, she pretends to lose them, you go on a date, ask the mother, it's all very proper." I keep browsing the limited supplies "Not like these Brit Pop lads and Moshers" she shouts.

Half-dead Fred growls, "Just wanting to get lasses drunk and give them a finger."

"Easy now Fred!" Apron Lady swipes at him again as he gets his cue to leave.

"Leave me be, I'm off to read me Sunday paper anyway," Half-Dead Fred mumbles as he waddles off towards the door.

"Sunday papers?" I ask moving towards Apron Lady to avoid the stench of Fred.

"He's a bit slow with his newspapers," Apron Lady tells me. "I just put them aside for him to read in order. Don't think he even realizes. I'd hate for him to miss out on what's going on."

"But he's a day behind? How is he not already missing out on what's going on?"

"He's a bit more than that love. He don't have a telly either, so best he just thinks its August or it will confuse him."

"Sure, whatever," I sigh as Fred and his stench finally reach the door.

"Ta-ra Fred," Apron Lady bellows.

I put my supplies on the counter: a loaf of bread, some cheese, a tin of corned beef and a jar of mustard and point towards the liquor shelf. "Bottle of the Bells whisky please, and 20 Lambert and Butler please."

"I would ask who the lucky lady was, but I think I

know!" Apron Lady winks again.

"Do you have any onions or lettuce?" I ask.

"What for?"

"What does it matter?" I take a breath. "Sorry. It's for a sandwich if that helps at all."

"We should do" Apron lady starts to rub an imaginary beard on her chin.

"Try in the fridge next to the mixed-race peppers."

"The what?"

"The mixed-race peppers on the bottom left."

I decide not to enquire any further and head back to the fridge where I spot a pack of onions hiding behind the mixed peppers. No lettuce though, but I'm surprised at the variety to be honest.

"I do like an onion" Apron Lady smiles. "They are the avocado of the north."

"That's everything thanks."

"Sure you're not forgetting anything?" Apron lady smiles before bellowing "Kelly!"

"Really I have to be heading home," I plead.

"Kelly! Your lad is here."

Oh fuck, when did I become her 'lad'? I better nip this in the bud right now.

"Who?" I hear Kelly shout from upstairs.

"Your lad!" Apron Lady shouts back, "the one with t'keys!"

I'll just put a stop to this right now. I'll be blunt. They may not like it, but I can find another shop anyway. I can hear footsteps coming down the stairs, so I scoop my shopping into my bag so I can make a quick exit after I stop all this crap once and for all.

The footsteps get louder until Kelly appears at the doorway behind the counter. She's got a black dress on, hugging her slightly curvy figure. Her blonde hair is styled and just resting on her shoulders. She looks incredible.

"Alright?" She says nonchalantly.

"Yeah," I reply.

"Okay," she purses her lips, "Is that all?"

"You off out somewhere?" I ask.

"Christmas party. Well once I finish me shift," she says, glaring at Apron Lady.

"Oh, just go! Don't worry about me love," Apron Lady beams at her incredibly attractive daughter.

"Thanks, I'll go get me shoes." Kelly turns to leave.

"Hold on!" I snap, breaking out of my daze and stopping her in her tracks. "Do you fancy going for a drink tonight?"

"Where have you been? I just said I'm off to a Christmas Party."

"Tomorrow then?" I ask.

"Yeah fine, I'll meet you at the Dog and Gun around..."

"Maybe not there," I interrupt. "How about The William IV, around this time okay?"

"Fine." Kelly gives the slightest smile and disappears back upstairs to what I can only imagine is some sort of alternate reality where the previous Kelly is lost.

"Scrubs up well R'Kelly," Apron lady gushes.

31

I open up Eddy's front door and I'm immediately hit with the stale stench of beer and freshly smoked weed.

"Evening," I shout, closing the door behind me.

"Leave it unlocked mate, I'm getting a pizza," Eddy shouts from somewhere.

"I bought stuff for sandwiches," I shout back.

"Fuck your sandwiches!" I hear a voice shout back. Not one I recognize.

I walk down the hallway glancing into the games room on the right. Nobody in there. Then the pitch-black lounge where I can just about make out a few bodies strewn around, most still alive but clinging to either a drink or a joint.

"I'll just put this stuff in the fridge then," I call into the room.

"Cool," Eddy shouts back from somewhere near the projector.

I walk straight on into the kitchen and toss my bag onto the table knocking over a few cans and empty snack packets. I grab my supplies from the shop and shove them into the fridge, picking up a bottle of Stella whilst I am there.

"What are you watching?" I shout as I use my hand to force the cap off the beer with the edge of the counter.

"American Pie," Eddy shouts back, as I edge into the dark lounge, trying to avoid my fallen comrades beneath me. I take a seat on the same sofa me and Bea had been sharing the night before and light a cigarette.

"How was work? Was your head okay?" Eddy asks, emerging from a beanbag.

"Shit," I say, taking a swig of my beer. "Really Shit."

"Don't go back then," a voice I recognize says behind me. I turn to double check, "If it's so shit, then what's the point in going back?" Bea says, taking a seat next to me and immediately throwing her long legs to rest on top of mine.

"Bea, nice to see you."

"Aw. Did you miss me?" She asks sarcastically.

I point at the projector. "Has he shagged the pie yet?" I shudder remembering Gordon acting the scene out with Tina's handbag, taking the leading role of the pie.

"He's fucked the pie; some girl got her tits out. Nothing much really" Bea says grabbing my cigarette from my mouth.

"Still not smoking then?"

"Why are you obsessed with me smoking? Pervert." Bea chucks a cushion at me.

"Can we rewind it back to the scene with the tits? Ray missed it," Buttercup chips in.

"I'm fine thanks," I chuckle.

"She got her bra off quick that girl," Bea jokes.

"I'm good with bras, me," Buttercup comments.

"How so?" I ask him.

"I can un-clip them with one hand; sort of my party trick."

"Bollocks!" a girl next to him laughs.

"I can!" Buttercup argues.

"Go on then," the girl challenges, shifting her back to the half laid down Buttercup. He puts his hand up the back of her top and within seconds he's done. "Bloody hell!" she gasps.

"See," Buttercup grins.

"That's impressive," Bea nods.

"I am an expert with bras," Buttercup boasts.

"I have to say I am impressed," I tell him.

"The trick is practice," he winks. "My mum said it was important to learn so she made me practice on her until I got it right."

"Eurgh! Fucking hell Buttercup!" Bea groans.

"That is wrong mate," Eddy sighs. "Typical Buttercup, building us up to let us down."

"Sicko," the girl next to Buttercup snaps and moves to a different beanbag. There isn't much any of us can say after that demonstration from Buttercup.

"I'm starving," Eddy moans, breaking the silence.

"I can make you a sandwich if you want?" I offer.

"Fuck your sandwiches, I want a pizza" the voice from earlier whimpers from a red beanbag. Not sure what he has against my sandwiches.

"Who is that?" I ask Eddy.

"I don't know," Eddy replies, looking around the dark room.

"What is your job anyway?" Bea asks me.

"I work for the council doing admin for planning and environments."

"Sounds thrilling," she replies. "Why was it so shit today?"

"I have to put a proposal together by Thursday on the restructuring of the department. If they pick mine, I get promoted to supervisor, if they go with this dickhead Tim's plan then he gets it and I probably join the redundancy list."

"Supervisor, ey, get you." Bea takes a drag on what is now her cigarette, "Who's this dickhead Tim?"

"Just a bellend who works in the Transport admin. He should have told me all this last Friday but didn't and then made it seem like he did in front of everyone today."

"I'd have knocked him out," Bea quips.

"Pizza!" Eddy shouts at the sound of the thud on the door. "Just come in mate, it's open," he shouts. The door thuds three more times followed by the ring of the doorbell. "Come in!" Eddy wails from his beanbag chair not wanting to have to move.

"Lazy bastard doesn't want to bring it in," the mysterious voice in the corner moans.

The door opens and is followed by the thud of it shutting. Eddy and the other stoners are perched up like meercats. I can see that the mysterious voice was Big Nick now as his humongous frame moves into sight at a sloth like pace from within the red beanbag.

"In the lounge," Eddy shouts as the footsteps get louder and I can sense someone stood behind me.

"Well look at this great big pile of twats."

I turn my head around.

"And here's the twat king." Clive stares down at me, clad in a large sheepskin coat his smirk just about visible under his walrus like moustache.

"What are you doing here?" I ask.

"Could ask you the same thing," he snorts.

"You know why I'm here. I'm staying here. Why the fuck are YOU here?" I snap back.

"What are YOU doing though?" he frowns motioning at me and Bea sat together on the sofa, her legs still draped over mine.

"Having a beer and watching a movie. What do you want Clive?"

Clive bends down and picks up a carrier bag. "Here." He chucks the bag at me some of the content spilling onto my lap.

"Oi watch it!" Bea snaps.

"Bills?" I ask Clive holding a letter up.

"Your stuff." Clive barks.

I sift through the letters and the odds and ends in the bashed-up carrier bag. "What the fuck is this Clive?"

"Like I said, your stuff. Get it sorted lad."

"Hold on... this is just a bag of bills?"

"And some other stuff of yours," Clive snorts.

I pick out an NME magazine I had been in the middle of reading before all this kicked off, a Pearl Jam tape that has been in the stereo in the kitchen, a beanie hat, a PlayStation controller and finally a couple of photo frames one with a picture of me and my grandparents and the other mine and Debbie's wedding photo.

"What am I supposed to do with this?" I hold out the PlayStation controller. "Did it ever occur to you that this may need to be plugged in somewhere?"

"I'm not to blame," Clive asserts.

"And why all these?" I wave the bills at him.

"Your responsibility lad, your house."

"My house? Are you taking the piss now Clive?" I toss the bills back it him. "What do I care if they don't get paid?"

"Well I'm not paying them!" Clive barks back.

"Get Debbie to pay them then, or both of you get the fuck out of my house!" I shout.

"Don't be daft lad," Clive spits, his moustache trembling and the vein on the side of his red face now throbbing. "You have no idea what my Debbie is going through!"

"You're right I don't! Because she won't speak to me and you won't tell me what's going on! It's like I'm married to Joseph fucking Stalin!"

"She's crying herself to sleep and you are here drinking, smoking, doing drugs with some slapper on your lap!"

"You fucking what?" Bea springs up.

"You heard me," Clive snarls.

"Don't go speaking to me like that!" Bea snaps at Clive, "I'm telling you now I won't put up with any of your shit."

Clive laughs and moves towards Bea. "Listen here. I am not going to take orders from you little girl!"

I hear a sickening crunch and feel a warm splash across my arm as Clive's nose collapses into the middle of his face. I look over at Bea, blood splattered across her face and chest and beaming with a huge smile.

"Jesus!" Eddy hops up out of his beanbag.

"You broke my fucking nose!" Clive wails dropping to his knees and holding what was his nose, blood dripping from the cavity.

"You deserved that," Bea tells him, "I did warn you."

Eddy runs over holding a box of tissues. "You broke his nose!" Eddy gasps at Bea.

"It's his own fault. He was being a dickhead," Bea says, nursing her sore hand.

"You broke my nose! What's wrong with you?" Clive sobs on the floor.

Eddy is picking out individual tissues and placing them on the floor in front of Clive to try and soak up the blood. "Ray, go get a towel mate."

"Get something for my face!" Clive snaps.

"Get it yourself," Bea tells him. "I'm going to wash my hands."

I grab a towel and some toilet paper from the downstairs bathroom, tossing the towel to Eddy and handing a scrunched-up bunch of the paper to Clive.

"I'm a qualified first aider," Buttercup shouts from the lounge.

"What should we do?" Eddy shouts back.

"Hospital," Buttercup advises.

"Who's sober enough to drive?" Eddy shouts to no response.

"Where are we going?" Big Nick manages to mutter.

"Hospital," I shout back.

"Fuck the hospital, where is the pizza? I though he had it," Big Nick points at Clive.

"He doesn't have the pizza." Eddy tells Nick.

"Bea broke his nose," I add.

"Not surprised, should have brought the pizza," Big Nick summarizes before settling back into the red beanbag.

"I'm calling Debbie, give me your phone Clive," I demand.

"No! my car's outside. I'll drive myself. Sod the lot of you."

"All clean!" Bea announces as she skips into the room. "Is he still here?" pointing at Clive.

"He's just leaving," I tell Bea.

"I'll be calling the police about this," Clive growls as

he rises to his feet. "And you!" he points at Bea.

"Careful," Bea warns Clive.

"Sod it!" Clive surmises and storms out of the front door, turning back to flip everyone the middle finger.

"What a nice old man," Bea says as she waves goodbye to Clive.

32

"Why does your job mean you need to get up at such an inconvenient time?!" Bea complains as my alarm wakes her from her second night in my bed.

"All jobs start early," I mumble hitting the alarm to turn it off.

"Mine doesn't," Bea moans and wraps the duvet around her head.

I lean down to my pack of cigarettes and pull one out of the pack, lighting it and feeling the soothing warmth of the first cigarette of the day. Bea reached across to take it from me. "Don't mess with my first cigarette of the day. If you want one I'll pass you one."

"Alright grumpy," Bea says, motioning for the pack. She lights a cigarette herself and pushes the duvet down from around her neck, lying topless next to me.

"I might just leave work today and stay here," I say, staring at Bea's exposed chest.

"Why? You're up, might as well go."

Not sure if Bea realizes that she is currently

making me feel I have other things I'd probably rather be doing than work. It amazes me the power a pair of breasts have over a man. If Debbie had come over last night and just flashed her breasts, I'd probably be having cornflakes with her at the breakfast table now. "If I don't go, we could hang out together today if you want?" I tell her.

"I have training today with Big Nick," she shatters my dream, "Should really go home too as my parents are probably wondering where I am."

"You live with your parents?" I ask her.

"What gave it away? We don't all have multiple houses Ray."

"I seem to have to break into all of mine though." I take a long drag of my cigarette, "I better pay those bills Clive brought over."

"Why?" Bea asks sitting up, "after he came over here like twat demanding you pay them? I'd set them on fire and post them back through the letter box."

"If nobody pays, then I default on the payment and that could affect my credit score."

"Oh no! Your credit score! How will life go on? For a guy who thinks the world is ending in just over a week your priorities are pretty fucked up. What do you imagine the new world to be like? Everyone dividing land and resources based on their fucking credit score?"

"Hang on," I sit up, "you have been reading my checklist?"

"Oh, the list that starts with 'Checklist for the End of the World' in big bold letters? Yeah, I did give it a glance. Strangely enough it piqued my interest."

"What do you think about it all?"

"I think you're spending too much time solving work issues, pissing around with bills and worrying about your credit score. None of that is one your list," Bea laughs.

"Part of me is slightly relieved you read it. It's not something that's easy to bring up in conversation really. You don't think I'm a bit crazy?"

"Yeah, I usually sit around in bed half naked with people I deem as 'crazy'. You're no crazier than the rest of us Ray."

"Fuck the bills!" I announce, taking a final drag of my cigarette and launching myself out of bed "Fuck Clive!" and "Fuck work!"

"That's better," Bea winks.

"Well not fuck work as I'm going, but less emphasis on work."

"Sure," Bea says sarcastically.

I start to throw on my work clothes and pick up my phone from the floor. One new message; not from Clive but from Kelly.

Lookin 4ward 2 2nite xx

I'd forgotten all about it. I feel shitty now, especially with a half-naked Bea in my bed. We hadn't 'done anything' in that sense but still I felt a bit guilty.

"What's up with you?" Bea asks.

"I just got a text through. I'm supposed to be going on a date with a girl tonight. If it's a problem I can cancel it."

"Why would I care?" Bea snaps. "It's not me you're married to Ray."

Not sure how to take that. I'm also now feeling guilty about what I am doing to Debbie. "It's just, you know? This..." I motion to the room.

"What?" Bea asks slightly confused.

159

"Well what this is? What's going on here?"
"Have fun figuring it all out," Bea laughs,
throwing the duvet back over her head.

33

Tina's hands are shaking as she is struggling to control Gordon's theatrics. She is biting her top lip and blinking rapidly as Gordon struts in front of her canvassing the crowd for imaginary votes as he puts forward his party manifesto.

I can see Tina getting frustrated. She puts a lot of effort into organizing the Christmas party and has a lot of pride in those aspects of her job. She like to feel appreciated and part of a team.

Gordon seems to be winding up now. "All I am saying is that we all want this to be a party where we can all have a bit of fun and let go a little. Don't bother with the sit-down meal, stick a buffet out for us all to graze on and the rest behind the bar." He refrains from taking a bow even though we all know he wants to and just takes his seat sipping at his now cold coffee.

"That's all very well Gordon but the restaurant is all booked; we will lose our deposit," Tina squeaks.

"It's only a fiver! Let the blood sucking capitalists

keep it!" Gordon bellows.

"Well you haven't even paid yours yet Gordon either. So far, I have only had fifteen pounds. I have paid the rest. Over fifty pounds out of my own pocket," Tina fires back.

"Here!" Gordon reaches into his wallet and pulls out a five-pound note, "Take it!" he extends his arm out to Tina.

"Regardless, it's too late to change plans now Gordon. It's a lovely restaurant and you can still order drinks there if you want them."

"Where is the restaurant Tina?" Annabel asks.

"It's just outside of Halifax. I've organised some taxis from the office at five o clock, will cost around…"

"How far" Gordon interrupts.

"I don't know the specific miles Gordon," Tina snaps back.

"What is the place called?" Gordon asks.

"It's called La Petite Maison and its absolutely beautiful food," Tina gushes.

"No! What is the place called where the restaurant is! Where are you dragging us to woman!" Gordon barks.

"It's in Leeds."

"Leeds!" Gordon roars. "Bloody miles away! Once we have paid for the taxis and the overpriced French nosh we will have nothing left for Christmas!"

"And what do you suggest we do at such short notice?"

"Let's go to the William and stick our deposits along with the party fund behind the bar. I'll have a word with the landlord and get him to put on some sandwiches for us."

"Why didn't you suggest this earlier Gordon? We

had a meeting about this back in October and all you did was sit there reading your newspaper!" Tina wails, almost in tears.

"I trusted it was all in good hands! I didn't expect to be dragged to Leeds for some fancy overpriced French meal," Gordon splutters.

"Next time YOU organise it!" Tina yaps as the door flies open. It's Tim.

"Hey guys, can you keep it down in here? I'm trying to work on my proposal next door and its quite important, so please either wrap this up or keep it down," he says with a condescending tone as the room falls silent.

"Sorry mate, we will keep it down in here. You go back to Mein Kampf now." I smile at Tim. I can't have everyone pussyfooting around him because they are scared of him trashing them in his proposal.

"Thought you would be working on yours too? Or have you already thrown in the towel?" Tim smirks back.

"Do you have anything to offer on the Christmas Party Tim? If not then feel free to leave," I smirk back as Tim scowls and closes the door.

"At least he had the balls to tell us!" Gordon scowls at me.

"Yes, at least he gave us that much," Tina adds.

"You really think Ray knew about all this and didn't tell you?" Annabel says standing up. "Ask yourselves what is more likely? Tim heard about the changes and didn't tell Ray as he was supposed to so he could get a head start on this proposal crap and make Ray look bad in front of everyone, or Ray knew and didn't tell anyone?"

I flash Annabel a smile. "Also, minor point but I think

the world is going to end as we know it in around ten days," I add "so I have had a think on it all and I really don't care if I keep my job or not."

"Exactly a reason to not bother to tell us," Tina pouts.

Annabel sighs, "Come on! You were all in that meeting and saw it with your own eyes! Tim made it obvious that he wants to be the manager or head supervisor whatever it is on offer. He just wants to be in charge. He called some people 'dead wood' for Christ's sake! He is a vindictive sociopath."

"Tim is really creepy," the new office temp pipes up, "I'm pretty sure he smelt my hair in the lift."

"Who hasn't brushed against someone else in the lift?" Gordon shoots back.

"You need to report that," Annabel tells the temp. "And if you ever brush up against me in the lift, Gordon, I will cut your balls off!"

"Can we get back to the party please?" Tina implores.

"I thought Gordon was organizing it now?" the temp asks.

"Well, if I must I'll happily go and chat to the landlord now." Gordon stands up, "If you will excuse me."

"Sit down!" Tina yaps.

"Am I organizing this party or not?" Gordon bellows.

"Can we just move onto point two?" Tina asks pointing at her flip chart.

"All that was point one? The last hour?" Gordon whines.

"Point one is the venue, and to be honest it doesn't look like we have agreed on that so perhaps we should discuss it for a bit longer until you understand, Gordon,"

Tina scolds.

"Well, if you are intent on dragging me to Leeds then count me out," Gordon stands and heads for the door.

"We all need to make the effort Gordon! You might enjoy yourself," Tina shouts after him.

"I will request my five pounds back then, Tina, as I will be enjoying a few beverages across The William after work on Friday, but I will not be going for a fancy meal in Leeds," Gordon surveys the room, "and you are all welcome to join me."

Tina is breaking now. "Please Gordon, can you just co-operate with me? This might even be our last party as a team!"

"Well I for one have seen the redundancy package on offer and think we would be fools to turn it down!" Gordon bellows.

"I thought that after that horrible news yesterday at least we would be closer as a team and in the back of my mind I knew we had this party to look forward to but it is obvious that nobody cares about it or our jobs," Tina's lip is on full quiver now, "so I will cancel the booking and leave you in Gordon's capable hands. Hopefully I will get some of my deposit back." Tina picks up her belongings and heads straight past Gordon towards the door.

"I don't feel very well after all this," Tina quivers. "I will be going home now and taking the rest of the day off."

"Course she is," I mouth to Annabel as Tina coughs and leaves the room.

34

The William IV isn't as busy as it was on Saturday. There are a few tables occupied but I had my pick of most of them when I got here about ten minutes ago. Zombie by The Cranberries is playing on the jukebox. I'd seen them live at the Cardiff Arms Park back in 1995. R.E.M headlined the bill but I'd wanted to go to hear Dolores' beautiful voice. It was another sign of the changes happening around the world that a brand-new Millennium Stadium opened in June, replacing the stadium I had once stood in.

I'd ordered a pint of lager to sip on whilst I wait for Kelly and ruminate about the day. Tina had made good on her promise and was gone by the time we all made it back to our desks. She had done the sulking teenager routine numerous times now and each time it seems to last longer, albeit this time I do have some sympathy for her.

Gordon had played everything off as if Tina had had a breakdown in the meeting room, playing down his own part in the coup and making sure to act it all out to the canteen staff before leaving for the day.

Tim had spent the whole day locked in the other meeting room; blinds drawn, working on his proposal. We hadn't spoken apart from our quick spar earlier which had made the day go much quicker, but I couldn't help wondering what he was going to put forward to the boss on Thursday. She is due to call us both with her decision before the party, if there even is a party now.

I'd brought my checklist with me to tie up some loose ends. I'm pretty confident I have everything on there I need and, using the pareto principle, I should be able to get 80% prepared in 20% of the time; then it's just the other 20% to worry about when the time comes.

"Alright," Kelly says approaching the table, "you got a drink then?"

"Let me get you one," I say rising out of my chair. "What would you like?"

"Smirnoff ice please," Kelly replies, taking off her coat to reveal a tight sleeveless hoodie over her stovetop pants.

"Sure," I say making my way to the bar. Kelly had tied her hair up in half up half down pigtails a bit like 'Baby Spice', not quite the elegant look from yesterday.

"Pint of Carlsberg and a Smirnoff Ice please," I ask the barman. Different staff on tonight than the weekend and less busy, so they seem a little more relaxed. I feel more relaxed than this time yesterday too and starting to enjoy myself. "Have one on me too," I say to the barman, reaching into my pocket for my now thick wallet. After work I had gone to the cash machine and emptied my bank account of the few hundred I had left in there. I'll go into branch tomorrow and get my savings that I have put away for a rainy day. This is my rainy day.

"Cheers mate," the barman smiles, "I had a pint too. That's six quid forty please." I pay the man and head back to the table.

"Ta," Kelly says as I hand her the drink and a glass with some ice and a straw in it.

"How was your day?" I ask her.

"Not bad thanks," she says, popping the straw into the bottle and taking a sip. "Worked in the shop in the morning and went to see a film with mates this afternoon."

"What did you see?"

"The Sixth Sense."

"Any good?"

"I liked it, but my mate didn't get the end, so she asked for her money back. They refused her and said the ending is what it is. My other mate tried to explain the ending to her and people in line overheard and went to watch Inspector Gadget instead."

"I had two people at work nearly kill each other over the Christmas Party plans," I laugh.

"Why would they do that?" Kelly asks.

"Just because its free money from the 'party fund' and they both want to do different things with it."

"That's sad. It's free at the end of the day and they shouldn't be so selfish."

"You're right. Did you have a good time at your do last night?"

Kelly takes a sip from her straw and thinks, "Yeah, it was ok. It was just the end of college one and some people got really drunk and started fighting so me and my mates just left and ended up in the Dog and Gun."

"You looked amazing."

"Thanks," Kelly says shyly, "What's that you were working on when I came in?" she asks.

I hesitate a moment and decide I might as well share it with her. "It's a checklist."

"What? Like a to-do list?" She asks.

"Yeah, a to-do list, things I have to do before the end of the world."

Kelly stops mid sip and looks at me. "The end of the world?"

"Yeah, a checklist for the end of the world."

"And when's that then?" she chuckles.

"A week or so. Well, January 1st to be precise. I think all the world's computers are going to get messed up by the change in date from nineteen to twenty, and they are all going to revert back to 1900 instead of hitting 2000, causing chaos everywhere."

"Bloody hell," Kelly exclaims. "I read about all this in the papers, but I didn't think it was that serious." She points to the list, "What do you need to do then?"

"Well, I've got five main categories on my list, and there are a few things below each category that I need to tick off to complete it."

"Bit more intense than a shopping list then," Kelly laughs.

"It's just how my mind works. I have always needed to compartmentalize things into achievable goals, otherwise I just can't get anything done."

"You lost me there," Kelly laughs.

"Split things up really and put them together, like on a shopping list I'd have all the freezer stuff together."

"Right. What have you got on there then?"

"Shelter, Food and Water, Security, Belonginess and Esteem," I show her.

"And how to you buy Belongingness - whatever that is?"

"The stuff underneath those is what I need to complete the category, and some things I can't buy."

"So, belongingness, how do you complete that one?"

"Well, it's the need to feel part of a group, so the subcategories are friends, intimate relationship and love."

"Oh shit, you're part of a cult or something aren't you?" Kelly says, moving back in her chair slightly.

"No. It's probably the wrong example to use now anyway. Think of it as me trying to make sure I am not alone or isolated. No matter how much you think you will be fine on your own, you will always need a sense of belongingness."

Kelly looks less scared now. "And how do you tick that off?"

"I'm throwing a housewarming party on New Year's Eve and if it all goes to shit, I'll have my crew already assembled without them even knowing."

Kelly leans forward and whispers, "This is a really weird date."

35

The wind has a bitter chill now as Kelly and I walk back towards the paper shop, her home, and the five pints I had at the pub are definitely keeping me warmer than I would have normally been. I can see the shop sign down the road. Kelly has been smiling a bit more since we stopped talking about the impending end of civilization as we know it. She definitely perked up a bit after we moved on from that. Now, walking down the street with her hand in mine, she is practically beaming. Not bad for a first date that started off with her thinking I was recruiting her into a cult.

"Did you have a nice time?" I ask her.

"Lovely thanks," she smiles.

"Me too," I smile back as we approach the shop.

"I had a great time. Thanks for the drinks and everything." Kelly lets my hand go "Something is bothering me though, and I need to say it, otherwise I will just be asking myself all night."

"Is it the cult thing?" I smile through gritted teeth.

"No, your list and all that, it's fine, it's part of you."

"Okay, thanks," I say, slightly intrigued now.

Kelly looks up at me. "You said I looked amazing last night," Kelly says looking down, "Well, I appreciate that but you haven't said anything tonight and that's kind of what I expected."

"What do you mean?" I ask.

"I'm not stupid. You only got interested in me yesterday when you saw me all made up for my party. Before that you wouldn't even talk to me," she says slowly and looks down. "In the shop with my hair tied up, in my comfy clothes, that's me," she looks at me and points at herself, "this tonight is me. I won't be that made up glamorous girl every time you see me, so I want to know you like me for who I am."

I take a deep breath and take Kelly's hand. "Kelly, I do like you for who you are. I don't know how much yet but it's a first date. I can be a narcissistic dickhead sometimes, but I am not like that all the time."

She smiles and then takes my other hand. "Can I ask you another question?"

"Of course," I say.

She points to my left hand "Are you fucking married?"

36

"He won't be much longer," the smartly dressed lady informs me as I sit in my ripped jeans, hoodie and stolen parka in my local branch. I'd started to play Snake on my phone to pass the time until the battery died. I was positive I had put it on charge last night, so must be something wrong with the charger. I'll pick another one up anyway, as It will be good to have a spare when the world ends.

It's starting to drag on a little bit, all the waiting here. I only had the day off to do Christmas shopping. The council gave everyone a day before the Christmas break every year seeing as we work right up until Christmas Eve, but even though it's a freebie I still don't want to spend it with the cast of Fraggle Rock.

There are two other people here waiting with me who are hogging the daily papers; the woman to my left who seems to know everyone who walks in and out of the front door and the man sat opposite me who keeps snorting mucus back into his throat every couple of minutes.

"Hiya Brenda love," the woman greets yet another friend, acquaintance or former lover - who knows? "How's your Albert's colon in the end?" I decide to reach for my walkman that is somewhere in my bag. "Tell him I said hi. I don't get out much nowadays, especially with this Y2K bug floating around." I decide not to say anything and just press on with listening to my recently returned Pearl Jam tape. I wonder how Clive is.

I get a tap on my arm midway through Evenflow and it's the lady next to me, not the person I wanted trying to get my attention. "Can you turn those musical earrings down? I can't hear myself think!"

"I'll just turn them off," I tell her, wanting to mention that all I have heard is bits and pieces of her life story for the past half an hour.

"It's terribly inconsiderate," she berates.

"Look, they are going in the bag."

"No respect for personal space."

"Look, I'm sorry I offended you but to be honest I put my walkman on because all I could here was you chirping away to every knobhead who comes in here."

"Language please," the man opposite me butts in.

"You got the wrong waiting room mate. This is the bank, doctors is down the road," I snap back.

"Excuse me?" the man spits.

"You, sniffling and snorting every ten seconds, so loud even the homeless fella outside the front has pissed off somewhere else."

"If you must know I have a cold," he says smugly, going back to his borrowed newspaper.

"It's not that Y2K bug is it?" The woman next to

174

me asks, grabbing her scarf over her mouth in panic.

"That only affects computers. It's not even a bug and you would think the amount of people you speak to, someone would have fucking told you that by now," I snap back at her and she lowers her scarf and goes to sit next to the man opposite. I catch a glimpse of the back of his paper 'Rivaldo wins Ballon D'Or'. That's one of the footballers from the bet I found in the parka. Wonder if the other two came second and third.

"Can I have a look at that paper mate?" I ask my new enemy.

"No," he replies hiding his face with the paper.

"Mr. O'Riordan," the smartly dressed lady announces, "if you will follow me."

I try and steal a glance at the newspaper whilst I move towards the lady. It's too small. I can't read anything, but I can hear the chippy woman who was set next to me mutter something about being 'first'. Screw her. I've come to get my savings; she's probably only here for a chat.

I follow the smart woman to the back of the branch where she points me into a small room containing a very obese man in a suit. There are no windows or any natural light at all in here which makes the whole room quite claustrophobic.

"Mr. O'Riordan?" the obese man greets me.
"Yes."

"Hello, Mr. O'Riordan, or can I call you Ray?"

"Call me either. It's my name, that's what they are used for."

"Okay, I'll stick with Mr. O'Riordan."

"Why?" I ask.

"I beg your pardon?" he chuckles.

"Why, why are you sticking with Mr. O'Riordan. Is it because you think I'm in a bad mood and don't want to further anger me?"

"Well, no it's just…….."

"I'm closing my accounts regardless so call me Dinosaur Shitpants if you want."

"Let's just take a look at the accounts," he smiles, causing his three chins to evolve into four.

"Has anyone told you why I'm here?" I ask.

"Yes, they have sir," he replies, brow covered in sweat.

"Well, can we just crack on with it then please?"

"Can I just talk you through some options?" He smiles.

"Listen mate, I'm sure you're a nice guy but I came here to shut down my savings account and take the money out, now and in cash."

"Can I just show you some ISA's we have on offer?" He pushes a brochure to me.

"You know why I'm here, I know why I'm here, I made a conscious decision to do this, I can make decisions by myself you know. I wouldn't go to Woolworths for a CD player and expect to be shown the different types of pick and mix, let's just do what I came to do please?"

The obese man nods his head and starts clicking around some buttons on his computer. I can hear him breathing which is quite unsettling.

"What is the reason for closing your account?"

"Impeding end of civilization as we know it or end of the world, whichever fits best."

The obese man tilts his head and squints slightly before carrying on, "And would you like the balance in cheque or transfer?"

"Cash," I stress.

"Sorry sir but we can't do a cash withdrawal from this type of savings account. It will need to go into your bank account."

"Why?" I ask.

"It's just the terms and conditions of the account you have."

"Fine," I say.

"Would you like the paperwork sent to the address we have?"

"No. I mean I have moved."

"Okay, do you have the address and a utility bill maybe?"

"I don't know the address and I don't think there are any utilities there."

"Right, I'll need to confirm your new address to issue out any paperwork."

"Just send it to the one on there. I still own the place," I gasp, running out of patience as my day I'd reserved for prepping seems to be half wasted already.

"Well that's all done for you sir, two thousand three hundred and fifty-six pounds has gone to your checking account. Anything else I can help with today?" The obese man wipes his brow.

"Yes, I'd like to withdraw "two thousand three hundred and fifty-six pounds from my checking account please."

37

The rain is starting to pick as I head through the cobbled flooring of the massive open air Piece Hall, a Georgian cloth market that had stood the test of time and past attempts to bulldoze it in favour of a car park. I decide to dash across the length of grass for shelter underneath the large stone balcony of the first floor, to have a look at how much cash I now have to start shopping for my supplies.

I open the tobacco tin that I took from the kitchen drawer during my raid of my own property. I take the elastic band off the roll and count the crisp tenners - one hundred and seventy pounds. I add that in my head to the three hundred and forty from my bank account and the two thousand three hundred and fifty-six from my savings - two thousand eight hundred and sixty-six quid. In normal circumstances a decent amount of cash but I'm going to need a bit more than that if I'm going to get the supplies I need from my list and also fix up the farmhouse basement - my 'bunker'.

I pull out the slightly wet piece of paper from my pocket with the name of the antiques shop I need. The unit is somewhere on the first floor and the lady at directory enquiries couldn't be more helpful than that. I pull out my phone to give the number she gave me a try but my phone is now completely dead. I'll need to get that charger too.

I head to the stairwell in the corner of the Piece Hall. It's dark and damp and smells slightly of piss. I head up the stairs and pass a teenage couple making out, one of which shouts "Get lost weirdo!" at me. I can't tell if it's the girl or the boy; he's young enough to not have his bollocks drop yet, and I would shout back to explain the irony of them calling me weird but I am slightly out of breath now.

I look across the vast stone balcony in front of me, dotted with shops in what were formally rooms for cloth merchants back in the 1700's. We had studied it in school and as a kid I'd spent hours down here with my grandparents, hiding in the abandoned rooms and visiting the market that was held in the centre on a weekend. I spot the 'Antiques' sign halfway down the balcony and assume that's the place I need to go.

The room is dimly lit, and I can just about squeeze through the walkways as various bit of furniture and other items protrude outwards at different intervals, blocking parts of the path. "Hello," I half shout, trying to get the attention of anyone who is still alive in here.

"Hello?" a confused voice shout back, "who is it?"

"A customer." I reply.

"What do you want?" the voice enquires.

"I've got some stuff to sell."

"Let's have a look then," the voice says. "I'm by the counter."

I look around and can see about six desks and another four or five bureau style things. "Which one is the counter?" I shout.

"The one I'm stood behind," the voice shouts back, as I try and guide myself through the maze of accumulated shit.

"What are you selling?" the voice shouts.

"Don't worry, its only small items," I shout back, nothing big. I can see you're full to the brim."

"Don't be daft lad. I'm low on stock here," the voice chuckles.

I finally see the owner of the voice to my right. He looks a bit like a tortoise; his bald wrinkly head creasing with a smile, his tiny but stodgy frame in a knitted green tank top over a mustard coloured shirt, his huge glasses making his eyes look like the Manga characters in Japanese cartoons and comics. He's sipping a cup of steaming hot coffee. I look around and can't see where it would have come from.

"Let's have a look then," he beckons me towards him.

"Just some family heirlooms that I won't be needing anymore," I tell him as I place the old coins and stamps on the counter.

"Lovely!" he exclaims as he starts to look through the stamps first with some tweezers in his chubby little fingers. "Whoever these belonged too knew how to keep them proper," the tortoise smiled. "People come in here with stamps stuck to all sorts of stuff. Thing is, once the stamp has been licked and stuck it loses most of its value. Keeping them in these little plastic pockets has kept their value."

"Great," I reply, staring at an old Air Raid Shelter sign on the wall. Not too interested in the analysis, just the amount he's willing to pay me would be nice.

"Now these stamps are in lovely condition, that tobacco tin was the perfect home for them away from grubby oily hands too," the tortoise smiles.

"How much are they worth then?" I push.

"Well, they will be worth less to me because I don't collect myself, but I will be able to sell these on, possibly at auction, which will lower the price again." The tortoise separates four stamps from the rest. "These four are the prime collectible pieces. The other lot are good, but I'd buy them as a job lot."

"Great, how much?" I push again.

"For the George V brown half a crown, fifty quid. For the horizontal Edward VII one-pound stamp, two hundred. The Edward VII ten shillings, seventy-five quid and the five shilling one I'll do fifty." He folds his arms and stands back, smiling.

I count up the figures in my head, not having any idea of their worth but trying to act cool and calm. "Three hundred and seventy-five in total there then. What about the other lot, the bundle?"

"Twenty-five for that lot." He points with his chubby finger, "Four hundred cash for the lot today." I instinctively shake my head and go to pick up the stamps. "Hold on!" he wobbles, "that's a good offer," he smiles back at me.

"Thanks, but I'll take my chances and try elsewhere." I have no intention of taking these stamps anywhere else.

"Wait, we haven't even looked at your coins yet!" tortoise man flaps.

"Well, take a look and make me an offer. Make

it quick though, I have stuff to do today."

Tortoise man moves the tin to a separate area of the counter and takes out the felt bag with the coins in, carefully untying the string and gently placing the four coins on the suede counter mat. He is immediately drawn to the large silver one. "Edward VII Coronation Coin, lovely," he grins moving his wrinkly head closer to the remaining three. "A Britannia farthing, and a couple more of Edwards: a silver sixpence and a half sovereign. Not bad condition. Who's were these?'

"My grandmother's," I tell the tortoise man. "She gave them to me just before she died back in 1992."

"Well she knew a good coin. The farthing isn't worth anything really, but the rest are lovely pieces." He pops the farthing back in the tin, guess he's not bothered about that one. "I'll give you eighty for the coronation coin and twenty a piece for the other two. You can keep the farthing." He folds his arms again, this time less of a smile.

"Okay, one-twenty for the coins, four hundred for the stamps, call it six hundred for both and you have a deal," I stick my hand out.

He declines my outstretched hand. "Most I can do is five fifty for the lot," Tortoise man stubbornly says.

"Five fifty and that Air Raid Shelter sign" I counter.

"Deal."

38

The streets of Halifax town centre are packed full with shoppers. I can see women with prams, old ladies with shopping carts, groups of young girls with butterfly clips in their hair followed by groups of lads, some still rocking curtains, all ticking things off their Christmas shopping lists. I have my list in my pocket too, but it's slightly different from everyone else's.

I'd popped into The Old Cock pub after leaving the Piece Hall to have a couple of pints and meet Eddy. He wasn't there and my phone was out of battery, so I had my one pint and left. I'm in that awkward state now where the one pint wasn't quite enough and yet I didn't really have any excuse to stay as I was on my own and carrying an Air Raid Shelter sign Plus, it is only midday, so I decided it was probably best to go. I'm thirsty again now and still have a lot to do before I can officially call it a day, but a quick detour to Fagin's to find Eddy won't do any harm as I'm limited in my purchases today - I don't have anywhere to store what I buy and no means of transporting it home.

Down a dingy back alley, just behind the local McDonalds, I reach my destination. Fagin's Bar is tucked underneath a nightclub and sandwiched between three buildings in a little prohibition style hideaway. I'd first discovered it popping down for a few pints with mates after school, but Eddy was a 'local' here and had hired out the nightclub above on a number of occasions for parties until he got lazy and started using his own house.

"Pint of Heineken please," I ask the barmaid who smiles back and goes about getting my pint ready. She has a lip ring like Bea, and also a couple of tattoos down her left arm. "One seventy-five please love." I count out some change from the pocket of my stolen parka and take my frothing pint from her. Maybe I should give the parka back, or at least the betting slip.

"Alright mate."

I turn around and see Buttercup stood behind me with a pint. "Hiya mate, just popped in looking for Eddy."

"He just nipped out for a McDonalds," Buttercup tells me, "He gets pretty hungry when he's had a couple of joints."

"Yeah, Frosties sandwich was always his favorite at Uni," I tell him, taking a long gulp of my pint, "that and a pint of Lilt."

"Heard you pulled the other night," Buttercup says.

"I wouldn't say pulled, but I did hang out with Bea for a while."

"Did you shag her?" Buttercup asks.

"Erm, no I didn't," I stutter. "We did have a nice time though."

"She's lovely, Bea," Buttercup smiles. "I always fancied her. Think it's that look 'cos she's half Indian." Buttercup sips his pint, "Wish I was half something, Italian maybe, or Australian. Everyone in my family is from Mixenden. Well, my Uncle is half Huddersfield but that's about it."

"She's great," I reply, not sure what else I can add.

"Not in here love," the barmaid shouts to Eddy as he appears at the door holding his bag of McDonalds.

"I'll be tidy," he pleads.

"Sorry, no exceptions," she replies as a dejected Eddy takes a seat on the big wooden table on the cobbled street outside.

"What's all that about?" I ask Buttercup.

"Two blokes got into a fight over a McDonalds Apple Pie a few weeks back. One of them got badly burned on his face when the other jabbed it into his cheek. Blanket ban on McDonalds now."

"Sorry mate, I was late and I have no phone battery," I shout out to Eddy. He is scoffing down the last of whatever he has bought and managed a thumbs up back to me.

"What phone you got?" Buttercup asks.

"Nokia 3210," I tell him.

"Can I play snake?"

"Phone's dead, mate. I just said."

"Oh yeah, perhaps next time," Buttercup sighs.

"It's all gone," Eddy tells the barmaid as he tosses her the brown paper bag.

"Oi! Sort out your own rubbish you knobhead!" she jokes back and hands him a half drank pint from behind the bar. He must have left in a hurry.

"Do you know who came second and third in

the 'Ballon D'Or'?" I ask Eddy.

"Nice to see you too and no I don't," he replies.

"Rivaldo won it," Buttercup says.

"What about Beckham and Shevchenko?" I ask Buttercup.

"Beckham won the treble with Man United this year," he offers.

"I need to know who came second and third."

"Well Bayern Munich came second in the Champions league and they don't play a game for third. In the Premier League..."

"Not for the Treble - in the Ballon D'Or," I interrupt Buttercup.

"He knows everything about football does Buttercup," Eddy says.

"Well clearly not everything," I sigh.

"Well, we don't know then! How's the shopping going anyway?" Eddy asks.

"Just got this so far," I tell him pointing to the sign.

"Buy that, today did you?" Buttercup asks.

"No, I thought I'd just bring it out with me," I snap back at him.

"I kind of imagined stockpiles of food, guns, swords, that kind of stuff," Eddy says as he reflects on the sign. "What about cigarettes and booze?"

"Mate, I literally have my two hands and this rucksack to carry stuff," I argue.

"So, you chose that sign? Not the best start for a prepper mate," Eddy analyses.

"What are you preparing for?" Buttercup asks.

"The end of the world."

"Definitely going to need more than that in my honest opinion," Buttercup tells me. "The sign is non-essential. You want to focus on the essentials, mate."

"I'm getting to it! I'm going to pop into Woolworths and WH Smiths next, then Tesco, Kwick Save and that electrics store by the Portman and Pickle pub." I gulp at my pint as Eddy laughs and Buttercup looks concerned.

"When's the world ending then?" Buttercup asks me.

"Well, it's the Y2K bug so New Year's Eve," I tell him.

"That's going to put a damper on people's parties," Buttercup bemoans, shaking his head. "Not very well planned is it? Has anyone confirmed this? Or is it still subject to change?"

Eddy laughs and spits out some of his pint. "Don't worry Buttercup, everything will be fine." He points to a large man in a leather jacket and a flat cap in the corner booth. "If you want Ray, that's the fella who sorts me out with all my duty-free stuff. He can get cigarettes, tobacco, booze, usually around a quarter of the price you pay in the shops here."

"I could do with a supply for myself and to use as currency too," I contemplate.

"First the Euro and now this. I don't know what is wrong with the good old British Pound," Buttercup sighs.

"I'll think about it," I tell Eddy.

"Well it looks like you're doing a fantastic job so far, so I won't be offended if you don't need my help!" Eddy laughs pointing at my sign.

I gulp the last of my pint down and pick up my sign. "I'm off then, thanks for the company." I flip Eddy the middle finger.

He flips one back and laughs, "Don't skip WH

Smith's now mate. You don't want to be stuck without post it notes and highlighter pens when the world ends."

39

I'm tired of shopping now. It's only two in the afternoon, and all I have bought is an old Air Raid Shelter sign, but I am flagging and it's partly to do with the alcohol, I am sure, but mainly I just can't stand shopping. I need help with this.

I have been pushing an empty trolley around Woolworths for at least half an hour now. I put in some plates and glasses but decided there was no way I'd carry them all home so put them back and did the same with the bedding I just put in the trolley minutes ago. It's too big, I decide, and abandon the trolley by the toy section, rescuing a similarly abandoned basket that will be more realistic in terms of what I can get back to Eddy's.

I don't need to worry about food items. I'll be getting all that with Annabel with her Espace next week. Bea has also said she wants to go with me when I get the security items as it sounds 'cool'. She seemed to enjoy the idea of picking an axe for the firewood and other tools that can double up as weapons. I said I'd meet her in B&Q tomorrow after work, but she won't go there as it gives her bad memories. Some lad at school used to call her Bea & Q and she broke his wrist, so we are going to Do it All instead.

I decide to just go with my gut and start adding things to the basket I know I can carry; matches, packs of lighters, candles, plastic plates and bowls, some cups, a shelf load of painkillers. I'd actually made money so far this shopping trip which is odd and the three thousand five hundred and sixteen quid in my parka pocket is starting to feel heavy.

I'm going on the rule that if something does happen, then I will need an initial amount of time to survive. If everything is blown up or people are rioting and looting, I need to be able to sit that out in my farm and wait until normality is restored. It's a shame I can't do that with work right now - I still need to get my proposal sorted.

"Oi!" I suddenly hear a voice shout. I look down the aisle and I search for the voice. "Oi! Wanker! That's my fucking parka!" I didn't recognize him at first due to the new black eye patch, but I drop the basket as it's the landlord from the Dog & Gun.

I immediately dart into the next aisle and then back down the one in front of that, hoping he will be running the opposite way.

"Oi! Come here!" I can hear him bellow. Sounds further away which is a good sign. I move to the aisle to the right of me and it's time to make an important decision.

"Get back here you bastard!" I can hear him shout. He sounds like he is making his way to the front entrance near Market Street. "You cost me two grand you wanker!" he shouts, definitely towards the front entrance. I decide to head for the back exit. I grip my sign and start sprinting towards the back of the store, pushing past a group of lads who are in a queue at the electronics counter and expertly dodging a lady with a pram by the café. "Oi!" I can hear him shout, too far away to catch me as I ride down the escalator to the exit by the Car Park, the one-eyed bastard still shouting in the distance.

The Piece Hall is back in front of me now. I could go back in there and find an empty room to hide in. It's too risky, especially as there was nobody there earlier. I turn left instead, leaving the town centre further behind me. I know the perfect place to lie low away from the landlord. It's right in front of me; Blockbuster Video. Doubt the one-eyed bastard will be coming in here anytime soon.

40

"Please tell me you have a newspaper from yesterday?" I plead to Kelly.

"Yeah, we got Fred's stashed away on his pile." She reaches down and grabs a copy of The Mirror and places it on the counter.

"I love you! Thank you!" I shout at Kelly to her surprise.

"Ooh slow down lad, you've only had one date," Apron lady scolds.

I flick through the back pages and spot the picture of Rivaldo. Scanning the article underneath, I spot the words I wanted to see; Beckham came second and Shevchenko came third. "Yes!" I shout, making Kelly and Apron Lady jump.

"What's the matter with you?" Apron lady grimaces at me, "Your team score a goal or something?"

"Just won a bet, that's all," I smile at them.

"You shouldn't gamble. It's a waste of money," Kelly says.

"I didn't," I chuckle as Kelly and Apron Lady look at me with confusion.

"How did your shopping go anyway?" Kelly asks.

"I bought this sign," I lift it up to show them "Air Raid Shelter, to go on the door to the bunker."

"Bunker?" Apron lady gasps.

"Ray is preparing for the end of the world, Mum," Kelly says

"And that's all you got? Never let a man do the shopping, that's what I say," Apron Lady chuckles heading upstairs.

"What is your mum's name?" I ask Kelly, feeling that it would probably be best to not have to refer to her as 'Apron Lady' if we did end up going on another date.

"Beryl," Kelly says still laughing.

"Beryl, stop being cheeky!" I shout up after her. Feels nicer to call her by her real name, humanizes the apron somehow.

"I can see why your wife is divorcing you now," Kelly chuckles.

"Her loss," I say pointing to my sign.

"See you have finally taken the ring off," Kelly says pointing to my left hand.

"Yeah," I nod, "Nearly got me punched by you the other night so I thought it was for the best."

"Sorry about that," Kelly says, "it's just a bit of a shock seeing your wedding ring after such a nice date."

"I wasn't exactly hiding it or wearing gloves all night. I just forgot to be honest, which is probably why I knew it was time to take it off."

Kelly smiles, "It wouldn't have been me that punched you. My mum heard it all and keeps a baseball bat under the counter."

" Don't think she'd need the bat," I smile back.

"Why don't you grab some food from here? Tins and Rice and Pasta and that?"

"Not at the prices you charge," I reply.

"Oi!" Kelly nudges me. "What's wrong with our prices? You keep coming in here!"

"I'm joking! I just need to get quite a lot."

"How much exactly are you expecting to fit in that backpack of yours?" Kelly laughs.

"I'm doing my big shops later. Annabel is lending me her people carrier when I do the food shopping next week."

"Who's Annabel?" Kelly asks.

"She's a friend from work."

Kelly looks at me with questioning eyes. "Only a friend?"

"Yes, only a friend."

The little bell on the door to the shop pings. We both turn to look and are greeted by the smiling face of Michael, the homeless man from outside.

"Is it alright to use the toilet Kelly?" Michael asks.

"Yeah no probs, you know where it is," Kelly replies.

"Cheers love," Michael says, stepping into the shop. "Alright Ray?" he smiles, walking past me and behind the counter, glancing at my big metal sign.

"Yeah, good thanks mate. Just bought a sign."

"Nice. Vintage that is," he replies before heading upstairs.

"How do you know Michael?" Kelly asks.

"Just spoke to him outside the other day, nice guy."

"Yeah he is. It's bad what happened to his

194

business. He fitted out this shop you know," Kelly says.

"Did you know him before he started sleeping rough?"

Kelly nods. "Yeah, he's been around the town for years. Used to go up to watch Halifax at Thrum Hall with me dad."

"Shame he's sleeping rough now. Has he got anyone? Any family?"

"No," Kelly sighs, "wife packed up after he lost the house, and he did have a daughter my age. I was in junior school with her, but she went off years ago, no idea where."

"Twenty Lamberts please," I change the conversation quickly as I hear Michael coming back downstairs. Kelly looks at me with confusion until she realizes the reason for my sudden change in topic.

"Ta love, see you later," Michael smiles at Kelly as he leaves the counter area.

"Here mate, I might have something you'd be interested in," I say to Michael

"Oh aye, what's that then?" Michael replies.

"Do you fancy a job?"

41

"Here comes Ray Mears!" I hear Eddy shout as I stumble through the front door with my Air Raid Shelter sign.

"Who is that?" I shout back, not knowing what pop culture insult he is throwing my way. Annabel had been banging on about him too at the farmhouse.

"The fella off World of Survival. He can catch a deer with only a packet of cigarettes and an old Air Raid Shelter sign," he laughs.

"Well it's going to have to do as I'm moving in tomorrow," I tell him, dumping my bag and my sign down on the kitchen floor. "Do you have a Nokia charger?"

"First of all, everyone has a Nokia charger," Eddy chuckles, "but seriously why so quick with the move? Tomorrow? That's a bit out of the blue."

"I can't say here forever mate, it will have been a week come tomorrow. I'm drinking and smoking more than I have in years being back living with you, plus I have got someone coming up to the farmhouse to start some work on it."

"Who? It's Christmas in two days mate!" Eddy says offering me a beer.

I take the beer from him and take a long gulp. "A homeless man who lives outside the paper shop."

Eddy nods, obviously thinking things over. "And he's going to live in your house?"

"No. He's doing work on the basement, putting up some divider walls and making it livable."

"The homeless guy?" Eddy asks.

"Yes! And just because he's homeless doesn't mean he can't do the job. He used to have a carpentry business. Kelly's family know him. He's a top bloke."

Eddy rubs his head. "But do you see how strange this is?" He takes a swig of his beer. "I just need to know you know this isn't normal."

"When have we been normal Eddy?"

Eddy sighs and nods back. "Well, I hope it works out. Did you manage to get anything else apart from your sign?"

"Yeah, a Land Rover."

Eddy seems lost now. "A Land Rover? As in the vehicle type?"

"Yeah, Kelly's dad was selling one and I've bought it, given Michael the keys so he can start getting stuff up there today. He's going to set up a tent in the barn and stay there whilst everything is finished."

"So, you have bought a Land Rover, given it to a homeless man you have just met who will live in your barn?"

"Yes."

Eddy stands up and walks towards the fridge to grab another beer. "And it's me who's bad influence?"

I shrug my shoulders and grab my pen and paper from my bag, picking up my beer and walking towards the games room.

"Ignore the mess. I'll clean it up," Eddy shouts. "Or if your mate isn't too busy and fancies a job? Don't have a Land Rover though."

The room is still full of the remnants of the three-day party. I shake off a beanbag next to the computer and collapse into it. The proposal is due tomorrow and the boss should let us know what is going to happen, basically mine or Tim's proposal, on Friday; which is going to be a bit awkward as it's the Christmas Party and there is no better way to start a Christmas Party than with a traditional group sacking. I assume we are still having the party. I don't have a clue what's planned now since Gordon's coup.

"The Dreamcast is disconnected, mate, if you're after that. The N64 is plugged in. Just swap them over," Eddy shouts from the kitchen.

"Nah mate, I'm working on that proposal for work," I reply.

Eddy enters the room and offers me another beer. I shake my head, so he keeps the two. "When is it due by?" he asks.

"Tomorrow," I tell him, wishing he would give me a little bit of peace.

"You got ages mate. Let's play some Ready 2 Rumble," he nags, offering me the beer again.

"I got a beer thanks, and I really need to get this done. I need to email it through tomorrow and the other guy has probably already emailed his across," I snap.

Eddy looks dejected and sinks back into the computer chair. "Why is it so important if you think the world is ending? Isn't that just a massive waste of time right now?"

He wasn't wrong, but I couldn't quite figure out why I was still doing it either. "What's with all the questions mate? Just leave me write this thing," I bite.

"At least let me help you," Eddy pleads.

"Look Eddy, this is important because, because …… I'm not sure why. I think it's because it's something Annabel was worried about and I have a chance to influence that and make things OK for her. Or maybe it's just that I want to fuck over Tim one more time before the world ends and, regardless of what my rationale or reasoning is, how could you help me? You spend all day drinking and smoking weed, playing computer games or partying. You don't even work much anymore, so how could you help?" I shout.

"Well we could read his fucking emails for a start!" Eddy shouts back.

I look at him, he's on the verge of tears. I feel like I have just kicked a puppy. "What did you say mate?"

"We could read his emails," Eddy says with his lip quivering.

"How?" I ask, sitting up.

"Well you know his email address, right?"

"Yeah, I think it's written down in my work folio."

"Well the council use a basic internet mailbox provider. It's not internal or a private network yet or that secure really. We just need his email address and this password cracker software my mate developed."

I get up out of the beanbag. "So, I will be able to see anything he has sent to the big boss?"

"Yeah, if we get in," Eddy says as I make my way

back with my folio.

"I can counter every one of his points without him even knowing!" I clap my hands together.

"Err yeah, if that's what you want to do. Personally, I'd send pictures of cocks to the boss, but up to you," Eddy giggles.

"Here," I push the folio in front of Eddy, "it's that one under 'Tim'."

"Okay. Now this software will try every available combinate of whatever words we put in the box below to try and crack the password. These are candidate passwords so throw some words, places, numbers he might use."

"Okay: Manchester United, Tim, Denim, Wanker, Twat."

Eddy looks at me with a frown.

"Sorry got carried away. Shagadelic, err he's 25 so 1974, he likes....."

"I'm in," Eddy smiles.

"What was it? Can you tell?" I ask.

"shagadelic69," Eddy laughs. "What's your boss' name?"

"Heather, Heather something." I rack my brain. I should know this, but I'd never really called her anything apart from Boss.

"Is it Slater?"

"Yes, that's it."

"There is an email from him to Heather Slater at 16:00 today, subject is Planning, Environment and Transport re-structure."

"That will be it," I say biting my lip, "it's got to be."

Eddy clicks open the email and offers me the computer seat and the spare beer.

"Cheers," I say, taking the beer, "for the beer and

this."

"No worries," Eddy says. "I can be of use sometimes."

I nod and start scrolling down the message.

Mrs. Slater,

Please see below my proposal for the re-structure of the Planning, Environments and Transport departments within Calderdale Council.

I have bullet pointed the key points below and included some supporting information at the foot of the email.

Currently we have 2 supervisory roles, one covering Planning and Environments and one for Transport both with 6 Full Time Employees (FTE) equating to 14 FTE within the department structure along with one temporary worker.

- Reduce the FTE to 3 across the Environments and Planning divisions equating to 50%. I believe this number to be sufficient to complete the work currently assigned under Ray O'Riordan's supervision.
- Similarly, in Transport a reduction, but of 2 FTE equating to 33%. However, the workload remains high and these colleagues would be replaced by temporary office workers with a £10,000 p/a reduction per employee.
- All three areas would report to me as Department Head with the Supervisor role becoming redundant; removing another 2 FTE, one being myself who would take up a role within the Department

Manager structure which is currently -1 FTE.

-   In total a removal of 7 FTE, 6 of which will be made redundant (one FTE, myself moving to the Department Manager structure) and the hiring of 2 new temp workers under Transport who will also proceed with the automation of our admin processes.

-   The new structure will have 7 FTE working under myself with three temp workers, reducing the annual spend on salary by around £100,000.

-   My recommendations for redundancy ahead of the formal review are: Ray O'Riordan, Tina Binns, Gordon Taylor-Smith, Steven Gligorovic, Simon Thompson and Annabel Shaw.

I re-read the bullet points and the names Tim has put forward, focusing on Annabel and the pit of my stomach starting to churn. I can't quite believe that he thinks the department will be able to function with half of the staff gone.

"What's it all mean mate?" Eddy asks.

"He's basically cutting the staff in half, making my job redundant too and recommending they don't keep Annabel." I push myself out of the seat and point at the screen.

"What? Why?" Eddy gasps, taking my seat at the computer.

"It's a power play. He's getting rid of the lifers like Tina and Gordon and anyone who is competition or disagrees with him, like Annabel. This will crush her."

"Are you going to propose they keep everyone?" Eddy asks.

"No, it's not possible. There needs to be a change. It just doesn't have to be as drastic as Tim is proposing. He just wants as blank a canvas as he can get and a promotion of course - the double-denim dickhead!" I sip at my beer, "I just need to make my proposal more appealing, and right now I think the only way it can be done is to play on Tim's weaknesses."

"Fucking hell!" Eddy gasps, pointing at the screen, "You have got to see this."

42

My head seemed a lot clearer this morning when I woke up. I'd finished the second beer Eddy had given me and then cut off the supply, working on my proposal instead and packing up my duffel bag ready for the early morning. I'd dropped it off, along with the Air Raid Shelter sign and some extra bedding Eddy had given me, into the Land Rover this morning. I'm pretty sure he just didn't want to have to wash the bedding, as it was the stuff I'd been using for the past week.

Michael had kept his word and met me bright and early outside the front of the store. Beryl, the artist formerly known as Apron Lady, had woken up especially and she had a tape measure, pencil and pad of paper Michael had asked for. She had also given us a coffee each in a Styrofoam cup, which was nice of her. Kelly was still fast asleep.

It was a stunning morning, crisp and brisk with the sun shining down to create little heat spots within the cold air. It was much colder up on the moors, but the view and the isolation were amazing up here.

I'd gone with Michael up to the farmhouse to show him exactly what I wanted doing. He was impressed with the structure of the place and said that it was cosmetics at best and a little renovation here and there to mask the fact it has laid abandoned for a number of years. A day or two's work at best.

"I think this will be the biggest job," I tell Michael as he follows me down the stone steps leading from the kitchen to the basement.

"And all this was hidden?" Michael asks.

"Yeah, under a rug under the table. And there is the outside entrance too. Saw a floating head on one of the photos and decided there was either something down here or plenty of bodies buried somewhere," I tell him flicking the light switch.

"Power down here too?" Michael asks.

"Yes. It's odd. No power anywhere else but down here it's fine. Checked all the electric companies and nobody is providing electric here."

"Someone must have piggybacked off the windfarm up the road," Michael suggests.

"Yeah, there is a picture somewhere of some of the commune members helping to build it, so makes sense they would steal the energy too! I'd feel better if we had a couple of generators though, just in case."

"I can pick those up for you," Michael says. "Mate of mine runs a hire shop, always has a couple too many, and going cheap, hundred or so each."

"That's great, I'll take three if he has them going."

"You won't need three, lad" Michael chuckles.

"I'm working on better safe than sorry," I tell him as we move further into the basement.

"No problem, three it is," Michael says, running his

hands across the wood paneled walls and then pointing at them. "Are you keeping the panels? What's the general plan for down here?"

"Well I want it sectioned off like a flat, so there is a kitchen, lounge and bathroom. Keep the growing area over there and add a big storage section at the back by the kitchen. And a bedroom, couple of bedrooms if there is the space."

"Right," Michael considers thumbing his beard, "Sounds like a bunker to me."

"Yeah, I've had that a lot."

"Well, it's certainly big enough down here, by the looks of things. Probably three times the footprint of the farmhouse." Michael sits down with his pad and pencil and draws out the room. "I'll need to measure up before we go but I'll,draw out a rough sketch for you."

"Cool, sounds good." I check my watch, noting that I had about an hour to get to work.

"What's the rush for this 'bunker' by the way?" Michael asks.

"Oh, before New Year's?" I ask and chuckle, "You will think I'm mad."

"Go on lad, spit it out," he laughs.

"Well, I think this Y2K stuff is going to be more serious than they are making out. Have you heard about it?"

"I have," Michael says. "I read a lot of the papers, as you probably guess."

"Well, you may think I'm daft, but I think it's going to be catastrophic, and the world is going to end as we know it in one week and one day."

Michael stops his drawing and starts to chew on his pencil.

"Crazy isn't it?" I tell him. "But that's what all the

signs are pointing towards."

"I don't think it's crazy," Michael says, standing up, "or that you're daft." He looks at me with his brown eyes wide and glazed over. "The world as I knew it ended for me a couple of years ago."

43

Michael had given me a lift to work in my new Land Rover before leaving with two grand in cash; five hundred quid for him and a grand and a half to make a head start on getting the materials for the bunker and also some backup generators just in case. I'm in early for once which is quite nice as it's quiet because nobody else is in yet.

I'm scribbling down numbers on a post it note, trying to budget my available cash. I'm going to invest some of it into getting a load of duty-free cigarettes and whisky from Eddy's mate, and doing the numbers I reckon I could spend around five hundred quid and get enough to supply myself but also use as currency when required.

It's time to take the plunge and text Eddy; better safe than sorry.

Hi mate can u ask ur mate for £300 of cigs n £200 of whisky

That should be plenty. If it's a quarter of the price then, by my calculations, I should end up with forty cartons of cigarettes at seven pounds fifty a carton of two hundred and around forty bottles of whisky if they are around a fiver as Eddy thought. This is assuming that Eddy's calculation of a quarter of the normal price is correct.

no probs

Short and sweet reply from Eddy. I need a bit more info than that though.

Can u ask where and when? N how much I get?

That should at least give me a little more to work off.

Yeah course

That at least ticks off a couple of items from my list if Eddy's mate can come through.

"Morning." Annabel smiles as she sees me. "Nice to see you here on time for once. After a promotion, are you?"

"Been up the farmhouse. Early start all around," I yawn.

"This morning?" she asks.

"Yeah, just got dropped off ten minutes ago by Michael."

"Who is?"

"The homeless fella outside the paper shop I go to." I take a sip of coffee. "He's nice. You'd like him."

"And he has a car?"

"No, a Land Rover. I bought one for him to use."

"It's too early for this, Ray," Annabel says walking to her desk behind mine "You bought a Land Rover?"

"Yeah, from the paper shop."

"You sure you're okay?" she asks me.

"It was for sale on the notice board," I explain.

"Ah, right, typical morning then," she chuckles and switches on her computer.

"How was it here yesterday?" I ask, thumbing a cigarette out of my packet.

"Tense." Annabel swivels around on her chair to face me. "Gordon was marching around telling everyone how he would spend the redundancy money if he got it and then nearly came to blows with Tina over this party." She takes a cigarette out of my pack. "Tina told him that she was over fifty quid out of pocket for the whole cancellation thing, so Gordon went and got her the cash."

"Why was she mad at that?" I ask lighting both mine and Annabel's cigarette.

Annabel takes a long drag. "Well, thing is, he only went and got the money from the petty cash for the tea and coffee. Later on, Tina went to buy some coffee and milk, noticed the petty cash was empty and started accusing the office temp of theft."

"Bloody hell," I chuckle.

"She stormed over to Tim who took her in a room to interview her and then interview the temp, all the while I was in there with them as the note-taker," Annabel chuckles.

"Didn't Gordon say he took the cash when saw all this going down?" I ask.

"Well, he left for The White Horse at lunchtime and only came back at three. We'd just finished the interviews and when he heard what was going on, he announced in front of the whole office that Tina had asked him to take it from there. Tina went ballistic and stormed off and the temp quit."

"I don't know if I'm glad I missed it or sad I missed it," I chuckle, as the office door booms open. Tim marches through, holding a briefcase in his right hand and a stack of folders tucked under his left. He spots me and gives me a look like you would give to a pair of Y-fronts that don't belong to you turning up in your underwear drawer; pure confusion and disgust.

"Too little too late," he smirks at me.

"You're using it wrong," I tell him.

"What?" He snaps back.

"The briefcase. The folders go inside, mate." I crack a smile at him, Tim just scowls and carries on marching to his desk.

"Better behave," Annabel clenches her teeth, "he could be my boss tomorrow."

I lean in towards Annabel. "If I tell you something, it can't go any further." She nods back at me in agreement. "Last night, me and Eddy managed to hack into Tim's emails."

Annabel's jaw drops as she moves closer. "How do you do that? Is that illegal or can you get sacked for it? What did you find?"

"I don't know the answer to the first two. Well, his password is shagadelic69 so there is that, but we found his proposal." I reach into my bag and pull out a copy of Tim's proposal email that I had printed at Eddy's.

Annabel starts reading and I notice her hands

are shaking a little, either anticipation or anger. She has started to shake her head and is taking huge drags of her cigarette so I can tell her reaction is the same as mine when I first read it.

"Is he for fucking real?" Annabel laughs and looks at me, biting the tip of her tongue.

"Just finish it," I say slowly and with hesitation as Annabel's head is shaking left to right more prominently now and I can see her mouth starting to screw up.

"What a bastard!" she says.

"Keep it down!" I tell her and look towards where Tim sits to see if he heard. Fortunately, he is lost in whatever it is he is doing, probably writing a proposal on how to further cull the Spice Girls and more efficiently smash up puppies.

"You need to tell people about this," Annabel says to me sternly and with some concern. "If people see this then..."

"They can't do anything," I tell her "It's perfectly fine. It's a proposal - a twattish one with no consideration for people but still what he was asked to do."

Annabel sighs and nods, "I guess you're right."

I reach into my bag and pull out the second print out. "This on the other hand….."

44

I hear Bea's bashed up Nissan Sunny before I see it. The exhaust is throwing out black smoke and hanging on by a thread, the volume on her stereo is turned up to max as Faith No More blasts out of her half open window. I give her a wave as she drives past the front of Do It All, her hardware store of choice, seeing as she is boycotting B&Q for personal reasons.

"Alright Bea?" I smile at her, careful not to appear too creepy as requested.

"Yeah, good thanks. Better we came here, not been in a B&Q since school, everyone kept winding me up, asking me where 'Q' was." She points at the sign, "See! Much nicer, a little rainbow going through a house."

I nod in agreement. "I got picked on at school for my name too."

"Ray?" She screws up her nose.

"Well it's actually Rain but I call myself Ray," I admit.

213

"Rain is a cool name, like Bea," she smiles. "Let's go in then."

"Hold up. Have you got a quid for a trolley?" I ask.

She sighs and pats down her ripped jeans. "Fucking highway robbery!"

"You do get it back you know," I tell her.

"That's not the point is it?" she grumbles, unzipping her coat to search the inside pocket. "Here," she thrusts the pound into my hand, "How's your shitty job? Obviously not paying you if you don't have a quid on you."

"It's shitty thanks," I chuckle and free the trolley from the trolley chain gang.

"It's getting chilly out now," Bea complains as we enter the warehouse like store.

"I know, I'll be setting up the fires tonight in the farmhouse," I tell her.

"Ah cool!" she exclaims. "I love an open fire, roasting marshmallows, melting stuff and chucking old toys into it," she smiles, almost skipping next to me.

"Well feel free to come in for a bit when we get back," I tell her.

"I could do. I don't have anything on tomorrow," she contemplates.

"Plus, you get to see the basement or bunker whatever it is."

"Sounds dodgy. I'm in!" she grins and pulls on my arm. "Come on, let's go."

"Whoa! Can we do this shopping first?" I ask.

"Oh yeah," she says, starting to pout, "Guess so."

I reach into my pocket and pull out my checklist, focusing on the section outlined as 'Security'.

Underneath there are the subcategories of 'currency', 'safety' and, finally, 'weapons'.

"What do we need to pick up?" Bea asks. "Is it all the building materials and shit for your dungeon?"

"No that's all taken care of, and please don't call it a dungeon," I reply. "We need stuff for Safety and Security." I point at the categories on the list.

"Like a gun?" Bea says with some uncertainty.

"Well, we can't get a gun as I have no time for a license, plus I don't know how to shoot one really and also it's a gun."

"My dad has a gun," Bea says nonchalantly.

"How does your Dad have a gun?" I ask.

"He has quite a few. Goes Clay Pigeon shooting with his mates from work. Shoots grouse on the moors. He's in the Elland Rifle and Pistol Club, first Indian to be President."

"Sounds like Rambo," I joke.

"He's not, but at least we know where to get some guns if the world ends. He won't mind anyway if he's dead," Bea says directly.

I look above me and ahead to see where the home security section is. I spot tools to my right so detour towards that first.

"Ooh, go down towards fencing," Bea points.

"Okay," I say, "Any reason why?"

"Yeah," she says, "we come down here when we get stuff for the deathmatch wrestling matches," she skips ahead of me. "Look."

"Nice," I say staring at the boxes of barbed wire.

"That's definitely something to go under your security category," Bea stresses.

"Good idea," I nod. "There is already some on the fences on the outskirts of the farm, but I could fix some to the window ledges of the farmhouse and barn."

"Or around a baseball bat," Bea smiles.

"Yeah. Or that," I agree, putting three of the big boxes in the trolley.

"This is fun!" Bea shouts, lifting her hand up for a high five. I slap it and turn the trolley back towards tools.

"What's next?" Bea asks.

"Tools," I let her know pointing ahead.

"You're a tool," she shouts, skipping off towards the tool section.

I try and follow Bea, but she's run off in the distance. I spot the axes on the bottom shelf in front of me and pick up three of the sturdiest looking ones. Next is a couple of Stanley knives and a selection of hammers.

I move towards the larger items. I need something long range that could do some damage, so pick up a heavy-duty floor scraper and check it for weight and range, getting some strange looks off an old lady holding a rake. It's decent so I grab two.

Hammers are good but something heavy and practical like a crowbar and a tyre iron would be a nice to have, so I stick those in my trolley which is now resembling an evidence locker.

"Ray!" I hear Bea shout in the distance. "Where are you?"

"By the duct tape," I shout back, adding ten rolls to my trolley. I start to read the back of a pack of lighter fluid when Bea appears at the bottom of the aisle holding a petrol-powered chainsaw.

She is beaming at me "Can I have this? Please?"

45

The sour faced checkout assistant is picking up each of our chosen items with a look of distain and confusion. He seems to be analyzing each one and what crime we might commit.

"Everything alright?" I ask him as he analyses a nail gun. "You do work here don't you?" I ask him as he decides to pass it across the scanner.

"Yes, I do," he replies, staring confusingly at a pickaxe.

"Well, you just seem to not recognize anything you are scanning, taking a good look at everything. Thought you might have walked in from Tesco by mistake," I pick at him as he hesitates over the Stanley knifes.

He is looking more worried than sour faced or confused as he scans the contents of our trolley: duct tape, axes, crowbar, tyre iron, lighter fluid, the chainsaw.....

"I'll need to see some ID please."

"Fine," I say reaching into my bag.

"Not you. Her." He points at Bea. "How old are you?"

"I'm two, you paedo!" Bea bites back.

"Got any ID?" The sour faced man says sarcastically.

"Yeah, in my fucking car that I own," Bea waves her car keys at him.

"Whatever," the man says, deciding it's not worth the battle and goes back to scanning a blowtorch.

"Think we will get all this in your car?" I ask Bea.

"Yeah, I reckon so," Bea replies.

"Are you sure you need all these hammers?" The sour faced man asks.

"Just keep scanning, you sad old bastard," Bea snaps at him.

"If we can't fit it all in, we can always leave the barbed wire for now and come back for it later?" I suggest.

"No, it will fit and if it doesn't we can leave you or maybe some of the Home Alone shit you picked up, like the tins of tar," Bea moans.

"That will be essential if we need to stop anyone coming down the stairs!" I moan back.

"How would we get back up the fucking stairs then?" Bea shouts at me.

two hundred and sixty-eight pounds please," the worried cashier announces.

I thumb through the wad of cash in my pocket and hand him two seventy. He proceeds to check every note for any signs of a forgery before handing me the two pounds change.

"I'll take that," Bea snatches the coins from my hand. "Pound I leant you plus interest," she smiles.

"You will get you pound back in a minute!" I sigh at Bea.

"That's what they all say," Bea smiles.

""What is it you're going to do with all this?" The sour faced man asks, "Or do I not want to know?"

"How are you still talking to us? We have paid, haven't we?" Bea groans at him.

The sour faced man looks more broken now. Bea has broken him down and I feel a bit sorry for him. "Sorry mate, we are preparing for the end of the world a week next Friday," I tell him.

"No need to be sarcastic, I was just trying to be nice," he shouts back.

46

The floor of the massive basement had been divided up with timber and, following the placement of it, I could see how the layout was going to look now from my viewpoint at the bottom of the old stone stairs.

Michael had split the basement up into seven sections: hydroponics, toilet, lounge, storage and two bedrooms. The toilet had stayed where it was, which was down to the right of the doorway I'd first used to get in here.

The hydroponics had been shifted from the far wall next to the lounge to the bottom right next to the toilet, but they were now sat in their own little area instead of nearly in the middle of the place.

The old lounge area was still bottom left, or the far wall opposite the toilet and hydroponics areas, and had kept the funky shag carpet and wooden paneling but was now sectioned off from the rest of the cold stone floor. The paneling had been trimmed to fit where the wooden beams were now fixed to the wall.

Next to the lounge on the left are the two would be bedrooms, both a decent size and comfortably fitting in the three military style cots in each. Could probably put in four at a push.

Finally, on the left, a decent size storage area, the same size as the bedrooms so could be converted to one if we don't need to store our food down here at any time in the future. Good thinking by Michael on that one.

The kitchen area is just to the left of the bottom of the staircase where I am stood. Michael has kept it open on to the hallway which has allowed for a table, a few more chairs, and an upturned tea chest currently, but it will look good with a couple more chairs and an actual table. Bea seems to be managing with the tea chest anyway as she polishes off her fish supper.

"Looks alright down here," Bea says with a mouth half full of chips.

"He's done a great job already."

Bea nods and takes a sip of her can of Dandelion and Burdock. "He's a pretty cool guy. Love the grunge look."

"He's homeless, Bea, I don't think it's a look."

"Whatever, looks cool anyway," Bea argues as she goes back to concentrating on her supper.

I hear Michael's footsteps behind me on the stone staircase. He had been fitting a new front door onto the farmhouse since we got back and hadn't touched his fish and chips yet.

"What do you think?" Michael asks standing next to me. "It's a huge space, six metres by ten."

"It looks great Michael. I can visualize it all now. It's really coming along."

"You are going to do walls, aren't you?" Bea asks Michael.

"Yes, there will be drywall," Michael chuckles.

"If it was me, I'd turn this place into a training room, like Stu Hart's dungeon. I could train you to wrestle then," she grins.

"I'm definitely having rooms," I tell her.

"Fine... I shotgun that room," Bea says pointing to the one next to the storage room.

"Are you going to be living here too?" Michael asks her.

"Haven't decided yet. I'm weighing up my options," Bea says, glancing in my direction.

"Well, there is a bit more to do down here. Probably be finished next Tuesday or Wednesday," Michael says sipping at his tea.

"Can you finish off the storage room first? Just so I can start moving stuff in there," I ask.

"Err, my bedroom first," Bea interrupts.

"No problem," Michael nods, "I'll need to look at the lighting down here too. Will need to fit a few more bulbs around to make sure each room is covered, but I'll get a mate who is a sparky to do that, then I'll crack on with the flooring and the drywall."

"How come there is electricity down here but not upstairs?" Bea asks.

"There is a cable and fuse box coming in from that porch like area behind that door by the toilet," Michael points, "I think it runs down from the windfarm. Ray said that some of the fellas that lived here worked up there."

"Can you get it working upstairs?" Bea asks.

"I can't. I'll ask the sparky, but more importantly he'll need to fit a backup diverted to the generators." Michael walks over to the second entrance and opens up the door. "They are in the outbuilding up that ladder.

Sparky will connect them up if you're happy with them up there."

"Yeah, probably best place for them," I nod.

"How are you doing for cash?" I ask Michael.

"All the materials so far down here, the drywall and laminate still upstairs, the new front door I've put on the farmhouse plus the tools and the generators came in at just over a grand," Michael tells me. "Still got the new kitchen, stove, toilet, sinks, paint and other finishing touches to consider after that, plus the cost of the sparky."

"How much more?" I ask directly.

"Well, that lot and the outbuildings too, like getting the barn fixed up a bit and tidying up the generator housing and you're spent-up I'd guess," he advises.

Michael had certainly made the cash stretch as far as he could. I don't think he had remembered to pay himself. "What about your wages?" I ask him.

"Well, I've been thinking," he says with some trepidation. "I'd happily take less than five hundred if you let me pitch the tent up in the barn for a while longer. Just a few months after I finish the job. It's getting freezing outside."

Bea punches me on the arm. "Let him stay in the house you knobhead!"

"No, it's fine!" Michael presses, "I prefer my own space."

"Michael, stay where you want for as long as you want but I'm paying you the five hundred." I take the wad of cash out of my pocket. I'm down two hundred and seventy from the trip to Do it All, Michael had two grand off me this morning, the Land Rover cost me half a grand, so I've spent around two thousand seven hundred and seventy quid today. I originally had about three and a half grand in the wad, so I should be left with around seven hundred and fifty now give or take a few quid that I spent on other important things like pints of lager. I count off the five hundred to hand to Michael and sure enough my once big wad is now down to just over two hundred quid. I still have the betting slip in the pocket of my stolen parka, but I still don't know whether to cash it in or return it.

"Here mate." I hand Michael the five hundred pounds. "Get the stuff needed and just don't spend any of your wages on it."

Michael nods and stuffs the cash in his pocket. "Think I'll have my fish and chips now," he smiles.

Bea chucks him the parcel. "Just warm it up in the imaginary microwave."

47

I still can't get over how amazing the views are up here. It's beautifully dark outside and so quiet. The moon is full tonight and is illuminating the moors in a hazy greyish purple tone. Sat by the window I can see nothing for miles in front of me. The fire is roaring next to me and filling the room with its warmth, the darkness perfectly interrupted in here by the flicker from the candles strategically placed next to our wingback chairs.

Bea is wearing one of my hoodies and is also wrapped up in one of the blankets from Eddy's on the wingback chair. She is engrossed in one of the books from upstairs, Moby Dick, and hasn't said a word in an hour at least. Michael retired to his tent following his fish supper along with the newspaper he had picked up this morning, so all I can hear are the crackles of the fire and the wind outside.

I have made good headway in writing down what is needed under the food and water section of my checklist. The water part shouldn't be too hard. There is a well and a spring that runs through the surrounding land; plenty to keep the taps running and in case of an emergency. Food is a different matter.

I've based the types of food I need to get on a list I found on an article Jeeves showed me after I asked him the question: 'food for surviving the end of the world'. I was quite surprised that there were hundreds of links for me to choose from. I didn't even expect one.

The amount I get I will need to base on it being full capacity here. Problem is, I don't know what full capacity will look like as I still don't know who could potentially be here when it all goes to shit on New Year's Eve - or if it will go to shit. So many variables right now.

I take out a cigarette and show the pack to Bea who shakes her head. I light the cigarette and draw in a deep lungful of smoke and feel the nicotine hit my system. That's another thing I'll need to think of; tobacco.

I try to enjoy the moment of complete silence and the smoke filling my lungs but keep thinking back to my checklist. Before food and water, I am going to need to tick off another section; Belongingness and Love.

I look over at Bea, all wrapped up and cozy in the blanket. She has the bottom left of her lip curled up under her teeth in concentration as she's reading her book. She actually looks cute right now, although I'd never tell her that.

I am pretty sure Bea is going to want to be here on New Year's Eve, even if it's just to laugh in my face when the world doesn't end. We have definitely got some sort of connection. She has kissed me on three or four occasions now and the last few have been pretty intense. We shared a bed and have been hanging out a lot together; perhaps she likes me more than a friend? I'm too afraid to ask really, and by asking she might confirm and where does that leave me with Kelly?

Me and Kelly have some chemistry and she is down to earth and grounds me a lot. Would she leave her parents behind and come up here? Probably not, but she would come up for a party and to see if the world is actually going to end. Besides she knows about my plan to use the party here as a way to ensure I have the people I care about around me and in turn my survival group if it all goes to shit.

What about Annabel? She has always been someone I can rely on. She is supportive and our friendship has always been strong and was built on trust. I would be lying if I said that I had never thought about what life would have been like if I had Annabel to go home to rather than Debbie. Now Debbie was no longer in the picture, why haven't I explored that option? Do I fancy her, or do I just like how she makes me feel? Has she ever thought of me as more than a friend? So many unknowns.

What about Eddy? I feel like one minute he is my rock and like a brother to me and then the next minute just out of control and I want to get away from him. He just takes way too many drugs to be effective or even function as a person sometimes. He is erratic and selfish but can be meticulous and selfless; it just depends which Eddy you get and that seems to be decided by how intoxicated he is and via what substance. I'd felt so much better today without the hangover encompassing my every move and decision and I can't risk letting myself get drawn into Eddy's bad habits again.

Debbie, of course; can I go through all of this and not even tell my wife what I am doing? She has made it very clear, or at least Clive has made it very clear, that we are over and she doesn't want anything to do with me. But things were good once. She was there for me when my grandparents died, when I got chucked out of Uni and when I had my nervous breakdown after my mother died. We shared our lives for eight years, and were even planning a baby up until last week. How can I erase that from my memory? And how can I live with myself if something happens on New Year's Eve and I don't do anything to protect her?

Is it really who I want around me? Or who is useful to me? I'm the one picking and I can't help but think I'm being driven by my narcissism, or driven by my cock and my ego is taking over sometimes. I know I need belongingness, a social group, people to work with, argue with, laugh with, live with to fulfil my needs as a human. The problem is, I need to decide who those people are and get them here before the world ends.

I toss the last of the cigarette into the fire and consider pouring myself a whisky, immediately shaking my head and reminding myself how different I had felt without the hangover and without the constant dread; it had been replaced by confusion and uncertainty and I'm not sure I would be able to sleep tonight but it's worth it.

I look over at Bea on her wingback chair. She is drifting off and looks so peaceful. I check the time on my watch: 11:03, probably best to start thinking about turning in for the night. Better have a piss first.

Due to the blocked toilet, we have been going outside like animals. Not so bad for me and Michael but Bea had already made it clear she was never coming back until the situation was rectified.

I chuck my coat on and open the new farmhouse

door, admiring its finish and the smoothness of the new locking system. It's pretty cold outside now. I hope Michael is okay.

"Shit!" I shout as my phone beeps and shocks me, it's so quiet out here.

It just keeps beeping. I grab it out of my pocket and the 'missed call' number is just going up and up and up. I check my messages and have twelve new texts. What the fuck is going on?

Before I get chance to read anything the phone starts ringing.

"Hello?" I answer with some uncertainty.

"Where the HELL are you?"

Fuck, it's Debbie.

48

I'd taken the Land Rover straight to the Royal Halifax Infirmary after Debbie told me what had happened - well more shouted and screamed what had happened, but I got the idea.

They had been woken up by a noise downstairs and Clive had gone down thinking it was me sneaking in again. When he had got downstairs, there was an intruder with an eye patch who had attacked him and demanded to know where I was; the one-eyed bastard landlord.

I'd got to the infirmary just after midnight, and after searching through the old Victorian maze of a building for half an hour I'd just found Debbie in a small room off one of the wards standing vigil over a sleeping Clive.

"Shit, his face looks a mess Debs, I'm so sorry," I reach for her hand as Clive lays asleep in the hospital bed in front of us.

She snatches her hand back and scowls at me. "His face has been like that for two days since your little tart broke his nose." She nurses Clive's head. "He's broken his ribs and his foot. They are keeping him here to make sure he hasn't got any internal damage."

"Debs, I'm sorry, I feel terrible. I hope he's okay."

"He's in hospital on life support. Of course he's not okay," she snaps.

I look around the bed searching for a life support machine but there doesn't seem to be one and Clive isn't plugged into anything. I decide to leave it.

"Did you see who did it?" I ask Debbie.

"No, but I heard him, Ray, and I heard what he was shouting at my dad. He was demanding to know where you were," she cries, "He was shouting for you. Wouldn't stop hitting my dad until he told him where you were hiding out. Why do you think I called you?"

I feel a pang in the pit of my stomach as Debbie berates me, not sure what I can say or if anything will make a difference.

"Who is this man Ray? Who is this man who has assaulted my father? Physically, emotionally and sexually?"

"He sexually assaulted him?" I ask Debbie.

"He hit him on his cock, Ray. It's swollen and very painful for him." Debbie says through tears.

"I wouldn't really count that as sexual assault, Debs," I tell her as gently as I can.

"I don't care what you think, Ray, just tell me who this man is and why he is after you."

I can't tell her who he is. It would open the door to a clusterfuck of trouble. Police would be called and that would not be a good thing right now. What would stop the one-eyed bastard from turning me in?

"Who is he Ray? What have you done? What

have you stolen from?"

"Stolen?" I ask.

"Well I don't know? Do you? He was shouting about you costing him money on some bet, somebody called Parker. I don't care really! I'm not the police Ray."

I think I know why he's so annoyed, but I can't tell Debs. "Look Debs, he sounds like a local nutjob to me and I have no idea why someone would be after me," I lie.

"The police want to speak with you," Debbie says bluntly. "They want to know your current address. I gave them Eddy's, that's still correct isn't it?"

"Yes," I lie again.

"What about the commune?" Debbie says, looking at me dead in the eyes.

"So, you did open the letter."

"I don't want to discuss that right now," she bites back.

"Maybe I want to discuss it Debs?"

"No. We are not discussing anything to do with us tonight Ray. My father is what is important right now."

I bite my lip and walk towards the window of the room. The one-eyed bastard said 'Parka' and mentioned two grand. He must mean that betting slip I found in the pocket. I look at my phone and decide to send a text to Eddy, just in case.

If Police ask Im staying with u

I slip my phone back into my pocket and look at Clive. His face all bruised, battered and swollen courtesy of Bea, his ribs bruised and wrapped in bandages because of the one-eyed bastard landlord and his bat, and then I look down to his broken foot in plaster. "How did he break his foot?" I ask Debs, "Did the guy punch him on the foot?"

"It doesn't matter how it happened," Debs snaps at me.

"Did he throw him or something?" I ask.

"No, he didn't throw my Dad," Debbie sighs.

"Well how did he break his foot?" I press.

"He broke it here okay!?" Debbie snaps "He insisted on waving me back whilst I was trying to reverse park and I ran over his foot."

"Poor Clive," I say shaking my head and trying to stifle a giggle.

"It doesn't change the fact that somebody attacked him, Ray. They broke into our house and broke his ribs, and they were after you."

"Debs, I have told you, I don't have a clue who could have done this. I'll happily talk to the police if they want to speak to me. I feel terrible about what has happened to your dad." I walk over to her and take her hand; she's still wearing the wedding ring. "Can I do anything to help out?"

Debbie sniffles and wipes her eyes. "You can cook Christmas Dinner at the house on Saturday because dad isn't going to be able to do it now."

49

I'd just made my third cup of coffee. It is gone nine and I am still the only person in the office. I am enjoying the peace and quiet of the office in the mornings and it has been a good time and environment for me to clear my head before the day to come.

Bea had slept through my late-night excursion and was unaware of anything that had happened. Michael had heard the Land Rover leaving and then returning but didn't ask any questions. When I woke up a few hours after getting back to the farm it was like it had never happened, just a bad dream, or a nightmare, where I had agreed to cook Christmas Dinner for Clive and Debbie tomorrow.

As far as I know, Bea is still at the farmhouse. Not sure what she would be doing there as I only have the books upstairs. Michael had dropped me off again and gone to pick up the rest of the supplies that are needed.

I take out the folder from my bag and take out the poly-pocket containing my proposal. I pull out the crisp pages and thumb through it one more time; I don't think I am even that worried about how work will all pan out now, I haven't thought about it for a few days and I have bigger things to think about. It's too late now but I just want to make sure I am doing the right thing.

The silence is broken by a santa suit-wearing Gordon carrying a box of what look like top shelf spirits. I am pretty sure of that because they still have the optics on.

"Here comes Santa Claus!" bellows Gordon to an empty office.

"Morning," I nod at him.

"Where is everyone?" he asks.

"Late, I guess. People don't usually get in till later on Christmas Party day," I tell Gordon, sipping at my coffee.

Gordon puts the box down and puts his hands on his wide hips. "Well this is not how I imagined it." He looks at his watch, "When are most people here then?"

"I have no idea Gordon. I've only been here this early once before," I smile.

"Right," He barks, picking up his box, "I'll be back in an hour or so. Don't tell anyone I was here," he storms off.

Back to the beautiful silence.

I slide my proposal back into the poly-pocket and back into the folder. The other two poly-pockets in there are either going to help mine or destroy it; one poly-pocket containing Tim's proposal and the other containing the other emails Eddy hacked from Tim's account.

50

The food in the canteen is as bad as ever but the Christmas decorations draped over the drink's cabinet, coffee machine and buffet counter are making it seem a little less depressing in here.

"Got any poached eggs?" I shout into the space between the counter and the kitchen.

"No. It's Christmas Eve," a gravelly female voice shouts back.

"Didn't have any yesterday though," I reply.

"Don't do eggs on a Thursday," the gravelly voice tells me.

I don't think I am going to get any eggs today so settle on two slices of brown bread. I take the slices across to the big industrial toaster which has some baubles and tinsel wrapped around it.

"Is this toaster a fire hazard?" I shout to the gravelly voiced woman.

"What's wrong with it now?" she shouts back.

"It's covered in tinsel and baubles, aren't those

flammable?" I ask.

"I'm not a bloody scientist!" she shouts back. "If it bothers you, have an apple!"

I dump my tray back in the holder and give up on the canteen. Probably should eat something before the party though; perhaps it will take Annabel's mind off everything if we left here for a bit. She is currently following me around and isn't particularly hungry, just nervous and worried about the boss delivering her verdict on my proposal today.

"Do you want to pop out and grab something to eat?" I ask Annabel.

"Not hungry," she replies.

"Well, it's way past breakfast and most places will be shutting here soon. It's Christmas Eve."

"I'll just have some of those sandwiches Gordon mentioned."

"I wouldn't count on him organizing those, Annabel."

"This is so annoying!" Annabel strops.

"Look, the boss said today, so it will be today."

"Has she said when she will call you?" Annabel asks.

"No, she didn't but said it would be some time in the morning."

"Go back to your desk then! It's ten to twelve!" Annabel pushes me towards the lifts.

"I have my mobile so she can get me on that," I chuckle.

"What if she doesn't want to call your mobile because it's more expensive?"

"She has her phone paid for by the council, Annabel, I'm sure she's not going to be bothered about a couple of quid ringing me."

"How are you not bothered by this?" Annabel shakes her head at me.

"I am bothered! I'm tense and nervous but also hungry and I can at least do something about that now."

"How can you eat when you're nervous? I couldn't even force anything down right now."

"Well, if I'm going to be drinking, I will need to have eaten something. It's nearly midday now and we started drinking around this time last year."

"Just don't drink then!" Annabel smacks my arm.

"I haven't had a drink in two days, well two beers the other night," I tell her.

"Holy shit," she replies her eyes distracted at something over my shoulder.

"Is that for me or whatever you're staring at?" I turn around and notice the boss strolling through the front door of the building.

"Morning Ray, Annabel," she says sternly.

"Morning Heather," Annabel replies as the boss nods and makes her way to the lifts, pressing the button and getting in alongside a waiting Sadsack. Annabel turns to me, "That's not a good sign," she winces.

"Actually, I think it's a very good sign," I smile back.

51

The boss and Tim had been in the meeting room together since Annabel and I had got back to our desks. Annabel had been called in by the boss around half an hour ago which had led Tina to come over and ask me what was going on - specifically why the boss had come down today and what it had to do with Annabel now. I had told her honestly that I didn't know. I had an inclination, but I wasn't going to go broadcasting that around the office for which Tina would have been a perfect medium to do so.

"Here comes Santa!" Gordon bursts into the office once again in his Santa suit and holding a box of liquor.

"Shhh!" Tina scolds Gordon as everyone keeps their heads down. "The boss is here!"

Gordon looks disappointed, probably mainly due to his entrance with the booze not getting the desired reaction twice in one day; he'd probably rehearsed that all evening.

I look at my empty coffee mug. I stand up and stretch, deciding that it could probably do with a refill seeing as the heavy drinking has been delayed. Probably not the best idea to start handing out booze whilst the boss is here.

"Ray," I heard from down the office. It's the boss, "Can you come in please?"

I nod and start to walk towards the room, my co-workers glaring at me then glancing away as I notice. I feel like I have somehow forgotten to put on any clothes this morning.

I open the meeting room door and see Annabel and the boss sat on one side of the big table and Tim at the other. Annabel is biting her top lip whilst Tim is sat arms folded and shooting me the most sickening glare I have ever seen, even worse than Debbie last night after I had hospitalized her father for a second time in as many days.

"Take a seat," the boss points towards the empty chair in the middle of the table. "We have covered most points already so I don't think this will take long."

I take the designated seat, looking again towards Annabel who is still biting her top lip and scribbling something on a pad in front of her, and back towards Tim who has turned his face slightly away from me now.

The boss is writing something down on her pad in front of her too and I'm just sat here doing an awkward half smile thing with my mouth closed. All I can hear is the clock on the wall ticking and the scribble of the pens.

"Ray," the boss turn to me, "I have brought you in to discuss the email you sent me yesterday. I'm sure you know why Tim is here and Annabel is here as witness and also as note-taker."

"Okay," I reply.

The boss straightens her shoulders. "The email you sent me contained not only your proposal for the re-structuring of the department but also this," she slides across a copy of the emails Eddy found on Tim's account. "First, I want you to talk me through what these are."

I pull the printouts towards me and glance at them. I have read and re-read them numerous times so have no need to see them again. "These are emails that I found on Tim's account."

Tim scoffs, shaking his head.

"And how did you get access to Tim's email account?" The boss asks.

"I hacked into it looking for his proposal."

Tim starts to laugh, "You hacked into my email? Rubbish!"

I turn to Tim. "I used a password breaker; just put in some words that you think might be in the password and it tries all different combinations."

Tim scowls "You're lying! Bullshit!" He looks at the boss and points at me. "You believe he is suddenly some computer hacker and hacked my emails? It's obviously a forgery."

"Your password is shagadelic69."

The colour drains from Tim's face.

"Plus, I have a printed out copy of your proposal in my bag."

Tim starts to fidget and points at me, "That is gross misconduct." He is getting angry now; his face is red, and he is sweating under that denim jacket. "Breach of privacy and gross misconduct, a sackable offence."

"I'm interviewing Ray. I do not need your input," the boss tells Tim sternly.

Interviewing... Fuck.

"Can you confirm the content of the emails?" she asks me.

"Of course. First there are emails from Tim to his friend at the temp agency rating temps out of ten in a number of categories."

Tim's face has gone a deeper shade of red now, more purple.

"Followed by emails from Tim sent to one of the temps from that agency here at the office, offering her a contract extension in exchange for a date."

"Those are is just a bit of fun between us all!" Tim argues.

"Anything else?" the boss pressures.

"Yes. The first one I noticed actually, which is an email from Tim to his friend at the temp agency with new bank details for his cut of the wages we pay the temps. He's been skimming money."

Tim's face has lost its purple tint now and lost all colour.

Annabel knew most of this when I had handed her the emails yesterday, but her mouth is hanging open, probably due to my Colombo like performance.

The boss picks up the stack of emails and shows them to Tim. "These show that for every ten pounds we paid per hour to the temp agency you and your friend skimmed two quid of that." She waves the emails at Tim who is sat in silence now. "I called the agency and they had each of the temp workers down for eight pounds an hour salary, five to the temp and three to the agency. That's eight pounds Tim; what happened to the other two?"

"This is bollocks. He has clearly had access to my emails for a long time and been planning this!" Tim points at me, "He's admitted hacking my email. This is something he has planned!"

I just smile and look at Tim. It's quite nice to see him squirm a bit and not be that cocky bastard clad in double denim.

"Look," the boss says sternly, placing her hands on the table and staring at Tim, "you can either resign right now or I can tell you about the conversation I have just had with both your mate at the temp agency who loves to sing like a canary and the poor girl who used to work here." She pauses as Annabel is struggling to jot everything down. "After that we can start the proper disciplinary procedures if that's the route you want to go down."

Tim's face drops, he shakes his head and turns to me, "You're a dead man."

"What is it going to be Tim?" the boss demands.

Tim grabs a piece of paper from the pile of emails and gestures for a pen. The boss hands him one and he starts writing his resignation.

"There!" he slams the pen down and pushes the paper towards the boss, "I resign."

"Thank you, and I accept your resignation." The boss places the piece of paper in her folder. "I'll walk you out of the building. Leave your stuff. We will want to have a look at it all before we post it to you."

"What about him?" Tim points at me. "He hacked my emails! That's gross misconduct! He should resign!"

The boss smiles at Tim, "He already has."

Now Annabel's jaw really hits the floor.

52

The White Horse is jam packed; it's afternoon on a Friday and it's Christmas Eve, so it would be weird if the pub wasn't packed wall to wall. The fireplace is full of crackling red-hot wood and the old oil radiators are blasting out heat which has made the old windows fill up with condensation, so nothing outside can be seen. We are in our own little isolated world and Gordon even came through with the sandwiches.

Everyone seems in a happy mood. Not sure how much of it is shock from what happened or relief from what they feared could have happened. After the boss had escorted Tim from the building and Annabel had picked her jaw up off the floor, the boss has come back to our department to announce that they were implementing my proposal which would see the reduction of three members of staff: Tim, Gordon and me.

Tim, of course, had resigned and was lucky to leave with his shitty denim jacket, whereas myself and

Gordon had accepted voluntary redundancy and were currently awaiting a nice big payday next Thursday; the day before the end of the world.

The department did need a bit of trimming, but Tim's plan had been too extreme and obvious now everyone knew why he was such a big fan of bringing in more temp workers. I felt bad about not telling Annabel the truth about my proposal. I was worried that she would talk me out of it or get her hopes up for something that for some reason wouldn't happen.

The tapping of a knife on a pint glass is just barely audible over the noise of the pub crowd as Gordon raises to his feet, his portly belly now sticking out at us from an undone button on his shirt.

"Colleagues and friends, I believe with all of us here and still slightly sober it is the opportune time for us to raise a toast!" Gordon bellows over our crowded table, some banging their glasses on the table in agreement and some cheering.

"Stand up then!" Tina shouts across at Annabel who is sat next to me. Annabel blushes and then smiles as she can't hold it any longer.

"Go on stand up!" I nudge her. She starts to stand and the crowd egg her on.

Gordon waddles over and puts his big wobbly arm around her shoulder. "Ladies and gentlemen, please raise your glasses to the new Department Manager of Planning, Environment AND Transport!"

"Thank you everyone," Annabel says over the cheers, reclaiming her seat next to me.

"Today has just been an insane mix of ups and downs! I have had an adrenaline rush all day!" Annabel says to me reaching for her cigarettes on the table.

"I knew it would all work out," I smile at her.

"You are still a bastard for not telling me anything," Annabel says, lighting her cigarette, "I won't forgive you for leaving me on my own here either," she jokes.

"I have other things to do, plus the world is ending a week today so I'll only be unemployed until then; not even long enough to claim benefits." I take a cigarette for myself. "But if it doesn't end then the right person is in charge," I smile at her.

"Drinks are on me!" Gordon shouts as he starts to try and squeeze his massive frame through the crowd.

Annabel points at him, "You made Gordon very happy too."

"He's not going to last the computer era much longer. I saw him the other day trying to write an email in Microsoft Paint!" I laugh.

"Ray!" Gordon shouts from the bar, "Are you having one this time?"

"No thanks, I'm still fine," I say pointing at my glass of lemonade.

"You are serious about cutting down then?" Annabel says looking at my sad looking lemonade.

"Yeah, it's best for now," I smile, "my lows don't seem as low and my highs seem to last longer."

53

The moon is bright again and illuminating the road in front of me. The bus had dropped me off just outside Hebden Bridge, and I had traversed most of the four miles from the bus stop to my farm. I'd called Bea but not heard back from her, so I didn't know if she was at the farmhouse or had gone home; it was Christmas Eve after all.

I'd left my former colleagues in good spirits. Tina and Gordon were even dancing together on the old wooden floorboards of The White Horse as I waved my goodbyes. Everything I had accumulated in the past six years working for the Council was now either in the bin or the side pocket of my backpack.

It was a strange feeling as everyone I'd worked with for so long, and had spent most of my time avoiding or ignoring, suddenly didn't seem too bad; perhaps I just I didn't see past my own ego to notice the needs and wants of others around me, or perhaps it's because I'm not drunk.

I don't know when I'll see all of them again. If the world ends next week, or if it doesn't, I'll see Annabel at some point to do my food shopping for my list. Hopefully at my New Year's Eve party too, when I ask her. The others I'm not too sure about, apart from Gordon.

I'd accepted an invitation from Gordon to go to his local amateur dramatics' performance of "Cinderella" the day after Boxing Day. He'd palmed me two tickets and said I could invite whoever I wanted. I didn't particularly want to go myself, so I'm not sure if I could put anyone else through the pain.

I can spot the outline of the farmhouse and the barn now; the big metal gate should be a minute or so away on the left. The moors are frosty tonight, and I can feel the crackle beneath my feet as I half walk on road and the grassy verge.

I take my phone out to check for calls or texts as the signal is iffy in the house, only seem to get anything with the door open in the Kitchen or by the window upstairs. I spot three new messages, hopefully one is from Bea. Nope, all three from Clive.

GET HERE EARLY WE R HAVING TURKEY

U WILL NEED TO PUT IT IN

PICK UP BISTO N WINE

If I didn't regret agreeing to cooking Christmas Dinner for my soon to be ex-wife and her father before then, I did now, as apparently neither of them were in a fit state to even pop in the Turkey before I got there to do the rest. Where am I going to get Bisto and wine from on Christmas day?

    I can't see any lights shining from the farmhouse or the barn. The Land Rover is there but I can't see Bea's Nissan Sunny; she might have parked it round the other side of the barn again though, and she was complaining birds were shitting all over it. Michael must be asleep in the barn or working downstairs. It's just gone midnight so I wouldn't be surprised if he had gone to sleep, but I hope he managed to pick something up for himself to eat as I have nothing to offer him tonight, or myself.

    "Michael? Bea?" I shout as I open the new front door. "You two still up?" I can't hear anything, but the light is on in the basement. I hesitate as I walk down the old stone staircase. The first thing I notice is there is a brand-new toilet where the old one used to be, a hand basin and some of the drywall has gone up. The storage room is a room now and the bedroom next to it that Bea shotgunned earlier also has four walls and a door. As I walk past the bedroom towards the lounge area, I smile to myself as I see Michael fast asleep on one of the chairs.

    I chuck a blanket over Michael and move back to the completed bedroom. I quietly open the door and find Bea tucked up on one of the cot beds wrapped up in some bedding I had never seen before. Next to her is a pile of books and two big duffel bags. Looks like Bea has moved in.

54

The cot I have made my bed for the night in is shaking. I can feel movement either side of me. I pull the duvet away from my face and see Bea's face smiling.

"Wake up!" she shouts "It's Christmas!"

"What time is it?" I ask, noticing at the angle I was at I could see perfectly down her pyjama top.

"No idea, like nine?" Bea grins, pushing down on the cot to make it move. "Get up! It's Christmas!" she hops off me and throws my packet of cigarettes and lighter at me, she's got a pair of my boxers on and her pyjama top is actually one of my t-shirts.

I grab my watch from the side of the bed. "It's half six Bea," I moan.

"I don't have a watch - you need a clock here somewhere," She replies.

"What about your phone? Don't you have a clock on there?"

"No idea, it's dead anyway, I need to charge it." She throws a t-shirt at me. "Come on! It's Christmas!

Stop being so grumpy!"

"Merry Christmas," I smile at her as I stretch and take a swig of the water next to my cot.

"Come see the tree!" Bea squeals, leaving me on my own again as she runs downstairs.

I slowly throw some clothes on and check my phone. No messages from Clive or Debbie yet. I'd need to be down there at around nine to pop the turkey in so I could have had an extra hour in bed.

"Come on!" I hear Bea shout from downstairs.

I slowly take the stairs down to the ground floor of the farmhouse and pick up some firewood so I can boil some water on the cooker for my morning coffee.

"What's taking you so long!?" Bea shouts from the basement.

"I'm starting the fire up in the range to boil some water," I shout back down to her.

"We have a kettle down here you knobhead," Bea shouts back, "I brought one up yesterday."

I abandon the firewood and take the old stone steps down to the basement. In the corner of the lounge area where Michael had been asleep in a chair last night, there is now a small artificial Christmas tree covered in some tinsel and baubles.

"What do you think?" Bea smiles at me.

"It's cool," I smile back as she hands me a coffee.

"I put it up this morning. Was going to get it ready last night but it took me and Michael ages to finish off the drywall." Bea points to the loose plug, "It does light up but there isn't any more sockets down here."

"It looks great, doesn't need it Bea," I tell her whilst taking a seat on one of the armchairs. "Where did

251

all this stuff come from?"

"My parents' house." She points to the kitchen table. "We now have a kettle, toaster and a Microwave."

"Won't they miss the stuff?" I ask.

"Nah, they are over in India for Christmas so they will be pretty stuck there if they survive the end of the world."

"True," I nod. "Are you staying up here for now then?" I ask her, blowing on my scalding coffee.

"Is that a problem?" she replies.

"No, it's just it came out of the blue a little bit," I tell her, taking a sip of my coffee in the awkward silence.

"What are we doing today then?" Bea asks.

"Well there's a problem," I sigh.

"Oh, so there IS a problem?" Bea stands up, putting her hands on her hips and rolling her tongue over her lip ring.

"I said to Debbie that I would go over and cook Christmas Dinner."

"Why the fuck would you do that?" Bea snaps.

"Her dad was hospitalized and she asked and I..."

"I know he was hospitalized. I hospitalized him!" Bea laughs, "Why does that mean you have to cook them Christmas Dinner?" she frowns.

"It wasn't his nose this time. A one-eyed bastard attacked him in the house."

"One-eyed attacker? What is this? Scooby Doo?!" Bea shouts.

"I hit this guy with a cricket bat a week or so ago and looks like I damaged his eye. I also stole the parka I've been wearing from him, which had some cash and a

252

betting slip in a pocket. He was looking for me because of all that, and also that the bet came in. Clive thought it was me sneaking into the house and was in the wrong place at the wrong time."

Bea considers what I have said and sits down in one of the armchairs.

"I'll go to my aunties then. I was supposed to be there anyway," Bea pouts, "and you're leaving Michael here on his own, are you? Like a dog?"

"Well yeah, he's not a dog. If anything, he's more like a cat, disappears all day and goes to his tent to eat and sleep, just gets on with it. Plus, I'm paying him to be here and to finish the work."

"Hitler had a bunker too you know," Bea snaps.

I walk towards the stone stairs to go gather my things. "I'm sorry Bea, I know it's not what you had imagined but I have to go and do this. I didn't want to ruin today for anyone, please believe that."

"Okay," Bea says, her head still down.

"I'm going to go get my stuff ready," I tell her.

"Do you want your present now or when I get back?" Bea points at a large box hidden behind the tree.

"You didn't have to get me anything. I haven't got anything for you."

"It's a Christmas, housewarming and thanks for letting me live here present."

"Thanks," I say and smile at Bea, "I'll open it when we are both back here."

55

"What do you want? We're shut!" Apron Lady bellows from the upstairs window.

"It's me, Ray," I shout up to her, "Any chance of opening the door?"

"It's eight a clock on Christmas day! We are shut!"

"Is your Kelly in?"

"We are closed love," she shouts down, sticking her head out of the window "and R'Kelly isn't up yet."

"I am now," Kelly shouts, sticking her head out of the next window along, "what's all this about?"

"I just wanted to say Merry Christmas," I shout back to them.

"You've heard of a phone, haven't you?" Apron Lady shouts down.

"What else do you want?" Kelly asks.

"Well as you mention it, I do need some Bisto and some wine."

"I told you we are shut!" Apron lady bellows

before slamming the window.

"Hold on," Kelly sighs and shuts her window.

It's freezing outside today and all I have on my top half is a shirt. I have left the parka in the Land Rover just in case the one-eyed bastard is taking a Christmas Morning stroll. I can hear footsteps and then the unlocking of the shop door.

"Come in," Kelly sighs as she lets me in.

"Merry Christmas," I say as I walk into the slightly warmer shop.

"Stop all that will you. What is it you need?" Kelly asks with her arms folded over her dressing gown.

"I was going to come over anyway," I tell her "but my father-in-law gave me a list just before midnight. If I didn't bring this stuff, he would just bang on about it all day."

"Well it is nice to see you," Kelly smiles.

"I'm sorry Kelly, I wouldn't normally do this, but can I just grab some Bisto gravy granules and a couple of bottles of wine?"

"Why not, it is Christmas," she sighs as I start my hunt for Clive's items, quickly stuffing two bottles of red and two of white into my backpack and then scanning the shelves for the Bisto. "By the Pot Noodles," Kelly points as she sees me struggling.

"Thanks," I grab the Bisto but it won't fit in my bag. "How much do I owe you?" I ask her.

"Just call it twenty quid," she says sticking her hand out.

"Thanks," I say putting the Bisto down.

"You have saved the day." I take out a crisp twenty from my wad, placing the note into her soft open palm.

"Glad I could help," Kelly says sarcastically,

shoving the twenty in her dressing gown pocket. "You having Christmas Day at your wife's parents then? That's a bit odd."

"I'm cooking dinner at my old place. Debbie, my ex, and her dad are going to be there. Her mum and dad separated a while back."

"Like mother like daughter, or are you two giving it another go?" Kelly asks.

"No, nothing like that. Her Dad is just... well he's got broken ribs so can't cook and Debbie has never cooked, so she asked me."

"What about Michael?"

"Oh, he's fine," I tell Kelly, "He's working most of today. Bea said she was going to take him with her to her Auntie's."

Kelly scrunches her face up. "Who's Bea?"

"What do you mean?" I reply.

Kelly squints her eyes. "Well you said Bea was going to bring him back some food from her Auntie's; who is Bea?

"She's just been staying with me up at the farm, she's..."

Kelly interrupts me, "So, you are living with some girl up at your doomsday farm, cooking Christmas Dinner for your ex-wife and you come here to get booze from me?"

"And Bisto?" I smile trying to make her smile at least.

"Whatever, Ray, just take the stuff and go." Kelly starts moving me towards the door.

"Kelly! Come on, I'm just trying to do what's best!"

"What's best for who though? For you?" she says with sadness. "You were banging on about some

Annabel last time, now it's your ex and this Bea girl. Just go talk about them somewhere else." She pushes me out of the door and closes it with a bang.

"Kelly!" I call but to no avail as Kelly turns and walks away, right past my tub of Bisto that I have left on the floor.

56

It's quite surreal walking down my street again -
well, what was my street. It feels like a different lifetime
that I last walked down here. Everything looks the same
but feels a little different and I remind myself that it was
only a week or so ago.

The usual parade of twats who hang around
under the canopy of the old grocers are not there,
probably still in bed, I wish I was still in bed. I remember
standing under there in the rain the night Debbie
initiated the lockout, no idea what I was going to do or
who I could call. I'm in a similar position now really,
trying to decide who to drag along with me on my
journey to the end of the world.

I can see the feral kid with the football. He has
had a haircut, spikes now and got a new football shirt
on; a red Man Utd one now with 'Beckham' on the back.
He's still shouting "Cantona" with every kick though.

The other usual suspects are out and about; the
old fella who sits on his windowsill with a can of John

Smiths has got a Santa Hat on and he's upgraded to a Guinness and Pat is once again sat in a deckchair, can of Strongbow in one hand and a mince pie in the other.

I try my key in the door and it still works. I click the lock and open the door, the smell of Clive's Joop aftershave hitting my nostrils already as I spot him dressed in his Sunday best on my armchair.

"You're late!" Clive shouts from my usurped throne.

"Morning Clive." I try to smile, closing the door.

"Shut that door! Were you born in a barn?" he snipes.

"No, a manger," I reply.

"Don't be blasphemous on the Lord's birthday!" Debbie snarls. "And you're late, by the way."

"You already said, but please explain how I am late Clive?

"It's half eight!"

"But how can I be late when you didn't specify a time?" I ask him, throwing my bag down onto the sofa.

"I said early," he snaps

"It is fucking early Clive," I snap back.

"You missed the presents; you didn't have anything anyway, so no big loss," he smirks at me.

"Nice to see the scrapping has started already," Debbie says, making her way down the stairs. She's wearing a crop top t-shirt, showing off her trim figure, and long maxi skirt.

"Morning Debs, you look nice."

"Thanks," she says "You look a bit smarter than the other day too."

"He could have shaved and put a tie on. It is Christmas after all," Clive grumbles.

I ignore Clive and grab my bag. "I'll take the

259

wine into the kitchen,"

"Did you get red or white?" Clive shouts at me.

"Red," I tell him seeing if he will bite.

"I was hoping for a nice white," he grumbles.

Debbie screws her face up. "You only drink red usually dad?"

"Well, it's Christmas, nothing like a nice glass of white wine; but you didn't get any so I'll go without," Clive moans.

The kitchen looks different to last time I was here; the microwave isn't there and I can't see the toaster or kettle either. "Debs," I shout, "where's all the stuff from the kitchen gone?" The chopping boards, knife block and utensil pot have disappeared too.

"I've put them away in the cupboards," she says walking in.

"Why?" I ask.

"More space," she tells me.

"More space for what?" I chuckle.

"More space for cooking! Or making a drink or I don't know! Just more space!" she tells me.

"But you have to get everything back out to cook anyway!" I laugh.

"We have been managing fine thank you Ray." Debs spits as she takes the wine out of my bag. "You did buy white wine Ray," she tells me as she double checks the bottle.

"Oh yeah, I remember now," I lie.

"Dad," Debbie shouts, "Don't worry you can have your white wine. Ray did buy some, he just forgot."

"Oh... great," a disappointed Clive shouts back.

"Where is the turkey, Debs?" I ask, scanning the under-counter fridge.

"In the fridge," she tells me as she pours out two large glasses of white wine.

"Where about in the fridge?" I ask, scanning the shelves.

"It's the thing that looks like a turkey," she snaps.

I pull out a small polystyrene tray covered in plastic with poultry inside. "This?"

"Yes," Debbie nods.

"This is a chicken," I tell her.

"It's a turkey," she insists.

"Look," I point at the label on the top, "Small, Caged Chicken."

Debbie dismisses me. "Same thing. Chicken, turkey, who cares?"

I stare down at the saddest looking chicken I've ever seen, slightly bigger than my clenched fist and half the end of the feathers still stuck in the flesh.

"What's wrong with the turkey?" I hear Clive shout from the lounge.

"It's a chicken," I shout back.

"Same thing; get it on lad! Stick it in t'oven," Clive barks.

"If I stick this in now it will be ready in ten minutes," I snap at Clive.

"Well, less work for you Ray. Look at it that way," Debbie smirks as she picks up the glasses of wine. "The rest of the stuff is in the carrier bag on the bottom shelf. I'm going to go look after my dad."

I point at her glass, "Enjoy your breakfast."

57

I'd enjoyed the couple of hours alone in the kitchen, just me and a random selection of ingredients that Clive and Debbie had decided may possibly constitute a Christmas dinner.

Clive had only interrupted my chores to order me to set up the VHS player from the loft so he could watch our old VHS of Home Alone before he started Home Alone 2 that Debbie had bought him on DVD, along with a brand-new player. He'd asked if there was a Home Alone 3 but I told him there wasn't. I'm not risking having to sit through that.

I did notice that Clive hadn't touched his white wine, so I felt quite smug that his ruse to make me look bad had come back to bite him on the arse; he can be a knobhead sometimes. Perhaps I will stick Home Alone 3 on for him later, just before I leave, enjoy that fucker.

I'm craving nicotine now. I'm trying to cut down on how many I smoke a day, but I've been dealt a rough hand today. Debbie is smashing the wine already, Clive is being Clive and I'm stuck in here with this clusterfuck of ingredients feeling like I'm on a Christmas special of Ready, Steady Cook.

I'd found enough random ingredients to make a stuffing and jam as much as I could of it into the poor chicken's arsehole, so it's definitely time for a cigarette break. I grab one out of my pack and light it, opening up the back door to let some of the smoke go outside.

"Shut that door lad! I'll catch a chill!" Clive shouts from his throne.

"No, keep it open please, I don't want the house smelling of cigarettes again," Debbie instructs.

"Am I closing it or leaving it open?" I shout back.

"Go outside!" they both yell at me in unison.

I shut the door behind me and take a seat on the old wooden bench in the garden. I take my phone out of my pocket to check for messages. The battery is getting dangerously low again now. I have two new messages though, one from Annabel and one from Eddy. I open Annabel's first

Merry Christmas! Have a great day in your crazy sex dungeon! Xxx

I chuckle and try and think of something witty to type back.

Wish you were here xx

No that's a bit too creepy, I'll try again.

Santa is loving it down here! Have a great Christmas Xx

That will do. I hit send and go back to read Eddy's message.

Merry Christmas Santa comin wiv ur cigs n Booze Tues

Short and sweet but to the point.

Cool cheers Merry Christmas
I type back and stick my phone back in my pocket. There is a spare charger in the kitchen, I better stick it on charge before it completely drains.

I hope Bea gets in touch at some point today. I feel really bad about how things were left this morning. I should have let her know what my plans were, but I'd had no idea that she was going to move herself in and decorate for our first Christmas together. I don't even know what me and Bea are, if there even is a label. She has made it very clear that she doesn't see us as a couple, but she has moved in with me. She acts like she doesn't want any mushy relationship stuff, yet she sleeps in my bed, wears my clothes and snogs me from time to time.

Likewise, with Kelly, I feel bad, but she wears her heart on her sleeve; what you see is what you get. I just don't think it is right for me to drag her into all of this: ex-wife, bunker, random girls living in the bunker. It's not her and she made it clear this morning she isn't interested in me if I'm giving so much of my time to other girls. If I'm not at the right time in my life to commit to one person then I shouldn't keep pulling her into my life.

I flick the cigarette butt into an empty plant pot and push myself off the bench. It's time to stick the veg on and then chill out for a bit.

I slide back into the kitchen, trying not to let too much of the cold air in or the warm air out. I stick my phone on to charge and spot one of the bottles of white has now made its way into the bin. I know what the time is. I could check my watch too but for a laugh I decide to go for a cheap win, "How's the wine Debs?"

"Yeah it's okay thanks."

"Cool, what is the time?" I plant a seed, wondering if she will notice I'm picking up on her early drinking.

"Ten to eleven" she yells to me.

"The shop assistant did say the White Wine went especially well with Cereal" I tell her

"Oh, piss off! It's Christmas Ray" she shouts.

"Just need to find another three hundred and sixty-four excuses now Debs" I chuckle.

58

The dining table in the front room had been cleared, with the accumulated junk that had occupied it since last Christmas relegated to the floor. I'd dug out the old Christmas themed tablecloth and set a place for each of us, complete with a Christmas cracker each I'd dug out of the loft.

Clive had shaken his head when he saw my layout and insisted on sitting at the head of the table. I'd asked him where the head specifically was on a square table but Debbie had shifted his plate, knife and fork and cracker along with his cushion and untouched glass of white wine to the opposite end to where I had put him.

I'd brought all of the side dishes in, along with some cranberry sauce and randomly, brown sauce that Clive had insisted on and placed the turkey, sorry the chicken, in front of him to carve.

Clive looks at the bird and then up to me, "Well, it's not a very big turkey is it?"

"It's a chicken Clive," I remind him.

"Still it's not very big." He prods at it with the carving fork.

"You've overcooked it lad, it's shrunk," he moans.

"Just carve it will you, dad?" Debbie prods.

Clive turns his nose up and starts slicing off the meat. He chucks a breast and a leg on his plate, a breast on Debbie's and some shavings onto mine.

"Where are the wings?" Clive says lifting the bird up.

"There on the side, dad," Debbie points to the two shriveled up bits of cartilage and bone.

"Do you want a leg?" he asks me.

"Well I better had as there is fuck all else left on it," I reply, noticing Debbie's frown before she grabs the potatoes.

"How many roasties dad?"

"Four please," Clive says.

Debbie grimaces "Well there are only six, are you alright with two?"

"Why did you only do six you muppet!" Clive barks at me.

"It was hard enough to get six out of one potato," I contend, shaking my head.

"No Yorkshire puddings either?" Clive snivels in disbelief.

"You two did the shopping!" I exclaim. "I can't just magic them out of thin air!"

"Oh Dad, I am sorry, just try and enjoy it if you can." Debbie puts on her kid gloves to massage Clive's ego.

"It's alright love, don't get upset, you did a great job." Clive comforts Debbie, "Hey, let's do a cracker shall we?" Clive smiles for once picking up the little paper tube of disappointment.

Me and Debbie follow suit and pick up our crackers, now forming a triangle of disappointment between the three of us.

"One...two..." The bastard pulled on two.

"Wahey!" Clive exclaims," I won twice! What are the odds?" he chortles, reaching his wiry fingers in to one of the crackers to grab his prize. "A plastic moustache? Well that's no use," he grumbles.

"You could always shave yours off and use that instead. Less maintenance," I offer.

"Don't play the fool," he scolds, reaching into the second cracker and pulling out a thin red plastic fish. "What the bloody hell is this?"

"It's a fortune teller fish, Dad," Debbie informs him. "Read the bit of paper with it and it will tell you how the fish can read your fortune."

"Read my fortune? What a load of bollocks!" he scoffs.

"Give it here Dad." Debbie takes the instructions from him. "Put your palm out." Clive seems to hesitate but complies in the end. "Now I pop the fish in your palm and whatever it does will decide your fortune." I sit back and hope the fish jumps down his throat as Debbie places it in his palm.

"It's doing all kinds of stuff; what does that mean?" Clive barks.

"I think it's having a stroke," I tell him. "It means you're going to have a stroke."

"No," Debbie corrects me, "it's curling its sides over."

"It's turned over now!" Clive exclaims.

Debbie checks the instructions. "Curling sides

and turning over means you are... Fickle and False." She looks down, disappointed.

"Screw Mystic Meg. That fish has some crazy powers," I chuckle.

"Bollocks!" Clive shouts, tossing the fish across the table.

"Do you want to read the jokes instead Dad?" Debbie parlays, offering him the little piece of paper from her winning cracker.

"No, I'm hungry," Clive moans.

"At least put your hat on!" Debbie pleads as Clive gives in and pulls out the thin paper Christmas hat from the closest cracker carcass. He sees it's pink so tosses it to me with a smile, getting more luck with the yellow one inside the other remaining cracker instead.

I slide my hat on as Debbie continues dishing out the meal I have cooked us.

"Broccoli and cauliflower aren't cooked long enough," Clive comments.

"Sorry, it's just my weird thing that I do like to bite and chew my food rather than have it dissolve in my mouth like a pack of Skips."

Clive sneers and the peas, carrots, sprouts and parsnips get a similar disappointing review from him. He does, however, pick up four of the six sausages before firing me a puzzled glance from across the table.

"There are no blankets on these pigs," he points at the sausages.

"It was too warm in the fucking oven, so they took them off," I smile back.

"I think that's enough wine for you, Ray," Debbie snaps.

"What wine?" I ask. "I haven't had any. I've been busy cooking and setting up the VHS for you and your Dad." I look back at her, expecting her to hit me with another insult but she is smiling. Perhaps she is happy that there is more wine left for her or maybe even just happy I'm not drinking through this nightmare.

"Gravy," Clive clicks his fingers, not even looking up from his plate. I pick up the gravy jug and pass it over to him.

"What's this?" Clive stirs the spoon around the gravy jug with a befuddled look on his face.

"It's the gravy dad," Debbie tells him. "It's nice. I've had some."

"It's bloody light brown!" he whines. "It's all thin like water too. Oh no, this won't do."

"I couldn't get any Bisto so I made the gravy from the meat juices and some cornflour in the cupboard. That's proper gravy right there," I tell him, before going back to my dinner.

"Piss water, that's not gravy its piss water."

"Don't have it then," I smile at him. "How's the white wine by the way?" I gesture at his untouched glass.

Clive put's his knife and fork down and stares at me. "I specifically asked you to buy some Bisto gravy. That's all I wanted. The one thing I ask for and you don't even bother."

Debbie slams her fork down. "Dad! Give Ray a break! Please! He's just cooked you a Christmas dinner so either enjoy it or piss off back to the lounge!"

Clive bows his head like a scolded child and quietly picks his knife and fork back up. Debbie is exhaling quite deeply, and I look towards her and give her a half smile just to let her know I appreciate her taking my corner. She returns my smile, puts her hand on my thigh and mouths "Thank you."

59

Debbie had decided to drink Clive's wine after he threw in the towel and decided he couldn't hold out anymore. He'd asked for a glass of red, which Debbie has ordered and I had poured for him, which was the right time for the one glass I was allowing myself today.

The wine had opened the floodgates for the nicotine craving. I'd managed to have one during Dame Thora Hird's show about her favourite hymns earlier, and one an hour later during some show with Noel Edmonds handing out presents. When I returned, Noel had been abandoned in favour of Ace Ventura: Pet Detective, which was, all in all, a solid decision on Debbie's part.

Debbie has started to chill out a bit now, probably due to the bottle and a half of white she has drunk, but she's laid with her feet up now, her painted toes just next to me. She discarded the maxi dress for a pair of little cotton shorts. Her legs look amazing resting on the back of the sofa. I look at her and recognise the woman I fell in love with eight years ago.

Clive is fast asleep in my former throne. He retired to the armchair as soon as the last morsel of Christmas pudding had entered his mouth. He had insisted on watching the Queen at three o'clock and had even clapped before and after the speech.

The Queen had captured my interest as well this year when she said, "The sheer rate of change seems to be sweeping away so much that is familiar and comforting." She was bang on with that. It conjured up images of work, the Y2K salesman and my bunker, of course.

Alongside the messages around the devolution of the Scottish and Welsh parliaments and the refugees in the Balkans, she had said "The future is not only about new gadgets, modern technology or the latest fashion, important as these may be", to care for others saying that "Love thy neighbour as thyself," was still important and finally said she was looking forward to the new Millennium, wished everyone a Merry Christmas and "in this year of all years, a very Happy New Year."

I had considered telling Debbie about the bunker, give her the opportunity to be there if anything should happen, and also to laugh in my face if it didn't. I'm not sure on the legal aspects of all of this but, is half of the bunker actually hers? I look over at her, playing with her wavy blonde hair and nursing a glass of wine in her hands. She looks so peaceful and relaxed, no signs of the woman I have been so annoyed at for the past week.

I stretch my arms and push myself out of the sofa. "Just popping for a cigarette," I tell Debbie.

"Oh, just smoke in here," she relents. "Your

ashtray is on the windowsill."

I take the ashtray from the cold windowsill, popping it the arm of the sofa. I thumb a cigarette a toss the pack onto the sofa. As I sit back down, Debbie grabs one from the pack and shifts her position to lean against me. I light both our cigarettes and blow my smoke towards a sleeping Clive.

We both sit in silence as the film plays out in front of us. Only the noise of Clive snoring in the room and it feels quite peaceful and quite Christmassy for the first time today.

"It was like this when we first moved in here," Debbie says, slightly slurring her words now. "Nice and peaceful, just relaxing on the sofa."

"Your dad wasn't asleep in my chair though," I chuckle.

"Why couldn't it have just stayed like this?" Debbie sits up and looks at me. "Why did we have to grow apart so much so quickly, especially after the wedding."

"I don't know Debs, I can't answer that one." I stub out my cigarette. "I wish it had been different. I still don't really know how we have ended up like this."

"Me neither," she sighs and rests her head on my shoulder. I am contemplating if this is the right time to ask her why she kicked me out of the house.

"You seem different," she tells me. "Happier, less drunk and more driven," she says softly.

"Thanks," I reply.

"Perhaps it's not being with me that changed you back," she stutters.

"It's not you Debs." I stroke her hair. "I just feel like I have something ticking inside of me again, the power is back on."

"So, what changed?" she asks.

"I'm not sure," I tell her. Even after everything that's happened, I don't know. Is it the thought of everything ending that's driving me and I'm looking forward to that? Or am I finally just ensuring all my psychological, physiological and self-fulfillment needs are being met using the Hierarchy of Needs triangle, understanding exactly what makes us all reach self-actualization.

"Ray, what changed?" she asks again.

I sigh, stroking her hair again. "I think I just needed to stand back and take a look at my life and decide what I really want."

"And what is that?" Debbie says softly.

I consider my response as I don't really know myself. What do I want? Do I want the bunker and thought of a new life away from the mundane trappings and devastating sadness of the world as we know it? Do I want a new life with Bea, or Kelly, or Annabel; or do I want Debbie? Will I be happy if the world as I know it ends on Friday, or will I be happy if it doesn't?

"I think I know," Debbie says, leaning towards me. I can smell her perfume as she places her soft lips on mine, kissing me, first softly, then with passion and then just not stopping.

60

Clive is still fast asleep in my armchair. It's probably for the best. He most likely would have had a heart attack if he had seen what I had been doing with his daughter on the sofa an hour or so ago; perhaps I should have woken him up.

Debbie has changed into her pyjamas now and we are back together on the sofa where it had all kicked off. Debs had poured herself another wine after our moment of passion and was flicking the channels now. I'm still sipping at my only glass and keeping an eye on Clive, ready to make my excuses and leave if he wakes up.

"Have a look and see if there is anything good on?" Debbie points at the Christmas edition of the Radio Times.

I pick the copy up and remember holding it as a child at my grandparents, eager to circle my favourite upcoming shows for Christmas along with the toys I wanted from the Argos catalogue.

"Nothing much I fancy Debs," I tell her. "There is the Royle Family Christmas special at half ten, but I'll be long gone by then."

"Oh, okay," Debbie says, sounding slightly surprised.

"Sorry, I just assumed you would want me to go so I made plans," I tell her.

"How are you getting back to Eddy's though?" Debbie's asks. "I don't think I will be able to drive you in the car." She points at her wine.

I think for a second and then remember she thinks I'm at Eddy's. "I bought a Land Rover, it's outside, so I'll just drive up as I've only had a glass."

"A Land Rover?" she gasps, sitting up, "How did you get a Land Rover?"

"I bought it second hand," I tell her, taking a long drag of my cigarette.

"And where did the money come from?" she asks sternly.

"I used some of my savings," I say with some frustration. "What's with all the questions?"

"How much?" she snaps.

"Five hundred quid." I tell her. "Now please stop with the questions, I haven't asked you a thing about why you booted me out or wouldn't talk to me for the past week!"

"Well you have rocked up here in a Land Rover. Did you expect me to just let that slide by?" Debbie points a finger at me, "and I told you why before you stuck you tongue down my throat!"

"That's your explanation?" I laugh "That was as vague as it gets! And you kissed me Debs, not the other way around."

"There are bills to pay here, Ray! And you're

wasting our money on a Land Rover!" she yells.

"My money, Debs. I used my own money to buy it and how exactly did you expect me to get around? You have kept the car so what am I supposed to do? Give hand jobs for rides around Halifax?"

"Don't be disgusting!" she yells before turning her volume down, "And stop shouting. You will wake up my father."

I look at Clive passed out on the armchair and he could be dead for all I know as he hasn't moved for a few hours.

"You should have told me," Debbie scolds. "It's a lot of money and I'm sick to death of you hiding things from me," she spits.

"Like what?" I challenge.

"Like your mother leaving you a huge bloody commune in her will," she challenges back.

"I didn't know anything about that," I laugh.

"Bullshit!" she spits.

"I had a feeling that it was what she had left me as the envelope was so thick and it's all she had, but I didn't know for sure! I didn't want to know!" I argue.

"You knew deep down that she had left you something and didn't even discuss it with me, your own wife."

"So, you thought you would find out on your own?" I ask her. "When did you open it?" I push, "The day it arrived on the doormat? You couldn't wait to see what she had left me and think about how you could spend it."

Debbie moves right into my face and points at me. "I opened it the morning I locked you out of the house!" She prods my chest with her finger. "That's why I didn't want you back in here. I was sick of your lies and secrets so when you said you lost your keys, I took my chance and called my dad."

"Well I am glad it worked out so well! And I don't have to share everything with you!" I snap.

"Yes, Ray, you do, because we are married!"

"Okay, well how about this one, it's a fucking great one," I laugh.

"Don't shout Ray, you will wake my father," Debbie asserts.

"Sorry Debs, but you absolutely have to hear this secret!" I growl.

"I'm not staying at Eddy's, I'm living at the farmhouse on the old commune," I tell her.

She laughs, "I knew it." She shakes her head, "I knew there would be something going on with that place."

"Well there is but it's not what you think," I snap. "I didn't just move into my secret house after you locked me out. I walked about in the pissing down freezing rain for hours with no money or car until Eddy took me in. I had to break back in here to get some basic essentials and only then did I find out I even owned the farm which I've just spent the last week getting up to scratch to be able to boil a cup of water and take a piss!"

"So, you are wasting our money and our savings on a run-down piece of shit in the middle of nowhere?" Debbie laughs.

"It's my home now and it's coming along. I have people helping me. It will be great when it's done."

Debbie stares at me in silence before shaking her head. "And I suppose that little tart is up there with you?"

"Bea is there. Don't call her a tart, she is my

friend."

"Why are you even doing all of this?" Debbie asks. "This is your home, and you have given it up without even trying to get it back! Does all of this mean nothing to you now?"

I step back from Debbie and take a deep breath, "and I think this Y2K bug is going to end the world as we know it, and I am kitting out the farmhouse to live there for the long-haul, but either way I won't be coming back here."

"You are unbelievable," Debbie says with pure contempt. "Go grab your things and I never want to see you again."

61

The farmhouse is freezing. The fire in the lounge has only been going for a few minutes and sat in the large wingback chair next to it, even though I'm still fully dressed and in my boots and parka, I still can't feel my toes or fingertips.

I'd not seen Bea's Nissan when I had pulled into the farm. She usually parks it round the other side of the barn anyway. The lights being out in the farmhouse wasn't unusual as we only have the candles above ground but seeing the bunker empty and not finding Michael in the barn has made me feel incredibly isolated up here.

I'd tried to call Bea when I couldn't find either of them, but it went straight to the answerphone. She is terrible with her phone and probably doesn't want to speak to me either.

I reach down into my backpack and pull out the bottle of red I took when leaving Debbie's. I only took a handful of things but did manage to leave the stack of bills on a sleeping Clive. That will be a nice surprise for him when he wakes up.

I can't remember where I put the corkscrew, but it's got to be somewhere around here. I push myself up out of the chair and away from the warmth of the fire.

I step heavily into the kitchen as my frozen feet feel like blocks of ice in my boots. I see the picture on the wall of the group of people gathered outside the front of this very farmhouse, the life it once had inside it, people with a purpose and a meaning, people like my mother.

It was a shame that purpose and meaning didn't include me. She had made her choice. From what little I had been told by my grandparents and what I had managed to claw out of my mother the few times I saw her, there was no room for kids here. The children went to a farm further up the moors. I'd heard her refer to it as "The Garden" but that's about all I know.

I spot the corkscrew next to the pans and force the cork out of the bottle of red wine I've been holding. I don't have any glasses, just some mugs and tumblers that Bea had brought from her parent's place. I pour myself a small amount in one of the mugs and sip on it.

According to my mother, she didn't want me to go to "The Garden" until she had settled in here. I don't believe that; I think she was so drugged up on whatever it was she was taking that she didn't see any problem in leaving without me. She knew my grandparents would look after me; they adopted her so why not me? And unfortunately for her, when she tried to get me back, they told her where to go.

And she ended up back here until she died two years ago.

I sip at my wine noticing that I have gone through the mugful already. I'll only have one more. I pour the wine again, this time making sure I fill the mug to the top.

I take the picture off the wall and take it with me to the lounge, settling back into the armchair with my mug of wine and the heat of the fire. I look at the picture again and wonder, is one of those men my father? She had been hanging around here for years, taking drugs and living the 'free love' life. Fuck she even called me Rain, for fucks sake.

Do I look like anyone on this picture? I scan back and forth and can't see any major resemblance. I toss the picture into the corner of the room hearing the glass crack as it hits the stone wall.

My mug is empty again. I am starting to feel shaky and my heart is racing. I reach into my bag and pull out the bottle of whisky., I stop myself.

I stand up and go to grab the bottle of wine from the kitchen. It will be fine, it's Christmas for fucks sake. I abandon the mug and decide to just swig from the half empty bottle.

I take my phone out of my pocket. No new text messages since I left Debbie's and my signal is non - existent in this room anyway. I shove it back in, trying to forget that I had even checked. It should be obvious from the conversations I have had with Bea, Kelly and Debbie that none of them are too interested in what I am doing right now, or if I am okay. I'm starting to not care either.

There isn't much wine left in the bottle. I neck what's remaining and pick up the bottle of whisky instead, unscrewing the top and taking a swig before I close my eyes and listen to the sound of nothing.

62

The rain is hammering down against the frosty ground and, on occasion, the wind fires it against the windows of the farmhouse.

I'd been opening and closing my eyes for an hour or so now, in and out of disturbed sleep, full of vivid re-imaginations of fights and arguments from the past week.

My watch tells me it is half past nine in the morning, but it means nothing to me. I reach for my cigarettes and lighter to get some nicotine to try and help me.

I light the cigarette and take a deep drag, immediately coughing as the carbon dioxide makes me even more lightheaded, nauseous and panicked as my adrenal glands pump out adrenaline.

The coughing has alerted me to my headache and the horrible acidic feeling in my throat. I drank a glass at Debbie's and one or two when I got home? I open my eyes and stare at the half empty bottle of whisky next to my feet that tells a different story.

I check my phone: no signal of course. I push myself out of the chair to get to the front door and try and get any messages that may have come through.

I'm trying my hardest to smoke the cigarette and not be sick. My head is spinning now and I have pins and needles down my arms, right to the tips of my fingers.

The phone beeps twice. I press through to see them, and they are from Clive.

IM NOT PAYING UR BILLS

Not important right now, I don't reply.

DID U TAKE THE WINE?

Unfortunately, yes, I did, currently not worth a reply.

I close the door and leave my phone on the windowsill in the kitchen on loud. That way if anything comes through, I can hear it.

I collapse back into the wingback chair, nauseous, head pounding and riddled with guilt. The only solution is in front of me, so I grab the half empty bottle of whisky and take a gulp, feeling the warm liquid burn my already burnt insides.

I feel calm over my body and close my eyes.

63

I can hear a knock. It sounds like it might be the front door, but I feel too weak to get up. I take a swig from the bottle of whisky and try to pull a piece of the lace curtain to see if anyone is there.

There is a man, someone I don't recognize. His eyes are half hidden by tinted glasses and his body wrapped in what looks like a fur coat. He is holding a book in one hand and knocking with the other. I swig at the last remaining whisky and close my eyes again..

64

It's dark again now. I still feel bad but not as terrible as earlier.

I kick something by the door as I stumble into the kitchen and lean my body weight against the old stone walls. My healed wrist pangs with pain so I let go and crash to the floor.

My wrist is okay, but I've cut my elbow open, and there is some blood dripping down my forearm. I crawl to the old stone steps towards the basement and shimmy down them on my backside in the dark.

I feel for my duffel bag in the darkness of the storage room and start throwing out clothes. I'm starting to panic now as if it isn't there, then I'm in for a rough night.

I feel around inside the bag and suddenly feel the cool, round, glass of the bottle. I pull out a bottle of Jamesons whisky I was going to give to Michael. Suddenly a wave of relief passes through my body as I start pulling the plastic topper off and yanking at the plug with my teeth, leaning back against the drywall and exhaling deeply.

65

It's dark but I don't know if it's the dark of the evening I just left or the morning I have arrived in, or maybe it's just because there is no natural light wherever I am. I have my bottle next to me, so I take a sip and close my eyes again.

66

I can hear knocking again. I see some natural light shining down the old stone staircase which is in front of me. I check for my bottle of whisky and there is half left. I push it to one side; I need to return to the world.

I force myself up off the cold stone floor and I'm dizzy but less so than yesterday. I fill a tumbler up from the sink and gulp down the water. I immediately re-fill the glass and gulp it down again, taking my third refill with me for the journey back upstairs.

The knocking is getting louder now, and I can hear a voice shouting. I push the hair out of my eyes to each side of my face and check what I am wearing: still the jeans from Christmas Day and my boots. I must have discarded the Parka and shirt at some point.

I put the glass down on the table and walk over the front door, opening the lock as it flies into me.

"Where the fuck have you been?" It's Annabel.

The sound of another person's voice makes my head pound, and pins and needles shoot down my arms as the adrenaline kicks back in.

"Is that blood?" She gasps pointing at my arm.

"I don't know," I mumble.

"Are you drunk?" Annabel asks.

"I don't know," I reply.

"What have you been doing?" she demands as she closes the door.

"What day is it?" I ask.

"It's Monday," She says curtly, "morning."

"Boxing day?" I ask.

"No, the day after Boxing Day. You missed Gordon's pantomime last night. He was upset."

"Sorry about that," I say reaching for my water.

"What's that?" she asks, pointing at my drink.

"Don't worry it's water," I say and take a gulp down.

"What started all this?" Annabel sighs.

"I just had a row with Debbie and then just the picture of my mother." I point to the smashed frame. "I just started thinking about it all, all the history," I exhale deeply, "I just felt abandoned and alone again."

"Ray, you should have called me."

"I wasn't thinking straight, I'm still not really." I rub my throbbing head

"Have you eaten?" Annabel asks with some concern.

I need to think about this. "Err, Christmas Dinner was the last time."

"Can I make you something?" she shrugs her shoulders.

"I haven't got any food yet," I mutter, going to sit on my wingback chair.

"Well that's easy then, let's go and get some before the shops all shut early. I have the Espace and you need to stock up for the end of the world, although from looking at you it seems to have already happened." She shakes her head. "Get some clothes on and let's go. I'll buy you a bacon sandwich on the way."

67

I hold back the urge to vomit as Annabel drives us down the final windy roads leading off the moors before we get back to civilization. My head is pounding but I am hopeful the two ibuprofen and two paracetamol I downed before leaving will kick in soon.

I pull out my pack of cigarettes from my pocket and light one, immediately regretting the decision and going extremely lightheaded and sick. I breathe out slowly so as not to spray the mixture of acid, vomit and bile that has been building in my throat all over the dashboard of Annabel's car.

My phone beeps and I look down. It's Eddy.

10am tomorrow at Wainhouse tower for duty free

I'd forgotten all about my order. Bit of an odd place to meet for the 'exchange' but better than more people knowing about my farmhouse, I guess. I decide to message him back so at least it's confirmed.

OK cool

I try another drag of the cigarette but it's too much for me right now. I offer it over to Annabel who happily accepts it into her mouth.

"Are you feeling okay?" she asks.

"Not really," I mutter.

"You need to get some food down you and get some fresh air," she tells me.

"Yeah you're right," I tell her, "I need to get on with prepping too as I'm running out of time."

"Well, we can cover the food today, that's a big chunk. What else have you got left?" she asks.

I pull my checklist out of the pocket of my stolen parka. Along with it drops the creased betting slip to the floor of the car; should I cash it in?

"Come on then!" Annabel insists.

"Alright! Shelter is nearly done, I just need Michael to finish and also pick up the petrol and the propane. Food & Water we should be able to tick off today. Security is done, so just need to figure out how to tick off Belongingness and Esteem."

"How can you prepare for those?" Annabel chuckles.

"Esteem, I don't know. I'm struggling with it before the end of the world to be honest. Belongingness is being part of a social group, intimacy, friendships so will be whoever is there with me I guess." I look over at Annabel to gauge her reaction and I'm met by a blank face and silence.

"Your VIP list," she chuckles.

"Yeah, I guess so."

"Bit of advice; before you go asking people to go living in a bunker with you, wandering around drunk, half naked and covered in blood isn't the best look." She has a point.

"I still haven't decided," I say, hoping that she may open up a bit about being there with me. She's not biting. "Well, I'm having a New Year's Eve party so you're invited to that, if shit hit's the fan you can always grab a place in the sex dungeon."

Annabel laughs. "I don't have any plans so far, I'll keep you posted."

"I'll make sure you get the least creepy corner of the dungeon," I smile at her.

"Well at least there will be food down there," she smiles. "How are you going to tick off esteem then? Seems like an odd one."

I look at the 'Esteem' category on the list. It's the only one that I haven't got anything that I can really tick off underneath. All I have jotted down is 'prestige' and 'accomplishment'.

"I don't know really," I pause, "Maslow's hierarchy of needs said it was about the ego and there were two parts, lower esteem and higher esteem. Lower esteem being the need for recognition, status and attention from others and the higher being from yourself, like self-respect and so on."

Annabel laughs, "Well don't go on a bender for two days again. That's a good start!"

She definitely has a point this time. "I guess with esteem I'll only know if I've got there when I've ticked off the others. I mean, it is a hierarchy and that is the last one just before self-actualization."

"Which is?" Annabel asks.

"In a nutshell, it is reaching your full potential."

Annabel indicates to pull over and stops in front of a nearby bus stop. She sighs and puts her hand on my knee,

"Look, Ray. It's not any of my business to start handing out advice on what to do and how to live your life but you obviously are still feeling depressed about life as a whole and from what I can see all this, this prepping and moving into the middle of nowhere for the end of the world is your reaction to losing what you thought was a massive part of your identity: your house, Debbie and being flung with nothing into a world full of hysteria around a programming problem that may or may not fuck some things up." She takes my hand, "You are doing this to try and find your identity again. You have gone so deep into what you need that you're trying to fix every part of your life by splitting it into sections and that overall goal of yours, to reach your full potential. If you have to re-do everything then go for it, but just make sure you realise that the you that existed before all of this wasn't bad, or not worth anything. You were just doing what we all do."

"What's that?" I ask her.

"Just trying to get through life with what you have got." She smiles, "It takes a brave person to recognise when things aren't working and try to change, but your mother and that fear of being abandoned and alone, that's not something you did and it may be something you can never change."

68

Annabel's Renault Espace is packed full of food and other supplies as we pull up back in front of the farmhouse.

I am feeling a little worse for wear but, after the greasy bacon sandwich and a few cans of full fat coke, I definitely feel better than I have the last few days. I breathe a sigh of relief as the car pulls to a stop and I am now back in a safe place, away from the busy crowds of the Netto in town and also with enough food for six people for three months.

"Do you want to get the door and I'll start unloading?" I suggest.

"Yeah sure," Annabel smiles, "I might check out your new toilet too."

I grab a couple of the big bags and follow Annabel to the front door. She unlocks it and I dump the bags by the range cooker.

"What the fuck!" I heard Annabel shout as she moves towards me and grabs my arm.

"What the fuck indeed," Bea comments back as she emerges from the basement.

"Who the fuck are you? Do you know her Ray?" Annabel panics.

"Who the fuck are you?" Bea challenges. "Is this your wife then?" she glares at me.

"Calm down Annabel, I know her, she lives here," I explain.

Annabel looks at me, "She lives here?"

"Yeah, I do, so who are you?" Bea squares up to Annabel, so I interject.

"Bea, this is Annabel who I work - sorry, worked with. Annabel this is Bea, she lives here now." They both look at each other with some uncertainty until Bea stick out a hand which Annabel decides to shake.

"Where have you been?" Bea asks. "We came back here and found blood on the floor, empty booze bottles and the downstairs storage room trashed."

"I was shopping. Where have you been for the past two days?" I ask Bea.

"Like I told you, at my Auntie's. I invited Michael because it didn't feel right leaving him here on his own. Some of us aren't selfish bastards like you."

Michael emerges from the stairs. "Hiya, sorry I was so long, we just didn't want to rush back. It was lovely at Bea's auntie's. I've not eaten that well in years either. What happened here?" he asks.

"Ray happened here, that's what," Annabel scolds. "I found him shirtless, covered in blood and still half pissed."

"You said you were cutting down," Bea snaps.

"I was, I just had a really shitty day and then being here alone."

"Whoa! Don't put this on us. You were here

alone because you decided to cook dinner for your ex-wife instead of us," Bea shouts.

"I'm sorry. I had an impossible choice to make," I sigh.

"Well, it's all worked out alright in the end," Michael smiles, "I'll go and grab some of the bags. I've tidied up the storage room, so I'll stick them straight in there," he says as he whistles past.

"Do you want a cup of coffee?" Bea asks.

I nod, "Yes please."

Bea scoffs, "Not you. Her. Annabel would you like one?"

"Err yeah go on then," she smiles.

"We don't have milk or sugar so it's black or nothing," Bea tells Annabel.

Annabel nods, "Yeah that's fine," as Bea descends back into the bunker.

"So, are you two...?" Annabel asks with raised eyebrows.

"No, we…. To be completely honest, she stayed in my bed at Eddy's a couple of times and all we did was kiss and she stayed here once and decided to move in," I explain. "It wasn't planned, it just happened, and we are not an item or anything."

"I'm not your wife, Ray," Annabel tells me.

"She said that too."

"Well, if that's what you want then fine." Annabel takes out a cigarette. "If she's on the VIP bunker list then who am I to judge?" I detect a hint of sarcasm as she lights her cigarette.

"Annabel, she is a great person and has been amazing around here and look what happened when she wasn't around the other night. I need people like you and I need people like her."

Annabel hugs me. "Next time you need someone please fucking call me." She lets me go and kisses me on the cheek. "People care about you, Ray, and end of the world or not, you are not indestructible."

69

I'm drinking for pleasure rather than to mask a deep-rooted pain. A day's work has put me back on a more balanced level and I'm enjoying sipping a whisky in the almost completed bunker of my farmhouse.

Annabel's help with pulling me out of the abyss to do some food shopping at Netto had allowed me to fully tick off another item on my checklist, leaving three left before the end of the world: Shelter, Belongingness and then Esteem.

Michael had cracked on with the bunker and we were now fully walled in with drywall in each room. The bedrooms had been given a woman's touch by Bea and Annabel with completely different results and I'd put away all of the food in the storage room and the two small fridges that were in the new kitchen area down here.

As Michael had finished off each room they were sealed in darkness until the sparky comes to do his bit, but with the four of us and a couple of candles it is beautifully peaceful and calm in the new lounge.

Annabel nudges me, "You need some wine glasses."

"All he had was mugs until I brought some glass tumblers up," Bea interjects half distracted by her book.

"I'm not holding a dinner party down here," I tell them, "plus I'm out of cash now so unless Michael has any left over, this is it."

"All the money you gave me is accounted for," Michael says, "Just the propane and the petrol to pick up tomorrow and pay the sparky when he eventually gets here too."

"That's it then, no more money." I go back to my whisky.

Bea put's her book down. "What about... I don't know... stuff to do?!"

"Yeah, like maybe a radio at least?" Annabel agrees.

"With what?" I stress.

"Your redundancy payoff?" Annabel suggests.

"Won't be here until payday," I tell her.

"Thursday is payday and that's only three days away." Annabel smiles smugly.

"Shopping spree!" Bea shouts, punching the air.

"Well, save some just in case the world doesn't end," Annabel stresses. "Prepare for that outcome too."

"We can get some stuff on Thursday," I concede "but nothing too expensive or useless."

"What are you going to spend money on after the world ends?" Bea says with a hint of annoyance.

"I was going to just take it out, buy some silver bars and stash the rest here somewhere."

"Boring!" Bea shouts, "Like this book! It's shit! It's nothing like that one about the whale I just read."

"What's it about?" Annabel asks her.

"Just some guy banging on about teaching the children and looking after his garden. It's just boring," Bea moans.

"Just pick another book then," I laugh,

"I want to know how it ends," Bea whines.

"How would you pay people for stuff if the world ends?" Annabel asks me.

"Rent boy," Bea laughs and I give her a dismissive glare.

"Believe it or not my arsehole won't be in huge demand, so Eddy is hooking me up tomorrow with some cheap cigarettes and whisky."

"Should you be buying tons of whisky after what just happened?" Bea asks.

"It's there for any eventuality," is all I can offer.

"Well, so far, out of the three of us staying here, it's only you that drinks anyway. Michael doesn't, I don't, so if the supply starts running thin we will know exactly who is to blame," Bea smiles.

I stare at my whisky. "Well, it is my money and I think it is a wise investment, unlike spending it..."

"Hold on," Annabel interrupts, "If you have no money left how are you paying for all this tobacco and whisky?"

"Hey, that's a good point," Bea says sitting up, "I like you Annabel."

Annabel smiles. "If you're all spent up, where is all this reserve money coming from?"

"A bet," I sigh, "a bet that has come in."

"The bet that wasn't yours's and that you stole from a one-eyed bastard landlord?" Bea questions as Annabel looks extremely confused.

"Yes, you are right Bea."

"Do I even want to know?" Annabel shakes her head.

"The guy assaulted me and stole my credit card, so I took his parka and the betting slip was in the pocket."

"The guy you hit with a cricket bat?" Annabel raises her eyebrows.

"That's the guy," Bea chirps in.

"Just give him the stuff back, Ray. If it's that much money then he deserves to have it back," Annabel says with disbelief. "How much are we talking about?"

"About two grand," I tell her, based on his threats to me as I fled Woolworths.

"I say, keep it and fuck him!" Bea chuckles.

"I'd give it back," Annabel says sternly,

"Me too," Michael adds.

"Okay! It's a redundant argument really as I need to pay for the cigarettes and whisky. I'll think about paying him back once I have my redundancy cash," I shout to calm the baying mob.

"Pussy," Bea snorts and goes back to her book.

70

I've been banging on the door of the bookies for around half an hour now. I'm running out of time to make it across to Wainhouse Tower to do the deal for the cigarettes and whisky I had ordered from Eddy's mate.

I bang three more times... nothing. The opening hours on the door are telling me it should be open by now. It's nearly quarter to ten now and nobody is answering or turning up to open the place up.

I check the betting slip in my hand; it's definitely a Coral ticket and I can't think of any other Coral branches nearby. I go back to banging instead.

"Hold up," an old man approaches me from behind, "nay point in banging lad, shop is shut."

"It says nine on the door," I point out to him.

"I'm not 'ere to argue, I'm 'ere to tell thee," He says sternly, "t'shop is shut!"

I look at the door, the hours posted and then back at the old man. "How do you know it's shut?"

"It's bank holiday you numpty," he laughs walking off.

He's right. Christmas was Saturday, Sunday was Boxing Day, so the bank holidays carry over. They are working off Sunday hours like Netto yesterday, fuck.

I look at my watch and I have about ten minutes to get up to Wainhouse Tower for the meeting. I'll have to go up empty handed because there is nowhere I can get half a grand at this short notice.

Michael had dropped me off before going to get the propane and petrol, Annabel is too far away, and Bea never has her phone on. What would I ask them for anyway? I could ask Eddy, but I hate people who take money from him because he is such an easy target. Nice guy with a boatload of cash.

I stick the slip back into my pocket and head towards the bus station. The bus shouldn't take more than ten minutes, but the timetable I looked at earlier is the wrong fucking one so I have no idea when the bus will even arrive or if there is one.

I take a cigarette out of my pack and fight against the wind to light it with my zippo. The warm smoke calms me for a second as I check my watch, hoping that time had suddenly gone backwards. It's now nearer to ten to.

Ahead of me I see a bus with "King Cross" on it, parked in the bus station. That's the one I want. I start to jog then decide to move into a sprint towards the bus as it's now turning out of the station. The traffic lights at the exit do me a favor and turn to red as I get within a hundred metres. Suddenly turning into Linford Christie, I power through, arriving breathless at the sealed doors.

The bus driver looks at me and then drives off.

71

Wainhouse Tower is towering in front of me as I take the gravel and grass path off the small road I have been walking down. I can see two vehicles ahead. Neither is my Land Rover so Michael must not have arrived here yet, even though I am half an hour late.

I push on up the steep path and look out at the gravestones ahead of me, the tower looming ahead and the derelict buildings that altogether were making this strange place on the outskirts of Halifax and Sowerby Bridge just a little stranger.

I spot some people just between the base of the tower and the graveyard. This must be Eddy's mate. There are three of them, all in leather jackets and around the same bulky size of the main man I saw in Fagin's and they don't seem impressed as they are all pacing around.

"Sorry I'm late," I call out.

One of the men turns to face me and looks like he's hit an imaginary wall as his nose is plastered against his face. "He's ere," he grunts back at the man I recognise who has a leather jacket on and the flat cap.

"Sorry, I got stuck in town and then the bus wouldn't let me on at a red light."

"Well, buses don't do that, it's dangerous and the driver would be liable for any accidents," Broken Nose says to me.

"Well, it made me late, sorry," I apologise.

"Eddy says you're preparing for the end of the world," the main man in the flat cap chuckles.

"Yeah, I am," I say sheepishly.

"What does all that entail then?" He smiles.

"Well, I have a place that's remote and I'm stocking up on supplies for the Y2K bug."

"It's good to have a plan B," he smiles. "These two 'ere are my plan B, just to let you know." He points at Broken Nose and another unnamed man I christen Ponytail.

"Right," I say breathing out heavily.

"How are you planning on transporting it though?" Flat Cap asks, noticing my lack of a vehicle.

"My mate is coming soon with a Land Rover," I tell him, "won't be long."

"Let's hope he's better at timekeeping them you," Flat Cap snarls at me.

"Again, I'm sorry. I had a little problem getting the money for the stuff from town," I explain.

"But you have the money now?" Flat Cap says with some certainty.

"I don't," I sigh, "Can we do this again tomorrow?"

"It's not a fucking tea party lad," Flat Cap snaps back.

"I'll have it tomorrow; it's just I went to the

bookies to cash out a betting slip for the money and it was shut," I plead.

"Course it was. It's Bank holiday," Broken Nose gasps.

Flat Cap holds a hand up to quieten Broken Nose. "And how much were you due to cash out on?"

"It's about two grand I think." I reach into my pocket, "Look, footballer of the year number one, two and three all in order."

Flat Cap motions Ponytail towards me, he snatches the slip from my hand and passes it back to Flat Cap.

Flat Cap looks down at the slip of paper. "Two grand you reckon?" he raises an eye to me.

"Yeah, around two grand," I assure him, "I'll have the money first thing tomorrow when the bookies open."

Flat Cap looks at the slip again and nods towards Broken Nose who walks towards one of the cars.

"This will do," Flat Cap smiles at me, pocketing the slip.

"Hold on," I struggle, "are you? That slip is two grands' worth!" I argue.

"Call it interest." Flat Cap grins as Broken Nose starts unloading the boxes from the car.

"That's four times what I agreed. Put it back in the car. I don't want it."

"You ordered it, you take it." Flat Cap folds his arms.

"But that's fifteen hundred more than the stuff's worth. That's full price!" I walk towards Flat Cap.

"Back off," Ponytail spits as he blocks my path.

"Please just give me until tomorrow morning," I

stress.

Flat Cap walks towards me. "See this tower," he points at the massive Wainhouse tower behind him, "some folk here said Mr. Wainhouse built it so he could look into some fella's estate on account of this fella bragging to everyone about having the most private estate in town." He smiles at me, "You got a nice little private place where you are. Don't go bringing anyone's attention to it, especially not mine."

I stand dumbfounded as Flat Cap heads back to his car. I hear the roar of the Land Rover coming up behind me and Flat Cap points at the Land Rover and whispers something to Ponytail.

"And, Ray, that is your name, right?" Flat Cap asks as I nod, "Make sure you tell me right now if this is all a game and I'll have no luck cashing in that bet of yours."

"It's not a game," I tell him.

"Cos other folk say that Mr. Wainhouse built this tower and spent so much money on it that he ran out completely and couldn't even build the factory next to it that had made him build it in the first place, so don't risk everything on one thing lad, you understand?"

"Yes," I reply sternly.

Flat Cap gets into one car whilst Broken Nose and Ponytail get into the other. Flat Cap gives me a little wave as he pulls around and back down the gravel path followed by his goons in the second car.

Michael gets out of the Land Rover and walks towards me "Everything go alright?"

"I hope so," I tell him.

72

The sparky had been and gone by the time Michael and I got back to the farmhouse.

He had been able to fit a separate light in every one of the new rooms and had hooked up a supply to the backup petrol generators above ground in the newly dubbed 'engine room'.

Bea had said that he was 'alright' but seemed slightly pervy and was a bit annoyed when she told him she didn't have any money to pay him as, in her words, it was 'not my fucking house you paedo'.

With my list of creditors growing by the hour and my life savings now consisting of the Britannia penny that Tortoise Man didn't want to buy, Bea had decided to go to her parents place and raid the freezer, leaving me and Michael to put the finishing touches on the basement, now bunker.

"If we finish laying this vinyl throughout, we can do the skirting boards then and leave the coving for tomorrow," Michael suggests with us both on our hands

312

and knees in the hallway of the bunker. "Probably be all finished by teatime tomorrow."

"Whatever you think is best Michael," I tell him, "What's left after the coving?"

"Just the tidying up really, nothing more to do down here. All the work left is in the barn and the engine room, just making them a bit more secure and safe and a bit of a facelift," he smiles.

"All that's left now is the people to live in here," I chuckle.

"Is that lass Annabel from the other night joining you here?" Michael asks.

"Good question," I sigh and take a sip of my tea. "I've dropped some hints but nothing yet. She did seem annoyed that Bea was here, so maybe she does want to move in."

"I can see why she would be," Michael chuckles.

"Why?" I ask him.

"Well if you had a nice house, car and someone told you the world was going to end and to come live in their bunker wouldn't you feel a bit confused? Especially if it was a good friend."

He has a point. "From that point of view, yes, I would hesitate."

"Who else is on your list?" He asks.

"Well I don't really have a list of people. I have ideas in my head, but I haven't asked anyone."

"If you don't ask lad, you won't get," Michael says sternly, clicking another piece of laminate in place.

"I didn't ask Bea or you," I point out.

"We didn't have our own place, though, did we? We both found something new and exciting here. Some people, you are going to have to sell them on it." He takes a sip of his tea.

"Well at least I have something to sell them on now," I smile, looking around at the basement that is definitely a bunker now.

"It's not just this though is it?" Michael looks at me. "It's being up here, away from all the crap going on down there. Once you get some veg planted and some animals or something, you could live up here, cut off from all the rubbish down there."

"I haven't really thought about that," I tell him. "Animals, that's a whole different ball game."

"Couple of chickens in the barn, I could sort that for you and look after them, a coop and a few bags of feed..."

I cut Michael off. "I can't afford it mate."

"Alright," he concedes.

"It sounds good, but I don't know anything about chickens or any animal really, haven't even had a goldfish."

"How about I sort it out?" Michael says, his head still down busy laying the flooring.

"I couldn't ask you to do that out of your money," I tell him.

"I'd like to, will give me something to do when I've fixed everything up," he smiles.

I'm not sure about this. I didn't factor cleaning up shit or slaughtering anything into my checklist, but he is right though, it does make sense to have a fresh supply of eggs and possibly chicken if I summoned up the courage. "I'll leave it up to you," I tell him.

Michael flashes me a grin. "Top lad, I'll crack on with that. There is a place selling chickens over near Haworth and there is still plenty of wood left but I'll pick up some pallets and save the good stuff."

"You go for it mate, whatever you think will

work." Perhaps this will give me something to get into too.

"Just one thing though," Michael stops working and looks at me, "if nothing happens, if this Y2K bug is nothing but a fart in church then what happens to all this?" he opens his palms up and out, "Are you giving up on this if it's life as normal?"

I inhale deeply and meet his eyes. "I think this is life as normal now, regardless of whether things change around me. I think I've changed too much to go back."

73

"Ray, Michael, give us a hand up here!" Bea shouts down the old stone staircase.

"Hold on, just finishing off the skirting," I shout back, and I hold the final piece for Michael.

"Hurry up will you," Bea shouts impatiently.

"Just hang on," I shout up as Michael narrowly misses my thumb with the hammer.

"Better go see what the urgency is," Michael chuckles as we stand up.

"I'll go up, you pack up down here and have a break for a bit," I tell Michael who nods back.

"Ray!" Bea shouts again.

"I'm coming!" I shout back, ascending the stone staircase into the kitchen.

"I've parked out the front, give me a hand," she shouts from outside now as I see her reaching into the passenger seat of her Nissan. The car looks packed to the brim.

"What have you got?" I ask her.

"Loads of useful stuff," she smiles, "and some dinner for tonight"

"Can't argue with that," I chuckle.

"Take these," she passes me two huge but light bags, "loads more bedding and pillows for the other beds."

"Are these off beds in your parent's place?" I ask her.

"No - well yeah, but they are spares," she sighs as I shrug my shoulders and take in the bags. "Just grab what you can," she announces behind me, putting down a television on the stone floor next to me.

"How much have you got?" I ask her.

"Just stuff to make it a bit less boring," she says, pushing me back out to the car

"Dumbbells?" I ask, picking up some weights from the boot of her car.

"Yeah, need to keep my strength up," she says, "could work on yours a bit too," she winks.

I put the dumbbells on the floor and scan the rest of the boot: board games, a football, cushions, rolls of posters; too much to take in. "It's like a jumble sale," I tell her.

"Ha!" she pretends to laugh back, "Car boot sale would have been funnier," as Michael appears on the doorstep.

"I'll just chuck these in the upstairs lounge as we are painting tomorrow," he smiles at Bea.

"Aw good idea, thank you love," Bea smiles back. She's never that nice to me.

"Oi fucker! Get moving!" She punches my arm and I wince as it genuinely hurts.

I grab what I can and start to move the assortment of items into the farmhouse's lounge by the front door. "Is all of this stuff from your parents' house?" I ask her.

"Yeah, it's just been in our garage, not being used, or in my room, like this," she picks up a pink rucksack and opens it up. "A SEGA Mega Drive, complete with a load of games," she beams," plus in there somewhere a Game Boy. Don't worry, I chucked a load of batteries in the bag, so I won't nick any of yours." She shoves the rucksack into my chest. "Go set it up!" I go to speak but she kisses me on the lips and skips past.

I turn to head back outside and see a man standing right at the top of the front field by the entrance gate. I don't think I recognise him but I'm sure I've seen the coat before. He's so far away, I can't quite make him out.

"I know that fella," Michael says standing beside me.

"Who is he?" I ask.

"He's from the place further up the moors," Michael says bitterly.

"Should I go and say hello?" I chuckle.

"No, steer clear of that lot," Michael stresses, turning back to unload the car.

74

"Are you going to play this now I've set it up?" I ask Bea who's wrapped up in the same blanket with her nose in a book.

"Hold on!" she yells.

"Michael is pissing around building a chicken coop and I've got no-one to play with on Streets of Rage," I toss a cushion at her head.

"I will break your nose Ray O'Riordan!" Bea growls back.

I'd set the TV up down in the wood paneled lounge in the bunker. It reminded me a bit of being a kid, sat in front of a small TV playing a video game, although back then it was the groundbreaking Atari 2600 and trying to stop E.T falling down holes.

I give up on Bea and decide to go fill up my glass with some of my new whisky. Worth trying it out anyway. I unscrew the top and pour a nice measure. It smells fine and after a sip it takes fine too. At least it wasn't a massive waste of two grand, wasn't mine to begin with either really.

"Do you want a drink Bea?" I shout to her.

"No," She replies curtly.

I grab my glass and head back to the lounge area, pulling out a cigarette whilst I'm standing. "I leave you alone now," I smile at Bea.

"I'm just getting to the good part," she whines.

"Alright! I'll leave you to it. Give me a shout when you want a game. It's nearly midnight by the way."

"Thank you, talking fucking clock," she sighs.

I walk past her and she grabs my hand, pulling it close to her mouth and giving it a kiss. I carry on to my seat as she lets it go, still not quite sure what is going on between us.

I pull my checklist out of my pocket along with my lighter, lighting the cigarette in my mouth and unfolding the list onto my lap. I grab a pen from the table next to me and skim through the items to see what I have left to tick off.

1. Shelter - Done
2. Food & Water - Done
3. Security - Done
4. Belongingness -
5. Esteem -
6. Self Actualisation

Still need to actually plant the seeds I have for the vegetables and that can't be done until the paint has gone on and dried, but it's all ready to go so it's only Belongingness and Esteem left to tick off.

Belongingness is next. I need to invite people to this party as so far, it's going to be me, Michael, Bea and possibly Annabel. I don't need lots of people, maybe two or three more, but who?

Eddy is a given. I should invite him and tell him there is a spot for him here if anything goes wrong. I haven't even thought about Dave. He is a twat, but I should try to help him too, but he's got kids and the noise would be unbearable. Plus, he's a twat.

Kelly. I like Kelly. She's considerate and sweet and she grounded me, but I don't think she is speaking to me anymore. Similarly, Debbie who I feel I should invite but just can't; it would be a mess if her and Bea were in the same room.

A lot of this depends on whether Bea is actually wanting to live here as an item. I still don't know if she actually fancies me. She has kissed me a few times but generally just berates and punches me. But she is here, and she made that move. I need to ask her.

"Bea."

"For fucks sake! I'm reading!" She groans and throws her head back. "What part of that sentence do you not get?"

"Look, it's important," I tell her.

Bea puts down her book onto her lap and looks at me.

"Are you here because you like me as in want to be with me?"

Silence from Bea as she bites her lip ring.

I take a long drag of my cigarette. "See the thing is, whoever I invite to stay here when the world ends, that depends a lot on how you see the relationship between us two."

"I told you before Ray," she sighs, "I'm not your wife."

"I know that," I tell her, "but we've kissed and

slept in the same bed and you have been in compromising positions around me."

"Compromising positions!" she laughs, "I'm not a fucking prozzy."

"Just tell me," I stress," do you want to be in a relationship with me, ever?"

"I don't believe in labels," Bea says sternly and goes back to her book.

It wasn't a no.

75

Michael has spent the morning sourcing chickens from a farm over near Haworth. He'd come back with a cock and four hens, much to Bea's amusement; she had taken a break from her book to ask him questions about his cock.

I'd finished off painting the bunker to allow him time to fulfill his need of Esteem and I was feeling some of my own in coating the hallway and grow room in a nice crisp white, the kitchen a moody red, and the bathroom in a colour labelled 'honey bee'.

I'd texted Eddy about the party on New Year's Eve and he was up for it. He asked if he could bring someone, which I had agreed to and immediately regretted as I realised I could potentially be surviving the end of the world with Big Nick or Buttercup.

The grow room which was full of the old hydroponics equipment was to be my new haven. I'd found a book in the old bedroom upstairs about growing veg and it seemed like the perfect hobby for me to take up to fulfill my lower and higher levels of esteem. Along with the chickens, this was going to be exactly what I need.

"Michael's cock is on your Land Rover," Bea shouts down from the kitchen.

I carry on cleaning the dismantled hydroponics pieces and ignore her.

"He's chasing his cock around the field now," Bea struggles to shout through fits of laughter.

I grab a cigarette and decide to go upstairs to watch.

"Michael..." Bea struggles to get out, "Michael... is...." she is belly laughing now, "He's caught his cock in your fence." She collapses to the floor in laughter as I see Michael had indeed cornered his cock and was now picking it up to put back in the back of the Land Rover.

Bea manages to get back to her feet and is wiping tears from her eyes. She can amuse herself quite well.

"You handle your cock like an expert," I shout to Michael who shoots me a disappointed glare as Bea collapses onto the floor again.

"I've nearly finished the coop, so hopefully all this crap about the chicken will stop then," Michael shouts back to us.

"Sorry mate," I shrug my shoulders.

"Wouldn't have been so bad if either of you had offered a hand," he tuts.

"I don't want to touch your cock. I don't know where it's been!" Bea chuckles and punches my arm.

"Grow up the pair of you," Michael shouts and walks into the barn.

"Are we having one of those chickens for dinner

then?" Bea asks.

"Erm. No," I tell her, "those chickens are for laying eggs, some for eating and some for more chickens when the cock is ready."

Bea stifles a laugh. "Fair enough," she says. "I'll cook us something then. How about a moussaka or something?"

My eyes shoot wide. "You can cook?"

"Course I can cook, you knobhead. Why do you think I brought all those spices and stuff from my parents' house? You can be so sexist sometimes."

"How is that sexist? It's the opposite of sexist!" I laugh.

"That right there is sexist," Bea scolds.

"I apologise," I bow to her.

"You are forgiven if you come with me to get the stuff. I know you are done with shopping, but I promise it will be fun."

"Alright. Deal. Will give us a chance to try out the oven too," I smile at her. "Michael!" I shout.

Michael sticks his head out of the barn and his face looks like he is expecting more cock jokes. "What now?" he snaps.

I raise my hands up. "We are heading out to get some stuff for a moussaka, that's all."

"Sounds lovely," he smiles.

"Don't play with your cock too much whilst we are gone," Bea shouts.

Michael shakes his head and goes back in the barn. As I turn to Bea, I spot the figure at the top of the field again, stood in the same place by the gate.

"You seen that guy before yesterday?" I ask Bea.

"No, but I probably wouldn't have paid much attention to a guy staring creepily at me as you do it all the time," she says.

"I'm sure I recognise him," I tell her. "I'm going over."

"No!" Bea grabs my arm, "Don't. He might think you're best buddies then and pop around for a cup of tea and some mutual masturbation. We don't want every weird psycho knowing what we are doing here. Let him perv from a distance."

She's right. I don't particularly want people dropping by. He can stay where he is but that's far enough.

"Shall I get my chainsaw?" Bea smiles.

76

"Basically, it's all about the oregano and nutmeg," Bea smirks as she races her Nissan Sunny around the tight streets of Hebden Bridge.

"Better in your moussaka than one of Buttercup's joints," I tell her.

"Joints are boring," Bea says, as she speeds through a corner, "lower your reactions." she adds, zooming past The Trades Club where my mother had apparently worked behind the bar for a number of years.

"Do you fancy popping in for a drink?" I ask her.

She sighs, "I don't drink! Plus, I want to get back and cook this amazing food."

"Just one," I plead, as she brings the car to a screeching halt and reverses into a space on the street.

"One drink and then back," she smiles, sticking on the handbrake and chucking the keys in her pocket. "Hebden is the lesbian capital of Britain you know, so I hope you aren't going in there to try and pull."

I get out of the car and look at the building with its name etched in stone, sandwiched between a large curved top window and the massive front door. I can imagine my mum walking through to start a shift whilst working a gig by Patti Smith or The Fall.

"What are you staring at?" Bea asks.

"Nothing. Just my mum worked here. I remember my grandmother bringing me once and my mum telling me the dancefloor was on springs."

"She was probably on springs with all that weed lying around, not the dancefloor," Bea says as we walk towards the front door.

It's quiet tonight, but still a three quid cover each on the door. Bea reluctantly reaches into her pocket and pays as I am still without money having given my last slither of hope to Flat Cap.

"What do you want?" Bea asks me.

"Whisky please," I say as I look around the rectangular room.

"No. Have something a bit lighter," she insists.

"Pint of lager then, whatever is cheapest and lightest," I smile, looking at the local artist playing guitar on the stage.

"Pint of lager please and a glass of water... tap," Bea tells the barman.

"It's smaller than I remember it," I tell Bea.

"I hate it when people say that," Bea scoffs. "Course it is because you were smaller. It's like saying your first pair of shoes kept shrinking as you grew older." Bea hands me my pint. "Cheers," she says.

"Cheers," I smile back and take a gulp of the frothy pint.

"They have photos behind the bar, perhaps your mum is on one," Bea points out.

I walk to the bar and lean over a bit to get a good look at the framed photos. I skim across and then back and then recognise a face. "I know that face," I nudge Bea.

"Your mum. Well to quote Cilla Black, 'Surprise, Surprise'," Bea says sarcastically.

"No, that one!" I point towards a photo on the edge. "And look, there is the same person next to my mother."

I get the attention of the barman. "Excuse me mate, can I take a look at that photo please?" The barman shrugs and hands it to me. It's my mother when she was probably around 18, two years after having me. She is dancing in a long, flowing, light dress and the man whose face I recognize has his hand around her waist.

"He must be someone from the commune too," I tell Bea. "I've seen his face on one of the pictures, I'm sure."

"Awesome," Bea says sarcastically. "Let's look at all the photos."

"Can I take this?" I ask the barman. "I'll make a photocopy and bring it back." He shrugs his shoulders and turns away. I take that as a 'I don't give a fuck'.

"Didn't you smash up the last photo of your mother?" Bea questions.

"Yeah, but I'm looking at it differently now. I can't change things that happened in the past."

My phone beeps in my pocket and I slide it out. A new text message from Eddy.

What the fuck did you do

77

"Eddy!" I shout as I barge through his front door. "Eddy, what the fuck is going on?"

"You tell me!" Eddy shouts, appearing from the kitchen, shirtless and his face and upper body covered in blood.

I gasp, "Fucking hell, what happened Eddy?"

"Oh this?" He points to his battered face. "This is a smashed in face, Ray. It's what happens when someone smashes your face in!" He brushes his blood-matted long hair from in front of his face, blood dripping from a cut somewhere on his forehead.

"Fucking hell!" Bea shouts as she enters the house.

"I know! Stop looking so shocked! It's freaking me out." Eddy pats his pocket for his cigarettes. I pull one of mine out and hand it to him.

"No!" he shouts and points at me. "Keep the cigarettes. That's the shit that caused all of this in the first place."

I step back. "What?"

"Your deal with Patrick," Eddy sniffles, blood falling from his nose. "You fucked him over and he thinks I'm some part of it."

"Patrick?" The pieces fit together, it's Flat Cap. "I didn't fuck him over, I paid him the fucking rrp!" I shout.

"Did you pay him?" Eddy says pointing a finger at me.

"I gave him the betting slip."

"You didn't fucking pay him then!" Eddy shouts.

"I gave him something worth four times what the stuff was worth," I argue.

"Well he went to cash it in the morning, and guess what? It's not even a bet! It's just some random guesses on a piece of paper from the bookies, hadn't even gone through the machine."

"But the guy said two grand!" I shake my head. "He shouted I'd cost him two grand."

Eddy looks at me. "Bit of advice, don't pay for dodgy stuff from dodgy people with a piece of paper you have no fucking idea where it came from!" Eddy sweeps his hand across the kitchen table and knocks all of the empty bottles off to a loud crash on the floor.

"What are they... Did the... where are... did you pay them?" I manage to stutter.

"Do I look like I fucking paid them?" Eddy laughs between cries. "They took my Dreamcast my Nintendo 64 and my projector screen and then beat the shit out of me."

"Where are they now? What do I do?" I mutter to him.

"They said they know where you live." Eddy shakes his head.

"How?" I ask.

"They marked your Land Rover, got the number plate and the address on it."

"Fuck!" I gasp. I grab my hand in my head "Fuck! Fuck! Fuck!"

"They left nearly an hour ago so I would stay away from your farm and warn Debbie if the Land Rover is registered there."

"It's not registered there. Fuck! I have to go! Bea I'm taking your car."

78

I could smell it before I saw anything, then the smoke was visible slightly in the dark sky and then the unmissable flames as I speed towards it up and down the steep roads.

I can hear shouting and sirens as I pull Bea's car onto the side of the road, yanking the keys out of the engine and slamming the door.

The flames are unmissable now, red, angry, and so loud I can feel the heat coming towards me and the nearby cars have all lost their layer of frost.

The flames are jumping out of the broken glass of the front windows. The door is no more. Charred on the pavement around ten meters from where it once was. I can see inside and the shadows of what is still burning and enveloped by the bright angry flames.

I can feel the acid building up my in throat. My hands are shaking and pins and needles are firing up in my arms and legs. I eat the adrenaline surge and sprint towards the burning shop.

The firemen are shouting something at me, but I can't hear them over the roar of the flames. I look at the building for an entrance point and can feel the fire starting to heat the skin on my face. I start coughing as I move towards the smashed window front and a hand grabs me on my shoulder pulling me back.

I fight against it, feeling stronger than I ever have and using the adrenaline to spot places that are open and accessible to get through into the shop. A second hand grabs my wrist now, the bad one and I wince in pain as it pulls me back.

I turn around and see two firemen pulling me and over their shoulders. I spot a girl shouting. It's Kelly.

"Ray!" I can hear her now as I move closer. "Get away from there!"

I turn back to look at the burning shop. I can't believe I had got so close to the fire. I touch my skin and it's red raw and sensitive. I touch my unshaven face and can feel the hairs have singed on the end.

"What are you doing?" Kelly gasps.

I stare at the fire and then at her, reaching forward and enveloping her in my arms.

"No one's in there," she says in my ear.

"Your mum and dad?" I ask.

"Mum is with the paramedics getting checked over. My dad is with her. He was at the pub across the road."

I squeeze her harder and exhale deeply. "What happened?" I ask.

Kelly sniffles. "We were just watching Corrie and I heard banging downstairs. I opened the door to the stairwell down to the shop and didn't see anything but smelt smoke. I grabbed mum and when we looked again there was fire everywhere. We called 999 and

334

went down the metal fire escape down the back."

"I can't believe this," I gasp "I am so sorry."

Kelly sniffles and hugs me tight. "How did you know about this?"

I exhale deeply again and let go of Kelly. "I was driving past and saw the flames," I tell her, feeling a knot form in my stomach as I lie.

We jump as a huge crash echoes from the shop, shooting embers and heat in every direction. I look behind me and see the first floor has collapsed into the ground floor shop now as Kelly bursts into tears.

"Move back please," a fireman directs us as we shuffle backwards.

I keep my arm around Kelly as a paramedic comes our way. Kelly starts to cry again at the sight of him heading towards her.

"Don't worry love everything is okay," he re-assures her. "Your mum is fine. She has just had a bit of a shock, as you probably have too."

"Can I go see her now?" Kelly asks through sniffles.

"Yes, your dad has taken her over to the pub. I told her I'd go find you," he smiles.

"Come on," I take Kelly's hand, "let's go see your mum and dad."

She turns to me, her face streaming with tears and her lip quivering. "Ray, I don't know what we are going to do. Just look at my home." Kelly starts crying.

I embrace her again and whisper, "I'm just glad you are okay."

79

Everyone is around the large wooden table in the old farmhouse kitchen. I'd managed to message Bea and Eddy to ask them not to mention anything about my knowledge of the fire, before heading back to Eddy's with a car full of cold, half-drunk victims.

"What happened to your face?" Apron Lady asks Eddy, as Bea dabs his wounds with some TCP.

"Probably fell off that moped. Bloody death traps," Kelly's dad, Bill, adds.

"Leave it you two," Kelly sighs.

Eddy shoots me a frown. "A mate of mine did it."

Bea had convinced Eddy to come with us back to the farmhouse, probably at around the same time I was offering the farmhouse to Kelly and her parents to stay in until their insurance got in touch with a hotel. We'd managed to fit all of us into Bea's car, aside from Eddy, who decided to take his Vespa moped.

"Not much of a mate then," Bill chuckles.

"No," Eddy snaps, glaring at me.

"Do you want a whisky Eddy?" I ask.

"Yes," he bites.

I grab the bottle and a tumbler, pouring him a glass and handing it to him. "Here you go mate."

He takes the glass and downs the whisky in one big gulp. "Another please." He slides the tumbler across the large wooden kitchen table.

I top him up again and watch as he downs that one too. "Eddy, take it easy now," I implore him.

"My head hurts," he moans.

"Shouldn't have been scrapping should you!" Apron Lady berates him.

"Mum, stay out of it. This has nothing to do with us," Kelly says, unbeknownst that the two are very much connected.

Bea chucks the TCP covered rag at me. "Dinner should be ready now."

"Thank you." Kelly smiles at Bea who does a half-forced smile back. Bea hadn't asked me anything about Kelly yet. I think the adrenaline is still pumping for all of us.

"I'll go get everything from the oven downstairs." Bea looks at me and points at the door. "Go see if you can find Michael," she orders.

"Perhaps he is messing with his cock in the barn," I giggle.

"Grow up!" Bea shouts at me. "There are ladies present," as she smiles down at Apron Lady.

I see the disgusted looks on Kelly and her family's faces and decide it's probably best to go out and look for Michael.

I close the farmhouse door and light a cigarette. It's frosty tonight and I can feel my singed skin tightening on my face where I had got too close to the fire. I walk towards the barn to give Michael a shout. He probably will be concerned about the fire. Perhaps I should have told him as soon as we got back but he can be hard to find as, just like a cat, he goes off on his own sometimes.

The barn is empty apart from the chickens, the cock and Michael's tent pitched up in the hay storage area now. He's not here.

"Michael!" I shout, just to make sure, but get no reply.

I abandon the barn and decide to check the engine room. "Michael," I shout, approaching the small outbuilding, "you in there?"

"Over here," I hear him shout back.

I turn and see him closing the gate at the top of the front field. "Where have you been?" I shout to him.

"For a walk," he shouts back. Odd time for a walk.

I take a drag of my cigarette and wait for him to get to me. He might be a bit shocked by what I tell him.

"You're out late," I comment.

"Just stretching the legs. Got bored with you and Bea gone," he stutters.

"Listen mate," I take a long drag, "Kelly, Beryl and Bill from the shop are inside. There was a fire."

"A fire?" he says with surprise.

"Yeah, at the shop. It's completely burnt it to the ground."

"Bloody hell," he shakes his head, "are they okay?"

"Yeah they are fine. They are in the farmhouse, about to have dinner with us."

Michael starts walking. "I better go see them."

I follow him back towards the light of the farmhouse, the smell from Bea's Moussaka now drifting out of the opened door. I see Michael hug Kelly and then shake hands with Bill and another hug for Apron Lady. He hasn't noticed the other guest, Eddy, yet but he's probably too concerned to notice anyone else right now.

"That's Eddy, by the way, Michael. My best friend." I point to Eddy as I close the farmhouse door.

"Hi mate," Michael smiles as Eddy waves back.

"Been scrapping?" Michael asks him.

"Sort of," Eddy replies, a little less bitter than earlier.

"Here we are," Bea announces as she brings the huge dish of moussaka up the old stone staircase with her.

"Smells amazing" Kelly says as Bea places it in the middle of the table.

"I'll dish up." Bea sticks a huge spoon into the steaming hot moussaka and dollops a healthy portion onto the plates in front of her.

"Grab a plate," she nudges, as she continues to keep scooping, "have some of the garlic baguettes too."

I look at Bea and smile. She has one of those 1950's style hair ties in her jet-black hair, her blonde streak just flicking down her face as she serves up. I've not seen this side of her and it's quite nice.

"Sorry love," Apron lady pushes her moussaka forward, "I can't eat this."

"What's wrong with it?" Bea asks.

Apron lady screws her face up. "It's not right, this Shepherd's Pie. It tastes funny. I think it's gone off."

Bea smiles at her, "It's a fucking moussaka!"

80

It's deathly quiet in the kitchen now. Everyone has gone to bed and it's just me and Eddy passing a bottle of whisky between ourselves.

Michael has gone to the barn. Kelly and her parents have taken the upstairs room. Bea is settled in her usual room next to the storage room and me and Eddy are still undecided. The silence isn't helping with that or any other decision.

"Didn't tell them a thing about the fire then? How you knew they were in trouble?" Eddy asks me.

"No," I sigh, "and keep your voice down."

Eddy sips his whisky. "You need to figure out how to pay Patrick before this gets even more out of control."

"I will. I get paid tomorrow, so I'll pay him," I snap.

"The full two grand?" Eddy checks.

"How is it two grand?" I sigh, "He sold me stuff that was worth five hundred!"

"If you had turned up with the five hundred Tuesday at ten as planned, it would have been," Eddy takes a sip, "but you didn't and he thinks you are trying to pull a fast one on him."

"But I'm not."

Eddy sighs. "Well, he's charging you fifteen hundred for making him think that."

"I'll go and get the money tomorrow morning from the bank and then if you give me his number I'll message him." I breathe out deeply. "And just don't mention any of this to Kelly."

Eddy pretends to pull a zip over his mouth and then re-open to sip his whisky.

"Eddy, I'm sorry I didn't mean for any of this to happen."

Eddy looks at me and nods.

I bite my lip. "I just lost track of my money and took a risk that wasn't worth it, but I thought it would be helpful for my prepping," I argue.

"What exactly do you think is going to happen?" Eddy says, sliding me the whisky bottle.

"I'll just pay him and that's the end."

"Not with Patrick, with this Y2K thing. What do you think is actually going to happen on New Year's Eve? One day from now," Eddy snaps.

I sit up defensively. "I don't think the world will have done enough," I reply, "there is too much going on out there to be sure we have caught it all."

"You're wrong then," Eddy scoffs, sipping his whisky.

"How the fuck is that then?" I challenge.

Eddy chuckles. "There were never any plans to fix everything, Ray," he shakes his head, "it was all about identifying what is wrong and fixing it, so there is

341

an element of prioritisation to that."

What do you mean prioritisation?"

"There was never any plan or possibility of fixing everything."

"Well were fucked then," I scoff.

Eddy sits back. "Some old dear is going to have a computer somewhere that she has never used and it's going to be running some ancient software older than us and undoubtedly something will not work on it come 1st January."

"But if that computer is in a power plant or an air traffic control centre?" I argue.

"Then it's already been fixed," Eddy sips his whisky, "it would have been prioritised."

"How can you be so sure? There might be one computer out there that fires off the wrong programme at the wrong time," I argue.

Eddy smiles. "I have re-written so much software these last four years in my spare time, along with all the other programmers and developers out there, so much money has been spent that it's pretty certain that all the high priority computers' hardware and software will have been fixed or will be closely monitored until it's safe."

"What about our computers at the council? The guy who came to our office told us they weren't ready, and we need to buy the software."

"That's because he's selling software, Ray," Eddy groans.

I sit back. "Better safe than sorry."

Eddy leans in. "I would bet my house that nothing on that disc you buy will have anything to do with changing a two-digit year to four, or making it so years are added as 365 days instead of +1. At best, it will identify something that needs changing or won't work but most likely it's a blank disk with a run programme."

I lean in to meet him. "Well at least I was trying to get it right. Look at Russia and Italy! They are hardly doing anything. What about their systems? A nuclear plant blowing up there would fuck us all up, look at Chernobyl!"

"They are aware though," Eddy argues. "They just aren't spending the same as the US and the UK, there is a difference. They have identified what is required and fixed it where it matters, not just a blanket approach which is why they haven't spent billions like the US, hundreds of millions like the UK and five hundred pounds that you spent which you should have given to Patrick!"

"Well, I can't help that now and I still think it's better to be prepared and safe up here than in the middle of a town if it all kicks off."

"But it won't kick off. We have known about the Y2K problem for years." Eddy grabs my pack of cigarettes." It's the legacy software that's the problem; companies running software and have no clue how it works, don't have process maps or records of anything, That has been the challenge, that is Y2K and in the high-risk industries that has been fixed."

"Like I said," I light my own cigarette, "if it's not, I'd rather be prepared when everything kicks off."

Eddy lights a cigarette. "You know something Ray, if it does kick off it will probably be more of a problem next year."

"Well yeah, Saturday 1st January."

Eddy smirks and shakes his head. "No, 2001. See, where programmers have been adding years as +1, which was used for two-digit years, then 00 is actually a year that can be used as it's never happened. Whereas 01 …… that has happened."

"I don't get you. You're just being a dickhead now. I've said sorry, do you want me to kiss it better or what?"

Eddy shakes his head. "Just listen. Year 00 hasn't happened so it's likely the computers or programmes will just run as normal, year 01 however, that has happened so the computer or programme will think it's run whatever it is supposed to; year 01 is in the past whereas year 00 hasn't happened, so for a computer it could be in the future, so it would run what it needed to."

"Even more of a reason to prepare then," I tell him.

"So, I'll ask you again; what do you think is going to happen on New Year's Eve?"

I top up my whisky and take a sip. "I think that there will be issues with some computers. We will hear of it gradually throughout New Year's Eve as the celebrations pan from east to west across the datelines. Then, when it hits Russia, or Italy or somewhere big, something will break that causes chaos and life will never be the same again. The end of the world as we know it."

"You were correct until you got to Russia."

I shrug my shoulders. "Just leave me to it then, Eddy, go home and don't bother about it all."

Eddy rubs his sore head. "Look. I'll help and support you through this, but I can't sit back and watch you go headfirst into things and getting people hurt in the process."

"I'm not trying to hurt people, Eddy. I can't

control the kneejerk violent reactions that some people seem to have. I didn't start that fire and I didn't attack Clive."

Eddy sighs. "But it's your actions that are getting people hurt."

"I'll be more careful; it's nearly over now anyway," I stress.

Eddy laughs "What is? The world? Because I think you're wrong." Eddy sits back and glares at me. "Think about if it doesn't end."

"All I need from you, Eddy, is to be here when it ends and not question me. I know what I'm doing," I snap.

"I can't though!" Eddy shakes his head. "I can't let you say things are a certain way when in reality they are not. It's my job. I know about this stuff."

"Don't be a dickhead Eddy," I sigh.

"I'm not being a dickhead. I'm just trying to make you realise that this may not be worth putting people in harm's way."

"Harm's way? I'm trying to help people Eddy!" I argue. "I want you here with me on this."

"I will be." Eddy nods and downs his whisky. "Just be careful though. There is no guarantee that what you think will happen is what is going to happen. That is what I'm trying to show you here."

"I get that, Eddy, but regardless of if the world end or not, I'm not going back to how things were."

Eddy stubs out his cigarette. "I'm off to bed." He stands up and heads for the stone staircase. "Don't do anything stupid again. Don't do anything because you don't think there will be consequences, because there very well could be."

345

81

"Who is she?" Bea asks, with her nose still in her book.

"It's the girl I went on the date with last week," I tell her.

"She seems simple," Bea sighs.

"She's nice, don't be nasty," I tell her.

"Simple in like a basic kind of way, I didn't mean to be nasty," Bea says softly, "just doesn't seem your type, that's all."

"How so?" I ask, turning on my side in my cot bed to face her.

"Just seems simple. Just likes the normal stuff in life. Celebrates the ordinary, which isn't like you." Bea turns to face me. "Just doesn't seem your type, or bunker material."

I look at Bea, tucked up in her bed. I had decided to take my usual spot in her room rather than share a room with Eddy and potentially have another row.

"I don't think she is here by choice," I reply.

"That girl, Annabel, she is definitely your type, but I can't see it in Kelly. Just seems like a younger version of your wife."

I chuckle. "She is nothing like Debbie, plus Debbie was a wild child before we settled down."

Bea sighs. "Well Kelly just seems like the kind of person who would be happy living in that shop, having kids, taking pictures at Christmas, everyone in the same position with the same false smile year after year."

"She just wants a nice life. Something I've gone and ruined for her."

Bea shifts back to lying on her back and goes back to her book. I stare at the ceiling, thoughts racing through my head: Eddy, the fire, Flat Cap and the betting slip.

I'd need to go and get the money to pay Flat Cap as soon as the bank opened in the morning. I'd get the betting slip back off him and post it through the letterbox of the Dog & Gun for the one-eyed bastard landlord; then I should have finally paid off my bounty.

"What was your mum's name?" Bea asks me.

"Diana," I tell her.

"When did she die?"

"1997," I sigh "two years ago, just after Princess Diana, so, all I heard for months was 'Diana' and 'Dead' in the same sentence."

"Your dad is alive though?" Bea pries.

"No idea." I chuckle briefly, thinking to myself it was probably something I'd never even thought about.

"How much of your book do you have left?" I ask, changing the subject.

"I'm on the last few pages, but it's getting weird," Bea says with a frown.

"How so?" I ask.

Bea looks concerned and comes to sit next to

me.

"Bea what's up?" I laugh.

"It's just gone weird," she says quietly.

"How so?" I ask.

"Because I think it's about you."

82

The book isn't that big, around 150 pages typed and bound in a leather cover. There isn't a title or an author on the front or the spine, but when I open it, the first page has two words printed in the centre:'The Garden'.

"Where did you get this?" I ask Bea.

She rests her head on my shoulder. "It was on the floor in the kitchen, the upstairs one."

"I don't remember seeing this before," I tell her.

"It was on the floor to the left of the door. I found it the day I came back from my Auntie's," Bea says.

"What makes you think it's about me?" I ask.

She sighs. "Well, it starts off all boring, just this guy talking about his garden. Then he starts talking about a pregnant woman, Diana, who gives birth on a farm to a boy."

"That could be anyone Bea. It's a farm and Diana is a common name," I argue.

"Yeah. But then the boy is raised by

grandparents and she can't see him and all the people in this garden want to steal him and bring him up there to join them, but Diana won't let them."

"I don't think anyone tried to steal me, Bea," I interrupt.

"Listen!" Bea punches my leg. "Then this garden cuts itself off from the farm and won't let anyone from the farm in. It gets quite religious then, until this last chapter."

"Which is where I show up?" I ask.

"No!" Bea groans, "just listen."

"Hold on," I interrupt, "did you say this place was called The Garden?" I ask, remembering words from my mother.

"Yes. The Garden," Bea stresses.

"My mother used to tell me she was taking me there. It's another building around here, I think. What else does the book say?" I ask with urgency.

"Now you want to know." Bea rolls her eyes. "It talks about Diana dying and the farm passing to the boy. Everyone is excited that the boy, who they have just revealed is called 'Rain', will return. Look, it says there," she points to the bottom of the page, "'now it is certain the boy, Rain, will return". I thought it was just a gardening thing throughout until I saw it then." Bea stops. "That's where I'm at now. There's, like, one paragraph left."

I stare at the page and try to process what Bea has told me. "Fuck!" is all I can manage. "Why didn't you finish it?"

"Because you're always interrupting me when I'm reading!" Bea groans.

"Look, it sounds fucking creepily similar, I grant you that," I say, exhaling a deep breath.

Bea looks at me with half excitement and half uncertainty. "Do you want me to read you the end?"

"Yeah, I do."

Bea puts her head down and reads. "' Now it is certain the boy, Rain, will return. It's been nigh on three decades since he last stepped foot on this sacred soil, and much will have changed but the story and purpose remain the same. While my bones have weakened, his will have grown stronger. Our message is 'plant a seed and it shall grow'. This is to be the greatest of trees that we witness arrive out of nowhere to extend its branch to The Garden once more.'"

"That's some weird shit," I tell Bea. "You read a whole book of this crap?"

"Yup. Good ending though," she winks at me.

"Why did someone at the commune write a book about me?" I shake my head.

"Whoever did left you a note too." Bea shows me the back page of the book.

I take the leather book from her and look at the blank back page. In handwritten ink there is a message:

'I've been waiting for you Rain, meet me in the Garden'

and it's signed

'Teacher'

83

I couldn't sleep. The adrenaline from the fire had been dampened by the whisky and my argument with Eddy, but seeing that book and knowing that someone from the commune was nearby and 'waiting' for me just made me pace around the bunker, much to the annoyance of a tired Bea. I'd thrown on my parka and boots and left the farmhouse in the direction of the barn.

It's freezing tonight and the frosty ground is crunching under my feet. The barn is close now and I can see a light coming from inside. I reach the heavy doors and pull one open. I can see a light by Michael's tent. "Michael?" I shout.

"What's going on?" Michael shouts back. "What's wrong?"

"Nothing, I just need to ask you something," I shout back as he emerges from his tent and onto the wooden ladder.

"It's a bit early isn't it?" he chuckles, landing on

352

his feet.

"Sorry, I just had to ask I can't sleep," I mutter.

"Well go on then spit it out lad," he presses.

"That fella, the one who has been hanging out by the fence at the top of the front field, where is he from?"

"What do you mean?" Michael says.

"You said he was from 'further up the moors' and to 'steer clear'. Why would you say that? And what is further up from here?"

Michael sighs and kicks some of the ground beneath him. "He's from a place called 'The Garden', a commune a bit like this used to be. It's a couple of miles away from here."

The Garden, like my mum told me and from the book.

"There are people still living up there like they used to do here, all cut off from society. Difference being they don't ever interact," he pauses "well apart from one, the guy that was hanging around here."

"Can you show me where it is?" I ask.

Michael dismisses me. "You don't want to go up there."

"I need to go up there," I say sternly.

"Listen lad, I'm telling you it's not worth it!" he starts to shout.

I pace around and grab the book from my pocket. "Bea found this book. It mentions me, my mother and The Garden. I need to find out who wrote this and why."

Michael grabs the book and tosses it behind me. "They are messing with your head lad! That's what they do!"

I bite my tongue and consider my response. "I

need to find out," I tell him turning to pick up the book.

"My daughter, Jane, went up there," Michael shouts behind me. "She was seventeen and never came back. Police gave up when she turned eighteen, said she was an adult and could make her own choices. That man you saw found her and took her up there and I've only seen her through the fence since."

I take a deep breath and pick up the book. "I'm sorry about that Michael."

"I've been up twice since we got here, once tonight after you left for the shopping. I wanted to see her, and I finally did, through the barbed wire fence."

I show the book to Michael. "I need to know how they know all this shit about me and my mother." I put my hand on his shoulder. "Please, can you just show me where it is?"

Michael nods and walks towards his boots. "It's two miles north of here."

"I'll get the Land Rover ready," I tell him.

He shakes his head. "No, if we turn up in that they will spot us straight away. Best to sneak up and see what we can see first. It's quite a walk though. If you think this place is off-grid wait until you see The Garden".

84

The morning light is creeping across the moors and illuminating the structure ahead of us although it won't be long until daylight will fully brighten the sky for the day ahead.

From our vantage point in the tall grass above the site, I can see a tower shooting out of the middle of the complex like a blooming rose. The former Air Traffic Control tower, according to Michael.

Around the tower are smaller concrete buildings and what look like metal hangars or shelters. The whole site is fenced in by ten feet of steel fencing topped with barbed wire. A small cottage at the front being the only break in the chains.

"They obviously don't want anyone getting in here," I say to Michael.

"Or out," he spits.

"How the hell did they build all this?" I ask.

"They didn't. It's a former RAF and USAF Air Force station, de-commissioned around 1970. They bought it for a song, and nobody has bothered them since."

"What's that cottage doing there?" I point to what looks like the entrance.

"That's the gatekeeper's cottage, was here way before all this. They built around it in the 20's probably."

"I'll meet you back here. I'm going over to it to try and get in."

"Alright," Michael says, "just be careful."

I start to stand and move as Michael grabs my arm. "If they don't want you to leave then you won't be leaving."

I toss him my phone. "Just in case you need to call the police or something."

Michael nods and lowers himself back into the tall grass.

I walk at a normal pace along the frosty grass. My front is damp now from lying down and my hands are starting to get solid with cold but I'm more focused on getting to the entrance of 'The Garden'.

I am starting to see a bit more of what is around me as it is around 8am now and the sun is starting to rise. I spot a cracked and overgrown road running perpendicular to the cottage. It seems to stop halfway across the moor and probably used to connect this place to the rest of the world.

I am close to the cottage now and can hear a radio playing. It sounds like classical music of some sort, but I can't quite make it out. I decide to stay hidden as best as I can and move closer to the cottage wall. I can hear the music clearer and it sounds like Mozart's Requiem.

I move to the side of the cottage and peer into

the side window. There is a man sat in a chair with his back to me, reading a book. I move back around the front of the cottage as close to the wall as I can get and hear the click of the radio turning off.

The front door is two metres to my left, so I edge over and give it two big knocks with the iron doorknocker. I move back to my position against the side of the cottage and wait to see who comes out.

The door opens with a creak, but nobody exits the cottage. I slowly edge towards the door and peek inside. The man has gone. There is nobody in here.

Edging inside, I can see the whole room now. The cottage is just this one huge room with a window either side and on the front. There is a metal door at the back that looks heavily secure but right now it's slightly open. Whoever left here has made sure I can follow.

I push the heavy door and it opens onto the main compound. I can see the buildings in more detail now, one either side of the massive tower and the metal shelters dotted around the site. There are flower beds and vegetable patches in-between all the structures, ponds and pens for animals too.

I walk through the heavy door and look to my right and see a man sitting on a bench, the same man that has been stood at the top of the field by my front gate; the same coat I remember seeing in a drunken haze during my bender and he's holding the same leather book as I have in my pocket.

He looks at me through his tinted aviator glasses and smiles. "I've been waiting for you, Rain."

85

I stand in silence staring at the man. He is wearing the massive fur coat I remember seeing through the window, along with the tinted aviators, but also a plain grubby vest and khaki pants. He is still smiling at me and twirling a daisy between his thumb and forefinger.

"Did you bring your book?" he asks with a deep Irish accent, dipping his glasses.

"Who are you?" I ask curtly.

"I'm glad to see you, Rain. Let's take a walk through the garden." He stands and smiles.

"I'm not taking a fucking walk with you. Tell me who you are!" I snap.

The man laughs and tosses the daisy to the floor. "If you read the book you should know that, Rain."

"Tell me who you are or I'm leaving now," I stress.

"Here, I am known as 'The Teacher'."

"What the fuck does that mean?" I snap. "Why

have you been watching me? What is this fucking book and what do you want?"

"See, I'm 'The Teacher'." he smiles, "I have the answers you are looking for."

"Answer my questions then," I fire back.

The man looks up to the sky and exhales. "I've been waiting for this moment for a long time."

"I'm going," I snap.

"Okay, okay." He walks towards me. "I have been to see you. I wanted to know if you recognised me."

"Why would I recognise you?" I ask, and he takes off his glasses. It's the man from the pictures with my mother.

"Because I'm your father."

86

"You probably have a lot of questions, but most of the answers can be found in that book," the man says in a thick Irish accent, as I stand in silence.

"You're my father?" I ask him, double checking I heard correctly.

"Yes!" He grabs my shoulders. "I am your father, and I haven't seen you in twenty-six years."

I still can't find any words. I'm rooted to the spot and face to face with the man that has been a huge question mark in my mind since I can remember. I have thousands of questions I need to ask him, but I can't even speak right now.

"Rain, I've been waiting for you and you're finally here!" he shouts.

I take a cigarette out of my pocket, my hands shaking, and just about manage to light it. I close my eyes as I take the first drag and when I open them, he is still in front of me.

"This is just the start son! We have so much to

talk about!"

I take a drag of my cigarette and breathe out slowly before punching him as hard as I can in the face.

He doesn't fall over, just barely flinches and clicks his jaw. He laughs and holds his hands up. "I know you are probably very confused and angry." He looks at me "I'll allow you that."

I drag on my cigarette and shake my sore hand. I'm shaking inside and check my hands to make sure I'm not visibly shaking too much. I am though.

"Let's go walk through the garden and I can show you everything here," he smiles at me walking back toward me. "Rain, come with me, I have been waiting for you to come here."

I move backwards. "Get away from me."

"I am your father, Rain. We can be together now."

I shake my head. "I'm leaving."

"You just got here!" he growls.

"You have had twenty-seven years to talk to me,it's too late now," I snap.

"I wanted to, Rain, I really did," he tells me. "I was kept away by your mother, and then her parents, and then by society. We can't leave up here! The world is different down there now. There is no place for people like us."

"So, you just sat here writing a book and hoping I would turn up?"

"I knew once Diana died and you inherited the farm, you would turn up on these moors. I have walked past the old farmhouse every day since I heard she passed away, wanting to give you this book."

"Why not just talk to me? Why write a fucking book?" I bark.

"I wanted you to know about me, about this place before I spoke to you. I was hoping you would understand, and the book tells you what you need to know! It's not just for you, everyone here has read it and they are excited to have you back," he smiles.

I scoff, "It was a stupid fucking idea."

"You showed up, didn't you?" he raises his eyebrows.

"Mainly because I wanted to know why the fuck some creepy ex-commune member was stalking me and writing about my life!" I shout.

He shakes his head. "I wrote that book so you would know us when you read it, and everyone here would know you when you arrived." He puts his hands on my shoulders and smiles at me; "You're home now, Rain."

I back away.

"I'm not staying here," I laugh.

"This is your home, Rain, you should have been here all your life! But you can be here now with me and everyone else," he stresses.

"I'm going back to the farmhouse. That's my home," I say curtly.

"Fine!" he smiles, "we can connect the two like it used to be. You run the farm and I'll look after the garden."

I laugh and look at him dead in the eyes. "I'm not having anything to do with whatever this is." I gesture around. "Where is everyone?" I point at the buildings. "Where are the people you keep up here and won't let go? Where is Jane? She hasn't left for years."

He looks at me with a serious glare. "I told you, son, we can't leave here. Society has changed."

"No!" I shout. "They can't leave here because

you won't let them."

"I won't let them?" he shouts "*They* don't want to!" he plays with a rosary that lays around his neck "I have saved the people here, saved them from all the shit you have run away from and they know I won't let them come to harm"

I look at him and think of the farmhouse, the bunker. Am I doing the same thing?

"All this is wrong!" I shout. "You are hurting these people, not saving them!"

"And what about you, Rain?" he purses his lips, "Are you hurting the people with you? Or saving them?"

I toss my cigarette on the floor.

"Do not disrespect the garden, son." He picks the cigarette but up and crushes it in his hands.

"See, stuff like that. It's just weird!" I shake my head.

"I had hoped this would be different." He turns away from me.

I laugh, "Me too! I'd always imagined you turning up and we'd go for a beer. You would take me to watch the cricket or something and we would talk about how you and my mother met, and why you were never around and then we would hug and exchange numbers." I open my arms. "All this? Didn't even cross my mind to be honest!"

He turns back around. "Your mother and I had a brief but loving connection. There were no couples or marriages or any of that capitalist society driven bullshit when we met, we had turned on, tuned in and dropped out. You were supposed to be here with the other children, but she never brought you. When she came to live with us she left you, and that was her choice not mine."

I stare back at him. "Maybe she made the right choice."

"We are not that different son. I built that bunker that you are living in with my own hands. I've seen what you have done to it. I've seen your list. It's just like how we started up here," he smiles.

"You broke into my home?" I shout.

He sighs. "It was my home long before you were even born son. I wanted to see what you were doing there and, if anything, it gave me more hope that you were finally coming home," he says calmly. "That book is about you, Rain. It tells you who you really are."

I don't know if I'm angry or scared. I take the book out of my pocket and toss it on the floor. He looks down at the book and shakes his head, looking up at me with sadness and anger in his eyes.

"This book isn't about me, it's about you," I say, turning away.

"It's coming, Rain," I hear him shout behind me, "You have seen it yourself! the end of the world! no more authority controlling our lives. Once again, we will truly think for ourselves and be free! And I'll be here waiting for it! But you walk out and I am done waiting for you!"

I turn to face him again.

"Goodbye Dad."

87

The hike back to the farmhouse had mostly been in silence. I'd told Michael that I hadn't seen Jane. I'd never be going back to that place, but I was glad I had gone. I hadn't mentioned anything about the strange man who refers to himself as 'The Teacher' being my father.

I'd hopped straight into the Land Rover on my return to the farmhouse, messaging Flat Cap with a new meeting time and place before going into the town to empty my account of my final wages and redundancy payment.

I'd called into Millets outdoors shop to pick up a last few essentials, and ended up spending nearly three hundred quid whilst I waited down the clock for the meeting. Apart from the cash for Flat Cap, I'm going to stash the rest.

I check my watch. It's one o'clock and Flat Cap should be here soon. I'm sat on my own in an old train carriage opposite the Eureka children's museum. I didn't want anyone coming with me. Following the words from Eddy and then hearing my father's word's echoing through things I had said and done in the past few weeks, I am done with dragging people along with me and putting them in harm's way.

My phone beeps and I look down at it on the table in front of me. It's from Eddy.

Goin bk 2 mine 4 some stuff, see you 2morro

I look out of the window to my left and I can see three bulky men in leather jackets. This should be them. I'd picked this spot as the carriages made it secluded but there were enough people around that Flat Cap wouldn't try anything in such a busy open place.

Broken Nose is the first to enter the carriage, followed by Flat Cap and then Ponytail. Flat Cap takes a seat opposite me with only a table separating us. Broken Nose stands behind him in the aisle with Ponytail taking his spot behind me. I'm trapped here now.

I start to feel my heart beating faster. Sweat is forming on my brow and in my palms and the all-familiar pins and needles have arrived in my arms and legs.

"Let's get down to this shall we?" Flat Cap says.

I go to speak but can't get the words out. I suddenly am very aware of feeling trapped and claustrophobic in this carriage. I try to push the window open at the top for some air, but my hands are shaking.

"Are you on drugs or something lad?" Flat Cap looks at me.

I try to get the words out, but I can't and start breathing heavily

"He's having a panic attack," Broken Nose says, folding his arms as Flat Cap just looks at me.

"It's basically the body's reaction to a dangerous situation," Broken Nose tells Flat Cap. "It's adrenaline that's causing this, based on the mind's natural reactions to a fight or flight situation," Broken Nose adds.

"What do we do?" Flat Cap asks.

"You open the window. We will move back a bit, give him some space," Broken Nose directs.

We all sit and stand in silence. I look up at Broken Nose and I start to feel like it's fading now. I notice I'm breathing more deeply now; the pins and needles have gone and I wipe the sweat from my forehead.

"I'm okay," I mutter. I'd never heard it called a panic attack.

"Sorry. I haven't slept," I apologise.

"That won't help," Broken Nose tells me, "lack of sleep can have severe impacts on your mental health."

"If he's alright, can we carry on?" Flat Cap interrupts and then looks at me. "Go on then."

I reach into my pocket and pull out a wad of cash. "Two grand," I tell Flat Cap as I put it on the small table and push it towards him.

Flat Cap picks it up and thumbs through the crisp twenty-pound notes.

"There are a hundred twenties; count them if you want," I tell him.

Flat Cap chucks the wad to Ponytail who I hear snap off the elastic band to start counting.

"Would have been a lot cheaper for you a few days ago," Flat Cap smiles.

"That shop you burnt down," I take a deep breath, "That wasn't mine."

Flat Cap laughs. "What are you talking about?"

"You burnt someone's shop down, thinking it was mine and it wasn't," I say sternly.

"How do you know we burnt anything down?" Flat Cap dismisses with a grin.

"Well, that shop belonged to a nice hard-working family who are now homeless. I just wanted you to know that," I tell Flat Cap. "Are we square now?"

Flat Cap looks at Ponytail who seems to give a signal. "Yeah, we are done," Flat Cap smiles standing up.

"Can I have the betting slip back?" I ask him.

"What do you want that back for?" Flat Cap laughs.

"It's not mine," I reply, "I need to give it back to someone."

Flat Cap shakes his head and draws the slip out of his bulging leather wallet. "Here!" he slams it on the table. "Perhaps that family would still have a nice little home with a shop underneath if you hadn't gone stealing dodgy betting slips." He smiles, "I just wanted you to know that."

88

I shove a tenner, a pack of Embassy cigarettes and the betting slip back into the pocket of the stolen parka. I look at the dilapidated sign of 'Do un' above and remember that first night when I had come in here, hoping for some shelter, and ended up on the path that has led me back here.

I push open the heavy door and immediately get enveloped by the stale cigar and cigarette smoke. I spot the ruddy faced man adorned with gold chains and the skinny man in the oversized coat shouting to himself in the corner.

"Is the Landlord in?" I shout at the young girl cleaning the bar.

"No," the young girl snaps. "Do you want a drink?"

"When's the Landlord due back?" I ask.

"It's Landlady." She points to her bulging chest.

I look around and make sure I am in the right pub. I definitely am, as there is a patch of unstained wall

369

where the cricket bat had been protecting the wall from the stain of the clouds of cigarette smoke.

"Does a big burly fella with a lion tattoo on his arm work here? May be wearing an eye patch?" I ask.

"He's gone," she says curtly as she wipes down the brass on the pumps.

I scratch my head. "Do you know where I can find him?"

"No idea," she snaps. "I haven't seen him since I kicked him out."

"He's your husband then?" I ask, hoping to leave this stuff with her.

"No. He was my boyfriend," she stops cleaning the bar and looks at me, "but he was treating this place like his own social club. It's a bloody mess and he was walking around calling himself the landlord when it's my family pub. Assaulting customers, stealing from drunks, and my till."

"I've got his coat here," I point to the parka under my arm, "can I leave it on the coat stand?"

"No. I don't want any excuse for him coming back in here. As far as I'm concerned, he's barred and you can tell him that when you see him."

"Okay, no problem, any idea where he will be?"

"No. Probably a pub somewhere acting like he owns the place," she snaps.

"That's very helpful," I tell her.

"You're the fella from the other night!" The ruddy faced man at the bar shouts. "I knew I recognised you."

"What fella?" the landlady asks.

"The one that clocked your fella with the Cricket bat," he stirs.

"That was you?" she snaps.

"Yeah," I say with some hesitation, "sorry about all that."

She looks me up and down. "Well do you want a drink or not then? Cos if you do it's on the house."

89

I can't see any lights shining from the farmhouse or the barn as I close the gate behind myself and the Land Rover. I can't see Bea's Nissan Sunny either, but she is still parking it round the other side of the barn as the birds are still shitting all over it. Either everyone is downstairs, or they are still out. I hadn't expected them to be out all day but then again, I didn't expect to be out all day either.

I get back in the Land Rover and park it up in front of the farmhouse.

"Bea? Michael? Kelly?" I shout as I open the new front door. "Hello?" No reply, but the light is on in the bunker. I spot a piece of paper on the kitchen table.

Thanks for everything, hope your meeting in town with the bank went okay, Bea is taking us to the hotel. Kelly X

I smile and grab my glass from last night, pouring myself a large measure of whisky. I pull a cigarette out of the pack and light it, pulling out my phone from my pocket to send Bea a text.

wen u bk?

I take a drag of my cigarette and hear a phone beep. Bea must have left her phone here. I shake my head and grab the bottle of whisky before starting to descend the stone staircase. After today I need to have a chill out in one of the comfy armchairs.

I get to the bottom of the stairs and suddenly I see Bea covered in blood and slumped against the back door of the basement. Her hands are above her head and tied to the long vertical door handle.

"Fuck!" I gasp, "Bea!" I shout, dropping the whisky and the cigarette as I move towards her. I get to her and start to untie her hands from the door handle as I feel a thud across the back of my head.

I wince as I roll to my side and can feel the blood trickling down my face from a gash on my head somewhere. My vision is blurry, and I can see little white dots flashing though the haze as I try to open my eyes. I can see legs in front of me, slowly walking towards me and I blink trying to regain my vision. Through the cloudy haze, a hand grabs my collar and yanks me upwards.

"Hello mate," the one-eyed bastard former landlord greets me. "Found you in the end."

90

"Your stuff is upstairs, just leave us alone" I mutter.

"That's not going to cut it anymore," the one-eyed bastard chuckles.

I touch the back of my head and feel the damp warm blood on my palm. I look at it dripping down my wrist and reach for the handle to pull myself up to a seated position against the hydroponics room door.

"You had this coming. How does it feel?" he sneers.

"Painful," I mutter.

He draws back the cricket bat in his hand and hits me again on the knee. I scream as the pain shoots down to the tips of my toes and burns my thigh.

"The amount of shit you have caused me!" he shouts. "My money!" He kicks my side. "My Mrs!" He kicks me harder, "and my fucking eye." He boots me in the face.

I slide down onto my side again. I can taste blood in my mouth now and spit it across the floor. A bit hits his white trainers.

"And now my shoes!" he sighs and stamps on my hand as I groan with agony.

"What do you want?" I ask him as I pull myself up into a seated position.

"I'm going to do to you what you did to me. I'm going to keep hitting you with this bat until you lose sight in one of your eyes, then I'm taking your girlfriend away," he points at Bea, "and I'm taking my two grand somehow."

"You never had two grand," I tell him as I stand up, pain shooting through my body. "Well, the tenner in the pocket, but the betting slip was a dud."

He frowns at me. "What?"

"I've still got it. It's upstairs. I tried to cash it in, and tried to give it back to you but neither worked," I chuckle as blood drops onto the floor.

"Bollocks!" he shouts.

"I was with your ex an hour ago. I was trying to give it back. She told me she'd kicked you out and you'd been nicking off customers," I smile.

"Where is it then?" he asks. "Show me."

"Your coat is on the table upstairs. Everything is in the left-hand pocket."

"Show me," he grunts.

I hobble towards him and start ascending the stone staircase as he shoves me from behind. "Quicker," he demands as I hobble as fast as I can, clearing the final step and pointing to the parka on the table.

"Look," I gesture as he takes his big ham hock hands and starts to fumble around the pocket, pulling out the pack of cigarettes, the tenner and the betting slip.

"Look on the bottom of the slip," I tell him,

"there are no times and dates printed. It never went through the machine.

The one-eyed bastard looks devastated. He also looks angry so I am not sure if I will also be a one-eyed bastard very soon. He scrunches up the slip and drops it on the floor, shaking his head.

"You have no idea how dead you are," he snarls at me and then turns to the stone staircase next to him. "Oh and look here, your girlfriend has come up to watch," he grins as Bea reaches the top of the stone staircase.

He stares at me picks up the cricket bat and smiles, "This will be fun."

His smile disappears as a loud bang resonates in the kitchen. I look over at Bea who has a rifle in her hand and then back at the one-eyed bastard who has jumped across the table and is on the stone floor.

"Merry Christmas ya filthy animal!" Bea shouts.

"Fucking hell!" I gasp, as Bea cocks the rifle again.

"What the fuck!" the one-eyed bastard yells from behind one of the chairs. Bea kneels down and meets his glance under the table.

"Hello," she waves.

"Put the gun down, love," the one-eyed bastard pleads.

"This?" Bea points the gun at him, making him squirm and kick at a nonexistent object whilst trying and pull another chair in for cover.

"Yes, put it down for fucks sake," he yells.

"Nah, I think I'll keep it," she smiles at him. "Ray, go and get something to tie this one-eyed bastard up with."

"Was that from Home Alone?" I manage to ask

Bea.

"Yes. It's an awesome film. We should watch it later," she smiles. "Now go and get some fucking rope or something."

91

Looking down on the one-eyed bastard struggling in the boot of Bea's Nissan Sunny was an odd sight; his good eye bulging out as he tried to say something, wriggling around like a toddler in a fit of rage.

"Since when have you had a gun?" I ask Bea.

"It's not mine, it's yours," she frowns.

"I don't own any guns!" I snap.

Bea sighs, "I got you one for your Christmas present. You never opened it."

"So, you left a loaded rifle in a box in the bunker?" I stress.

"It wasn't loaded! God, I do know something about guns," Bea sulks.

"Where did you get it?" I ask.

"It's one of my dad's. He has loads so he won't miss it."

I go to shout but notice the blood caked all over her face and neck. "Let's just leave it. Look at your face! Are you okay?" I ask, moving her now pinkish blonde streak out of her face.

"Me?" She points at herself, "I'm fine!"

"He's bust your nose pretty bad," I grimace.

"Oh no," she laughs "I did that when I head-butted him. Hit him so hard I must have knocked myself out. That's when the bastard tied me up."

"Well, he's dangerous, so we need to figure out what to do with him," I frown.

"Can't' we just drop him by the police station?" Bea asks.

"No, there are too many questions then and he will most likely end up back here with or without the police."

Bea bites her lip ring. "So, we just leave him in the boot?"

"Yea, for now," I look around, "nobody comes around this side of the barn and it's far enough away from the farmhouse."

"Where is the gun now? I whisper.

"In the car, in the back on the floor," she says.

I frown, "Right, well, give me the keys and let's just lock everything up here for now."

"Cool." Bea slams the boot shut, locking it with her keys and tossing them to me. "Don't think I have Home Alone on any of the tapes I brought," she sighs. "Fancy a game on the Mega Drive?"

92

Michael had come back from wherever he had been when I nearly got beaten to death with a cricket bat. I'd assumed that he had gone up to The Garden again to try and see his daughter but, knowing Michael, he could have just wandered for hours.

There had been a few questions about our faces but he seemed happy enough with the explanation that Bea had tried to teach me how to wrestle in the basement and we had both ended up hitting our heads on the new laminate flooring. More than happy to eat his dinner and go back to his tent in the barn.

Kelly had texted me to say that the hotel was very posh and having its own party so it would be unlikely that they would make it to mine. I'd decided that it was probably best that I stay out of their lives from now on.

I have finally got to relax in my comfy armchair, with a newly poured whisky and cigarette dangling from my mouth. Bea is button smashing her way through the final opponent on Street Fighter 2 and despite it being twenty-four hours until the end of the world, everyone is pretty calm.

I think it's time, so I pick up my checklist up from the table next to me. I look at Bea, totally relaxed after a crazy day, being knocked out, tied up, holding a man at gunpoint and stuffing him in the boot of her car. She looks so at peace, just smashing the shit out of Mabson.

Whoever else ends up here, Annabel, Eddy or even if it's just the three of us, I'm certain that we can survive anything. I grab the pen and tick off Belongingness.

I move down to Esteem and put a big tick next to that. I feel good about myself and despite the horrible stuff that has happened in the last fortnight, there isn't anything I would have changed.

"Fuck yeah!" Bea shouts as M.Bison falls to defeat and 'You Win' flashes on the screen.

"Well done Bea. Didn't even need a gun this time," I joke.

Bea scoffs, "That gun saved your ass."

"It did help but we still have to decide what to do with him," I tell her.

"Find a massive hole and drop the bastard in it," Bea smiles.

"That's murder Bea. Kidnapping is one thing, but I draw the line at murder."

"We could just drive him really, really, far away and let him go. My friend's dad did that with a cat once. When I found out I smashed up his car."

"He'd probably find his way back, Bea," I chuckle.

"Can we decide tomorrow?" she moans. "It's

late and my face hurts. Pass me that whisky."

Bea takes a swig, swills it and spits it down the nearby toilet. She's been using it to numb the pain in her front teeth.

"That's minging. I don't know how you drink that stuff," she says, screwing up her face.

"I need it after the day I have had," I say, taking a sip.

"Oh yeah. How did it go paying off the Yorkshire Mafia?" she laughs.

"Fine thanks. It's all sorted."

"You haven't told me anything about that other commune up the moors," she complains. "Michael had a right face on him all day after that."

"Just some oddball who used to live here," I tell her, unsure how much to divulge right now. "He wrote about me, but it was really about him. He won't be coming around here again."

"You have had a bad day," Bea pouts, "but chin up! It's the end of the world tomorrow."

93

For the last day of civilization as we know it everything seems pretty normal, if you forget about the man tied up with duct tape in the back of Bea's Nissan Sunny.

I'd sown the first of the seeds in the hydroponics planters set up in the bunker and Bea had started putting up some decorations she had bought for the party. Michael had emerged from the barn early on to let the chickens out, so had either been out 'til late last night or had slept through the fighting, gunshot and ensuing chaos.

It has been raining on and off and Michael had been hanging around the barn a lot, but I had made it across to Bea's Nissan twice to give the one-eyed bastard some water. He called me a 'cocksucker' the first time and then a 'dead motherfucker' the second. I had to ask him if he meant I was dead or if he was referencing my dead mother to which he looked confused, so I taped his mouth back up.

I'd just set up the two crank handle radios I'd picked up from Millets, one in the upstairs kitchen and one just now in the downstairs lounge, both tuned to BBC Radio 4 who are covering the celebrations throughout the day.

Annabel had texted me to let me know she was coming over after she had stopped in on Gordon's party. She asked if I wanted to pop in, but I had declined, not telling her that I'd probably rather spend an hour in the boot of Bea's Nissan with my new mate.

Eddy was due at some point in the evening but hadn't confirmed who he was bringing yet. He had asked for a plus two but considering I was already worried about his plus one I told him I didn't have enough space, which would be true if Kelly was coming but since her text yesterday it seemed like she was going to enjoy a classy night at the hotel.

"Come have a look at this," Bea shouts from the top of the stone staircase.

"Give me a second," I shout back finalising the tuning on the radio. I down what's left of my cup of coffee and head up to see what Bea has created.

"Cool isn't it?" Bea points to the wall behind me that separates the upstairs lounge and kitchen. A large piece of fabric is nailed into the place with 'Checklist for the end of the world' written in big black letters.

"It's pretty awesome," I chuckle.

"Look, I've put your categories below in red." She points below the letters, "Shelter, Food and water... you get the idea."

"It's perfect, Bea," I smile.

"Oh, and this one." She grabs my hand and takes me out the front and points to the lounge window. She has covered it completely from the inside with a massive poster reading: 'We are all fucked'.

"You have outdone yourself again," I tell Bea.

"Have you fed the animal recently?" Bea asks.

"No, but he will need some food at some point." I grind my teeth. "I'll take him something out when we put the party food out later."

Bea groans. "Yeah, sure his mood will turn seeing a cocktail sausage and a pineapple and cheese stick."

"Let's just deal with it later," I say flippantly, moving back inside out of the rain.

"What time is everything supposed to end then?" Bea asks.

I sigh. "It's complicated."

"Fucking hell, even the apocalypse can't be simple," Bea moans.

I exhale deeply. "Well, it's starting in about ten minutes."

"Ten minutes?" Bea shouts. "Thanks for the warning!"

"Don't worry, we will get drip fed stuff hour by hour as different countries and places hit the New Year. Kiribati will be the first to celebrate the millennium at 10 a.m. our time. They changed their time zone and everything to be the first. Even called one of their islands 'Millennium Island'."

"I can't decide if that's cheating," Bea mutters.

"The United States have a warship called the 'Topeka' straddling the International Date Line too."

"Now that's cheating," Bea says sternly.

"After Kiribati, we move through different countries every hour, 11 a.m. New Zealand then 1 p.m. Sydney, 2 p.m. Adelaide, 3 p.m. Tokyo, 4 p.m. China, 6 p.m. India and then the big one at 9 p.m., Moscow."

"How is Moscow the big one?" Bea asks.

"Because they haven't done much preparation for this," I tell her.

"They always have to be the bad guys," Bea frowns.

"Well, their President, Boris Yeltsin, resigned this morning so who knows what is going to happen. Some guy called Putin is in charge now," I tell Bea.

"Are we after Russia then?" Bea asks.

"There's a few more places at 10 p.m. Jerusalem being a big one for all the religious fanatics. 11p.m. is close to home so France, Italy, Spain until ours at midnight."

"And that's when we will know we are either fucked or not fucked?" Bea asks.

"Not quite," I wince as Bea throws her head back in annoyance, "we then go the other way so 2 a.m. is Brazil, 3 a.m. Argentina, 4 a.m. Newfoundland Canada, 5 a.m Eastern United States."

"I get it," Bea interrupts. "When does it end then?"

"Samoa is the last country to celebrate, at around 11 a.m. tomorrow."

"Well let's hope it starts in Kiribati," Bea scoffs, "because I'm bored of the apocalypse already."

94

It didn't start in Kiribati. Bea had decided she wanted to tick off the countries as we got to the hour, so she had nailed another piece of fabric to the wall with all the times listed on it. By the time she had finished putting it up we could already tick off Kiribati and New Zealand. Michael had come in for a cup of tea when we heard reports from Australia that everything was working as normal and Bill Gates was celebrating on a fucking yacht in Sydney Harbour.

When it was Japan next, I was nervous, but it passed. Same for China and for India but they had come and gone. It was Moscow next but geographically most of Russia had already celebrated the millennium as it stretches all the way to Japan and has eight fucking time zones.

I don't know if I feel dejected because Bea and Michael are starting to look at me differently. I can see them pulling faces but trying to talk to me like a kid who came last in every race on sports day, or if I feel frustrated that I might have got this all wrong. One thing I don't feel right now is any sense of regret though and that is keeping me balanced and my esteem high.

The glare of an approaching vehicle illuminates the candle lit kitchen. I stand and peer out of the net curtains as the headlights stop shining. It's Annabel's Renault Espace.

"Who is it?" Bea asks.

"It's Annabel," I say, opening the front door of the farmhouse.

Annabel locks her car and gives me a wave. "Sorry I'm later than expected. It all kicked off at Gordon's," she points to the back of her car. "Can you give me a hand?"

I walk out to meet her as the rain soaks my crisp white shirt.

"Nice to know we are all fucked," she smiles pointing at the farmhouse window. "Can you get my bag from the boot?" she points.

"Sure," I say, walking round to the back of her car and popping the boot open. She has brought a small suitcase.

"Thought I'd be prepared," she smiles at me. "Wish I'd been prepared for the shit that just happened at Gordon's though," she sighs.

"What happened?" I ask, lifting her suitcase out of the boot and slamming it shut.

"Tim showed up." She makes a face with clenched teeth.

"What!" I laugh. "Did he think he would be well received?" I lug the suitcase towards the farmhouse.

"No, I don't think so," Annabel says, following me. "He turned up half drunk and started shouting about how we were all 'losers' and told us to 'go fuck ourselves,'" she laughs.

"Bloody hell," I gasp as I put the suitcase down in the kitchen.

"Yeah, and he tried to start a fight with Gordon until one of Gordon's massive sons intervened and nearly decked him," she laughs. "He was shouting and swearing a lot and mainly about you."

"No surprise there," I sigh, closing the door.

"Good job you didn't come because he was drunk and looking for a fight," Annabel tells me as she puts her bag of booze on the kitchen table.

"Who's this?" Bea asks.

"Tim that used to work with us. Ray got him sacked and Tim was at this party I was just at, looking for him." Annabel takes off her coat to reveal a blue babydoll dress that matches her choker. "Gordon and his son managed to kick him out in the end. Never seen him so angry though."

"Drink will do that to you," Michael quips from his armchair in the lounge.

"Is Eddy coming?" Annabel asks, looking around the room.

"That's probably him now." I point to the window as headlights start to illuminate the room again. I go to the window and the brightness stops but no car.

"Not him, just a car driving past," I say, dropping the curtain again.

"Hope they don't go too far up the moors," Bea chuckles.

"Why's that?" Annabel asks her.

"Some former commune psychos still live up there a couple of miles away. Like a cult," Bea says, grabbing a handful of crisps from the bowl on the table.

"Ones that lived here?" Annabel asks me.

"Yeah, some of them. Looks like they had a falling out years ago. They posted a book through door about it, even mentioned me in there," I chuckle.

"That's some creepy shit Ray," Annabel frowns. "Can I look at the book?"

"I left it there when I went up with Michael, told them not to come near here again." I pour myself a whisky. "Think they got the message."

"Moscow in one minute," Bea announces as she turns up the radio.

"What's going on in Moscow?" Annabel chuckles.

"They are hitting midnight now," I tell her. "Bea's put a checklist of her own up on the wall, see." I point to the list of countries.

"And your checklist has pride of place too. Very cult like actually," Annabel jokes as I get a knot in my stomach just hearing the word cult.

"What's it saying on the radio Bea?" I call over.

"They have hit midnight now. Just that really." She bites her lip ring.

"It's the bit now that's the waiting," I tell Annabel. "They will start doing the checks on some high priority areas like nuclear plants and banking systems. Even Russia want to know if something has actually happened."

"Then we wait till the next hour and tick it off," Bea smiles.

"Cool," Annabel chuckles. "Can I have a glass or something? I brought white wine."

"Yeah, I'll grab you one." I head downstairs to grab Annabel one of our new wine glasses from Millets - plastic of course.

It was nice to see that Annabel brought a suitcase. Not only does it mean she doesn't think I'm batshit crazy, but she might even want to be a part of what we have here. The main uncertainty, of course, being whether the world is going to end or not, because right now we are nine hours in and apart from some minor glitches, nothing has gone wrong.

"Eddy's here," Bea shouts from upstairs.

"I'm coming up now," I shout back heading up the old stone staircase. As I get to the top, I see that Eddy has brought Buttercup with him and a carrier bag full of booze. Nothing else.

"Alright Eddy, Buttercup," I nod.

"Alright," Buttercup nods back as Eddy puts his carrier bag on the table, retrieving a can of Stella from it immediately.

"Everyone, this is Buttercup," I point, considering what the end of the world with Buttercup might look like.

"Hiya," Annabel smiles. "Why do they call you Buttercup?" she asks.

"Don't know really," Buttercup says, grabbing himself a beer.

"It's because he builds people up," Eddy chuckles, "and then let's them down."

Annabel laughs, "and then worst of all you never call?" She smiles at Buttercup.

"I do, I called Eddy earlier," he stares gormlessly, "what you on about?"

"Didn't bring a bag then, Eddy?" I ask.

"Why would I bring a bag? It's only one night." He takes a sip of his beer, obviously still pissed off at me for the beating he took.

"Still sulking?" I joke with him.

"Don't worry about me, mate," he takes another swig, "there's some random bloke parked at the gate at the top of the field. You did pay Patrick, didn't you?"

"Yeah," I say, rushing to the window. It's hard to see anything. I can't spot a car.

"Are you winding me up?" I ask him seriously.

"No, I'm not." He points through the window. "Just by that gate at the top."

"Bea, get everyone downstairs, I'm going to have a look." Bea jumps up and starts signaling to the staircase.

"Let's go!" she says, motioning with her hands.

"Show me where," I say to Eddy.

Eddy laughs. "I'm not getting involved in your shit again."

"Just stand watch by the door then," I ask.

"What the fuck is going on Ray?" Annabel frowns.

"I'll give you a hand," Buttercup volunteers.

"Just please someone keep an eye out from the front door and let Bea know if there's a problem," I stress. "Annabel, Bea, Michael just stay downstairs please. If it's who I think it is, I don't want him talking to any of you."

95

I power forward across the muddy, slippery front field. The parka I have been wearing is locked with the one-eyed bastard in the boot of Bea's car, so my white shirt is getting sodden now.

I can see a car as I get closer. It's pulled off into the grass verge on the left, just after the gate. There are no lights on outside or inside the car but if it's who I think it is, he won't want to be seen by me.

I walk through the open gate and turn to face the car on my left. It's a newish black BMW. I edge closer and peer through the rear window. There is one figure in the driver's seat. I don't think he can see me. I walk closer and see the rear lights come on. The engine starts and the car shoots back towards me. I jump up and to the right as the car skims my left leg and flips me slightly mid jump. I hit the hard tarmac with a thud.

I groan slightly as the wind has been knocked out of me. Fortunately, I landed on my left-hand side after being flipped slightly and not on my neck or back. I sit up and see the car stopped in front of me. A figure emerges from the driver side …. it's Tim.

"What the fuck Tim?" I shout, holding my sore left arm. Tim is still drunk. He is swaying a little bit but functional enough to be able to drive here, knock me over and walk towards me.

"What do you want Tim? For fucks sake you just ran me over with your car! That's fucking insane!" I shout.

Tim walks towards me, still not saying a word but staring at me dead in the eyes.

"What's your fucking problem Tim?" I yell at him.

"Shut up," he snaps. "You deserve this for everything you did," he screams.

I stand up and brush the gravel off my left-hand side. "Fuck off, Tim." I start to walk back to the house.

"Oi!" he shouts. "Don't walk away from me." He starts to follow me.

"Tim, just get back in your car and fuck off and I'll forget this ever happened," I snap.

"I'm talking to you!" Tim shouts, slightly slurred.

"Tim, back off and go home. Do not get anywhere near my house," I yell, marching back to the farmhouse.

Tim is still following me and getting closer.

"Tim, just go home!" I stress.

He walks up to me and pushes me backwards.

"Think you can fuck around with me?"

I stand up and Tim pushes me again. This time I don't slip.

"Think you're better than me?" he sneers, pushing me harder again as I backtrack towards the barn.

"Look, I don't want to fight you, Tim. You fucked

up at work. All I did was let people know what was going on. You were going to cost people their jobs!" I snap back.

"You fucking messed everything up!" Tim pushes me again but stumbles into the muddy ground. I am next to Bea's Nissan now and I fumble in my pocket for the keys. I manage to stick them into the door and grab the rifle from the floor. Tim is a couple of metres away now, so I point the rifle at him.

Tim stops and does a double take at the rifle. He looks at me and then back to the rifle.

"Just go home, Tim," I stress.

"Is that a gun?" He points to the rifle.

"Yes," I say sternly.

He starts to laugh. "You won't fight me and expect me to believe you will use that."

"Eddy!" I shout.

"Now you're bringing your friends as back up? Pussy. Just fight me," Tim slurs.

"I told you to just go home," I stress as Eddy and Buttercup appear behind Tim.

Tim turns round to look at them.

"Look like two more pussies to me," he sneers.

"Is that a gun?" Eddy asks, with an open mouth.

"Go back inside, pussies," Tim slurs at them and turns back to me. "The little lost orphan boy, never working hard but being given everything, jealous of me, like your wife," he laughs. "No wonder she left you. You're pathetic."

"Just go home," I tell him. "This is your last warning."

He walks towards me and grabs the barrel of the gun. I yank it back and manage to hit him over the head with the butt, causing him to stumble down.

"Grab him!" I shout as Eddy and Buttercup grab an arm each.

"What now?" Eddy asks.

"Are you going to shoot him?" Buttercup looks up at me with his doe eyes.

"Just take him to the boot!" I yell.

"Get the fuck off me!" Tim thrashes.

"I know self – defense, me. Don't push me," Buttercup yells back at him.

"Get off me!" Tim yells, elbowing Buttercup.

"I warned you!" Buttercup shouts before pulling his arm back and punching Tim in the balls.

"Whoa! What the fuck?!" Eddy gasps and Tim's eyes bulge.

"I warned him," Buttercup says as Tim collapses into the foetal position.

I walk around the three of them and open the boot, grabbing the duct tape from next to the sleeping one-eyed bastard.

I start taping his legs and then force his arms behind him as he is still weak from Buttercup's nut shot. He offers some resistance but it's fairly easy as he is so pre-occupied by the pain searing in his ballbag.

"Why are you taping him up?" Eddy asks.

"Lift him up with me," I direct.

"Where?" Eddy stressed.

"Boot of the car," I point. Eddy grabs one arm and I grab the other as we drag Tim towards the boot.

"What the fuck!" Eddy jumps back dropping Tim as he notices the one-eye bastard in the boot.

"What are you doing?" Tim manages to moan. He spots his fellow prisoner tied up in the boot. "Who's that? What are you doing?!" he wails. "I'll go, I'll go, I'll go home now!"

"It's too late," I tell him, peeling off a piece of tape and slapping it on his mouth. I think he is saying "please". He looks like he is, but I can't hear him properly. He tries to turn but Buttercup and I lift him off his knees and fumble him into the boot, waking the one-eyed bastard up in the process.

"What the fuck is this Ray?" Eddy says slowly.

"Well they both started it and at least they have each other for company." I look at them both staring at each other and yelling muffled words as I close the boot.

96

I toss my ruined white shirt into the wash pile by the storage room and grab a clean t-shirt from the pile. Bea sticks her head out of the bunker lounge as Eddy and Buttercup arrive at the bottom of the stone stairs.

"It's all sorted now," I smile at Bea.

"He's lost the fucking plot," Eddy shouts.

"What's going on?" Annabel comes into the hallway now.

"Nothing. It's fine now," I say curtly, putting on my clean t-shirt.

"Who was it?" Michael asks.

"It was Tim from work," I tell them. "It's fine though."

"Tim?" Annabel gasps.

"He must have followed you up here, but it's sorted now." I grab a bottle of whisky from the storage cupboard and take a swig.

"Fuck. Has he gone?" Annabel asks.

"No, he hasn't gone has he Ray?" Eddy snaps.

"Well, where is he?" Annabel stresses.

"He's in the boot of Bea's car," I tell her.

"Sorry, he's in the car?"

"In the fucking boot, tied up," Eddy shakes his head.

"Well at least he has company," Bea smiles.

"You knew about this?" Eddy asks her.

"Well yeah, it is my car," Bea tuts.

"Sorry Ray, but I'm with Eddy here, you can't just lock Tim in the boot of a car," Annabel shouts.

"It was quite easy actually," Buttercup contributes. "There's two of them in there, if you missed that part."

"Who is the other person?" Annabel looks at me with her mouth open.

"The one-eyed bastard landlord," Bea chips in.

I take another sip of whisky. "Look, I'll sort it out now."

"How?" Eddy asks. "Gonna shoot them with your rifle?" He stirs.

"What rifle?" Annabel looks at me.

"Bea bought me a rifle," I tell her. Annabel looks at Bea who meets her with a big smile.

Annabel shakes her head. "This is not right."

"I know," Eddy agrees. "I'm going. Come on Buttercup."

"Just let me sort it," I shout. "Give me five minutes to have a drink and a cigarette and I'll drive up the moors somewhere and let them both go." I light a cigarette. "Michael will you give me a hand?"

"Err, this is a bit out of my league lad," Michael says, scratching his head.

I take a sip of my whisky and look at Michael. "You know these moors. I need you."

97

South Africa, Greece and Jerusalem had all celebrated their New Year's Eve whilst I was trying to convince Annabel and Eddy that instead of leaving, it was in their best interests to stay in the bunker with the guy with gun who has two people tied up in his car. Not an easy sell.

Michael is driving Tim's car, ahead of me in Bea's Nissan. I needed someone to come with me to help shift Tim and the one-eyed bastard out of the boot and I needed that person to be Michael as he knew the way to our destination.

I have the radio on, and it's just struck midnight in France, Italy and Spain. Just one hour until midnight here and so far, no problems. I don't think that it bothers me that nothing has happened. I think people will look at me as if all my preparation has been for nothing when in reality, I have built myself a new life.

I can see Michael ahead signaling left. This must be the road I had seen when we took a trek a few days ago. I can see the Air Traffic Control tower ahead of me and, just as Michael expected, our arrival has caused a flurry of lights in the distance.

It's a couple of minutes down the broken road. Potholes have merged into potholes, so Tim and the one-eyed bastard are probably not having the best time in the back. It will be all over for them soon.

Michael pulls the BMW to a stop outside the cottage at the front of The Garden. I do a quick U-turn in Bea's Nissan and reverse backwards to where he has parked.

I get out of the car and walk towards the boot. I pop it open and Tim and the one-eyed bastard are both staring at me. The anger has turned to fear now, and I can understand why. Michael joins me at the boot and helps me lift Tim out first, carrying him across to the front of the cottage.

The one-eyed bastard is a bit heavier and we just about manage to carry him before dropping him next to a wailing Tim. I look at them both and wonder if this is the right thing to do. But it's only a split second before I walk backwards and stare up at the light.

My father is in the tower staring back at me. He looks slightly confused and on edge, for sure. I point towards the BMW and then the tied-up parcels of Tim and the one-eyed bastard and hold my father's gaze for a second. He nods back and I turn around immediately.

Michael is already in the Nissan. He hasn't said a word and then I realise he might have seen Jane somewhere in the grounds during all this.

"It will be alright. We'll get to her one day," I smile at him.

He keeps his head down as I put the car into gear. The radio clicks on and the sound of fireworks being let off fills the car from the radio broadcast. I pull another U-turn and start driving away from The Garden. The fireworks on the radio are interrupted by silence and then a stern voice starts to speak. 'This is coming to us as a breaking announcement.'

98

My earlier transgressions seem to be forgotten as Michael and I enter through the front door of the farmhouse. Nobody looks up or says a word, their attention drawn to the radio in front of Eddy on the kitchen table.

Buttercup, Annabel and Bea are sat around the large kitchen table too. Nobody has uttered a word so far and the radio is turned up to full volume, drawing everyone's attention. I chuck my leather jacket on the back of Annabel's chair and she doesn't even budge. The radio in the Nissan had cut out shortly after the announcement started, so I'd floored it trying to get back here.

"What's going on?" I ask to a wall of silence.

"What's happening? What was the breaking announcement?" I circle the table.

"Someone say something!" I stress.

"Shut up!" Bea groans. "We are trying to listen!"

I light a cigarette and stand behind Bea and

Annabel. The radio is saying words I recognise but I don't know the context, so I just can't figure out what is supposed to have happened.

"Eddy," I look over at him, "what are they saying?"

"Something in France," Eddy mutters. "Some systems have started crashing and wiping account balances to zero, personal accounts, business accounts."

I move over to him. "Anywhere else? Or just France?"

"Only France have reported anything. They started their checks at 11 p.m. our time and found something about half an hour into it. People are probably scrambling around checking our banking systems now."

"How do we know if it will affect the UK too?" I ask him.

"We don't yet," he says, "too many variables; like what the system is, who owns it, where is the mistake in the software, is it linked to anything. Even if I was sat in front of a bank's computer now, I wouldn't be able to tell you anything in fifteen minutes."

"I thought you said all the high-risk industries had been covered?" I ask him.

"They have," he sighs and swigs his beer, "just seems something slipped through the cracks."

"Is it too late to go and get a bag?" Buttercup asks.

99

"What do we do?" Annabel says, standing up and gesturing for one of my cigarettes. I hand one to her.

"Not much we can do now," Eddy says solemnly.

"Well, we do have a bunker, so that's a bonus," Bea adds.

"How did you know this would happen?" Annabel asks me.

"I didn't really," I shrug, "just thought it was likely, and as I was already starting over I just thought it would be worth being prepared, I guess."

"Look, we don't know how serious it is yet," Eddy argues.

"Well it's five to midnight and it's all we are talking about!" Bea stresses. "At least we are somewhere safe and not crammed in front of the millennium fucking dome, like sheep."

"It's safe up here," I say to Annabel.

"I might even get to use my chainsaw!" Bea

grins.

"I feel like I'm in some sort of weird dream or on a prank show or something." Annabel takes a long drag on her cigarette. "I mean, what do we do?"

"Nothing we can do!" Eddy shrugs his shoulders. "Just wait and see."

"So, is the world ending then?" Buttercup asks.

"In what context Buttercup?" Eddy says.

"As in the end of the world and we all die?" Buttercup tells him.

"Well at the moment, no," Eddy sighs. "It's a banking glitch. It sounds serious but the worst-case scenario is that there aren't any records of who has what and where."

"That sounds bad," Annabel says.

"It is," Eddy says, reaching for the whisky bottle now.

"Like you said though," Michael chips in, "nowt we can do."

The room goes silent. Annabel is pacing with her cigarette, Eddy has his head in his hands, Michael is sat in the armchair just staring at the wall, Buttercup is staring at Bea and Bea is biting her lip ring.

I take a swig of my whisky and light a cigarette as the sound of Big Ben chiming comes through on the radio. Everyone joins in the count but with more worry and apprehension than the excitement and cheer of normal, 9, 8, 7, 6, 5, 4, 3, 2, 1...

00

Me and Bea are sat on top of the Land Rover staring up at the night sky. It's hard to comprehend the vastness of the universe beyond what we can see. Infinite planets, stars and universes that stretch for an infinite distance and yet this moment feels so unique and important to me.

It's my moment, pure mindfulness. I am fully within it, and it is within me. I can hear sounds clearer, smell Bea's sweetness stronger and see much clearer. I feel fulfilled and enveloped within my own self-actualization.

The sky looks the same as in the millennium just gone. Perhaps it will be the one thing that always remains a constant. No matter what happens to me, to the farmhouse, to the country or to the world, there will be that same pattern above me in the sky that will bring me back to this moment.

I put my arm around Bea and pull her close to me, pulling her blonde streak back so I can see her eyes.

She looks at me and I kiss her on her lips, softly until it feels right to stop.

She smiles a different type of smile to me. I've never seen it before, but I like it, and she seems at peace.

She rests her head on my shoulder and I clasp her hand in mine as we continue to stare up from the horizon into the stars, wondering when we will see the planes falling to earth from the skies.

ABOUT THE AUTHOR

J.R. Rickwood is a former stand-up comedian and writer of observational humour, this is his first book.

For original artwork including the illustration on the cover of this book, more information on 'Checklist for the End of the World' and upcoming novels please visit.

www.JRRickwood.com

Please subscribe to the mailing list for upcoming news.

Printed in Great Britain
by Amazon